Rafael Sabatini, creator of s̲ was born in Italy in 1875 and educated in both Portugal and Switzerland. He eventually settled in England in 1892, by which time he was fluent in a total of five languages. He chose to write in English, claiming that 'all the best stories are written in English'.

His writing career was launched in the 1890s with a collection of short stories, and it was not until 1902 that his first novel was published. His fame, however, came with *Scaramouche*, the much-loved story of the French Revolution, which became an international bestseller. *Captain Blood* followed soon after, which resulted in a renewed enthusiasm for his earlier work.

For many years a prolific writer, he was forced to abandon writing in the 1940s through illness and he eventually died in 1950.

Sabatini is best-remembered for his heroic characters and high-spirited novels, many of which have been adapted into classic films, including *Scaramouche, Captain Blood* and *The Sea Hawk* starring Errol Flynn.

TITLES BY THE SAME AUTHOR
ALL PUBLISHED BY HOUSE OF STRATUS

FICTION:

ANTHONY WILDING
THE BANNER OF THE BULL
BARDELYS THE MAGNIFICENT
BELLARION
THE BLACK SWAN
CAPTAIN BLOOD
THE CAROLINIAN
CHIVALRY
THE CHRONICLES OF CAPTAIN BLOOD
COLUMBUS
FORTUNE'S FOOL
THE FORTUNES OF CAPTAIN BLOOD
THE GAMESTER
THE GATES OF DOOM
THE HOUNDS OF GOD
THE JUSTICE OF THE DUKE
THE LION'S SKIN
LOVE-AT-ARMS
THE MARQUIS OF CARABAS
THE MINION
THE NUPTIALS OF CORBAL
THE ROMANTIC PRINCE
SCARAMOUCHE
SCARAMOUCHE THE KING-MAKER
THE SEA HAWK
THE SHAME OF MOTLEY
THE SNARE
ST MARTIN'S SUMMER
THE STALKING-HORSE
THE STROLLING SAINT
THE SWORD OF ISLAM
THE TAVERN KNIGHT
THE TRAMPLING OF THE LILIES
TURBULENT TALES
VENETIAN MASQUE

NON-FICTION:

HEROIC LIVES
THE HISTORICAL NIGHTS'
ENTERTAINMENT
KING IN PRUSSIA
THE LIFE OF CESARE BORGIA
TORQUEMADA AND THE SPANISH
INQUISITION

The Lost King

Rafael Sabatini

HOUSE OF
STRATUS

This edition published in 2001 by House of Stratus, an imprint of
Stratus Books Ltd., 21 Beeching Park, Kelly Bray,
Cornwall, PL17 8QS, UK.

www.houseofstratus.com

Typeset, printed and bound by House of Stratus.

A catalogue record for this book is available from the British Library
and the Library of Congress.

ISBN 07551-154-4-9

Contents

PART ONE

PART TWO

Contents (contd)

PART THREE

PART ONE

Chapter 1

His Majesty

Anaxagoras Chaumette, the Procurator-Syndic of the Commune, had asserted with ostentatious confidence that he would take a King and make of him a Man.

In the comely, flaxen-haired lad of eight who sat on the sofa, swinging his short legs and expressing himself, with a volubility occasionally incoherent, in the language of the gutter, the Citizen Chaumette contemplated the success of his noble alchemy. It confirmed him in his sincere belief that even such corrupt and unpromising material as Royalty, possesses a latent fund of honest, genuine humanity, which, if pains are taken, may be brought to the surface.

Here the pains had been taken, on Chaumette's prescription, by Antoine Simon, the sometime shoemaker whom he had appointed preceptor to the royal child. A broad lump of a man, tricked out in the fine blue coat adopted as the proper livery of an office that carried emoluments amounting to some ten thousand livres a year, Simon leaned with possessive airs upon the back of the sofa. He was proudly conscious that he deserved not only the approval of Chaumette for the triumph of his tutorship, but also of the Citizen Hébert for the obvious care with which he had inculcated the unspeakable lesson his pupil was at this moment delivering.

Hébert, the dainty, foppish sewer-rat who edited with such elaborate obscenity that organ of the Cordeliers, the *Père Duchesne*, sat gravely listening, exchanging ever and anon a glance with his gross bespectacled associate. Now and then, when there was a failure in the monotonous volubility of His Majesty's recitation, Hébert would coaxingly interpose a leading question that would renew the flow of that terrible stream.

At the table, beside Pache, the burly, impassive mayor, who in some sort presided, a young municipal officer named Daujou, acting here as secretary, was writing rapidly. His lips were compressed, and there was a horror in his eyes. Long afterwards he was to tell the world that he did not believe a word of the utterances he was recording.

At moments the virtuous Anaxagoras, his sensibilities outraged, would blow out his fat, sensuous lips, and show the whites of his eyes behind his spectacles. Thus he advertised his dismay of disclosures by which Hébert was to ensure the triumph of the Republican austerity for which he battled.

This fervent zeal of Hébert's had taken alarm, as is well known, at a whisper that by the approaching trial of the Queen, the Committee of Public Safety hoped to bring Austria to negotiate for her deliverance. Should that Messalina be let loose again upon the world? Not as long as he had a pen and a tongue for whose utterances in the cause of his sublime idealism nothing was too foul.

In a foam of obscenely virtuous fury he had harangued the Jacobins. "In your name I have promised the head of Antoinette to the sansculottes, and I will give it to them if I have to go and cut it off myself."

Consumed by that same burning zeal he had sought the Public Prosecutor. Tinville had thrust out a dubious lip over the Queen's dossier. "It's a poor case at best, my friend. There is hardly enough to make conviction certain. And there are political considerations against pressing even the existing charges."

Hébert consigned political considerations to the nethermost hell. Theirs was a righteous, enlightened age that had made an end of political trickery. Additional charges must be discovered so as to baffle the traitors and intriguers who dreamed of an acquittal.

To discover them he sought his friend Chaumette, a man in whose bosom he discerned the glow of as pure a flame of Republican altruism as in his own.

I find it odd that in seeking additional charges with which to bring that unhappy woman to the scaffold, Hébert should have made no use of that atrocious piece of scandal for which the brother of the late King was primarily responsible. The Count of Provence had resented from boyhood his cadetship and the fact that the crown, which he believed himself so fully qualified to wear, must go to his elder brother. The protracted childlessness of Louis XVI kept him for a while in the hope that Fate would yet make amends to him. Then, seven years after her marriage, Marie-Antoinette gave birth to a daughter, and three years later to a son. But even these events did not cause him to despair. It was soon apparent that the sickly son could not live, and it began to look as if no further children would follow. At the end of another four years, however, in 1785, the healthy, robust Louis-Charles, who was so soon to become Dauphin, made his bow to the world, and frustrated his uncle's last hope.

The Count of Provence was a curious compound of astuteness and stupidity, of dignity and buffoonery; but I will not do him the injustice to suppose that he did not first persuade himself of the truth of the scandal whose dissemination he zealously furthered. We are so prone to believe that which suits our purposes, and particularly charges that are damaging to those whom we dislike; and dislike was as strong as it was mutual between the Count of Provence and Marie-Antoinette.

Could it be believed, he plaintively asked his intimates, that a marriage barren for seven years should suddenly of itself become fruitful? Was it not at least suspicious, and was it not manifest that Count Fersen's attentions to the frivolous Queen were too assiduous to be honourable? Could anyone seriously doubt that the handsome, devoted Swede was Her Majesty's lover, and that Monsieur the Dauphin was a bastard?

That slander, discreetly hushed yet venomously active, spread from Court to city, from Versailles to Paris. With the scandal of the necklace and the ribald inventions concerning the Queen's relations with the Polignacs, it supplied yet another weapon to those who strove to bring the monarchy into contempt.

The Count of Provence in his fatuity, and until he took fright and fled the storm, had actually displayed Jacobinistic leanings. It was his silly hope that the men of the new ideas would on those grounds and in his own favour exclude the Dauphin from the succession.

There was matter here for Hébert, since in all times the adultery of a queen has been high treason. But perhaps treason to a throne could not logically be made to count for much with a people who had destroyed the throne, or perhaps the accusation was not loathly enough to satisfy Hébert's political prurience. Instead, he preferred another and grosser iniquity which he claimed to have discovered in the Queen's conduct.

He discussed it with Chaumette. Chaumette, this squalid adventurer who had lived impurely ever since, at the age of thirteen, he had been kicked out of an ecclesiastical college, was overcome with horror. He had buried his peasant face in his coarse red hands.

"Forgive this weakness. In spite of the loathing with which kings inspire me, it still remains that I am a man."

After that obscure outburst, he mastered his emotions, and went to work. He schooled Simon in the lesson in which Simon in his turn was to school the boy; a boy kept in a half-fuddled state with brandy, so as to dull his naturally keen perceptions; a boy who had been taught to deck his utterances freely with every obscenity in the language, until the speech of the gutterlings had come to replace upon his innocent lips the courtly diction of Versailles.

Listening now to the boy's depositions, Chaumette had as much cause to be satisfied with the manner as Hébert with the matter of them. Each hoped confidently that all present would be properly impressed. There were, besides the boy, nine of them altogether, in that room on the second floor of the Temple Tower, which had been inhabited by Louis XVI during his captivity, and was now a part of the lodging of Simon and his wife and their charge. It was a well-appointed chamber, for neither in his furniture nor in his table had the late King been unduly stinted. On a settle in rose brocade that was ranged against the wall, two members of the Commune who were that day on duty, Heussé, a chocolate-maker, and Séguy, a doctor, sat listening in shocked gravity. In the background, Jacques Louis David, the pageant-master of the Revolution, the painter whom the generous patronage of Louis XVI had rendered famous, occupied a tall-backed chair, with young Florence la Salle, his most promising pupil, on a stool close beside him. They sat with their shoulders to the window, which was placed so high in the wall that a man might not look out of it save by standing on a chair, and La Salle, his legs crossed, rested an open sketch-book on his knee.

He sat tapping his teeth with the butt of his pencil. Lost in a dreamy wistfulness, his wide-set, luminous, dark-blue eyes pondered the boy. Thus until a prod from David aroused him. The master set a finger to the drawing La Salle had made.

"More weight in that line," he growled under his breath.

He grunted approval when it was done, a smile on his hideous face, so scornfully twisted by the cyst that defaced his upper lip. "You see how it changes the value of the whole? What a sense of depth is gained? Less drawing, Florence. Fewer lines. Only those that really count." He touched the young man affectionately on the shoulder, and rumbled on. "The likeness could not be truer. You have the trick of that. If only you would cultivate austerity. Austerity."

"I will try again," the pupil murmured. He turned a page of his sketch-book, and shifted his stool away from the master's chair, ostensibly so as to obtain a view of his subject from a fresh angle.

But he did not at once begin to draw. His rather saturnine face as expressionless as a mask, he continued from under his black brows to study the boy who still chattered his vile lesson.

The little King, small for his age, and plump, was dressed in a green carmagnole, with a tricolour cockade plastered on the breast of it. His round, fair-skinned face was unnaturally flushed, its winsomeness marred now by the childish jactancy of the boy who apes the airs and manners of a grown man. There was an unnatural glitter in the blue eyes under their high-arching brows, an unpleasant lack of control about the slightly hare-toothed mouth, from which those men were drawing the falsehoods that should send his mother to the guillotine.

Suddenly, whilst considering him, La Salle was vouchsafed that wider, deeper vision the lack of which David was forever lamenting in him.

"You are a great draughtsman, Florence," the master had told him more than once. "But for all your draughtsmanship you will not be an artist until either wit or emotion informs your work."

In a flash he had perceived how either might inform it here. In this wretched besotted boy he discovered a subject for cynical, soulless humour or for profoundest tragedy, according to the spirit of him to whom the artist's vision was vouchsafed.

His pencil worked rapidly and surely; and, with an economy of line that presently delighted David, he accomplished a sketch that was at once a portrait and a story.

Whilst he had been working, the boy's depositions had come to an end. Pache, the mayor, had cleared his throat to ask if that were all, and Chaumette, the atheist who had invented the Goddess of Reason, called now upon the Divinity he had been active in abolishing, to bear witness that it was more than enough: a supper of horrors possible only within the ambit of the canker of Royalty. Thereupon Pache had opined that they had better come to the confrontations, and Daujou was sent to fetch Marie-Thérèse Capet from the floor above just as La Salle completed his sketch.

In the pause Hébert had risen and had sauntered round to look over La Salle's shoulder at the drawing. He had mincingly commended it. The student paid no heed to him. He sat bemused, apparently insensible even to the word of praise that David let fall. But Hébert was insistent and desired others to share his artistic satisfaction.

"By your leave, citizen," he said, and took the sketch-book from La Salle.

He carried it to the table, and leaning forward between Pache and Chaumette invited their attention to it.

Chaumette adjusted his spectacles. He looked from the sketch to the boy, and back again to the sketch. He made a chortling sound.

"The devil's in his pencil," he approved. He nudged his neighbour. "Look, Pache."

But Pache, swollen with the importance of his office and its functions, perceived in this an unpardonable levity. Irritably he thrust the sketch-book away from him.

"Don't pester me with these trifles. Have you no sense of our purpose here?"

"Trifles!" said Hébert, as he gathered up the book. "This is not a trifle. Futurity may account it a historical document." And superciliously he added: "A pity that you have no culture, Pache."

He was restoring the book to its owner when the door opened again and was held by Daujou for Madame Royale.

La Salle's compassionate eyes studied this slight, pallid girl of sixteen, dressed in deep mourning, between whom and the boy on the sofa the resemblance was remarkable. She had the same flaxen hair, white skin and blue eyes, the same arching brows, so marked in her case as to lend her countenance an expression of perpetual astonishment. Her softly rounded chin lacked the dimple that was impressed in his, but the lines of the mouth were very similar, and there was the same forward thrust of the upper lip.

From the day when first she could stand on her own feet she had been an object of the deepest homage. The noblest and greatest men and women of the kingdom had formally ranged themselves at her passage through the galleries or avenues of Versailles, had stood to receive her commands, had bowed low or had curtsied to the ground in humblest reverence of her august rank. Only the irrefragable consciousness that by right of birth nothing less was her due, sustained now – child though she might be – the almost disdainful self-command with which she confronted the ostentatious disrespect of these coarse men. In her eyes their offensive attitudes diminished not her, but themselves. From what she was, from what she had been born, no grossness in their conduct could detract.

Only for a moment had she shown a sign of dismay, and that was when first her glance alighted on her brother, and she beheld the green carmagnole and gaily striped waistcoat worn at a time when decency dictated that like herself he should have been in mourning for their lately martyred father.

After that she disdainfully confronted these men who remained seated in her presence, so as to mark the equality of which they were apostles. Pache as well as the two functionaries on the settee even retained their cockaded hats, in the band of one of which – Heussé's – were displayed an identity-card – his *carte de civisme* – and a card of membership of the Jacobins. Séguy was smoking, and Chaumette, suddenly fearful lest his bareheadedness might be misconstrued, reached for his hat with its bunch of tricolour plumes, and clapped it over his flat, ill-kempt black hair. It was with a voluptuous thrill that this creature who knew himself for a part of the scum that had been cast to the surface of the revolutionary cauldron, savoured an office which enabled him figuratively to set his heel upon the proud neck of this delicately nurtured daughter of a hundred kings – those kings who filled him with loathing because he could not rid himself of the base persuasion that they were beings of a different and superior order of creation.

He leered now at the girl over his spectacles. But her attention was again upon her brother, whom she had not seen since he had been brought down, three months ago, from that room on the third floor of the tower, to be placed in the care of Simon. She had taken a step towards him, and had seemed about to address him. Then she had checked, deterred and bewildered by the subtle change she detected in him, and by his very attitude.

He was swinging his legs again, not buoyantly as before, but petulantly, his expression now sullen and morose. From the depths of his infant soul there arose, as if evoked by her candid glance, a vague consciousness of guilt for which she might call him to account. Hence came an indefinable resentment of the presence of this sister whom he loved. She might have broken through that barrier had not the harsh voice of Pache suddenly commanded her attention.

"Thérèse Capet, attend to me if you please."

She stiffened at the insulting form of address; but since to protest would be to derogate, it was in silence that she squarely faced him, thrusting out her chin.

His interrogatory began. He questioned her closely touching relations held by herself, her mother and her aunt, with two commissioners who, false to their duty, had become parties to an attempt to rescue the Queen, engineered by that intrepid adventurer Jean de Batz. They had been denounced by the then custodian of the Temple, a man named Tison, who was now, himself, a prisoner there. Pache's questions, however, aimed at discovering more than had been admitted by Tison.

To his admonition that she should be careful to speak the truth, her only answer was an indignant stare. Against the rest she entrenched herself in ignorance. Baffled by her calm denials the mayor at last threw himself back in his chair and spoke to the municipal beside him.

"Read the depositions of the little Capet. Perhaps they will revive her memory."

Once or twice whilst Daujou's colourless voice was reading her brother's frank incrimination, not only of those two generous friends, but even of the Queen for her endeavours to seduce them from their duty, she turned bewildered eyes on the boy, to be met by a derisive grin.

"Have you anything to say now?" Pache asked her at the end. "Do you confirm the truth of your brother's testimony?"

Again her grave, reproachful glance sought her brother. It had the effect of increasing his resentment.

"You know that it's true," he exclaimed petulantly. "All true. All the sacred lot of it."

Perhaps what shocked her most was the barrack-room adjective on the young King's lips. The eyes she turned once more upon her questioner were as hard as was her voice.

"I confirm nothing. I have no knowledge of these matters."

"How is that possible since your brother knows them?"

"It may be that his memory is better than mine."

"That's all you have to say, is it, my girl?"

Chaumette moved behind Pache. He came to stand squarely over him.

"Let us pass on. Give me the depositions."

Pache did more. He surrendered his chair and his place at the table to Chaumette.

"There is something much more serious, much more lamentable, much more horrible." Thus the Procurator-Syndic, settling himself into the seat and polishing his spectacles. Slovenly of dress, with his ragged collar, his dirty foulard untidily knotted, his false air of naiveté, this blood-hound of the Commune had something of the air of a village schoolmaster.

He set the spectacles on his nose, cleared his throat noisily, and began to read. There were not more than a dozen lines. But it is to be doubted if any other dozen lines ever penned were packed with so much infamy as these accusations of a mother by her own son, a child of eight.

Chaumette set the document down, and leaned forward, his elbows on the table. "You have heard. You will not pretend of these, too, that they are matters outside your knowledge. Living all closely together as you did up there, you must be aware of them. Do you acknowledge it?"

She was bewildered. "Acknowledge? But acknowledge what?"

"The truth, of course. What I have just read to you."

"But I do not understand what you have read." The utter candour of her eyes made it impossible to suppose that the impatience in her voice was histrionic.

"You must make it plainer," said Hébert. "What the devil is the good of veiling things? Let us have it frankly. We live in frank times."

The Procurator-Syndic was indignantly distressed.

"By God! Is it not enough that I must soil my lips with allusions to such turpitudes, without shaming me into discarding all pudicity? However, since you play the innocent with me, my girl, I suppose that I must master repugnance and come down to plain terms."

But even when he had done so, the pure innocence of Madame Royale remained for some moments unenlightened. At last, however, the full horror and bestiality of his meaning burst upon her mind. A flush arose and deepened in her softly rounded face from neck to brow. Chaumette might now relish the conviction that insult had pierced her panoply. That flaming countenance, that trembling lip, the tears that suddenly filled her eyes were to him so many welcome signs that at last he had seared her disdainful insensibility.

"You do not answer," he complained, and by the words spurred her into a royal passion. She stepped forward. The tears fell away from eyes that were now aflash.

David nudged his pupil. "Seize that! Quick! Thus, at three-quarters, as you see her."

La Salle plied his pencil, but ineffectively and merely because it was easier to obey than to explain to David that he was neither an animal nor a machine. Meanwhile the girl's voice rang out.

"Answer, do you say? Do you dare to expect it? What answer can there be to lies so foul, to invention so shameful, so vile, so horrible?"

"Yes, yes," said Chaumette. "Foul and vile and horrible, we agree. I am shamed in mentioning these things. But inventions? If so, they are not ours. The words I have read are your brother's; the matter of them is, I think, beyond the invention of a child of eight."

"My brother's!" That was indeed something momentarily overlooked. The reminder suddenly checked her. She turned to him, Sitting there flushed and sullen, observing her furtively, like a dog that fears the whip, conscious of misbehaviour even without understanding the nature of it.

"What infamy!" she cried. "These lies cannot be yours."

He rocked himself on the sofa, his air mutinous as before.

"Yes. It's true." Simon leaned over him, encouragingly, to pat his shoulder. "You know that it is all true."

There was the sound of her fiercely indrawn breath. "Wretch! You don't know what you are saying."

"Oh yes, I do. I know what I am saying, and I know that it's true. So do you."

"He can't! He can't know." She had swung again to face her torturers. Piteously her eyes looked from one to another of the eight men within the sweep of her glance. But all save two were either cold or mocking, and the two – David and La Salle – did not meet her anguished look. Both heads were bent; David's over his writing, for he had been setting down her words, La Salle's over a portrait that he was merely pretending to sketch.

Chaumette looked at Hébert for guidance. Hébert thrust out a nether lip, and shrugged. "She is obstinate, of course. No use wasting time."

"Very well." Chaumette took the written sheet from Daujou. He beckoned Madame Royale forward, dipped a pen, and proffered it. "Sign there, if you please."

She looked at him, dubiously, suspiciously. Then she scanned the document, assured herself that it contained no more than the questions put to her and her replies, and in silence she signed it.

Daujou rose to reconduct her, and at the same moment, as she stood back from the table, the little King, seeing her about to depart, slipped down from the sofa and sidled timidly up to her. He loved her; he had missed her sorely these three months, almost as sorely as he had missed his mother, and more than he had missed Aunt Babet. He was lonely and hungry for affection. Simon and his wife were gruffly kind to him, and habit by now had inured him to their coarse ways. Similarly, now that he had grown accustomed to it, he was no longer resentful when the men of the Temple Guard tossed him from one to another, blew tobacco smoke in his face, and called him Charles. Indeed, he had come to enjoy himself amongst them, playing the man amongst men, drinking sweetened brandy, learning the language of the rabble, so rich in blasphemy and indecencies, and the ribald patriotic songs they delighted to teach him. To the child who previously had lived by rigid forms, there was in all this an exciting emancipation. But there was no warmth to replace the love of his mother, his sister and his aunt, from whom three months ago he had been rudely ravished.

The presence of Marie-Thérèse had gradually made him aware of it. The dim consciousness that in some incomprehensible way he had offended her, increased his sense of loneliness and urged him to a caress that should close the gap between them.

Thus, plaintively, he approached her now. She was unaware of it until she felt his fingers seeking to entwine themselves in her own. Startled, she looked down into that upturned face on which there was a piteous little smile. Instantly her expression changed. She snatched her hand away, and recoiled from him.

"Don't touch me! Don't dare to touch me! Don't dare to address me!" she breathed fiercely. "Little monster! Never will I forgive you this. Never!"

He stood abashed, at gaze for a moment. Then a sob shook him, and his eyes filled with tears. At the same instant a hand fell upon his shoulder. The burly Simon, who had followed him from the sofa, spoke in a rough, coaxing voice.

"Come, Charles. Come and sit down with me. They're going to fetch your Aunt Babet."

The child looked through a mist of tears after his sister, as, moving stiffly, her head high, she passed out of the room.

"She was angry with me, Citizen Simon," he sobbed. "Why was she angry with me?"

Simon patted his shoulder to soothe him. "Pay no heed to her. Sacred little aristocrat."

Chapter 2

Jean de Batz

In the evening of that same October day Jean de Batz, Baron of Armanthieu, sat writing briskly in a cosy, even luxurious, room in the Rue Ménars, behind the Hôtel de Choiseul. He worked by candle-light, the curtains drawn, the fire burning brightly, the room suffused by a fragrance of pine from the fir-cones that were freely mingled with the blazing logs.

This incredible man, the most active worker in the royalist interest in Europe at the time, was of an audacity that no other secret agent has ever paralleled. Almost he seemed to disdain precautions. He rarely troubled to veil his identity, showed himself freely wherever his occasions took him, and came and went with a fire-walker's apparent indifference to the dangers of the ground he trod.

Where others of his kind writhed with frantic but futile violence when the net closed round them, de Batz quietly cut his way through the meshes with golden shears. No man was ever better versed in the arts of bribery, and no man ever employed its corrupting power on so vast a scale. Apart from the gold with which he was well supplied he commanded a supply of the Republic's paper money which was inexhaustible because it came from a printing-press of his own, secretly established at Charenton. These forgeries not only equipped him with unlimited means; they served the further royalist purpose of accelerating the terrible depreciation of the paper currency.

His agents were everywhere. Every transaction of the Committee of Public Safety was known to him at once from Sénar, its secretary, who was in his pay; and, with the exception only of the Revolutionary Tribunal itself, there was not a government department some of whose officials were not bribed to serve him. If success had not waited upon an attempt of his to save the King, and another, later, to deliver the Queen and her children from the Temple, this was due to the malignity of chance, which had presented him with obstacles that could not have been foreseen. That he continued at liberty, practically unsought, although he was known to be the author of these and of other capital offences against the State, is a sufficient proof of the power of the resources with which he hedged himself.

In his person he was a stiffly built man of middle height, good-looking in an imperious way, aggressive of nose and chin and lively of eye. He had cast off coat and waistcoat, and he sat now in frilled shirt and black satin small-clothes, his lustrous black hair as carefully queued as in the days before the coming of sansculottism.

He wrote diligently, with a glance ever and anon at the ormolu timepiece on the mantelshelf, until he was interrupted by the sounds he expected and his elderly servant, Tissot, ushered in the Citizen La Salle.

De Batz sat half round in his chair, so as to face his visitor.

"You are late, Florence."

La Salle loosened the bottle-green riding-coat that had been tightly buttoned to his slenderly vigorous body. He removed his conical hat and shook out the lustrous black hair which he wore long, *en oreilles de chien.*

"It was a long affair, and I didn't stay to the end. David couldn't wait. The Convention is discussing the Law of Suspects tonight, and our Lycurgus must be in his place. Being at the Temple only by his favour and as his acolyte, I had to depart with him, just before Madame Elizabeth was examined by those muck-rakes."

He was by habit slow of utterance, with a drawl that brought a sneering, half-humorous note into his most sober speech. It went well with the frank boldness of his pallid face and with the strong mouth, cast in lines of bitterness which laughter merely emphasized.

"What happened?" asked de Batz.

"Conceive the worst and you will still not have plumbed the depths of the ordurous invention of these gentlemen." He rendered in disgust an account of what he had witnessed at the Temple. "The boy did not know what he was saying. It was a lesson learnt by heart, and his wits were fuddled; a consequential, self-assertive little braggart, playing the man. Before they've done with him, those scoundrels will have gangrened his soul. And then the girl. When their filthy hands rent the veil of her chaste innocence she suffered one of those shocks that change a whole nature. In her anguish she was vixenish to that unhappy boy. It was all horrible. To see children so used!" He pulled his sketch-book from his pocket. "Perhaps emotion for once lent me the vision that David says I lack." He laid the open book before de Batz. "What does that tell you?"

But the Baron, deeply stirred, had no eyes for La Salle's drawing.

"This foulness is Hébert's. He must make sure that the Queen does not cheat the guillotine."

"Isn't it enough to murder her, without bespattering her with their mud? Is God asleep?"

"God? What has God to do with it?" There was a tragic scorn in the Baron's muted voice. "The worst insult ever offered God was the assertion that He made man in His Own Image. Man! Malicious, greedy, hypocritical man, vulnerable to evil at every point. Realize the truth now, whilst you are young, Florence, for it will save you from many errors: men are not good."

His eyes fell, at last, to the sketch, and his attention was instantly caught. He shook his head over it. "A tragic picture. Poor child!"

La Salle almost forgot the tragedy in pride of his art's presentation of it. He cited David's commendation of the power of the drawing, pointing out the telling lines, as if by comparison the sufferings it mirrored were of small account. He wasted breath; for to de Batz all that mattered was the message of the portrait, and not the terms in which that message was conveyed.

That pathetic picture of the sweet, boyish face half veiled in a sly leer moved him fiercely.

He spoke suddenly, on a gust of passion.

"God helping me, whatever the cost, if I have to tear down the Temple walls with my hands, I'll have that child out of it. Florence, I shall depend upon your help."

La Salle's eyes widened. He made a dubious lip. "It will be difficult."

"And dangerous; all things worth doing are one or the other, and often both. But nothing was ever more worth doing. Can I count on you? You know the place. You have been there."

La Salle possessed audacity in plenty, but no rashness. He was cold, logical and unsentimental. As one of the Baron's chief agents, he had done daring and skilful work. To enable him to do it this pupil and associate of the ultra-Republican David postured before the world as an advanced and active revolutionary. He was ostentatiously a member of the Jacobins and the Cordeliers, and he had won election to the Council of the Commune as one of the representatives of the section in which he dwelt. Thus he watched events at their source. Thus, in quest of information, he had been able to persuade David to take him that day to the Temple, on a pretext of making sketches that might be of some national importance.

The present proposal, however, seemed not only desperately hazardous, but foredoomed. He hesitated, his black brows contracted.

"I am ready for anything short of the impossible."

"Good. Between us we'll make this possible."

They discussed it further over dinner: for La Salle stayed to dine with de Batz, at a table that was generously spread, as were the tables of all who could afford the unconscionable prices to which food had soared. Scarcity and starvation were for the unfortunate populace, whom the revolutionists, the ideologues and the self-seekers had gulled with promises of wealth for all. There was, of course, for the indigent a dole, that usual concomitant of national decay. It was to be earned by attending sectional meetings. But it amounted to only forty sous a week, and what relief could be obtained from this when bread stood at thirty francs a pound and the bottle of wine that had cost eight sous in the days of tyranny could not be bought for less than twenty francs? The restaurants of the Palais Royal did a brisk trade; the theatres and gaming-houses were well patronized; the men who had made the Revolution grew wealthy, and feasted; but the people for whose deliverance it had been made, sank, under the rule of these despots from the gutter, to depths of wretchedness unknown in the days of the despots on the throne, and in this state they would continue for as long as credulity tightened the bandage over their eyes.

It was to this that de Batz alluded when he said: "Until I succeed, these wretched dupes, their heads stuffed with cant, their bellies empty, will continue to make sanity impossible."

"Which reminds me," said La Salle, "that I have not the price of tomorrow's dinner."

"That is the normal state in which you visit me."

"Oh, it is not only when I visit you. I am practically without resources. My boots leak, my – "

The Gascon interrupted him. "You had a thousand francs from me a week ago."

"And what's a thousand francs? Or don't you keep a watch on the depreciation of the assignat? A thousand francs today is less than the value of a gold louis. Besides," he drawled, "isn't it your faith that the more of this paper of yours is put into circulation, the sooner the government will be embarrassed?"

"You're always specious. But I'm not thinking of the money only." Gravely his piercing eyes were levelled upon La Salle's baffling countenance. "I sometimes wonder whether you work for the cause or for the money that you get from me?"

La Salle was moved to smile. "The foolishness of that unnecessary question! I work for both. That should be manifest. Without your money how am I to live, since the Revolution took all that I had, even to my expectations when it guillotined my uncle and confiscated his property. Count me venal if you choose. It should be enough to justify confidence. I must work for the cause of monarchy because in the restoration of the monarchy lies my only hope of the restoration of my property and also because failing that I shall have to be a painter, although David says that I lack the deeper vision that makes the artist. In anarchical society there is no living for a painter, unless, like Jacques Louis David, he can design its pageants. So let my obvious interestedness, present and future, dispel mistrust of me where my less obvious virtues fail to do so."

"Faith, you're frank. And hard. Oddly hard for one so young."

"We age quickly, we who live in this hotbed of decay; and we harden. We are not even ashamed to become escrocs and ask for money, as I do. What the devil is the purpose of pride, Jean, when your boots leak?"

To mend them the Baron gave him that night not a bundle of forged notes, but a handful of genuine gold louis. He was cynically frank about it.

"You have suddenly become too valuable to be risked, Florence; and there are risks in false assignats, even when they're as good as mine. There's a boy to be rescued from the Temple, and you are better fitted for the task than you may suppose. As you've realized, to save a king for restoration to his throne is for you the surest way of becoming a Court painter."

"Always provided that I don't meanwhile leave my head in Charlot's basket." La Salle pocketed the gold. "It's as well to look at both sides of a medal. Let me know what's to be done as soon as you've decided."

That decision, however – the evolving of a plan – took de Batz three months to reach. In the meantime the unhappy Queen, to whose other crimes had been added the damning charges of which her own son was made the unwitting author, had ridden to the Place de la Révolution in the tumbril, and David, from a window in the Rue St Honoré, had done in a few masterly strokes that swift, terrible, heartless sketch of her which all the world knows today. He displayed it in his atélier, in the northern pavilion of the Louvre, and to La Salle in particular offered its virtuosity as a model.

La Salle was still working on a portrait of Louis XVII from the three sketches he had made at the Temple, and he achieved in the end a picture which closely resembled the portrait Kucharsky had painted some eighteen months earlier. David condemned it as mere competent craftsmanship, which may have been unduly harsh, for the likeness was of a remarkable fidelity. To please the master, La Salle tried again, on a larger canvas, and was still more severely damned as academic.

David missed the leer, the slyness which in one of La Salle's sketches had so delighted his warped soul. But in the portraits not all the master's vitriolic scorn could bring his pupil to reproduce the evil truculence of which the boy's face had shown that momentary glimpse. La Salle tried yet again, this time on a reduced scale, producing what was scarcely more than a miniature. In all he worked on that one subject for the best part of three months, until he knew every line and plane so well that he swore he could paint the little King's portrait with bandaged eyes.

And then one day he was seized by the humour of it that whilst all about him the world was in convulsions, with the enemy legions on the frontier and the guillotine reaping a daily harvest just beyond the Tuileries Gardens, he should be bothering about a painted face, and his master about railing at his shortcomings.

That was when the call to action reached him at last from de Batz.

Chapter 3

Joseph Fouché

It followed from this collaboration between de Batz and La Salle that one day early in Nivôse of the Year Two of the new Era of Liberty – which is to say towards the end of December of 1793 of the obsolete Christian Era – the young art student climbed to the third floor of a dingy house in the Rue St Honoré. Of the young woman with the comely, careworn face who opened a door to his knock, he inquired for the Citizen-Representative Joseph Fouché.

It had happened that at the very moment when de Batz reached the decision that Chaumette was the man upon whom to commence the intended operations, Joseph Fouché had suddenly returned from a republicanizing mission in the Nivernais. He had come to Paris so as to defend himself from a suspicion of moderation bruited against him by Robespierre.

This unexpected return and the circumstances of it had brought de Batz to the opinion that Fouché would better serve their aims. He had watched this man's career, and had closely informed himself of his history.

Educated by the Oratorians for a professorship, Fouché had for seven years exercised that calling in Oratorian institutions. He had taught mathematics at Niort and logic at Vendôme, and in 1783 at Arras he had held the chair for physics, to which thereafter he assiduously devoted himself. A passionate student of aerostatics, he had in 1791 made a balloon ascent at Nantes, which had thrilled the inhabitants with wonder and terror. There in '92, he had married, thus abandoning all notion of the priesthood, of which he had already received the minor, revocable orders. At the same time abandoning pedagogy for politics, he had won election to the Convention as the representative of the Lower Loire. He was, de Batz informed La Salle, the very prince of opportunists, a man without convictions, always the servant of circumstances, and likely always to be on the winning side, since his immense intellect and alertness should always enable him to foresee it. Whilst men had been leniently disposed towards the late King, Fouché had offered unanswerable arguments of leniency; when the main body of opinion swung round, Fouché discovered reasons that left him no choice but to vote the King's death. His mission in the West had been begun with unparalleled ruthlessness and had so continued for as long as he saw in ruthlessness the key to advancement. When his lucid mind, clear of the fanaticism, the brutality, the cowardice that clouded so many revolutionary spirits, perceived the first signs that the nation was becoming nauseated with slaughter, he adopted moderation. So, whilst he lighted no more fires and shed no more blood, to a government which – less quick to perceive the change in public feeling – still desired a policy of ruthlessness, his reports continued to be written in blood and fire.

Robespierre, however, was not easily duped, and Robespierre watched him closely and jealously, as he watched any man who showed signs of ascendancy; for Fouché's activities had already made him famous. His intellectual strength inspiring confidence, an ever increasing party was forming about him, in which Anaxagoras Chaumette – himself an idol of the rabble – was a leading spirit.

Not only did Robespierre perceive in Fouché a potential rival to be destroyed, but there were other more personal reasons for this rancour. In Arras, during his professorship, before the Revolution, a friendship had been established between the lawyer and the Oratorian. Fouché had lent him money. And it was almost as hard for Robespierre to forgive this as the fact that Fouché had left Arras without remembering to marry Robespierre's sister. He was suspected of having seduced her. It was probably an unjust suspicion, for Fouché, intellectually superior to any such thing as a moral sense, was yet by nature of the singular austerity that goes with such cold minds.

Lastly, the sometime Oratorian, now a flagrant atheist, accounted it within his mission to dechristianize the province of his commissionership. In collaboration with Chaumette, he had invented the Goddess of Reason and the ceremonials of that cult, mummeries which were repugnant to Robespierre the Deist.

It was Chaumette who had sent word to Fouché of the clouds out of which a thunderbolt might suddenly be launched upon his head, and Fouché had posted straight to Paris so as to confront his critics.

He had not only answered them, he had crushed them, temporarily at least, under specious arguments presented with the turgid oratory which they understood. And he brought more than arguments. He piled upon the floor of the Convention great stacks of gold and of silver: crosses, chalices, patens, ciboria, candlesticks and the like, the spoils of the churches of the West, and such baubles as the ducal crown of the house of Mazarin. All this, he announced, he had assembled so that it might be melted down to buy boots and bread for those who fought the battles of the nation.

"That is our man," de Batz had told La Salle. "He is in a situation of danger and difficulty, as he knows. Whilst he perceives the change that must come and is aware of the peril of waiting too long before declaring himself, yet he perceives, too, the danger of a premature declaration. Meanwhile, all that such a man can do is to watch and to arm. He will refuse no weapon that presents itself; and I trust to his acuteness to value the power of the weapon that we offer."

And so La Salle had climbed those stairs in the Rue St Honoré, and had been admitted to the single shabby room that the pro-consul occupied; for the arched alcove into which the bed was thrust could hardly be counted as a separate chamber. Nevertheless, Fouché's wife attempted to make it so count when she retired into it and pulled a tattered screen across the opening.

La Salle might then have supposed himself alone with Fouché, but for the fretful crying, the coughs and gasps of the ailing child the citoyenne could be heard endeavouring to soothe.

The pro-consul had risen from a seat by one of the two grimy windows that overlooked the street. He had been writing in a note-book, which was now closed upon his forefinger. He stood waiting, a tall, very thin, delicate man, reddish of hair. His shaven face, long, narrow and well featured, would not have been unattractive had it been less worn and pale. It was the face of a man much older than the three-and-thirty years the ex-professor counted. In the glance of the pale eyes, low-lidded and sleepy-looking, there was something sinister and chilling, whilst the mouth, thin and straight, informed the intelligent that here was a man whom it would be difficult to win by sentiment.

"You wish to see me, citizen?" His manner was coldly courteous, his voice thin. He suffered from the handicap in a man of State who must also be an orator, of a weak throat, and he had not yet recovered from the strain he had yesterday put upon it in the tribune of the Convention.

La Salle, a little disconcerted by the unexpected sordidness of the surroundings in which he discovered this great man, made a quick recovery, bowed hat in hand, and delivered himself of the well-considered opening.

"It was my good fortune to hear you yesterday in the Convention, and I hasten to pay my homage to your pure republicanism, and to express what all thoughtful men must feel – our comfort in the knowledge that we possess so stout a champion to do battle with the liberticides."

Fouché considered him gravely for a moment. Then: "It is good of you, citizen," he said, "to climb three pairs of stairs so as to tell me this." There was a bitter-sweetness of suspicion in the tone.

La Salle's smile was apologetic. "I have yet another motive."

"It had occurred to me."

"I am a painter, citizen-representative, a student still, but one who hopes to exhibit in this year's Salon, and the hope would be likelier of fulfilment if my subject were of interest in itself. I trust that you discover nothing unworthy in my seeking this adventitious aid."

The pallid face of the man who was never known to miss an adventitious aid to the attainment of any aspiration, displayed a smile that was like wintry sunshine on a frozen pool. "No, no. But why come to me? I know nothing, I fear, of art. My leisures, like my labours, have been given all to science."

"But it is your portrait I desire to paint, citizen-representative." He pulled a sketch-book from one pocket, a pencil from another. "If you would permit me as a preliminary to make a drawing... The reverence, citizen, in which I hold your idealism would inspire me to – "

"Yes, yes. I know all that. I am not, I hope, a man to refuse what is so easily granted. But this will take time, and I am leaving Paris again at once. I return to my duty in the West." He drew forth his watch. "I am afraid we must postpone this affair of yours."

La Salle's face reflected his dismay. "It will take so little time. I work so quickly. Just a preliminary drawing and some notes, from which I could prepare my canvas against your next visit to Paris."

The dull cold eyes were watching him. "But if you work so quickly what would be gained?" And he went on: "You are a student, you say. With whom do you study?"

"With Louis David."

"Ah! A great painter. In the classical tradition, they tell me." His manner relented. A bony, translucent hand, very long and prehensile in the fingers, waved the young man to one of the only two deal chairs in the room. "Sit down. I can give you half an hour, or a little longer, if that will serve."

"Oh, excellently, excellently! If you will sit there, citizen, your profile to the light. So. Now, if you will turn a little towards the window. Not quite so much. There. That is capital."

His pencil worked briskly, and for some moments the task completely absorbed the artist. But when the main lines were down, enough to make a show, he ventured, whilst still drawing, upon conversation.

"It grieves me, as it must grieve every patriot, citizen, to hear that you are not to remain in Paris. You are wanted here. To combat the corruption that is about."

Fouché did not answer. He sat as if wrapped in thought. After a moment's concentration on his sketch, La Salle resumed.

"There are queer stories. One hears things in the ateliers and in the cafés. They may not be true, but they make a man uneasy."

"What sort of things?" asked the dry, thin voice.

"Some that it is hardly safe to repeat. And some... For instance, the latest rumour is of a plot to kidnap the little Capet."

He expected a question that would open the way for him. But Fouché did not come to cues. "That is as inevitable as its failure," he said. "It has been tried. No need for alarm as long as Chaumette has charge of the Temple."

"I hope not. Indeed, I hope not. I am relieved to hear you say so." La Salle worked on, his wits seeking another line of attack. "Yet considering the temptations one is rendered uneasy."

"What exactly are the temptations?"

This was better. It supplied the opening needed. "The price that the enemies of France would pay for the possession of the person of the so-called Louis XVII."

"That could not tempt a patriot. He is not athirst for gold. His needs are small: iron, bread and an income of forty crowns."

La Salle sighed. He stole a glance round the sordid room.

"If all patriots were as you, citizen, there would be no grounds for uneasiness."

"All patriots who are not like me are not patriots," said Fouché. "But if you are seriously perturbed, you should see the Citizen Chaumette. He is responsible for the Temple and its prisoners." He drew forth his watch again. "I hope that your sketch is finished. My time is hardly my own."

Then La Salle understood that his aims were suspected, and that without even troubling to ascertain their nature, Fouché was purposely making it impossible for him to pursue them. He accepted a defeat which no insistence could avert. With a word of apology he worked on in silence for some moments.

Fouché rose with him when it was done. "May I see your drawing?"

La Salle proffered the book. The sleepy eyes considered the page.

"Yes," was the odd comment, "you are an artist." He turned aside to call. "Bonne! Come and see this picture of me."

She came, a gentle, timid woman, and a flicker of interest lighted her dark, careworn eyes as she looked at the portrait. It pleased and was flattering, because La Salle, whilst faithfully recording the comely lines of the countenance, had completely missed – as David was scornfully to point out to him tomorrow – the elusive repellent force contained in them.

"It is beautiful," she exclaimed. "So like you, Joseph, that it almost speaks."

"If it does that, it is not like me at all."

"He jests, citizen. He is like that," she reassured La Salle, her eyes on his grave, attentive face.

"I had hoped to paint a portrait, citoyenne. But that must wait until we meet again."

Thus maintaining the pretence, and with many compliments, he took his leave.

"A charming young man," said Bonne-Jeanne.

"Oh, charming," her husband agreed. "Charm is a spy's best stock-in-trade."

"A spy?" There was real fear in her glance. "Was he a spy?"

"It is at least probable. A pupil of Louis David's. Louis David a worshipper of Robespierre, devoted to him body and soul. Robespierre, spreading the ground with snares for me. There seems to be a chain. And he talked to me of plots, as I expected he would, when I allowed him to remain. We had better be making our packages, my girl, and get back to the West."

The child in the cot grew fretful. Care deepened in Bonne-Jeanne's face. "Couldn't we wait for two or three days? Little Nièvre is so ill."

Pain contracted his eyes. He set an arm affectionately about her shoulders. "For little Nièvre, too, it will be better that we get away from these drinkers of blood. Wild beasts are cruel only because of their stupidity and fear. So it is with men. Only the stupid and the craven are cruel."

Yet in Lyons, when he got there, he wrote his name in fire and blood, so that he made it infamous for all time. And he did it with a full consciousness of what he did; practising cruelty not because he was either stupid or cowardly, but because, so as to hold his position until he could make of it a stepping-stone to mastery, he must not in the present temper of the government be moderate.

Chapter 4

The Seduction of Chaumette

"You should see the Citizen Chaumette," Fouché had said to La Salle, and as if acting on that advice it was Chaumette, after all, whom he sought upon the morrow.

Loitering in the hall of the Tuileries for the purpose of waylaying the Procurator-Syndic of the Commune, the young painter was himself hailed by the great man and drawn out of the crowd.

"What's this you were telling Fouché of a plot to kidnap the little Capet?"

"Oh, that! Probably an idle rumour."

They came out on to the steps of the palace.

The December day, although sunny, was cold, and perhaps on this account the attendance of idlers in the courtyard was less than usual. There were a few odd groups, chiefly of the out-of-work starvelings so plentifully produced by the attempt to build Utopia. Women preponderated – noisy, aggressive harridans who shared the general illusion of emancipation which had made of every fishwife a politician. Two or three newspaper-hawkers were shouting the contents of their sheets, announcing the daily discovery of a plot against the Republic by either Coburg or the perfidious Pitt. Beyond the gateway, in the Carrousel, a swarm of beggars whined, some flaunting their sores or their crippled limbs, so as to move compassion. Their presence annoyed Chaumette. He denounced them to his companion as being assembled and paraded by aristocrat intriguers, so as to discredit the Republic by creating an illusion of misery.

In the Rue St Nicaise they had some difficulty in getting through a mob of angry, raucous women that besieged a bread-shop and fiercely resisted the injunctions, and even the pikes, of four sectionary officers who strove to range them into an orderly queue. La Salle inquired ironically, was this another illusion resulting from reactionary juggling?

"The women," Chaumette answered him, missing the irony, "are getting out of hand. They have been encouraged to play a part for which they are not fitted. Their place is in the home, bearing children to defend the fatherland. The law will have to see to it. But this aristocrat plot of which you were speaking…"

"I spoke of no aristocrat plot. I don't think aristocrats are concerned in it."

"You don't suggest that patriots are conspiring to steal the boy? What could they do with him?"

"Do you really ask me that?" It was to be presumed that La Salle's laugh was at the simplicity of Chaumette. "Have you thought, my friend, what his imperial Austrian uncle might be willing to pay for the boy's person? Certainly not less than a million, probably five millions, possibly ten millions, and in Austrian gold, Chaumette, not in assignats. There's a short cut to affluence for anyone who desires affluence, to power, perhaps, for anyone who desires power. For if the forces of reaction should yet prevail and the Republic be engulfed, what would be the position of the preserver of the King?"

The sudden gravity of Chaumette's peasant face provoked fresh laughter in La Salle. "You begin to see that there would be motive enough. Look to your prisoner, Chaumette. Look to your prisoner."

"So I will, name of God! You shall tell me more. You shall give evidence of this before the Committee of Public Safety."

"I have no evidence. That is, I do not know enough to denounce anyone. I have heard several named. But it is all so vague. It would be terrible to bring suspicion on any man by naming him in these circumstances."

"It would be more terrible to leave the Republic exposed to peril. Better even that some innocent heads should fall." Chaumette was patriotically intransigent. "You shall come before the Committee and name those you have heard mentioned."

La Salle shook his head. "In that case I should have to begin by naming you."

"Me?" Chaumette sucked in his breath. "Name of God! Me?" He stood still. They had turned the corner, and were standing before the portals of the Opera. A chestnut-seller approached, crying her wares. She removed the rusty shawl swathing the pan she bore in the crook of her arm, and proffered the boiled fruit. Chaumette in that moment of irritation dismissed her with peremptory contempt, and so provoked a storm of abuse in the course of which, and in spite of his sash of office, she cursed him for a pig of an aristocrat.

Chaumette dragged his companion on, out of range of her invective.

"These women! Name of God, these women!" He halted again. "You were saying that I am named by these calumniators." He was livid.

"Less unreasonably than others."

"How? What do you mean by that?"

"The Temple is the prison of the Commune. You are the Procurator-Syndic of the Commune, the only man in Paris with free, unchallenged access to the Temple at all hours. In your case, at least, there is the opportunity. Does it not follow, once the silly rumour is afoot it must attach itself to the one man who is in a position to perform the thing?"

"I see." Chaumette was thoughtful. He stroked a stubbly chin. "I see," he said again, so slowly that La Salle, watching him with his dreamy eyes, wondered whether already the subtle poison was at work. "What others did you hear mentioned?"

"They are great names. Names best not uttered."

"But to me? In confidence?"

"I am not to be dragged before the Committee to repeat them. Nothing could be more dangerous. Denunciation of something probably untrue might serve to inspire traitors. After all, five or ten millions in gold might seduce a good many patriots from their duty."

"That is true. Name of God! How true that is! No, no. There shall be no premature denunciations. I give you my word. Now, whose names have you heard?"

"Barras, for one," La Salle invented shamelessly.

"Faith, if it's true of any man, it might be true of him. A sensual, spendthrift sybarite, with his horses and his women. He'd grab at a million or two to feed his lusts, the damned rotten-souled aristocrat. Bah!" He spat ostentatiously. "Anyone else?"

"One other." La Salle lowered his voice. "Robespierre."

Chaumette jumped as if he had been stabbed. Startled out of his poise, he became, in his excitement, dangerously indiscreet.

"God of God! If Fouché should be right, then, that this mincing *Monsieur de* Robespierre, with his powdered head, his silk stockings, and his fine coat, is at heart an aristo."

"Fouché says that, does he? A shrewd man, Fouché. I'ld pay heed to what he says, which is not to say that I believe that Robespierre has thought of possessing himself of little Capet."

"But he might, considering what's to be gained, as you've made me understand. Name of a pig! He might."

"Keep a good watch at the Temple, Chaumette." He came to a standstill. "Here we part. David is expecting me at the atélier. Apropos, and speaking of Fouché, I made a sketch of him yesterday. I must show it to you. And one of these days perhaps you'ld let me paint your portrait, Chaumette." His dark eyes discarded their dreaminess as they now appraised the Procurator-Syndic's lumpy features. "A fine subject, my friend. An inspiring countenance. I speak as an artist, you understand. That noble, lofty brow. It is Roman. The pure lines of that well-cut, resolute mouth. They would come easily. Not so easy to reproduce the fire, the sublime light of those eyes, to seize the nobility, the elusive nobility that informs the whole. Difficult. But so worth attempting. You must let me try, Chaumette."

"My dear La Salle! My friend!" Chaumette was purring under a commendation in which flattery was not to be suspected, since it was an artist who spoke in academic terms. "But when you will. Command me freely."

Thus, the insidious La Salle created the occasion to pursue the seduction of the Procurator-Syndic.

And he lost no time. On the following day – warmly commended by de Batz, from whom he extracted another ten louis on the strength of the progress made – he carried canvas, easel, and paint-box to the second floor of a house in the Rue Filles Saint-Thomas, where Chaumette had his lodging. The Procurator-Syndic was housed with comfort and no more luxury than became a prosperous patriot. For prosperous he was. Besides the emoluments of his office, his earnings were considerable as a pamphleteer. His home was conducted for him by the comely buxom Henriette Simonin, whom he had probably married.

La Salle made friends with her at once. He possessed without exerting it a considerable attraction for women, and here he was at some pains to please. Because she complained to him of the bareness of the walls of their sitting-room, he threw off between the sittings which Chaumette gave him some four or five paintings, which included the Execution of Louis Capet and the Death of Marat, the latter being little more than a plagiaristic reproduction of David's famous picture.

She hovered about when he was at work, and saw to his comforts, sometimes with a bavaroise, and sometimes with coffee and a petit-verre of noyau of Phalsbourg or of liqueur of the Isles (that was really made in the Faubourg St Germain). And very soon the intimacy he cultivated with her, produced the increased intimacy he desired with her husband, so that long before the portrait was finished, La Salle had become the close friend of the family. With this advantage there were also disadvantages. The assiduity of Henriette's attendance when La Salle was painting, made it difficult to talk of the affairs that supplied the real motive for the artist's presence. Some opportunities there were, however, and one at least that Chaumette, himself, deliberately made, sending his wife on a marketing errand that must ensure her absence for some time.

La Salle was expecting this, for with the collaboration of de Batz the ground had been carefully prepared.

Chaumette sat to be painted in all the panoply of his exalted office – blue coat with gilded buttons, a tricolour collar from which hung a brass tablet on which the Rights of Man were inscribed in minuscule characters, a tricolour sash, a sabre which he had never drawn, and an empanached hat, from under which his hair hung down in black, untidy wisps. With his broad, coarse, moist face, he looked to La Salle like Impudence travestied as Majesty.

He was thoughtful for a time on that day when Henriette had been so carefully dismissed. Then, suddenly, he broke the silence.

"Barras was at the Temple yesterday."

The painter instantly suspended his labours, but his surprise was merest comedy. The visit had been suggested to Barras by that other of de Batz's agents, Sénar, the secretary of the Committee of Public Safety. He had ventured the opinion that the Public Safety should inform itself of the conditions in the prison of the Commune, in which two State prisoners of such consequence as the Capet children were confined, and Barras had been prompt to act upon it.

Having conquered his simulated stupefaction, La Salle asked: "By your authority?"

"By an order of the Committee of Public Safety, which I was not even required to countersign. That is an abuse that shall not occur again."

La Salle's eyes were owlishly grave. "What did he want there?"

"Ah! What? Apparently he did no more than look round. He went into the boy's apartment, and then up to the women's on the next floor."

"Alone?" There was alarm in the question.

"No, no. Simon went with him. A faithful watchdog that."

Silence followed. Abstractedly, La Salle mixed some colour on his palette. When at last he spoke, it was as if he were thinking aloud. "I wonder if…after all…there was anything in that rumour."

"It is what I am wondering." Chaumette did not require to be told to what rumour La Salle alluded. "And I'ld give a deal to know. Ah, fichtre! The fool wastes his time, anyway."

"In your place, Anaxagoras, I should make sure of it."

"I have made sure. With my regulations the thing would be impossible. The boy would be missed at once."

"I suppose so, and yet… Queer things are sometimes done. Say, now, that a substitute were provided."

"A substitute? You want to laugh. Where would they find a substitute?"

"Millions can find anything. After all, it is not so difficult to find a substitute for a child of eight. Likenesses are common at that early age, before character has moulded features."

"And now you want to frighten me, I think. But you've forgotten Simon."

"On the contrary. I've remembered him. He could be bribed. There are millions to be spent, remember."

"Rubbish! Simon could not be bribed."

"He could be removed, then. Say that Barras desired to remove him. With the weight of the Committee of Public Safety behind him, could he be resisted?"

"Let him try. I shall know where we stand then, and I'll take my measures."

La Salle's countenance reflected a grave concern for his friend Anaxagoras. "In your place, I should not wait. As Procurator-Syndic, you are responsible for the safety of that child. Have you reflected, Anaxagoras, that if these scoundrels were to succeed in stealing him, your head would pay for it? And, on my faith, there never was a moment when the temptation could be greater. Things go none too well with the army in the Vendée; on the frontier we are reeling under the blows of the despots." Excitement kindled in him, he gesticulated a little wildly, palette and mahl-stick in one hand, paintbrush in the other. "An opportunist – Barras or another – wanting to make himself safe in the event of a counter-revolution, might go to any lengths to obtain possession of that child. If that happened, Anaxagoras, the guillotine would provide a collar for your neck. Name of a name, my friend! I shudder for you already."

Anaxagoras was stirred to the murky depths of him. He heaved himself out of the chair, putting an end to the sitting for the day.

"You may be right, name of a dog!" He paced to and fro, his hands behind him, his ridiculous sabre clattering about his heels.

"I'll double the vigilance, treble it. And the Commune shall pass a decree that no one – not even members of the Public Safety – be admitted to the Temple without my order."

La Salle's eyes shone. "Almost you reassure me, my friend."

"Almost!" roared Chaumette. "Almost? By all the devils, isn't it enough?"

"Perhaps my affection for you makes me overanxious."

"But what more can I do? What more can I do?"

"Oh, nothing. Nothing."

"There's no conviction in your tone. You say, 'nothing, nothing', as if you meant, 'something, something'. Ah, name of a dog! Be frank with me. Can I do more?"

They stood squarely before each other, La Salle's countenance the very image of gravity. "No, I suppose you can't. That is, short of… Ah, bah!" He dismissed the thought.

"Short of what?" Chaumette was insistent.

"It's not worth mentioning. You'll account it fantastic, and yet… the more I think of it… It's the one way to make sure that no one will steal the brat."

"What is?"

"To forestall them. To steal him yourself."

"Steal him myself! Are you mad?"

"Yes. It must sound mad to you. Perhaps it is. And yet…and yet… if you were to take him quietly away and hide him somewhere, somewhere that no one could suspect… I suppose it's impossible."

Staring at him, a frown of thought came slowly to replace the empty amazement on Chaumette's low brow. Then he shrugged, and swung aside. "Fichtre! Mad!"

"I knew you would scorn the notion. Yet it is the one sure way to make yourself safe, say what you will."

Chaumette became annoyed. "And if it were discovered? How safe should I be then?"

"Safe enough. Safe from everybody, so long as you could produce the boy. As safe from the wrath of the Republic as from that of the Monarchy if it should ever come to be restored. And that's another reason that had not occurred to me. But there!" He turned abruptly aside, to pack up his brushes. "I suppose the sitting is over for today."

But Chaumette was suddenly at his shoulder, breathing fiercely.

"I hope you are not suggesting that I should play the game you attribute to Barras."

"I, attribute a game to Barras? Oh, come. What have I said? I attribute nothing to anybody. I point out to you a possibility, what I should probably do if I were in your place. But then, perhaps I am a coward, Anaxagoras. I lack your dauntless courage, your Roman soul. Nothing short of the assurance of safety would let me sleep of nights. That's all."

It was enough. Enough to give matter for serious thought to the fierce revolutionary who, for all his moments of audacity, was at heart a coward. For twenty-four hours he was haunted by La Salle's crafty phrase, "As safe from the wrath of the Republic as from that of the Monarchy if it should come to be restored."

On the morrow, when the young painter came to put the finishing touches to the portrait over which he had so deliberately delayed, he found Henriette again absent, and was in no doubt of the reason.

And no sooner had La Salle settled to his work than Chaumette broached the subject.

"I've been thinking of what you said yesterday, Florence, about the little Capet. You made me angry. Yet it was good advice you gave me for all that, if I could but follow it."

"What difficulty do you find?"

"Several. First, there's Simon, the custodian of the boy."

"That's not a difficulty. You appointed Simon. You can dismiss him."

"And then? He would have to be replaced."

"True. But you could create a slight gap between Simon's departure and his successor's arrival. That would be the moment to make the change."

"Oh yes. The change. That's the second difficulty."

"Less of a difficulty than the first." La Salle stood out from the canvas, and faced the sitting Procurator-Syndic. "To be quite frank, I was led yesterday to say that to substitute a child of eight was an easy matter, by the fact that only last week, whilst hunting for a model, I came upon a child of about the same age who might easily serve as a substitute for the little Capet with anyone who didn't know him very well. The same pale, puffy countenance, the same straw-coloured hair and blue eyes."

"Yes," said Chaumette, with heavy sarcasm. "And at the first word he utters… "

"He's a deaf-mute," said La Salle, and startled Chaumette into a hard, suspicious stare.

He went on after a short pause. "That, in fact, is how I came to notice him. He is being exhibited for his infirmity – by a one-armed beggar who pretends to be his father – with a placard on his breast to announce the affliction. That sort of child can be bought, or, at least, indefinitely hired, for two or three hundred livres. I don't say that he's a duplicate of Capet, or even that he resembles him much. But he's pallid and plump and yellow-haired and of the same age, and so he broadly answers to the same description."

"Descriptions of the little Capet include some singular peculiarities," said Chaumette heavily. "There are odd vaccination scars, the veins on one of his thighs are grouped into the image of a dove – just like that damned order of theirs of the Saint Esprit – and his right ear is deformed; the lobe of it is twice the size of the left one."

"But the new custodian and the commissioners on duty don't need to be told all this, and, anyway, the child won't walk about naked, with his hair cut short."

Chaumette sat hunched in his chair, his chin in his hand, his face dark with thought. The obstacles over which he had sighed in secret during the past night had suddenly disappeared. Yet he hesitated to go forward.

"You talk of this beggar-child as if you had but to go and fetch him."

"Provided I possessed two or three hundred francs, that is probably all I should have to do. Anyway, I could try, if you should decide."

"Decision is not so sacredly easy. There are a lot of things to be considered; a sacred heap of things."

"Shall I see, meanwhile, if I can get the boy?"

Chaumette looked scared. "If you were very cautious you might. Yes. That can do no harm. We can consider then, when you've ascertained if he's to be had."

"You can trust me, Anaxagoras," La Salle assured him, and applied himself so vigorously to the portrait that he finished it that day. There was no need to prolong sittings which had accomplished their object. Chaumette had gulped the bait. The first and most difficult stage of the plot was overpast.

Chapter 5

The Puppet-Master

As he had baited the trap, so did La Salle guide the steps by which the trusting Anaxagoras should enter it. He had an answer to every objection, an easy way round every obstacle. There were not a few of these in the tortuous course that he had chosen, and more than one of them had at first seemed insurmountable even to the sagacity of de Batz.

When La Salle had supplied the answer to the last of the questions raised by the Procurator-Syndic, this functionary paid him what he supposed was a high compliment.

"Sacred name! You've as calculating a mind as Fouché, and he was once a professor of mathematics."

The deaf-mute was, of course, traced, and being precisely what La Salle had said, the pretended child of a professional beggar, there was no difficulty whatever about obtaining possession of him at a cost to Chaumette of three hundred livres. In fact, possession of him had already been obtained by de Batz in anticipation.

The next step was to get rid of Simon and his wife, and again it was La Salle who indicated how it should be done.

Chaumette, by now entirely under the dominion of this masterful young painter with the drawling, weary voice and the languid, ineffective manner, followed his directions with punctilious fidelity. At a meeting of the Council of the Commune on the last day of the year, he proposed a decree making it illegal for any man to hold simultaneously more than one office in the public service.

La Salle was in his place on the Council, and so was Antoine Simon, who was also a member, as one of the representatives of the Temple Section, and a person prominently in the public eye in those days, as the preceptor of the young Capet.

Chaumette crushed opposition at the outset by raising the question to those grave, lofty grounds of principle on which, as every hypocrite knows, few men dare to display hostility in public. In inveighing against the holding of more than one office, he denounced as a bad citizen any man who sought to multiply emoluments at the State's expense.

For that evening the matter did not go beyond the stage of debate. But that was enough deeply to perturb the spirit of Simon, who foresaw the unpleasant effect for him of the proposed decree.

Descending the stairs after the meeting he found La Salle at his elbow.

"My good Citizen Simon."

Simon, who had ever been friendly disposed towards the young painter since their acquaintance began on that October day in the Temple Tower, returned the greeting with a gruff cordiality, and they passed out into the street together.

La Salle felt his way delicately.

"There will be a deal of grumbling if this notion of Chaumette's should become law."

"I suppose that membership of the Council will be counted as an office," Simon grumbled.

"Assuredly, since it carries emoluments."

Simon's oath was all the comment La Salle required.

"Ah, my dear Citizen Simon, it is a sad truth of human nature that when men are given the means they always become despots. They arbitrarily impose their will and their fancies upon those who are in subjection to them. They care nothing for the injustices they may do in savouring the voluptuousness of power."

"Name of a pig, but that's the truth, Citizen La Salle. What is to be done?"

"Hope that this mischievous decree will not be passed. That is all at present, my friend."

It was certainly enough to ensure that when the decree should be passed, it would be La Salle whom Simon would seek for comfort in his dismay. They were not kept waiting for the event. It took place at the very next meeting of the Council, when the vote compelled by Chaumette made it illegal for any man to fill two offices simultaneously, and expressly for any member of the Council to hold any other appointment, whether or not it interfered with his attendance. Simon could hardly credit that the catastrophe had overtaken him of resigning the custodianship of the Temple, with emoluments of six thousand francs a year for himself and four thousand for his wife.

It was Chaumette, himself, who had appointed him to that enviable office. It was Marie-Jeanne, Simon's wife, who had deserved it. A sturdy, muscular woman, very feminine of nature, despite the masculinity of her appearance, a good housewife, with a natural aptitude for nursing, she had given herself to the care of the wounded men of Marseilles who had been housed in the Cordelier Convent after the attack on the Tuileries. For this she had deserved well of the nation and particularly of the Commune; and Chaumette had rewarded her by bestowing upon her husband a custodianship for which Simon otherwise satisfied the Procurator-Syndic's requirements.

The very memory of how the office had come to be bestowed upon him quickened Simon's resentment when he saw himself so abruptly and arbitrarily deprived of ease and consequence.

He sought out Chaumette after the meeting was over, and kept him in talk for some time, hoping, like the stupid man he was, that an exception from this harsh decree could be made in his favour. For this he pleaded. But Chaumette, wrapped in a legal sacrosanctity, shocked by so improper a suggestion, assumed a minatory tone. It did not become a good patriot to be so concerned with a profit to be extorted from the State. In fact, it rendered his patriotism suspect.

The simple, ignorant mind of Simon took fright at that dreadful phrase, and hurriedly he bade the Procurator-Syndic a good night. His fear, however, was not of a kind to cool his rage. On the contrary it was a wind to fan it, and he became as metal softened for the hammering to which La Salle was waiting to submit him.

The arch-intriguer, wrapped to the eyes in a cloak against the piercing night air, surged at the shoemaker's side as he was emerging from the Place de la Grève.

"And is it you, Citizen Simon? Well met, my friend. What do you say now? Was I right or not? This new decree will rob you of your rich deserts, as I feared it must."

In a snarl of infinite bitterness, Simon began to unbosom himself. "These sacredly fine patriotic notions! These... Ah, bah!" Caution and mortification, between them, robbed him of words.

"Believe me, I feel for you. For you and with you." The young painter's voice was rich with feeling. "A cruel decree. Wantonly cruel. I don't care who hears me. A piece of despotism. An abuse of power."

"No less," said Simon fervently. "Name of a sacred pig, no less!" And being encouraged, he discarded caution. "Vile despotism. Horrible tyranny. That's what it is. These sacred cuckolds in office take a lot on themselves. Sacred little kings! That's what they are: sacred little kings. But the people'll find them out. See if they don't. They'll be sent to end like the big one who sneezed into Chariot's sacred basket a year ago."

"How just is your anger, my friend! Almost – do you know? – this accursed decree seems aimed particularly at you."

"At me? At me?"

"Had it not occurred to you? Do you know another member of the Council whom it hits so heavily?"

"Sacred name!" said the foolish Simon. The monstrous vanity engendered by his custodianship made him easy to persuade. "But why at me?"

"Ah! There you ask me to explain a mystery."

"By God, you've said it. A mystery. They couldn't have found a man to do their dirty work better than I've done it. Look at the boy. You saw him three months ago, Citizen La Salle. Deroyalized. Completely deroyalized. That's what he is. That Messalina, his own mother, wouldn't know him if she could come back to look at him. Whose work is that? Mine, name of a pig. Mine! And yet they kick me out like a sacred dog. They get rid of me."

"That's it," said La Salle. "They get rid of you. You've explained it. You're acute, my dear Citizen Simon. It was to get rid of you that Chaumette passed that decree. You've set your finger on it. It leaps to the eye."

"The sacred swine!" said Simon.

"And why has it been done? Shall I tell you, or do you see it for yourself? You are too diligent, too watchful, too good a patriot. You get in the way of their dirty aristocratic schemes. Oh, it all becomes plain. Chaumette and his friends want to make themselves safe if a change should come, if the despots should return. They've no heart, no guts. Because things are going none so well, already they count themselves defeated. I've seen that for some time. It helps me to understand this piece of villainy. They just want to make themselves safe."

Simon was ready to believe any evil if only he could understand it. "How do the sacred scoundrels make themselves safe by getting rid of me?"

He heard La Salle's soft laugh in the dark, felt the clutch of La Salle's slim, vigorous hand on his arm. "Suppose," said the young painter very softly, "that they wanted to steal the boy. Would they not begin by removing you?"

"Steal the boy? Why steal him?"

"To sell him."

"Sell him? Who the hell wants to buy him?"

"Several people, beginning with his uncle, the Emperor of Austria. I could get you half a million in gold for him tomorrow. Perhaps more."

A flow of obscenity testified to the depth of Simon's amazement. He was like a man who, lost in impenetrable darkness, suddenly sees a light, so easy is it to believe the worst of those of whom we wish to believe it. He was still ejaculating recklessly when La Salle hushed him.

They were crossing the Rue Soubise, and a patrol of sectionaries was approaching from the right. The leader stepped forward, raising a lantern to the level of the faces of these two wayfarers.

"Halt there! Ah, it's you, Citizen Simon." He passed on to La Salle. "Your card, citizen."

La Salle drew it forth and held it in the light. It was scanned, and the patrol tramped on, leaving them free to proceed.

Simon resumed his objurgations, incoherent for a time, but at last coherently. The Citizen La Salle was right. It must be as he said. Chaumette was a grasping, greedy swine. He'd sell the boy to Austria, would he? Not whilst Antoine Simon could prevent it. This he vowed, calling several unspeakable divinities to witness. He would denounce the bastard.

"Come, come," said La Salle. "Take thought, man. Chaumette would have you under the knife within twenty-four hours. The crime he intends is plain enough to anyone who can reason. But what good is reason before the law? Why, I'd denounce him, myself, if I could prove the thing. But I'm not so mad as to lay my neck in the window of the guillotine for nothing."

"Do you tell me that I can do nothing? That I am to look on, to allow this infamy to take place?"

"My good Citizen Simon, you are on very dangerous ground. There is nothing in the world that you can do, short of anticipating them and stealing the boy, yourself; and that, of course, would be insane."

Simon gasped and gulped. "Insane? But would it be insane? If a thing is possible to them, why should it not be possible to me?"

"Come, come, my friend! A little calm. You are suggesting something terrible."

"I am proposing to save the little Capet for the nation. There must be ways of doing it."

"Of course there must be, or these scoundrels could not contemplate it, as you've said. But the difficulty is to discover that way. I wonder, now." He was thoughtfully silent for a moment. "Tell me, when do you leave the Temple?"

"What do I know? As much as you know about that. Perhaps in a week; perhaps in a fortnight."

"Well, well, whenever it may be, perhaps you are right after all. The wise thing may be to take the boy with you when you go. Wait! Listen."

Simon contained himself as he was admonished, and listened.

La Salle talked steadily all the way up the long Rue du Temple, and at every step Simon sank deeper and deeper under the spell of that subtle young gentleman's plausibility.

Late that night La Salle summed up the situation to de Batz in the Rue de Ménars.

"It marches, Baron. I hold the strings that make the puppets dance. I have persuaded Chaumette to have the boy kidnapped so as to forestall Barras. Chaumette has persuaded me to persuade Simon to do the kidnapping in the first instance. And I have persuaded Simon to do it so as to forestall Chaumette, and for half a million as a salve to his Republican conscience. All is in train. Somewhere between Simon and Chaumette I shall step in to dislocate the machinery. But up to that point it runs smoothly. Smoothly as the guillotine."

De Batz, that master of intrigue, looked at the lazily smiling young man with eyes of awe.

Chapter 6

The Hand-Cart

The 30th Nivôse, Year Two, which is to say, the 19th January, 1794, was the date appointed by Chaumette for Simon's departure from the Temple; and he had settled that no fresh preceptor should replace him. He explained himself to the Commune. The boy's tutelage had gone far enough. To protract it was a useless waste of national resources. The custodianship supplied by the four members of the Commune daily on guard there as commissioners, two of whom were changed every twenty-four hours, was all that would he required.

So well grounded a proposal was cordially agreed, and La Salle's machine continued to run smoothly. Marie-Jeanne had been brought into the plot, influenced less by the money to be made than by the rough goodness of the motherly soul encased in that coarse envelope.

On the afternoon of that 19th January, a day of fog and drizzle accompanying the thaw that had set in, the Simons were busy packing up in the Temple Tower.

Madame Royale, in the mémoire of her captivity, written during the last weeks of it, nearly two years later, tells us how she and her aunt, Madame Elizabeth, listening attentively to the unusual sounds on the floor below, formed the conclusion – a conclusion oddly accurate – that Louis Charles was leaving the Temple. It had long been the habit of these unhappy ladies to listen for sounds that should give them some indication of what was happening in the world beyond their walls, and particularly to the movements in the little King's chamber underneath. For days after he had first been separated from them – in July of '93 – they had heard him sobbing in his sudden motherlessness; for the child had been passionately devoted to the mother whom his unconscious lies had helped to send to the scaffold. Soon, however, after the fashion of tender, infant souls, upon which mercifully no impression can sink to any depth, he must have consoled himself; for they could hear him at play, stamping, shouting and galloping about the room; and they took comfort in the thought that, at least, he was no longer fretting. A little later on they could hear him singing the ribald and revolutionary songs that his new preceptor taught him: the *Marseillaise*, the *Carmagnole*, or, more commonly still, the terrible *Ça Ira*! He preferred this last because the revolutionary words were set to a melody with which he was already familiar, a sprightly contredanse that in the bright days at Versailles – now mere shadows on his memory – Marie-Antoinette so often played on the clavecin. As time and his corruption progressed he grew still noisier, though the listeners on the floor above never suspected that an excess of wine, which was forced upon him, accounted for the raucous bawling of songs that made them shudder. At least, he was not unhappy or maltreated. He was well housed, well nourished and well clad, and his little wants were freely supplied. He was given such toys as he craved, and when he was tired of romping, there were books, perhaps not very judiciously chosen, and playing-cards, of revolutionary pattern, of course, on which kings and queens were replaced by heroes of a republican order.

On this very day – this fateful 19th January – he was to be given a great pulp-board horse, as more satisfying to his imagination than the broom-handle on which he performed his equestrian exercises.

But it was late on that damp, foggy evening, something after eight o'clock, when the messenger from the toymaker trundled up to the portals of the Temple a hand-cart bearing the monstrous horse. This dirty-faced messenger, in carmagnole and clogs, a bonnet of rabbit's fur pressed over his brows, and a woollen scarf muffling him to the nose against the rawness of the air, was La Salle. His manners matched his appearance. He was truculent and surly, and when the guards halted him at the entrance he became abusive at the delay.

"Will you keep me shivering here all night with your imbecile questions? Very fine for you, coming warm from your fire in the guard-room, to harass a poor devil who's half frozen. Can't you see for yourselves what I've got, and haven't I told you where I am going? Carrying a toy to this pampered Capet whelp. Tramping through a couple of miles of slush on an errand like that! There's a job for a patriot!" He swore and spat. "And then to stand here while my feet freeze and you damned aristos give yourselves importance and clutter my senses with your silly questions! For that's what you guardsmen are — damned aristos. You don't impress me with your blue coats and your gaiters. Pampered minions!"

They made sport of his ill-humour, mimicked his grumbling and opened at last the grille for him. Grumbling still, he trundled his cart through the gateway and across the courtyard, past the Palace of the Grand Templar, which formerly had been the residence of the King's brother, the Count of Artois, and on through the trees of that miniature park to the lofty, grim tower with its extinguisher-roofed turrets, the whilom donjon or keep of the Templars.

The door at the foot of the tower stood open, and a rhomb of warm light was projected thence upon the drizzling gloom. From within came a jolly sound of voices and clinking glasses.

Leaving his cart before the entrance, La Salle clattered across the vestibule, and came to stand truculently in the open doorway of the great council hall in which the commissioners were making merry. For Simon, in accordance with the predetermined plan, had fetched a couple of bottles from the cellar, so that he might crush a final cup with the gentlemen of the Commune who had just come on duty. It was a chamber forty feet square, with a vaulted ceiling carried on groins that sprang from a central pillar. Near this pillar, an island of candle-light in an ocean of gloom, stood the table about which the five men were clustered: Simon and the four commissioners, all of them men of the artisan class, not one of whom had ever taken duty here before or was acquainted with the appearance of the King. Chaumette had seen to this.

"Hi, there!"

They turned at the angry hail, and saw La Salle standing under the lintel.

"Does no one answer the door in this sacred place? Must I stand in the snow until I get chilblains whilst you damned noblemen are guzzling in here?"

The burly Simon detached himself from the group. "Now then! Now then! Give yourself airs, don't you? Who the devil are you, anyway? The Czar of Russia or King George of England? And what's your business here?"

"I've brought a horse, a toy horse, for the spoilt brat of the late despot."

"Oh, that!" Simon's tone reduced the matter to insignificance. "Take it upstairs. Second floor. My wife's there. She'll see to it."

He turned back to the table and his companions, and La Salle went out grumbling. Presently they heard the clank of his clogs on the stone of the spiral staircase.

The Citoyenne Simon above heard it, too. She was standing in the open doorway of the boy's room on the second floor when La Salle appeared laden with his toy. Actually it was a hobby-horse, of the kind used in mock tournaments, the head and shoulders of the size of a pony's, the remainder a framework draped with the trailing housings of a charger. These draperies were gathered into a bundle, and the whole seemed unwarrantably heavy.

The big, mannish woman made way for him, her broad face solemn under the mob cap.

Within the room he set down his burden. He paused a moment to recover breath, glancing round. In a mahogany bed with a green satin coverlet the little King was peacefully sleeping.

In silence, whilst the citoyenne remained listening at the door, La Salle slashed away the network of cords that confined the housings.

He shook them out, took the horse by neck and tail, lifted it and tossed it aside, leaving on the ground a yellow-haired child of eight or nine, dressed in a carmagnole and little pantaloons.

The woman turned and leaned forward, peering at the child's pallid face, which glistened like wet ivory in the candlelight. She crept forward so as to obtain a closer view of the boy limp in the sleep into which an opiate had plunged him.

"Quick!" La Salle whispered. Through the grime with which he had smeared his face, his eyes blazed command. "Our lives depend upon it." He crossed in a couple of strides to the bed where the little King, similarly drugged, was soundly slumbering. He swept back the coverlet, picked up child and sheets in one bundle and bore it to an armchair. Then, waving the woman back to her sentinel post at the door, he swiftly stripped the garments from the other child, lifted him into the bed, composed him so that he lay on his side, and covered him with the bedclothes.

Next, with the swift, unhesitating movements of the man whose plans have been well considered, he picked up the King again, swathing the sheets about him in such a way that he seemed to hold no more than an awkward bundle of linen.

"Now! Let yourself be heard. Scold like a fishwife. Bully me into helping you to carry some of your belongings."

At once she made shift to play the comedy commanded. She seized a couple of packages that stood ready, and raised her voice to a pitch of raucous railing.

"Take up that bundle and carry it to your cart. Oh, you'll be paid for your trouble, never fear. Come on, good-for-nothing. Out of this!"

He started down the stairs with his burden, the woman clattering after him, her shrewish voice ringing through the tower. "Talk of fraternity! A lot of fraternity I see these days. A beast of burden is what I might be. There's that drunken man of mine at wine with those fine gentlemen of the Commune, leaving me to do all the removing. And if I ask a good-for-nothing oaf like you to lend a hand with my packages you must stop to ask if you'll be paid for the service. Name of a name! If I were young and pretty, you'd be ready enough to carry me as well as my packages. And if I were somebody else's wife that animal Simon wouldn't be leaving me to carry everything myself. I know you men. Lot of filth!"

Thus scolding, shrewishly, she drove him before her, down the winding stairs, he answering with increasing violence, calling the devil to witness that it was no part of his job to be carrying her noisome rags for her, and that if he were her husband he would find a bridle for her nasty tongue.

The noise they made and the furious insults they bawled at each other, produced first amazement and then hilarity among the commissioners in the council hall. La Salle went swiftly past the open door of it with his bundle, a man furiously driven; the woman, following close, checked in the doorway so as to make an obstacle to anyone attempting to come forth.

"What's to laugh at, you oafs? And you, Simon? Am I to carry everything and be insulted by this jackanapes with the cart whilst you drink yourself into idiocy with these fine patriots? Salaud! Is that what you're paid for? Is that your job?"

"Bah! My job's over, or will be when I've delivered the brat. Your job is to get on with the removal, and keep your muzzle shut, or I'll shut it for you. Get on there!" he thundered in final dismissal.

As if cowed, she waddled out, muttering imprecations.

La Salle had bestowed his bundle in the cart. He snatched from her the things she carried. "Come on, come on! We don't want to be all night." He flung the packages, bulky but light, on top of the sheet-swathed little body. "Anything more?"

"Plenty more. Wait there."

She re-entered the tower, and her voice was raised again in renewed railings at Simon.

"Well, well," said he to his companions, "I'd better be going, or that beldame will give me no peace. I'll make formal delivery of the boy. You'll want to see him, I suppose, before you sign the register. Come on then, citizens."

There was a general emptying of glasses, a last word of praise for the wine, one of them served up an unclean joke of a recipe for hen-pecked husbands, and, laughing together, they came out of the council hall and followed Simon to the stairs.

Midway up they met Marie-Jeanne descending, a chair hooked on to each of her arms. There was barely room to pass, but she contrived it despite their protests.

"Sacred drunkards!" she growled at them. "Make less noise. The child's asleep. There's a bundle of crockery behind the door. Fetch it down with you, Antoine. And put out the lights."

They obeyed her admonition, and went the rest of the way in silence. Treading softly they followed Simon into the King's room. Simon took up the candle from the table, and held it high, waving a hand to indicate the bed.

From the middle of the chamber where they had halted they beheld in that dim light a mop of yellow hair upon the pillow and the outline of a child's body under the coverlet. That was all; but it was all that they could have asked to see. One by one they nodded and withdrew.

Simon followed them down with the bundle of crockery. He had locked the door and withdrawn the key. As he came down he extinguished each of the lanterns set at intervals in the staircase wall.

Below he handed the bundle to his waiting wife, and led the way once more into the council hall for the last formality. There he surrendered the key of the King's room to Cochefer, one of the commissioners, and required the four of them to sign in the register the acknowledgement that at nine o'clock on the night of the thirtieth Nivôse of the Year Two of the French Republic One and Indivisible, they had received from Antoine Simon the custody of the person of Louis Charles Capet.

It was finished. Simon's last duty at the Temple was fulfilled. He was free to depart.

Outside, La Salle had piled the two chairs on the cart in such a way that they did not press upon the child hidden in the linen.

Across the stretchers of the chairs he now disposed the bundle of crockery, and by the time Simon emerged, carrying a lantern and buttoning his greatcoat, they were ready.

They set out through the slush of melted snow to cross the fog-swathed garden with its denuded, dripping trees. At first they went in silence. The Simons were scared now, conscious that their heads would pay for failure to get past the guards who had orders, as they knew, strictly to examine everyone and everything passing in or out of the Temple. Even La Salle, a man utterly without nerves, confessed afterwards to a consciousness of quickened pulses as they approached the gatehouse. But he kept his senses and remembered the comedy to be played, so that by the time they reached the courtyard the sounds of their discordant, scolding voices had already gone ahead to herald their approach.

La Salle was cursing the couple for having kept him waiting on such a night and for using him as if he were a lackey; the citoyenne was cursing her husband for a lazy drunkard who left her to fetch and carry as if she were a beast of burden; Simon cursed back at his wife, for a shrew who gave him no peace; and the two of them cursed the hand-cart man for daring to plague them with his reproaches.

Thus, all three shouting abusively together, they came across the courtyard towards the corps-de-garde.

A sergeant stood forward, three of his men behind him, drawn from the gatehouse by this discourteous rabble.

"Nice friendly party, aren't you?" he greeted them.

The three of them, talking at once, presented each his separate grievance. By gestures, growing more frantic, the sergeant sought to repress them, whilst behind him his men stood grinning. At last, out of patience, he added his voice to theirs in a roar.

"Ah, sacred name of a name! Do you want to deafen me, then?"

They fell silent suddenly.

"And is it really you, Citizen Simon? Have you been emptying the cellar before leaving? There," he ordered one of his men, "open the gate, Jacques."

Plaintively Simon began to tell the sergeant how ill-used he was. Fiercely his wife cut in to assure the sergeant that she had the misfortune to be married to a worthless salaud who had well deserved to lose his job. Whilst they talked the iron gate creaked on its hinges. La Salle pushed his hand-cart forward with magnificently surly unconcern. But the sergeant laid a hand on it.

"Not so fast, my lad. What have you got there?"

"What should I have but a parcel of filthy rags and shards, for which these good-for-nothings kept me waiting out there in the slush until I – "

"Oh, be quiet! Thousand devils! Are we to have it all again?" The sergeant shifted his detaining hand to the precariously poised bundle of crockery. It clattered under his touch. With a yell the vigorous Marie-Jeanne was upon him, her palms against his breast, thrusting him back.

"Name of God, you clumsy lout! Do you want to smash my bits of things, if you haven't smashed them already?"

"Softly, woman! Softly!" the sergeant protested.

"Do you go softly with your clumsy paws? I was only just in time. A little more and I shouldn't have had a plate left. What the devil do you want to go rummaging for, you great bear of a man? Don't you know we're removing? Or perhaps you think I'm stealing these chairs and this household stuff? Do you?" Menacing, the virago stood before him. "Is that what you think?" Shriller rose her voice. "We are honest folk, Simon and I. Always have been. If we hadn't been honest folk we'ld never have been given charge of the Temple Tower. And now, you slob in uniform, you as good as treat us as if we were pickpockets."

From under the smother of her abuse he was making feeble attempts to quiet her.

"Duty...my duty...the regulations..."

"Duty!" she crowed, and her laughter shrilled in wrathful mockery. "Officiousness! That's what I call it. Officiousness. You want to be important, like the gentlemen of the late tyrant's bodyguard. There's too much sacred aristocracy left in France. That's what's wrong with the country. Bold big men like you ought to be on the frontier, fighting the enemies of France, instead of manhandling inoffensive women and accusing them of theft. If I were to – "

The sergeant lost his temper.

"In the name of hell, Citizen Simon, if you don't take your harridan out of this I shall do her a mischief. Be off!"

"Harridan!" she screamed.

"Be off!" he roared. "Out of here at the double. March!"

He took her by the shoulders and thrust her, snarling and scolding, through the gateway.

La Salle stolidly pushed his hand-cart after her, whilst Simon, acting as rearguard, stayed to keep the sergeant's attention distracted by apologies for the conduct of Marie-Jeanne. But the sergeant wanted no more.

"Out of here, I've said. To hell with you both. I thank the good God I shan't see you here again."

Beyond the gateway, La Salle trundling his hand-cart over the cobbles broke blithely into song:

> "Ah, ça ira, ça ira, ça ira!
> Malgré les mutins tout réussira!"

Chapter 7

The Kidnappers

The new dwelling which the Simons had been constrained to find for themselves lay within a stone's throw of the Temple gates, a mean lodging consisting of three rooms on the first floor of the old stables of the Temple. La Salle's journey with the hand-cart was, therefore, a short one.

The maternal Marie-Jeanne, anxious to reassure herself that all was well with the drugged and half-smothered child, would have taken him up with them had not Simon opposed her. Nor did she yield readily. There was an exchange of real acrimony between them before she could be made to understand that not one moment longer than necessary must they keep the boy, lest some hitch at the Temple should bring investigators after them. Once the child were away, Simon cared not what questions might be asked him. He would know how to answer them.

So, at last, La Salle was allowed to depart with the bundle that contained the King of France. He carried it not more than forty yards down the deserted, mist-enshrouded street, to a hackney coach which waited there, as if to be hired. In this he deposited his bundle, climbed in, and the vehicle set off at a steady pace.

It was all as had been planned. On the morrow Simon was to seek La Salle at the address the painter gave him – No. 20 Rue Paradis –

there to receive a substantial earnest of the million that was eventually to come from a royalist source.

Of this arrangement, to which Simon was led to agree, not only out of faith in his good friend La Salle, but also because the peculiarly dangerous circumstances of the case offered him no safe alternative, Simon said nothing to his wife. Those same dangerous circumstances made it impossible to confide in anyone. Presently Simon would tell her that, menaced by perils, they must seek safety in flight. Pretending possession of just enough money for the journey, he would take her abroad, to Switzerland, Prussia, Austria, or even England, there to live on his million in the idle luxury of the aristocrats whom his noble republican soul abhorred.

Such was Simon's dream that night, when he accounted the gold as good as earned and his position invulnerable, whilst La Salle was speeding across Paris, bearing that precious child to de Batz. It was not, however, to the Rue de Ménars that the hackney coach was driven, but to a mean house across the river in the Rue du Cherche Midi, where the Baron and two other men awaited him.

In a well-lighted, cosy room on the ground floor, the child, delivered at last from his swathings, but still asleep, was set in an arm-chair before the fire; and whilst La Salle stood over and beside him with a justifiable air of triumph, and the two strangers (neither of whom was named by de Batz) pondered their King in round-eyed awe, the Baron went down on his knees before him. As he peered up into the flushed face, scanning its every lineament and feature, from the brow to which the yellow hair was clammily plastered, to the softly rounded chin with its suggestion of a dimple, the tears sprang to the eyes of that man whose nerves were normally of iron.

"My King!" he murmured. "My King! God of Heaven, I can hardly believe that I am not dreaming this."

Impulsively he got to his feet and went to fling his arms about the lazily smiling La Salle.

"Florence, my friend! How to reward you?"

"Oh, that! There's reward enough in the consciousness of the deed, in the satisfaction of duping those sons of dogs. And it was amusingly easy."

"Easy!" De Batz snorted fiercely. He addressed the strangers. "That is his way: to belittle everything that he does; to reduce it to its lowest terms."

"No need to explain him," said the elder of the twain. "We can perceive only valour and nobility in a man who could carry out so glorious an undertaking and place himself in such jeopardy."

"It's done, and that's the end of it," said La Salle. And in his indolent, drawling voice he gave them a brief account of the adventure, waxing humorous over the bad moment with the sergeant of the Temple guard.

When he came to take his leave, the Baron displayed a grave concern. "Is it safe for you now in Paris? These gentlemen are taking the King away at once into the country. You could go with them, Florence, and lie lost there if you think there is danger for you here. I have procured papers for you, in case – "

"My dear Jean, I have a most important appointment tomorrow with the Citizen Simon. He is expecting to receive a million from me. And there are my studies. Impossible to leave the Atélier David. Give yourself no concern. All the perils of this adventure are behind me. They were run tonight. The rest is nothing."

Not only de Batz, but the other two were disposed to be emotional, and La Salle, with that horror of emotionalism which persuaded David that he would never become a great artist, was in haste to be gone.

He slipped out into the murk of the January night, at last, to make his way back on foot to his shabby lodging near the Palais Egalité there to doff his carmagnole and bonnet of rabbit's fur and put himself to bed with the sense of something accomplished that should one day make history, and that in the meantime should enable him to ask de Batz for fifty louis. He reflected grimly that whilst the valour and nobility attributed to him by those gentlemen were very ornamental qualities, they were powerless to fill the belly of a poor devil of an art-student whom the Revolution had rendered destitute.

The following morning found him fresh and brisk, at work in David's atélier in the Louvre, a young man without a thought to trouble his assiduous pursuit of art. He worked diligently upon a portrait of one of his fellow students, until he was interrupted at about an hour before noon by a visit from Chaumette.

The Procurator-Syndic's morning had been an eventful one.

Anxiety had urged him to begin the day by paying a surprise visit to the Temple, for which he deemed it well to offer some explanation to the commissioners on duty there.

"Antoine Simon will have departed last night. I have thought that I should verify that he has left everything in order."

They assured him that this was the case. Chaumette put on his spectacles and turned over the leaves of the register. He inspected the acknowledgment, signed by these same four commissioners, that formal delivery had been made to them of the Capet children. He grunted.

"That's in order." He removed his spectacles and turned again to confront them. He took care to be casual. "Have you seen the tiger-cubs this morning?"

They had, said one of them, answering for all, and anything less like a tiger-cub than the little Capet was not to be imagined.

Chaumette scowled. "How?"

"He won't open his lips. A surly, mutinous, good-for-nothing little ape. We must have asked him a dozen questions, and not a word could we get out of him. He just stared at us, vacantly, like an idiot, or a deaf-mute."

"Ah! Sulking, eh? Well, well. And the females? Are they of the same humour?"

"On the contrary: as prim and docile as a couple of silly nuns, with their 'yes, monsieur', and their 'no, monsieur'. I told them that they should have learnt by now that there are no sieurs left in France, that we are equals and citizens, to which they answered 'yes, monsieur'. Nit-wits, I call them." And to emphasize his low opinion of them, the patriot spat upon the tessellated floor of the council hall.

"A rotten-hearted brood," Chaumette agreed.

He would not trouble to go up. There was not the need. But now that a permanent custodian had been abolished, the Commune was of the opinion that certain precautions were necessary so as to ensure against any attempts to kidnap the boy; since he chose to preserve a mutinous silence, he should be deprived by solitary confinement in future of the necessity for speech. Chaumette would send in a carpenter at once, securely to screw up the boy's door, opening a shutter in it through which his food could be passed in to him. After that no one should enter the room or unfasten the door without a special order from the Commune. The boy must learn to attend to his own wants. There had been too much pampering of this whelp of the Austrian wild beast. Finally he deputed two of the commissioners to see that his orders were promptly and effectively carried out that day by the carpenter who would be coming.

He took his departure from the Temple and, conscious of a mild excitement, went to climb the stairs of Simon's new lodging.

Simon, himself, opened to his knock, and for a moment stared chapfallen at this unexpected and unwelcome visitor in sash of office and with trailing sabre. Then he was thrust rudely back, and Chaumette, without waiting for an invitation to enter, stepped across the threshold and closed the door.

"Are you alone?" he asked. His manner was grim; under his lumpy, pendulous nose, his mouth was tight.

"My wife is marketing."

"Ah! And the boy?"

"Boy?" Simon lost colour. "What boy? I have no boy."

"Not of your own. No. But the boy from the Temple? The Capet boy? Where have you stowed him?"

"The Capet boy? Where have I stowed him? I?" Simon had already recovered. He knew his ground. His good friend La Salle had shown him how unassailable he was upon it even if this should happen. The little dark eyes twinkled in his broad red face. "You want to laugh, Citizen Chaumette."

The Citizen Chaumette, never prepossessing, became hideous with menace. "Don't play the fool with me, Antoine."

"It's you who play the fool, I think. You can't be serious."

"I am so serious that I'll have the sacred head off your shoulders if you don't get some sense into it quickly. You don't want to be denounced, I suppose?"

"But denounced for what, name of a name?"

Chaumette's effort at self-control was plain. "Listen to me, Antoine. I've just been to the Temple. The boy imprisoned there this morning isn't Capet. He's been changed."

"Changed? Changed! What do you tell me?"

"I tell you just that. So quit this mumming. Where's the child?"

"Why the devil should I know?"

"Because if you don't surrender him to me at once I'll have your lousy head in the basket within forty-eight hours. That's why you should know."

Simon laughed at him. "If you've been to the Temple, I suppose you've seen the register and the signatures of four commissioners. Then there's the guard who passed us out. They can tell you that we had no child with us. If the boy's been changed the commissioners must have changed him." Simon crowed. "That'll show you the folly of removing a good custodian. Unless," and his manner became suddenly sinister, "unless that was part of some dirty game of yours. By God! I have it. The commissioners last night were appointed by your juggling. Of all the foul intrigues! And to try to put it upon me so as to make yourself safe if it should be found out! Denounce me, will you? It's yourself you'll be denouncing. It's your dirty head that'll roll in the sawdust."

Chaumette's face was livid and evil. "I am going to search these rooms." He carried his hand to his sabre. "If you attempt to hinder me I'll cut you in pieces."

"Oh, I'll not hinder you. Search and be damned."

In a raging silence Chaumette made his search. Simon followed him from one to another of three rooms, mocking him the while. Raging, discomfited, persuaded at last that this rascally cobbler had turned the tables on him, he stalked to the door. On the threshold he turned.

"I'll have your head for this, you dog. By God, I'll…"

"Don't forswear yourself," Simon checked him. "Touch me, and I'll prick your bubble for you. You are the Procurator-Syndic of the Commune, responsible for the safety of the boy. Touch me, and I'll challenge you to produce him. If you can't, you know as well as I do what will become of you. So take my advice and hold your tongue. Good day to you, Citizen Procurator-Syndic."

"It'll prove a mighty bad day for you, you scoundrel," Chaumette answered him, which was merely a theatrical exit-line, for he went off in baffled, raging panic.

In this state he descended upon the Atélier David to drag La Salle from his work. He was white and shaking, the normal vigour of his coarse face all turned to flabbiness. He contained himself only until they were outside the Louvre, in the courtyard, which the persistent drizzle and the cold kept untenanted.

"Your fine scheme has gone all to pieces," he exploded at last. "That son of a dog Simon has wrecked it for his own profit. It should have been foreseen."

La Salle was bland. "Honest, myself," he drawled, "I seldom allow sufficiently for the dishonesty of others. I keep forgetting that, as a friend of mine insists, men are not good. But be precise. What, exactly, has Simon done?"

"The low bastard dares to defy me. He refuses to deliver up the boy. He has the effrontery to pretend that, for all that he knows, the brat is still in the tower." He seized the lapels of La Salle's bottle-green coat. "What do you know of last night's events? What happened?"

Gently, but firmly, La Salle disengaged the other's hands. His countenance was solemn. "So far as I am concerned, all happened exactly as I planned. The boy was brought away. The rest was for Simon."

"The blackguard shelters himself behind the register and the signatures of the commissioners. Says that if there was any kidnapping it must have been done by them."

"Could there have been a hitch?" wondered the innocent La Salle. "In your place, I should pay a visit to the Temple."

"I've been. I began by going there. I gave orders for the boy to be shut up in solitary confinement."

"Ah! Then you saw for yourself that the substitution had been made."

"I did not." Chaumette was vehement. "Sacred name! How could I see the boy? Do you think I'm an idiot? Should I have it said afterwards, when the thing's discovered, that I had seen the boy before ordering him to be shut up? What would be my position then?" And again he asked: "Do you think me a fool?"

"I'm not sure," said La Salle, and looked at him with interest. "Let me understand. Did you tell Simon that you knew that the boy had been exchanged?"

"Of course I did."

"Then I am sorry to say that you leave me in no doubt that you're a fool."

"Eh?"

"You told Simon that the boy had been exchanged. How did you know? The commissioners will testify that you did not see him and that you ordered him to be placed in solitary confinement. How will you explain that? By second sight? My dear Anaxagoras! My poor Anaxagoras! If Simon denounces you, you are a lost man."

Chaumette's jaw went loose.

"Death of my life!"

"Appropriate oath. Fortunately Simon will be as scared as you are of having to answer questions. So he'll not dare denounce you. The situation is a deadlock. There's that for your comfort."

"Comfort! Name of a name of a name! Do you call that comfort? Is Simon to succeed in this infamous swindle?"

"I understand your wrath. I sympathize. But after the blunder you've committed, I see no help for you." They were at the end of the courtyard. La Salle turned. "I think we are getting wet out here to no purpose. Keep away from the Temple in future, so that no one can ever say that you have seen the substitute. So long as you do that, and since Simon dare not talk, you should be safe."

"Then I was right, after all, in not seeing the boy this morning?"

"Oh no. You were not right. You were merely fortunate as things have fallen out."

"But if I had seen the child…"

"We are going round in circles, and I am getting wet." He lengthened his stride, and regained the shelter of the building, where Chaumette did not dare to protract the conversation. "If anything occurs to me I'll let you know. But, my friend, what is done is done. Summon the philosophy of your namesake to your aid. Au revoir, Anaxagoras!" And he went off to return to his easel, leaving the distracted Chaumette dully to wonder whether he was mocked as well as cheated.

La Salle, on his side, was thankful to be so easily quit of the Procurator-Syndic. Less easy was it to deal with the Citizen Simon, who sought him that evening at his lodging in the Rue des Bons Enfants; a very malignant Citizen Simon.

After beginning the day so excellently by a triumph over Chaumette which left Simon bubbling with malicious laughter for an hour and more, things had taken a disquieting turn. He had repaired in the neighbourhood of noon to the address in the Rue Paradis which La Salle had given him. At No. 20 he found an apothecary's shop, which was not at all what he expected. Nevertheless he inquired, to be assured that no such person as Florence La Salle was known at No. 20 Rue Paradis.

He came out of the shop with laboured breathing and an uneasy feeling at the pit of his stomach, the physical symptoms of the first dim suspicion that he might in his turn have to dance to a tune similar to that which with such relish he had piped for Chaumette.

At a loss he stood in the street, unmindful of the drizzle, until he remembered having heard once that La Salle worked in the Atélier David. He didn't know where that might be, but it was easily discovered, since Louis David was a member of the Convention. Simon took himself off to the Tuileries, and from an intelligent functionary elicited the information that the Citizen David's atélier was in the Louvre hard by. When eventually he reached it, he found that as a result of the bad light of the January afternoon all the students had departed. But an elderly slattern who acted as custodian was able to tell him where the Citizen La Salle was lodged.

Within less than a half-hour Simon was climbing the rickety stairs of the house in the Rue des Bons Enfants, and thumping on the painter's door.

He accounted himself in luck when La Salle himself opened to him.

"I find you, do I?" Simon was violent. "What sacred game do you play with me that you send me to a damned apothecary's in the Rue Paradis, where they've never heard of you? There's an explanation wanted, my lad."

The young painter stood very straight before him, and in the dim light his pallid face seemed cast in lines of mild surprise.

"The Citizen Simon, is it not? And you were saying?"

The languid tone was exasperating. Simon lowered his head and charged like a bull. A powerful, heavy man, he sent La Salle staggering halfway across the room. It was a moderate-sized, untidy, poorly furnished place. A truckle-bed was ranged against the wall, there was a table in the middle of the floor; a couple of chairs and a chest of drawers with a cracked marble top completed the furniture; a curtained recess did duty as a wardrobe. There was no carpet on the bare deal boards, and the only curtain on the single window was such as an accumulation of dust supplied.

La Salle, recovering his balance, backed away towards the empty fireplace, whilst Simon, closing the door, squared himself as if for combat.

"Now, my lad, will you tell me what the devil you meant by sending me to a false address? I'm not the man to suffer any sacred nonsense. So realize it."

Whatever effect his violence might have produced, it had certainly not disturbed the languor of La Salle's manner.

"Perhaps you'll tell me why you force yourself upon me and take this tone. I find it offensive."

"You do? You may find it more so soon. Don't you know what I've come for?"

"It is what I ask myself, Citizen Simon."

"What?" Simon advanced a pace or two. "Name of a dog!" The colour had darkened in his face; the malevolence had deepened in his little eyes. He was controlling the fury begotten of his misgivings. "There was talk between us of a million, to be paid me for certain goods I've delivered. At the Rue Paradis today I was to receive in earnest – a substantial payment on account of it."

"Oh, that!" La Salle laughed, like one who suddenly sees light. "But surely you didn't take me seriously! Surely you didn't believe in that million. That was a joke, my friend. I thought you understood."

"A joke!" The veins swelled up in Simon's head and neck. For a moment he may have been nearer to an apoplexy than he suspected. "You...you don't mean... What do you mean?"

"What I've said. Where did you suppose that I could find a million? My dear Citizen Simon, the deliverance of that child was a fine and noble deed. There is, I am told, an abiding joy in the consciousness of a good action performed. Let that be your reward."

There was an ominous pause, in which the room was filled with the sound of Simon's laboured breathing. Then he broke into speech so violently that bubbles formed at the corners of his thick lips.

"You dog! You toad! You mincing, aristocrat viper!" Hot upon the apostrophes came a torrent of meaningless obscenity, whilst the patriot crouched like a beast about to spring. "I'll break all the bones of your carcase."

A stout cane stood against one of the piers of the fireplace. La Salle snatched it up when the infuriated Simon leapt at him. He eluded the charge by springing aside, and as he sprang he struck. Simon caught the blow on his forearm, seized the cane, and wrenched it from the other's hand. It came away so easily that he hurtled backwards. Recovering, he hurled himself forward again, to check suddenly, on the very tips of his toes, with a gasp of fear. The point of a slender blade some two feet long was within an inch of his breast. Then he understood the miracle. La Salle's cane was a sword-cane, and Simon's wrench at it had merely brought away the scabbard from the steel.

And as cold and deadly as that deterring blade was the voice that now admonished him.

"A little rash, my friend, are you not? As rash now as when you believed that a million would be paid you for swindling the Republic, for betraying your fine patriotism, for selling your new-found gods. There's a Latin proverb you should learn. 'Ne sutor ultra crepidam.' Get back to your cobbling, Citizen Simon. Stick to your last. High politics require a different type of mind. Meanwhile, out of here! March!"

He advanced the steel. Simon recoiled before it. La Salle marched upon him. "I'll spit you like a lark if you don't move faster. Out of my lodging, you scoundrel, you paltry traitor, you kidnapper of kings."

The empty threat that the baffled Chaumette had flung at him that morning, the baffled Simon now flung at La Salle. "I'll have your head for this, you scoundrel. I'll see you guillotined before I've done with you."

He was answered much as he had crowingly answered the Procurator-Syndic. "Give me trouble and I'll find the way to denounce the piece of kidnapping you contrived. The proof of it is in the Temple, and they'll have your head for it, Citizen Simon. But I don't think you'll give me trouble."

The wretched cobbler, his dream of an affluent aristocratic existence brutally shattered, wrenched open the door and without another word went clattering down the crazy stairs. Chaumette was avenged.

Chapter 8

Farewell to Art

So little was La Salle perturbed by the situation for which he was responsible, that I cannot discover that he took any measures to protect himself, or altered in any way his normal mode of life.

Chaumette, compromised by his actions, dared not for his head's sake break silence, and was constrained actually to maintain, for Simon's profit as he supposed, the deception which he had practised for his own now thwarted ends. Simon, coldly defrauded in his turn by La Salle, could only utter a denunciation at the price of carrying his own head to the scaffold with the painter's. Even in the inconceivable case of an understanding between Chaumette and Simon, and of confidences between them which would reveal how cynically La Salle had used and swindled both, they would be powerless to move against him, since they could invoke no law that would not recoil upon themselves.

So in the months that followed, of which so far as La Salle is concerned the records are scanty, he calmly went his ways, working studiously at the Atélier David when he was not actively serving the monarchical cause. We have his own word for it that, aspiring to live by art, he was ready by every effort to promote the restoration and ascendency of aristocracy because he believed it to be the only social system in which art can remuneratively flourish. The amiable cynicism of this admission bears witness to his frank dislike of heroics.

It is on record that once, upon being reproached by an émigré nobleman, with the self-interest by which he explained his actions he had answered: "What then? Do you really find me unusual? Does not self-interest shape and colour the politics of every man and every nation? You gentlemen of the Army of Condé, so magnificently and heroically ready to shed your blood, and even more ready to shed the blood of others, in the cause of monarchy, will deny, of course, that you fight to restore the condition of things most agreeable to yourselves, or to recover the wealth and luxury of which the present order has deprived you. But do the facts deny it? In my way I have served the cause more signally and dangerously than on the battlefield. The only difference between us is that I am honest. I frankly avow the object of my labours. I do not wreathe my brow in laurel and cry to the world, 'Behold a self-sacrificing hero!' "

He pursued his serene way amid the strife and turmoil about him, regularly attending – as one of the representatives of his section – the meetings of the Commune, so as to watch and report to de Batz upon its measures and its reflections of the public temper, which throughout those early months of '94 was of a steadily increasing violence.

For these were the days in which the Revolution in a frenzy of autophagy was devouring its own body. The Convention was an arena that stank of blood. In the desperate struggle for mastery Chaumette led the Cordelier revolt against the growing power of Robespierre. He may have been stimulated to it by letters from his friend Fouché, who took care to find duties to keep him in the provinces until the Parisian battle should be fought out. Chaumette dragged with him the obscenely elegant Hébert, to learn with Hébert how fickle a thing is public opinion and how foolish it is to trust to popular favour. Hébert went to the guillotine in March. Chaumette followed in April, to the execrations of a foul mob in whose eyes one little week earlier he had been a demi-god.

Thus vanished one of those whose knowledge might have destroyed La Salle. Simon remained, a soured, fear-haunted, vindictive, but impotent Simon, who growled his blasphemies in reply to La Salle's unfailingly courteous greetings whenever they met upon the Council of the Commune. But soon Simon followed Chaumette. He went in the Thermidorean upheaval. His stupidity destroyed him. Unable to read the signs, he rashly mounted the tribune on the night of the 9th Thermidor, to incite the Commune to rescue Robespierre at a time when Robespierre was already irrevocably lost. Fouché, that man of the circumstances, had seen to this. Robespierre had summoned him to Paris, so that he might destroy him as he destroyed all whom he feared. It was the rashest act of Robespierre's life.

Fouché dared not disobey; but arriving at the very moment when a leader was the only thing lacking to those secretly in revolt against the tyranny of Robespierre, who was fast becoming a dictator, the coldly formidable ex-professor unobtrusively supplied it. It was the end of Robespierre and of the Terror with him. France could breathe freely again.

In the terrific emotional reaction that followed, thought was given to the prisoners in the Temple Tower. There were only the two orphans now; for the saintly Madame Elizabeth had been sent to the guillotine a couple of months before.

Discovery of the King's evasion and substitution must have followed immediately. For Barras, the sybaritic, nobly-born, base-hearted revolutionist, paid an early visit to the Temple; and Barras could neither have been deceived nor have kept the startling discovery entirely to himself. Yet general publication was impossible because of the storm it must provoke at home and abroad.

In its new emotionalism the Convention was shocked at the rigour of the imprisonment. It was scandalized to think of these two children, kept apart, in close confinement, without exercise and without attendance of any kind, so that Madame Royale of France (now in her seventeenth year) was under the necessity to make her own bed and sweep her own floor.

Harmand, the deputy of the Meuse, was sent by the Convention to visit the prisoners and to report. We have his own word for the boy's blank, unresponsive stare and utter silence under Harmand's succession of kindly, solicitous questions. But the obvious explanation never occurred to him, and he accepted a preposterous assertion made by someone, that the boy, coming to realize how his speech had doomed his mother, had made a vow never to speak again.

A liberal improvement in the conditions of the captivity of these admittedly guiltless State prisoners followed upon Harmand's report. They were to be reunited; they were to be accorded the freedom of the extensive gardens for exercise; suitable attendants were to be provided for them. We know that the attendants were provided, and that thereafter they enjoyed more solicitous treatment. Beyond this, however, there was no such change in the conditions as had been decreed. No communication was allowed between them, for the overwhelming reason that this must at once have discovered the terrible secret of the substitution, which the government was so desperately concerned to guard.

The government, indeed, found itself in a dilemma. In the turn of political events it was becoming daily increasingly difficult to justify the captivity at all. Very soon it must be impossible. The dilemma increased as time went on. It became desperate when negotiations for peace were on foot with Spain, and the Spanish Bourbon made it a condition of signing that his French cousin should be delivered to him. There was also a threat from England to land an expedition to reinforce the insurgent royalists in the Vendée, so as to procure the deliverance of Louis XVII.

By this time the Year IV was well advanced, and some eight months had passed since the extinction of the Terror.

De Batz, ever alert and active, and well aware of the government's quandary, watched the situation with the closest attention. In secret he was marshalling his forces against an opportunity to complete the work which Thermidor had begun, by proclaiming Louis XVII, who was carefully hidden no farther off than Meudon. In this he was assisted by none more ably and diligently than by La Salle, whom Louis-David now accused of losing interest in his studies.

Because of the affection which David had long since conceived for this pupil and because of the talent he perceived in him, the great master was profoundly annoyed and did not mince his terms.

"I've warned you already that mere facility in drawing does not make the artist. Drawing is a matter of the eyes and the hands. But art is a matter of the soul. And your soul is still asleep. I do my best to arouse it so that it may use its vision. But God knows I'm growing tired of labouring like Sisyphus on a lump of unresponsive stone. Your wits are elsewhere. You are getting into bad company. Last night I saw you supping at the Café de Foy with a group in which there was more than one notorious reactionary. If you are going to adopt politics, I wash my hands of you. It'll be your ruin."

La Salle thought, on the contrary, that it would be his fortune. If de Batz succeeded – and La Salle's confidence in the Gascon admitted of no doubt – de Batz should stand in future very near to the restored throne, and La Salle would stand very near to de Batz. He let artistic vision go hang for a political vision in which he saw himself one of the great men of the revived monarchy, one of the masters of the State.

And then – long before the royalist plans had reached a point that admitted of action – the dream collapsed as dreams will.

Barras and those other members of the government who were in the secret, finding Spanish insistence upon the surrender of Louis XVII an obstacle to the sorely needed peace, decided to remove it in the only way that remained possible. The child must die, and his passing must be plausibly encompassed. Accordingly, his death followed in early June, after an illness in which two doctors attended him. Never having known Louis-Charles in life, these and two other doctors who assisted them in the post-mortem were able to certify – and the exact terms are not without significance – that they had performed an autopsy on the body of a child, "whom the commissioners stated to us to be the son of the late Louis Capet".

The dead child was declared scrofulous and rickety, ailments of which the healthy Louis-Charles had certainly shown no symptoms. Still more remarkable was it that this dead child's hair was of a light chestnut colour, whereas the little King's had been pale yellow. But that it was the body of the son of the late Louis Capet was further certified by the two attendants appointed after Barras' visit and several others who had never seen Louis-Charles before the date of Simon's removal from the Temple. The only two persons in the Temple at the time of the death who were really qualified to identify him were carefully excluded. They were his sister, Madame Royale, who had never seen him since that dreadful day of the depositions, and the man Tison, who, once the custodian there of the royal family, was now, himself, a prisoner in the tower.

There was no obstacle to the official announcement of the death and to the official burial of the body, and the government could proceed upon its negotiations with foreign States without further embarrassment.

The news of the death of Louis XVII was duly conveyed to his uncle, the Count of Provence – now at Verona – and the Count of Provence was able at last to gratify that pruritus of kingship which once had led him in blind malice to bring a contribution of loathsome scandal to the forces which had accomplished the Revolution.

Madame Royale, however, was not informed of her brother's death until some time later, and it might have seemed significant to some that from the date of it, the freedom to leave her quarters and use the garden, decreed nearly a year earlier, was at last accorded to her.

Whether the child who died in the Temple was the unfortunate deaf-mute and half-imbecile boy procured to substitute the King, or whether, as is so widely believed, a second substitution took place, and a moribund child of similar age was brought there to breathe his last and deliver the government from its embarrassment, was not a speculation that preoccupied de Batz.

The event brought him not only dismay and disappointment, but a sudden well-founded fear for the safety of the child hidden at Meudon such as he had not known in the worst days of the Terror.

He explained it to La Salle.

"Having killed the King for reasons of State, they've committed themselves to see that he remains dead. They dread nothing more than a resurrection. Agents, who do not, themselves, know whom they are really seeking, are already in quest of the real Louis XVII. Sénar, without being aware of the real object of the search, has warned me of it. He supposes it concerned with some Bourbon princeling brought to France. Frankly I am frightened. We must make doubly sure of the boy's safety until the country is ready to receive back its King."

He had arranged everything. Among the foreign agents of the Powers interested in the restoration of the French monarchy, there was then in Paris an envoy of Prussia, Baron Ulrich von Ense, with whom de Batz was in relations. The Gascon had disclosed the truth to him, and von Ense had accounted himself honoured by the proposal that he should convey the young King to the Court of Frederick William III. Once Louis XVII were safe in Berlin, his survival could be proclaimed to the world.

That was the plan suggested to de Batz by his apprehensions, and in the execution of which he sought the assistance of La Salle. He made his motive clear. There were dangers in entrusting a child of such enormous consequence to the care of a single man. If anything should befall his escort, mishap or illness, the boy would be helpless, and discovery must follow. If La Salle would consent to go, the necessity of disclosing the dangerous secret of Louis-Charles' survival to yet another person would be avoided. Then La Salle was so much better fitted than any other for the task, because of the first-hand testimony he could afford of the escape, answering all questions that doubt might reasonably suggest. Lastly, to inspire confidence, there was the cool courage and ready wit of which La Salle had already afforded such abundant proof.

"It is asking a great sacrifice of you, Florence, I know. It will mean a lengthy interruption of your studies."

La Salle made little of the sacrifice. On the one hand his duty to his King imposed it. On the other, the ultimate reward of success seemed certain and considerable. Let him help to convey the little King to the Court of Prussia, and he would be clumsy indeed if he did not contrive to remain there in a tutelary capacity until the time came to return in triumph with the King whom he would have the credit and glory of having saved and preserved.

"It may mean the end of my studies with David, and so farewell to art. But for the Cause… What can I say? I'll go, of course."

Chapter 9

Pursuit

It was to be made evident that de Batz had taken his decision only just in time.

We do not know who amongst the members of the government were informed of the boy's evasion, but we know, at least, that Barras and Fouché were aware of it, and there is reason to believe that the forlorn hope of a hunt for him was set on foot by the latter. That the agents flung out in the name of the Sûreté Publique should have been told of the identity of the boy they were seeking was, as de Batz supposed, unlikely. The probabilities are that they were told that there was a royalist plan to set up a false Louis XVII, and they were bidden to scour the country for a yellow-haired child, otherwise answering a description supplied, who was not residing with his parents, who had recently made his appearance wherever he might now be, and whose custodians' account of their custodianship was not clearly and independently to be confirmed. From the outset it was regarded as a hopeless quest by those who set it on foot, and hopeless it might have remained but for one curious circumstance.

The boy was at Meudon, in the mansion of the famous banker Petitval, who although an open and devoted royalist had been in the difficult matters of finance of such value to the government that he had been sheltered from interference during the wildest phases of the Revolution. In Petitval's household the boy passed for a nephew of the financier's, a child whose parents had perished in the Terror, and so as to divert any suspicion of the lad's identity, Petitval had actually attempted negotiations with the Committee of Public Safety for the delivery to him of the prisoner of the Temple, who was already in his possession. By this crafty piece of duplicity he almost overreached himself with those in the secret of the King's evasion. The singularly astute Fouché wondered whether the request might not be just the strategical pretence that it actually was. He sent his spies to investigate, and they reported the presence in the Petitval household of a yellow-haired nephew of about ten years of age, who had been at Meudon for some eighteen months.

Thereupon, Fouché, accompanied by an energetic, resourceful underling named Desmarets, whose fortunes thenceforward were closely to be linked with his own, decided, himself, to pay a visit to Petitval.

That by the mercy of Providence he arrived there just too late was for him the fullest confirmation of his suspicions. Petitval, a middle-aged man of gracious manners, received the representative with bland courtesy. It distressed him not to be able fully to reassure the Citizen Fouché's obvious mistrust – though upon what it was founded the banker professed himself unable to surmise – by presenting his nephew; but unfortunately the boy had left Meudon only yesterday for Brussels, where his mother, Petitval's youngest sister, resided.

The statement of the boy's departure Fouché was able to verify. But when careful inquiries had discovered that the carriage in which he had set out with two companions had taken the road to Mélun, in a south-easterly direction, he knew that Petitval had lied to him on the subject of the traveller's destination. His suspicions became certainties. The vigorous Desmarets was launched in pursuit, with the fullest powers to enlist on the way such assistance as he might need so as to capture and bring back the fugitive.

The King had a start of twenty-four hours. But travelling without cause to fear pursuit, and therefore at no more than reasonable speed, it should be easy to overtake him before he could reach the frontier even at the nearest point.

The road to be followed by the fugitives had been discussed with Petitval, in whom La Salle met again the elder of the two men who had been with de Batz on the night of the evasion from the Temple. Movements of troops, Petitval pointed out, made the Rhine frontier undesirable. Attempts to cross it meant subjection to more than ordinary scrutiny. They must, therefore, prefer to make for Germany by way of Geneva, where every assistance would be rendered them by a royalist agent named Martin Lebas. Thence they would continue their journey through the Principality of Neuchâtel, and Bâle.

"And after that," said the Baron von Ense, who was entirely in agreement, "by way of the Black Forest. Righteous God! It is to go halfway round the world to get to Prussia." He was a large, blond man of fifty, powerfully made and active, with a deep voice and an air of consequence that was tempered by a roguishness lurking in his blue eyes. As a comrade in an enterprise of inevitable difficulties and probably dangers, La Salle formed the immediate opinion that he could not be bettered. From his carefully dressed head to his admirably shod foot he looked a man upon whom it would be good to depend.

Having uttered his half-humorous lament on the length of the journey which caution imposed, he submitted. De Batz supplied them with passports, which he had either forged or else obtained through one of his subterranean channels. In one of these the Baron von Ense was described as a Swiss chocolate-manufacturer named Hagenbach, travelling with his nephew; in the other La Salle was described as a clerk, under the name of Husson.

They took the road in a berline with four horses, and for three days they rolled smoothly and uneventfully towards the frontier.

The boy was no longer the dulled, half-sullen, half-truculent child whom La Salle remembered, and whose portrait he carried with him. For amongst his few belongings he had packed several of his sketch-books, which contained drawings of not a few revolutionary celebrities. These he thought might prove of value to him in Prussia.

He noted with satisfaction the change in the King's air and bearing. The puffiness and pallor acquired in confinement had now vanished. He was rosy-cheeked once more, firm of flesh, ready-witted for his years and of a winning gaiety. Whether from the force of heredity, or from the memory of those early days at Versailles when, from the moment that he could understand anything, he had understood that he was a person of tremendous consequence, he blended now with his gaiety a certain air of dignity and accepted as his due the deference shown him by his two travelling companions. At times he was reminiscent, and particularly of his imprisonment in the Temple, but only down to the date of his separation from his mother. After that his recollections seemed a little vague and blurred; but he allowed them to perceive that there were scenes that stood out acutely, some of which he described.

Often he spoke of Simon, and was sorry to hear that he had been guillotined.

"He was not bad," he told them, "except when he forced me to drink brandy, although I detested it and it made me ill. For the rest he was a droll fellow. Poor Simon."

Of Simon's wife he spoke with something akin to real affection and appreciation of the fundamental motherliness of her nature shining through her coarse exterior. To her he owed the alleviation of many a sorrowful hour in the days when he was first parted from his mother. Of his sister he was filled with tender concern for her continued confinement in the black tower of the Temple. When he mentioned her, or Aunt Babet or his mother, the tears filled his blue eyes.

A sensitive child he revealed himself to those two men, yet of a certain waywardness and with something coarse and wild – the impress of the Temple days – showing itself at moments through the recovered mantle of natural dignity.

They travelled at a good round pace, yet without that urgency for which they could not suspect the occasion. Now and then, on those first three days, they would alight, and for the sake of exercise walk for an hour or two beside the lumbering travelling carriage. The boy, however, tiring quickly, and being imperiously disinclined to sit alone in a vehicle moving at a walking pace, the two men came to an arrangement that would afford them the exercise they required. Each on alternate days should perform the journey on horseback, whilst the other accompanied the King in the carriage.

This decision was taken at Auxerre on the fourth morning, after breakfast, when the berline, ready to resume the journey, stood waiting for them before the door of the Petit-Paris Inn, where they had lain.

Von Ense span a coin, to determine whether he or La Salle should ride that day, and the coin settled it in favour of La Salle. The finger of benign Providence had controlled the spin. The post-house was next door to the Petit-Paris, and bidding them not wait for him, since in the saddle he would easily overtake them, La Salle went thither to hire himself a horse.

Unhurried, he watched them drive away, down the steep street of the dirty little Burgundian town, then turned to make his demand of the post-master, announcing that he was riding to Montbard.

A horse should be saddled for him at once.

He strolled out again, to wait in the sunshine of the June morning, and whilst he waited a dusty chaise came clattering to a halt before the door of the Petit-Paris. Out of it rolled three burly men, the heavy face of one of whom was familiar to La Salle. He recognized it for a face he had often seen of late in the hall of the Tuileries. This in itself may have quickened instinctively his attention, and prompted a closer inspection of their carriage. The thick dust that overlaid it suggested that it had been on the road all night. These travellers were suspiciously in haste; either pursued or pursuers.

Whilst La Salle leaned in watchful unconcern in the doorway of the post-house, the chamberlain came out of the inn to welcome the arrivals, and their leader, the man whose square, heavy face was known to La Salle, stepped forward to meet him with a question.

Was a party, consisting of two men and a boy, coming last from Sens, at the inn, or had it been there?

This was illuminating and bewildering. But La Salle did not give way to bewilderment. At a stride he placed himself within the doorway of the stableyard, lest the chamberlain turning in his direction should recognize him and announce him for one of the members of the party sought. Thence he listened for the answer he expected; that such a party had, indeed, lain the night at the Petit-Paris, and had in fact set out again for Montbard only a few minutes ago.

From one of the new arrivals he heard an oath, but from the leader, who was Desmarets, a laugh, and the rejoinder: "What matter? We have them now. No need to shatter ourselves. We'll breakfast whilst fresh horses are being harnessed. Come along." And they marched into the inn.

Within five minutes La Salle, tolerably well mounted, was going down the street at a trot that became a gallop as soon as he was clear of the town.

How they came to be pursued might be a mystery. But that pursued they were was no mystery at all. Had it not been for the blessed chance that had delayed his own departure their capture in the course of the day would inevitably have followed. He boasted afterwards that he took this preserving favour of Providence as a sign that high destinies awaited him.

He overtook the berline towards noon, some ten miles beyond Auxerre. He halted it for a moment, so as to tether his horse to the rear springs, urged the postilion to use whip and spur, and climbed into the vehicle to deliver his alarming news.

"Potzteufel!" swore von Ense, and looked to his pistols, whilst the little King stared round-eyed.

"If this," said La Salle, "is not to be another flight to Varennes with a similar ending to it, we'll need both speed and wit."

"Since we surely possess the one, we can surely make the other," said the Prussian, and he swore jovially. "Herrgott!"

"At the price of a little discomfort," La Salle agreed, and he explained that henceforth they must make use of no more inns, and neither eat at table nor sleep in beds until the frontier was overpast. He would take to the saddle again, and ride on ahead, to Moyers, to see that horses were ready for them the moment they arrived, so that no time should be lost in waiting for relays.

"Meanwhile no panic," he admonished them. "These mouchards have computed our rate of travel, and made too sure of us. That is our chance, and a generous one. For the rest, trust to me."

And trustworthy he proved himself by the resourcefulness which he exhibited when the berline came rocking into Moyers at three o'clock that afternoon.

At the post-house the relays were waiting for them, and as they drew up, La Salle's head and shoulders instantly appeared at the window of the carriage. "Keep back," he muttered. "Don't show yourselves. We'll leave no more traces until we can leave false ones. Hence these." He passed a mysterious bundle through the window. It contained a petticoat, bodice and mob-cap, which His Majesty was to assume between here and Montbard. "And here is food; a chicken, bread, cheese and a bottle of wine." He thrust a basket after the bundle. Then leaning forward into the carriage, he informed them of his arrangements.

He had found ten horses stabled at the post-house. Of these he was taking eight: the four that were now being harnessed to the berline, and another four for a post-chaise in which he proposed to follow them to Montbard. By thus virtually stripping the post-house of fresh cattle, he would delay their pursuers for several hours at Moyers.

"At Montbard you descend at the inn for supper," La Salle instructed them. "And so do I. But we sup separately and without recognition of one another. Thus the party sought, of two men and a boy, will have disappeared. Instead there will be a gentleman travelling with his daughter, and another gentleman travelling alone. That should suffice to destroy the scent."

The boy laughed in amused delight. This languid-mannered Monsieur Husson was proving an engaging wag. Von Ense, however, perceived an objection.

"And the passport, then? How do I pass a girl on that?"

"No need for the passport until you are at the frontier. By then His Majesty will have resumed his proper sex. The postilion is ready," he ended. "Away with you now. I'll sleep in the chaise between here and Montbard, since after that I shall be all night in the saddle, ahead of you again."

In that rickety, ill-sprung travelling-chaise La Salle arrived at Montbard an hour behind von Ense, just, indeed, as the Prussian nobleman was becoming anxious, not guessing that this had been in the other's calculations. As La Salle stalked through the common-room, bawling for supper, he knocked against the Baron's chair. He turned to apologize, and in bowing, muttered under his breath the single word: "Partez!"

Von Ense, having by now, as La Salle had observed, finished his meal, was prompt to obey that order to depart.

Just as the new arrival was being served, the Prussian called for the reckoning, ordered the berline, and passed out with his make-believe little girl.

La Salle heard the carriage roll away, and set about making himself conspicuous. To the landlord hastening up in alarm, he denounced the wine for Côte du Rhône.

"Name of God! Do you suppose I'll consent to drink this stuff in Burgundy? I would as soon drink ink."

It was the wine of the house, the host assured him. A sound enough wine and genuinely Burgundian. But what did the citizen expect at ten livres the bottle? – a wine that before the fall of the assignat they sold for eight sols.

The young traveller's indignation deepened. Had he asked for wine of the house? Or did he look like a starveling that they gave him no better? He dared swear they had not ventured to put such wine before that big aristocrat who had just walked out. Let the landlord search his cellar.

The landlord brought him a smooth, well-cellared Nuits. The traveller tasted it, and mellowed. This put blood into a man. It healed one of travel-weariness, and he was weary of travel. He was from Chartres, on his way to Grenoble, journeying on business for his father, a woollen merchant. He rambled on garrulously whilst consuming his supper, deliberately laying a misleading trail. Then he swept away as he had come, leaving a landlord glad to be rid of so noisy and insufferable a popinjay, evidently one of those parvenus thrown up by the convulsions of the times, and the very last person to be a member of the party which those gentlemen from Paris were pursuing.

He passed the berline at some time after midnight, in the neighbourhood of Flavigny, and he was waiting for it on the following morning in the hill town of Bussy, the last stage before Dijon. As at Montbard, they kept apart, nor had La Salle bespoken relays for them here, judging the urgency now less.

But towards evening, when von Ense came to Dijon, accounting that sufficient had been done both to outdistance and mislead pursuit, they reassembled and supped in company, the King once more restored to breeches. He was so tired that he could hardly keep awake at table, and on this account von Ense decided that they should lie the night at Dijon. La Salle disagreed sharply.

"If that had been the intention, it would have been prudent at least that His Majesty should have retained his disguise, and that we should have continued apart."

"Ah, bah! Thunderweather, Monsieur Husson! Are you the man to start at shadows?" And the Prussian's deep-throated, careless laugh belittled the notion of danger.

"I start at neither shadows nor substances, Monsieur le Baron. But a long and close acquaintance with danger has brought me a sense of the value of prudence."

"But look at His Majesty," the Baron insisted. "Almost asleep on his feet. No use to save him one way if we kill him another. Come, come!" he coaxed good humouredly. "Let the child sleep between sheets tonight."

Reluctantly La Salle yielded; but two days later, at Lons, with the end of the journey to the frontier almost in sight, he was to regret it, just as the Baron was to regret the false confidence which had lulled him not only that night at Dijon, but subsequently at Dôle.

La Salle's abiding uneasiness, quickened by these delays, had urged him to keep to the saddle and form a rearguard, so as to avoid surprises should the pursuers by any chance have picked up the trail. Riding at a leisurely pace on the Saturday morning on which they left Dôle, he reached Tassenière at noon, and paused there for an hour or so to rest and refresh himself. Then, on a fresh horse, he set out, again at an easy pace, to ride the twenty-five miles to Lons, where he was to rejoin the others that evening.

Five miles or so beyond Tassenière he drew rein on the summit of the gentle upland between the valleys of the Dorain and the Seilles. The day was warm but clear, and from his vantage-point he could survey the pleasant, rolling, fertile plains for miles in every direction. The air was sweetly fragrant, and it vibrated with the scarcely audible sounds of multitudinous invisible life; the play of sunshine on distant water fringed with feathery willows caught and charmed his artist's eye. To capture those tints and the elusive colour of those shadows, with the voluptuous sense of warmth in which they were contained, were perhaps a worthier achievement than anything that might come of dancing attendance on a throneless king. He fetched a sigh that was in itself an elegy on such reflections, and then he was dragged suddenly from dreams to reality, and the awakening artist was lost again in the adventurer. A mile away, adown the road by which he had ridden, a cloud of dust was rising.

Without alarm at first he decided that it would be prudent to ascertain what might be contained in that excessive dust. He edged his horse – a big, powerful animal, the very mount for an emergency – to the side of the road, where a screen of saplings would serve for cover, and there sat and waited. Soon he was able to discern that what approached was not a carriage, but a little troop of horsemen. His young eyes were keen, and the air, as I have said, was clear. At half a mile he could distinguish the accoutrements of seven dragoons.

What alarmed him, however, was that civilians were riding with them and that three was the number of these civilians. The fact was too suggestive to permit him to wait longer for a clear verification of his instant assumption.

He moved out of his shelter, clapped spurs to his horse, thanking God for its vigour, and was off, riding as he had never ridden before and as he hoped never to ride again. As he went headlong amain, his clear conclusion was that, the pursuers having found the scent again, had taken to horse, so as to make up for the time lost whilst at fault, and had enlisted military assistance so as to make doubly sure of their quarry when they should overtake it. These gentlemen from Paris must dispose of uncommon powers.

Conjecture now brought him face to face with something missed in all his careful planning. At Dijon, when the pursuers found that the quarry had suddenly gone to ground, and they were unable to pick up the trail of two men and a boy, there still remained the trail of the berline itself – a conspicuous yellow vehicle with black-panelled doors, which would have been described to them by the first post-master on this side of Meudon to whom they had addressed their inquiries. This was what La Salle now despised himself for having overlooked, he who was coming to pride himself upon a vision that took in every circumstance of a case. Had he but stayed to think how inevitable it was that an intelligent catchpoll would have sought information upon every detail, he would have been supplied with arguments against von Ense's slackening of speed to which they might yet have to attribute a defeat.

It was to avert this evil that he galloped, and probably the only thing of which he did not think was that if at the headlong pace at which he devoured the miles he should happen to break his neck, the King of France's last slender chance of escape would perish with him.

Within some three miles of Sallières he came up with the stage-coach that plied between Dijon and Lons. If he lost some moments in getting past the great lumbering machine, he gained in exchange an inspiration. When, a couple of miles farther on, he overtook the berline he ordered the postilion to pull up. At the moment he was thankful that the Baron von Ense should prefer a leisurely mode of travel.

His unexpected appearance startled them. What he had to tell them in a few briefly muttered words not to be overheard by the postilion startled them still more. Bitterly von Ense broke into self-reproaches. Generously he admitted that if only he had listened to Monsieur Husson's arguments they would not now be in this danger. What could they do against a troop of dragoons?

"You can do what I tell you this time," said La Salle.

The stage-coach hove in view a quarter of a mile away. "Take your papers and valuables and get down at once. You and…" He checked in time, for the amazed postilion was all attention. "You and your nephew will travel by the Dijon coach to Lons. It won't be comfortable in this heat, and it may be crowded; but at least it will be safe, for that is the last place in which these assassins will look for you." He lowered his voice to a murmur for the Baron's ear alone. "From Lons you will travel post, setting out at once. Then go straight on to Geneva without waiting for me until you reach it. I will rejoin you there at Lebas' house. But I may be delayed."

As they were climbing out, La Salle gave his attention to the post-boy. "Your part in what's to do, my lad, is to hold your tongue. You'll have heard that silence is golden. To you it may be worth five louis. Speech, on the other hand, you'll discover to be leaden. Say one word except as I bid you, and I'll see that it's your last." He pulled his hand from the pocket of his riding-coat and brought into view the butt of a pistol. "I hope we understand each other."

The postilion, an impudent-faced lad with a tip-tilted nose, shrugged his shoulders. "No need to threaten, citizen. I was never one to talk."

"Continue in that excellent habit."

La Salle walked his reeking horse into the middle of the road and raised his hand to arrest the approaching coach. The ponderous vehicle rumbled to a halt. Postilion, coachman and conductor, speaking all together, demanded objurgatorily the reason of this interference, whilst passengers craned startled heads from the windows.

La Salle pointed to the berline drawn up at the edge of the ditch and to the man and boy standing beside it. He was sparing of words.

"An accident to the carriage. These citizens are for Lons."

The conductor abandoned an incipient truculence. If that was all it could be arranged. But he must charge them the full fare from Dijon. He had no authority to split the rates.

"There you are," said La Salle to the Baron. "Everything arranges itself. Goodbye and a good journey."

Von Ense hesitated. His jovial face was grave. "But you, my friend?"

"I follow. Do not lose time. Goodbye."

The boy came to touch his hand. "You won't be long, will you, Monsieur Husson?"

"No longer than I can help," said La Salle, and meant it; for by his genial, easy-going nature the Baron whom he had judged so dependable was filling him now with misgivings.

Almost he thrust them into the coach, and after that stood watching the vehicle as it drove on. From the window the boy waved to him. He took off his hat and waved it in response, then he turned to the post-boy.

"Now, my lad, your five louis are half earned already. You'll be paid at Châlons."

"But I'm not going to Châlons."

"Oh yes, you are. And without arguments."

"I was hired for Lons," the lad insisted.

"But five louis await you at Châlons. That's a year's pay, isn't it? And, anyway, you're going there. Now, tell me: what is the first posting-place for Châlons beyond Sallières?"

"There's a post-house at Volant."

"How far is that?"

"About three leagues from Sallières."

"Your horses can do it. We relay then at Volant. But you will stop at Sallières to inquire the way to Châlons and the state of the roads. I desire it to be known that we are going that way, and I desire nothing else to be known. Remember it. Forward now, and ply your whip. I am in haste."

He climbed into the saddle, and in the wake of the yellow berline came into Sallières and to the gate-way of the post-house just as the stage-coach carrying von Ense and the King was drawing out for Lons.

Ten minutes later, having relinquished his horse and flung himself into the berline at a moment when there was no one at hand to see that the vehicle was otherwise empty, La Salle, himself, departed again to take the road to Châlons.

Chapter 10

Lake Léman

The yellow berline reached Volant without adventure, and, having relayed there, pushed on. Five miles beyond it the dragoons and the three civilians came to supply La Salle with the fullest confirmation of the assumptions upon which he acted. At the first glimpse of them now he leaned from the window for the final instructions of the post-boy.

"All that you will know, my child, when you come to be questioned, is that you are from Dijon, which is true, and that I have been your only passenger, which you had better believe to be true, if you want to make sure of the gold and avoid the lead. I'll say no more. I trust to your intelligence, which I hope is excellent."

The troop came on, and soon the carriage was enveloped in a pounding, clanking, shouting cloud of men and horses.

The post-boy drew to a standstill, as ordered, and at once the square-faced civilian who was in command, a man of short build, but stocky and active, flung down from his horse and sprang for the door of the berline. His voice was harshly exultant.

"You've led me the devil of a chase, citizens. But at last..." And there, having got the door open, he stopped short, upon discovering a single occupant in the vehicle. This occupant, a young man with a very languid manner, inquired almost without heat what the devil this violence might signify.

"But for your soldiers," he added, "you'ld be dead by now, for I must have taken you for a brigand – which is what you look like – and shot you at sight."

"Where the hell are your companions?" the stocky man stormed at him, whilst the other two civilians and the sergeant in command of the troop formed a peering background for him.

"Companions?" echoed La Salle. "You consider that I should have companions? What would you? It's a view I don't share. I happen to like my own company. So if that's all perhaps you'll allow me to proceed."

Desmarets' baffled rage was fanned by that mocking self-possession.

"Let's have a look at your papers."

"Ah! And now we are vindictive. We would like to persecute a poor, defenceless traveller for not being somebody else. But I happen to be neither poor nor defenceless, and I don't show my papers to the first rascal who asks for them. I'll know your authority first, my good man."

The red, white and blue card of an agent of the Public Safety was flashed in his face. "I am Desmarets. Ministry of Justice. Is that enough for you?"

"Too much, citizen catchpoll." La Salle's expression suggested that now that he possessed the man's description he found him an object of disgust. He sighed wearily as he fumbled in his pocket. "Really, such jacks-in-office as you almost make me feel that we have returned to the days of monarchical despotism. But here you are."

The agent took the passport of the Citizen Gabrile Husson, and studied it. Its perfect correctness increased his discomfiture, but he would not yet surrender. "You are the person designated here?"

"I've been under that impression."

"It says, 'travelling to Switzerland for affairs'."

"That is no doubt true."

"Then why aren't you on the road to the frontier? You are going away from it."

"Does my passport deny me that right? Does it say anywhere that if I choose to turn aside to visit a friend in Châlons I must not do so?" He dropped his airiness, and became stern. "Enough, Citizen Desmarets. You begin to exceed your authority, I think. Be good enough to give me back my papers and let me get on."

Desmarets, undecided, breathed noisily. One of his companions plucked his sleeve. "Aren't we wasting time, and just when it's most precious?"

"Wasting time!" Desmarets was savage. "What am I to do now with time? By God, if we've been following the wrong trail for two days, how are we to find the right one now?"

"I wonder," said the other, "if that fool at Montbard was really a rogue and deliberately described the wrong berline. That's where we lost them."

"What's the good of wondering?" He almost flung the passport at La Salle. "Here. Take your sacred papers. Bon voyage!" His tone made of the wish an imprecation. He slammed the door, stepped back, and waved the post-boy on, in a manner that seemed to consign them all to Hell.

The whip cracked, the berline began to move, and La Salle settled himself in the carriage. A smile was tightening his lips. He did not envy the diligent Citizen Desmarets when he got back to those who had sent him.

It was no part of his intentions to interrupt the journey to Châlons, as another might have done, now that the comedy was played. Suspicion might well remain in the mind of the gentleman from Paris, and for lack of any other thread to follow, and as a forlorn hope, he might still keep the yellow berline and its single traveller under observation. There could therefore be no thought of racing at once for Gex and the frontier. So on to Châlons went La Salle, and lay the night there, after duly rewarding the post-boy as he had promised, in addition to paying for having brought him out of his prescribed way.

On the morrow, with fresh relays and another postilion, he resumed his journey, which ran now by way of Bourg. Thence he doubled back to Chaleat, and eventually reached Gex over the Col de la Faucille, whence he had his first glimpse of the breath-taking grandeur of Lake Léman, in its wedge between the towering Jura Mountains and the massive Mont Blanc range.

It was a long journey, in which he lost time beyond his calculations, consuming upon it the best part of a week. This not merely because of the detour that he made, but because a deluge of rain accompanying a terrific thunderstorm rendered the roads almost impassable for a carriage. On horseback he would not have been seriously hampered; but he could not abandon the berline because it contained effects belonging to von Ense, which it was necessary to convey to him. On the last night that he spent in France, the night of the last Thursday in June, another storm broke suddenly over the land, a storm more closely connected with his fortunes than he could possibly suspect as he lay snugly in his bed at Gex.

On the morrow, which dawned calm and smiling, with a sun that rendered startling the white Alpine summits ahead, the yellow berline set out on the last stage of its adventurous journey, and in the late afternoon the red machicolated walls of Geneva came into view. They crossed the bridge over the Rhône towards sunset, and came to draw up in the courtyard of the "Black Eagle" on the lakeside.

A shabby fellow, who had been leaning just outside the porte-cochère, idly smoking, followed the carriage into the yard, scanned it attentively and then passed into the inn.

Stepping down from the berline, La Salle desired to be directed at once to the Rue de St Pierre, and the house of Martin Lebas, where von Ense and the King should be waiting for him.

This Martin Lebas, a French clockmaker who years ago had married a Swiss wife and had permanently settled in this city of clockmakers, had acted in Geneva throughout the Revolution with extraordinary devotion as a royalist agent, and he had been of inestimable service to many an embarrassed émigré who had contrived to slip across the frontier. He was in more or less constant communication with de Batz, and it was here at his house that it had been agreed that von Ense should pause, so that they might rest

awhile now that they were out of France, and definitely plan the long
route yet to be pursued.

La Salle found the Rue St Pierre, a steep acclivity up the hill on
which the old town clustered under the domination of the Cathedral
at the summit. It was a narrow street of half-timbered houses, with
deep overhanging eaves and pointed gables, the façades of some of
them crudely decorated with wood carvings, pious mottoes and
painted figures.

He had no difficulty in finding the place. Lebas' name, well
displayed over a wide shop-front, was clearly visible even in the
fading light. The house was in darkness; but then, dusk was only just
descending. He knocked, and stood waiting.

Turning on the doorstep whilst he waited, he had an impression
of two shadows, farther down the street, sliding suddenly into the
cover of a doorway.

Then a heavy step sounded within; there was the click of a latch,
the door swung inwards, and the light of a lantern beat on La Salle's
face, held high by a tall, middle-aged man.

"Monsieur Lebas?" inquired La Salle.

"He is from home." The man was curt.

"My name is Husson. I must be expected. I was travelling with –
"

He was interrupted. "Monsieur Lebas is not here. He left Geneva
this morning. He will be back on Sunday night or Monday morning.
If you want to see him come again then." And he added, significantly,
thought La Salle: "Certainly. Come again."

"Oh, but a moment. Even if Monsieur Lebas is from home, the
Baron von Ense should be here. It is – "

Again the man cut in. "Monsieur le Baron was here. But he too has
gone."

"Gone? Impossible! Gone where?"

"He has gone. That, monsieur, is all that I can tell you. The rest
you must ask Monsieur Lebas. Good night!"

The door was slammed in his face, leaving him between dismay
and resentment, in that steep quiet street upon which night was

descending. Ahead of him, as he turned his gaze, the great mass of Mont Blanc thrust above the deepening shadows of the valley a white, glittering shoulder still flushed at the summit by the vanished sun.

He stood there a moment, hesitating and angry. At last, mastering an impulse to hammer on that door again and demand some fuller explanation of the mystery he sensed in so much reticence, he turned away and went slowly down the street.

He must put up, it seemed, at the inn, and remain there for the next two or three days, until the return of Lebas should enable him to discover by what road he was to follow von Ense. He could not conceive what should have occurred to cause the Baron thus to quit Geneva without waiting for him. But something undoubtedly must have come to alarm him into flight.

With his hands deep in the pockets of his coat, his head sunk between his shoulders and his eyes on the ground, he lengthened his stride and in turning a corner collided with a man advancing from the opposite direction. The collision brought them both to a standstill, and La Salle found himself peering into the face of his recent acquaintance, Desmarets.

By the light from a shop window they remained a moment at gaze. Then with a murmured word of apology, betraying no recognition, La Salle side-stepped and passed on. That he was permitted without question to proceed served to deepen his mistrust. Desmarets did not desire to invite a recognition of which La Salle had been careful to betray no sign. But the presence in Geneva of that persistent bloodhound supplied the answer to the question La Salle had been asking himself at that very moment. Somehow the fellow had picked up the trail again, and had not hesitated to follow it even over the frontier.

La Salle was as aware of the audacity of French agents as Lebas would be. Geneva was too near the border, and in the course of the last three years the clockmaker would have been well aware of the many kidnappings of fugitives from France who prematurely accounted themselves safe once they stood on Swiss soil. Because of this Lebas would be wary and vigilant, and never so wary and vigilant as in these last days when his house had sheltered a king. He too would have his spies, who would have reported to him the presence of Desmarets and his fellow-catchpolls. The arrival in Geneva of these agents of the Committee of Public Safety would be enough to alarm the stoutly loyal clockmaker on his exalted fugitive's behalf.

Here, then, was the explanation of von Ense's premature departure with his royal charge, and perhaps also of Lebas' own absence. Possibly he had gone with them, to guide and escort them into safety.

Forewarned, forearmed. It remained for La Salle to take precautions against any embarrassing activities on the part of these fellow-countrymen of his. He would barricade his door at night, and sleep with pistols ready to his hand, and in the daytime he would avoid all solitary places such as ill-intentioned persons might choose for an act of violence.

For the rest, he was relieved in mind by the explanation he held. He supped with a good appetite, doing justice to the lake trout and the white wine of Neuchâtel, and he slept soundly.

In the morning he went forth into the sunshine, and sauntered on the esplanade, ravished by the loveliness of the scene, the vast blue lake mirroring the grandeur in which it was set, the foothills rising out of orchards and vineyards on the lower slopes to the emerald Alpine pasture-lands above, and above these again the Titanic rocky ramparts crowned by glittering heights of snow and ice. He moved towards the bridge that spans the Rhône at the outfall of the lake, a red sandstone structure with its angular roof borne on umber-coloured timbers and its pointed burnt-red turrets, so quaintly mediaeval to his French perceptions.

Near it a crowd was gathered about a boat that was moored to a jetty. Either the safety he sought that day in gregariousness or mere curiosity drew him thither. On the fringe of the crowd he became aware of a patter of steps behind him, quick and yet irregular, as of someone who came in faltering haste. He turned, and beheld a young woman sustained by a man who trotted breathlessly beside her, some urchins straggling in their wake. Both were woebegone and white-faced, and the woman was whimpering. Thrusting past La Salle on the edge of the crowd, the man became rough, and plied his elbows so as to open a way for the woman who was now clamouring piteously: "Let me come to him. Oh, let me pass! Of your charity, let me pass."

The little press opened a way for them, and closed it again as they went forward.

A young boatman in waistcoat and breeches, barelegged below the knee, was at La Salle's elbow. La Salle turned to him.

"What has happened?"

"A drowning," the man answered gloomily, and added: "That's the poor widow. They've just brought the body ashore."

"Two bodies," another corrected him, and went on: "Ah, Dieu de Dieu! They should never have attempted it. Everyone could see a storm was coming on. But the gentleman was in desperate haste to cross to Lausanne, and he offered to pay well. What would you?"

"Much good the gold will do them now," grumbled the first. "Four of them drowned like that within hail of the shore, and two young widows left to get a living as they can."

The crowd stirred suddenly. A lane was opening through it, and there was a hush disturbed only by odd commiseration and the heart-broken wailing of a woman. Through the press, with steady tramp, came two lakeside men bearing a body on a stretcher, the woman staggering distraught beside it, still upheld by the man who had opened a way for her.

They passed close to La Salle, and he saw that the dead man, supine and calmly smiling, had been young and sturdy. A second stretcher followed. The man on this was of stouter build, his tangled hair of a faded blond. La Salle started forward, his eyes wide with horror, the blood draining from his cheeks. The leaden-hued countenance into which he was staring down was the countenance of Ulrich von Ense.

He attempted to advance, but someone thrust him roughly back. His mind momentarily stunned by the shock of his discovery, he found no words on which to claim the right to stand beside that body. By the time his wits had cleared sufficiently, a part of the crowd had closed in behind that grim procession, the remainder was dispersing.

The young boatman he had earlier addressed was still beside him.

"You said that four were drowned," he commented, and the steadiness of his voice surprised him.

"Four," the man agreed. "Two were boatmen; brothers they were. One of them is the first of those they are carrying. Then there was the gentleman who hired them. His was the second of those bodies. And there was a boy; his son maybe. All four of them lost through rashness two nights ago. They haven't found the other bodies yet."

La Salle became aware of eyes that watched him. He looked up into the grim, square face of Desmarets. Paying no heed to him, he moved off mechanically, following the crowd.

Here in the radiant sunshine, by Geneva's mountain-encompassed, smiling lake, was the abrupt and cruelly tragic end of this adventure and of all the hopes he attached to it.

Fate, like the malignant jade she was, had swindled him whilst his back was turned.

PART TWO

Chapter 1

The Freiherr Vom Stein

A curtain falls on the tragi-comic story of La Salle in that moment in which death cracked the egg that held the embryo of a king-maker. It does not rise again until thirteen years later, by when the throne of France had been set up once more to be occupied imperially by that portent Napoleon Bonaparte, to the dismay and disgust of Louis XVIII, who for a moment had deluded himself with the belief that the Corsican would play by him the part that Monk had played by Charles II of England.

Not until the spring of the year 1808 can I discover in the available records a single clue from which La Salle's history may once more be traced. And then it is in the police records of Berlin that we pick up the trail. From this I assume that he pursued his way into Germany after the tragedy of Lake Léman, and notwithstanding that this would seem to have destroyed all motive for the journey. Perhaps he feared that Desmarets would make it dangerous for him to return to Paris, and it may at the same time have occurred to him that in Prussia he would find it easier than in France to live by his art. He may even have gone forward with intent to reach the ear of Frederick William, conveying to him the news of what had happened in Geneva, and, turning to account the part he had played in the King's escape, seek by means of it to obtain a footing at the Prussian Court.

These are conjectures. Whatever the intent with which he did pursue that journey, the evidence is all that he failed in it, failing also, it is to be supposed, as a painter, for when at last the police records discover him to us again, it is to inform us that he was arrested as a result of a fracas occurring in a gaming-establishment which he had set up on the first floor of a mansion in the Herbststrasse, in association with another Frenchman named Prigent.

In these records, and in all subsequent references to him, we find him calling himself *de* La Salle. I have little doubt that he was entitled to the ennobling particle. It is at least as reasonable to suppose that he dropped it in France during the Terror as an undesirable distinction in patriotic eyes, as to assume that he appropriated it after the manner of the adventurer who is at pains to improve the appearances of his social status.

Beyond the association with a gaming-establishment there is nothing disgraceful in the arrest to which he was subjected. He appears to have been quite passive in the fracas responsible for it.

Prigent, who acted as croupier to the faro bank that La Salle held, was married to an attractive woman whose conduct was not above levity. I suspect – it was alleged, if not proved, in the subsequent proceedings – that she was largely employed as a decoy for young men of fortune. In this rôle her success with a young officer of Uhlans, Hauptmann von Weissenstein, appears considerably to have exceeded what was necessary for the purposes of a gaming-establishment.

One night when von Weissenstein had been both drinking heavily and losing heavily, his conduct towards the lady became so flagrant that Prigent, who placed limits upon the extent to which for business purposes he was prepared to carry marital complacency, was moved to raise an angry protest. He was answered by a stinging insult from the white-coated officer.

"I'll suffer no insolence from any low French pander."

Prigent's face went red, then deathly white, and from his dark eyes there was a momentary blaze. He rose to his feet, and his voice shook with a passion which prudence and interest alike were urging him to control.

"You will leave this house at once, Captain von Weissenstein. At once."

The Captain laughed at him. "Only if Madame should order it. And Madame would never be so cruel. Eh, schatzli?"

She had drawn away, beyond the reach of his too audacious hands, and she stood, a tall, handsome figure, all white against a background of dull-red velvet curtains. Her eyes were wide and her red mouth loose with fear.

There were more than a dozen punters, all men of fashion, seated at the table. Two lackeys in yellow liveries, with powdered heads, stood woodenly at either side of a buffet at the room's end. La Salle in the dealer's seat had just taken up a fresh pack. In the general hush that had descended upon the room he set it down again, with the wrappers still unbroken.

It becomes necessary to make his acquaintance all over again. For the Florence de La Salle, aged thirty-five, of the gaming-house in the Herbststrasse in Berlin, was a very different person from the art-student of the Atélier David who had kept himself from penury and served his monarchical sympathies by acting as one of the Baron de Batz's coadjutors. The thirteen years that were sped since he followed von Ense's body to its grave in the Geneva churchyard and buried with him all his hopes of eminence as a man of State had not mellowed him. That already his appearance was that of a man of forty shows how hard he had lived. He was leaner than of old, and there was a suggestion of springy toughness in all his movements, which were at once swift and smooth. We know that he had been at the point of death from the smallpox, and that he owed his survival to the unrelenting care of a woman who had loved him, and who, taking the contagion, had died of nursing him. This was something that may well have contributed to the hardening of his nature, just as, had she lived, he must have been redeemed from his egoism, for he returned her love with a devotion that was ennobling him. It was to that care of hers, to the compresses which day and night she had renewed upon his face whilst he lay fever stricken, that he owed the fact that his countenance was scarcely pitted. Nevertheless it was oddly changed when he emerged from the attack. The skin had contracted, bringing the bone structure into greater prominence, lending a sharpness to features which formerly had been softly rounded, and his complexion had become of an abiding creamy pallor. His hair, which formerly had reached to his shoulders, was now cropped short, to conform with the prevailing mode, and whilst still black and lustrous, it bore from the brow through the middle of it a bar almost an inch wide, of purest white. This was another legacy of the smallpox, which by its oddness lent a certain distinction to an appearance that in the main was almost sinister.

As he sat now in his slightly raised seat at the faro table, in a double-breasted light-blue coat with silver buttons and a deep black stock of military type that set off the pallor of his face, with its calm observant eyes, he suggested the self-possession of the man who knows his world, the man who would be equal to any emergency, the man with whom it would be dangerous to take liberties.

Those calm eyes were set upon Prigent with a compelling steadiness, as if he would have guided him. But Prigent avoided the glance, angrily intent as he was upon the offending officer. Angrily he was repeating his former demand.

"Captain von Weissenstein, I have required you to leave this house. You will do so at once, or you will take the consequences."

"The consequences?" The officer looked at him with a sneering contempt that drove Prigent to madness. In his fury he snatched up his croupier's rake and struck the Captain across the face with it.

It was a vicious blow into which the man had put all the concentrated strength of his anger. Weissenstein reeled under it. Steadying himself, he stood for a moment open-mouthed, paralysed by astonishment, and there was blood on his face. Then, with a foul oath, he put his hand to his sabre and lugged it out.

They fell upon him in time, and wrenched the weapon from him, and in an instant the calm of that elegant room was turned into a bear-pit. Von Weissenstein struggled furiously in those restraining arms, Swearing that he would smash up this den of French thieves, and largely succeeding, for tables and chairs were going over, ornaments were being shattered, and windows broken.

The noise attracted a passing patrol, and when this came in – a sergeant and four men – to restore order, the arrests were confined to the three foreigners, whom von Weissenstein meanly accused of having swindled him. His military rank ensured him obedience and personal immunity.

For La Salle it was a disaster. After spending a night in jail, he appeared with Prigent before a magistrate, charged by von Weissenstein with keeping a disorderly gaming-house, in addition to which there was against Prigent the further grave offence of having assaulted an officer wearing the uniform of the King of Prussia.

It was in vain that four of those who had been present came generously to testify in the Frenchman's favour and to state the provocation which had led to the blow. The law might look the other way where gaming-houses were concerned, but when – as sometimes happened – they became theatres of disorder, something had to be done. Besides, this was the year 1808, the year following the Peace of Tilsit, by which Bonaparte had shorn Frederick William of Prussia of half his kingdom, humiliated the State and brought it to the verge of ruin. The feeling against Frenchmen was not of a character to induce a Prussian magistrate to take a lenient view of their breaches of the law.

The monstrous fine imposed upon La Salle appears to have been limited only by the known extent of his possessions. In addition he was sentenced to three months' imprisonment. His associate, Prigent, similarly fined and sentenced, was given in addition a year's imprisonment in a fortress for having struck von Weissenstein. Towards the woman they practised the gallantry of allowing her to go free and to enjoy the destitution to which her husband's sentence must reduce her.

La Salle would have served his term of imprisonment, and thereafter, probably submerged, would never have been heard of again, but for the circumstance that here in Berlin he had formed fairly close ties of friendship with a young councillor of State who occasionally came to play at the house in the Herbststrasse. This nobleman's name was Karl Theodor von Ense. He was the nephew and heir of that Baron von Ense who had perished with the King of France in the storm on Lake Léman.

In itself this explains the relations in which we find him with La Salle. Whether their meeting in Berlin had been fortuitous, or whether, as seems more likely, La Salle had sought him out, the young councillor conceived himself under a debt to the man who by clearing up the mystery of the uncle's disappearance had enabled the nephew to enter upon his heritage. Natural feelings, too, must have prompted gratitude in von Ense to La Salle as the only mourner who had followed the Baron's coffin to the grave at Geneva, at which his story had been duly verified. It is even possible that von Ense may have enabled La Salle, by financial assistance or otherwise, to set up his gaming-house.

Anyway, in the present ruin it was to von Ense that La Salle appealed from his prison, and von Ense at once went to his assistance. He was well placed to do so, for not only was he a councillor of State, but he was actually close in the confidence and practically the leading coadjutor of that great statesman Heinrich Friedrich Karl, Freiherr vom und zum Stein, who was now the virtual dictator of Prussia.

In the capable hands of vom Stein the State was being unobtrusively regenerated from the disaster of Jena and the Peace of Tilsit, which had left Prussia under the burden of a crushing war indemnity, its garrisons in the occupation of French troops until it should be paid. Inspired by a burning patriotism that knew no scruples whatsoever, there were no measures that vom Stein would not take to redeem his country from the nullity to which Bonaparte had reduced it, there were no infamies that would not bear in his sight a virtuous aspect if they contributed to that end. In the service of his country, no man ever believed more implicitly than vom Stein that the end justified any means. Whilst, on the one hand, labouring unsparingly to restore prosperity to his exhausted country, on the other he was quietly planning and preparing a national rising that should redress its wrongs, and he had entered into a secret alliance with Spain for mutual support when the time should be ripe. The condition imposed by Bonaparte that the Prussian army should not exceed ninety thousand men, he circumvented by replacements which were gradually having the effect of turning every Prussian capable of bearing arms into a potential soldier.

All this vom Stein was steadily and successfully accomplishing under the very noses of the legion of spies employed by Joseph Fouché, who, as Bonaparte's Minister of Police, was now, under the Emperor, the most powerful man in France.

Karl Theodor von Ense was one of the very small band of Prussian noblemen at work with vom Stein in these underground preparations for national deliverance, and it was enough that von Ense should ask the all-powerful minister that leniency be exercised towards a man whom he represented as his friend, and one whose sufferings and labours in the Bourbon interest would seem to proclaim an anti-Bonapartist.

La Salle was restored at once to liberty, his fines were remitted and his property restored to him, with the sole condition that he should henceforth respect the laws of the land that sheltered him, and not again open a gaming-house in Berlin.

Vom Stein had, naturally enough, been curious as to the origin of von Ense's association with a man whose mode of life seemed at first glance of a questionable character.

"Cannot the same be said of many another émigré?" asked von Ense. "Are there not enough French noblemen throughout Germany who are being put to all sorts of shifts to make a living? This is a poor devil of a gentleman who has suffered the loss of everything by the Revolution." That was the shape of von Ense's apology for La Salle. He continued: "The man has some talent as a painter. I have seen some of his work. At one time his hopes and aims were to live by his art. But your excellency knows the hardships of that road. Had it not been for a cruel trick that fortune played him, La Salle might today be in a position of eminence on the steps of a throne." And now, at last, came the story of La Salle's part in the flight of Louis XVII, which so fully explained the interest he commanded in von Ense.

"Ah, yes," said Stein. "I remember that you told me this before." And he swung at once to the obsessing thought with which he sought to link up every political occurrence. "I said then – did I not? – that those events explain the strong and growing belief in France that Louis XVII escaped from the Temple, and that the announcement of his death there was fraudulent."

He lapsed into thought and sat hunched in his great chair, a small, bald, wiry man of fifty, with a lined, sallow face. It was a remarkable face. The line of the jaw was long, and the mouth was a thin hard line. The brow was lofty, the black eyebrows level, and the heavy pendulous nose was flanked by keen, rather prominent eyes.

They sat in the white-panelled library of his mansion, the tall windows open to the garden, for the time of year was late May, and the tepid air was fragrant with the perfume of magnolias now in bloom.

Hunched in his chair, he was absently tapping his teeth with an ivory paper-knife. Presently he spoke again, quietly, wistfully, a man thinking aloud. "How different things might have been if that boy had survived! Bonaparte who would not play the kingmaker to Louis XVIII might easily have been constrained by public feeling to play it for Louis XVII. The Orphan of the Temple. What a rallying-point for an emotional nation in a state of penitent reaction!" He smiled with a touch of sourness. "Once I even dreamed..." He broke off. "But what do dreams matter? The business of a man of State is with realities, and the reality here..." He shrugged, leaving the sentence unfinished. "What was this Frenchman's name?"

Von Ense told him, and he wrote it down. "Frauenfeld shall hear from me at once. Your Monsieur de La Salle shall be set at liberty today."

There for the moment the matter ended. But a week or so later, von Ense being again with the minister, Stein asked him suddenly: "Your friend La Salle, does it happen that he is still in Berlin?"

"Yes, Excellency."

Stein seemed to hesitate. He ruminated, chin in hand. Then he spoke brusquely, "I should like a word with him."

"He will be most honoured. When will it suit your excellency's convenience to receive him?"

The minister did not answer. He moved to his writing-table, sat down, and from a drawer took a very thin volume bound in vellum. "Here is a little manuscript that set me dreaming once. It is a copy of a mémoire of Madame Royale, the present Duchess of Angoulême, the sister of that unfortunate boy Louis XVII. It was written by her during the last week she spent in the Temple, and it is a full account of her captivity there. Later on whilst at Mitau with her errant uncle, Louis XVIII, a Russian spy obtained access to it and made a copy, which he sold some time afterwards to one of my agents. I have regarded it as a curiosity of a certain historical importance. But it never occurred to me that it might one day be of political use. It is of interest to me at the moment because, as far as it goes, it supplies certain confirmations of your Monsieur de La Salle's story. When I come to question him, I may find that it supplies still more, just as he may be able to add considerably to the information the mémoire contains. And then, perhaps, I may have something to propose if I judge him discreet, acute, and courageous. Bring him to me at ten o'clock tomorrow, if you please."

Von Ense undertook the errand, and punctually at ten o'clock on the following morning presented his protégé to the minister.

The Freiherr vom und zum Stein received them in his library, seated in his tall-backed arm-chair at his vast mahogany writing-table, bare of everything save a silver inkstand and the vellum-bound volume he had yesterday displayed. For a long moment his hard, piercing gaze studied the rather singular countenance of his visitor, pondered its pallid calm, the luminous, compelling eyes and the queer streak of white in the thick black hair, considered the quiet elegance of his dress, and at last indicated a chair that would place him with his face to the light.

"Pray sit down. You too, Karl. For you may remain."

Then with his elbow on the table and his hand partly shading his brow, the statesman delivered himself fluently in French.

He spoke of the interest La Salle inspired in him for the part he had played in the escape from France of the unfortunate son of Louis XVI, and then came to question him at length upon the Temple prison, its architecture, the arrangements in the tower, the treatment of Louis XVII whilst imprisoned there, and the precise manner of his evasion and substitution. To each question as it came La Salle replied quietly, promptly, confidently, and fully.

Last of all he was asked: "Do you remember the date on which, as you say, the prince was smuggled out of the Temple?"

"Perfectly. It is one of the memorable dates in my life. It was on the 19th of January of '94."

Stein nodded. "Yes. That agrees. Madame Royale on that day was under the impression that her brother was being taken away. She formed this impression from the comings and goings which she and Madame Elizabeth heard on the floor below. Afterwards she learnt that this bustle was caused by the departure of the Simons only, and that her brother had remained in his prison until his death eighteen months later. Thus she has written," he explained, answering the question in La Salle's steady eyes. "But it is plain that she wrote merely what she was told, and not from knowledge of her own. It is odd that she adduces nothing from the fact that after that date in January of '94 she heard, as she tells us, no sounds from the room below, whence until then the noise made by her brother playing and singing had daily reached her ears. A want of deductive reasoning there, I think. The silence perfectly agrees with your story of a deaf-mute substitute."

He passed on to questions concerning the flight from France in the summer of '95, until La Salle's answers had supplied him with the entire story.

After that vom Stein fell into a long brooding silence, broken at last abruptly, by his sharp, rasping voice to ask yet another question.

"Monsieur de La Salle, may I take it that your loyalty to the legitimate kings of France continues unabated, and that you would lend yourself with zeal, even with enthusiasm, to measures for the restoration of the House of Bourbon?"

"To be quite frank, Excellency, my interest in politics perished on the day that I buried the State councillor von Ense's uncle. Since then I have been concerned solely with serving my own interests."

"None too successfully perhaps. Certainly none too worthily."

"Excellency, each of us lives as he can. Which is to say, as he must."

"I could offer you something better worth while to a man of your enterprise and spirit."

"You are kind, Excellency. If it is sufficiently remunerative, I shall be happy to accept."

"You make no other condition?" The question was sharp.

"I know of none other worth making, Excellency."

"Very well. That will serve." Vom Stein sat back in his chair, laid his finger-tips together and, speaking slowly and distinctly, advanced an astounding proposal.

"You will agree, I suppose, that the whole of Europe is held in a state of nightmare by this Corsican who has made himself Emperor of the French. His monstrous ambition has turned the world into a shambles, and no country has suffered more bitterly than mine. Every right-thinking man who is not a Bonapartist must sigh and pray for an end to this desolation, and must account any measures justified that will achieve this end. Any measures. Even the French themselves begin to groan under this man's despotism. In the sacrifices he demands, the orphans and widows he creates in his pursuit of what is called glory, the French begin to regard him as a punishment from God upon the crimes they committed in the name of Liberty. I tell you that France grows weary of this tyranny." He said it with an air of challenge, and paused, as if waiting for La Salle to take it up.

"I would venture to submit, Excellency," he was quietly answered, "that they are not yet so weary as to accept Louis XVIII in his stead."

"That is unhappily true. And there you place your finger on the main obstacle to a Bourbon restoration. The French are without interest in, or admiration for, the present head of that house, who is not of a stature to inspire sympathy or to command a following. But if to the emotional, hysterical people composing that nation – you will forgive these expressions, Monsieur de La Salle – could be presented a Bourbon king who was in himself an interesting, romantic figure, a figure rendered so by his sufferings, a prince whose supposed death from ill-treatment may be a little on the conscience of the people, and whose reappearance consequently would produce relief and arouse the desire to right a cruel wrong, then it might not be difficult to create for him so great and enthusiastic a following that Bonaparte's strength would be sapped. Even if his immediate overthrow did not follow, so much embarrassment would be created for him at home that Europe would have a respite from his filibustering, a breathing-space in which to consolidate against his further aggression. You follow me, I hope, Monsieur de La Salle."

"Perfectly, Excellency, and with full agreement. Unfortunately the lake will not give up its dead."

A thin smile tightened the line of the statesman's lips. "Suppose that he had never been drowned. Suppose that he had succeeded in reaching Prussia, Austria, or Russia, and were now to appear again – the Orphan of the Temple – to claim his own?"

"But to suppose that..." La Salle broke off. He had suddenly caught the significance of the peculiar tone the Freiherr employed. "I understand. But to set up a spurious Louis XVII... How many have there been since Hervagault tried that imposture in '98?"

"A multitude; but not one who possessed the necessary knowledge to enable him successfully to sustain the part. That knowledge you and I, Monsieur de La Salle, command between us." He tapped the vellum-bound volume with a forefinger that was of the colour of ivory. "Ill-informed and otherwise unlikely as those poor pretenders were, the following won by Hervagault and some of the others is enough to show what might be done by a candidate properly prepared."

He sat forward, and his tone became brisk. "That is the task I offer, Monsieur de La Salle. It is one for which you are peculiarly fitted by your intimate knowledge of what took place up to the time of the King's death and by your old associations with the royalist party, associations which you could easily resume.

"Before we go further, the question is: Would you be prepared to undertake what amounts to a service to humanity and would be a source of fortune to yourself?"

La Salle has made the quite superfluous confession that he was taken aback and even moved to indignation by the magnitude of the fraud he was so cynically invited to perpetrate. Outwardly he retained a baffling impassivity whilst he considered the terms in which he should couch his refusal. Before doing so, however, he asked a question.

"Assuming, Excellency, that we succeed in placing the son of a butcher, baker, or tailor on the throne of France, what then? Would it be possible to leave him there?"

The aristocrat in the Freiherr vom Stein revolted visibly at the thought. "Certainly not. It is not intended, sir, to perpetuate such a fraud, but merely to employ it so as to overthrow the present bloodthirsty usurper. Once our Bourbon revolution has been achieved, we withdraw this pinchbeck puppet and bring forward the legitimate King. That follows logically."

This certainly altered matters. But still La Salle's white face remained inscrutable to the statesman's searching glance. He had yet another question.

"The man for the part, Excellency? Have you found him?"

"I have not sought him yet. There, too, I should require your help."

"He should have yellow hair and blue eyes, a fresh complexion, arching brows, full lips, a small nose and a dimple in his chin. I do not think he should be tall. The boy was short for his years. And he would be better plump, or even stout. The Bourbons are a fleshy race."

"Is this your answer, Monsieur de La Salle?"

La Salle seemed to rouse himself to a fuller consciousness. He displayed his lazy smile, into which with the years had crept a certain craftiness. "It is not an enterprise to be undertaken rashly, Excellency. Give me a little time for thought."

"By all means. And here's to help you." He proffered him the vellum-bound mémoire. "Take it and study it. You will find that it will add to your knowledge of those intimate details with which it is so important to be acquainted. Then come and talk to me again."

It was three days later when La Salle returned, again accompanied by von Ense, who remained as before a silent witness of the interview. La Salle brought with him a portfolio from which on arrival he drew a picture and placed it before vom Stein.

"Here, Excellency, is something to help your search for a suitable man, so far as his exterior goes."

The picture showed an angelic face. It was so like the well-known portrait by Kucharsky that if you set them side by side you might suppose that both had been painted by the same hand.

Vom Stein stood up to consider it in a better light, holding it at arms' length. "Is this your work?"

"Yes, Excellency."

"I pretend to no judgment in art. But it seems to me of obvious merit."

"Your excellency will remember," said von Ense, "that I told you that Monsieur de La Salle is a painter."

"By choice," said La Salle. "But many other things by necessity."

Vom Stein nodded. "You painted this from memory?"

"Largely. But that is not surprising. The portrait is one upon which I worked so hard and reproduced so often that I could not forget it in fifty years. Besides, I have still my sketch-books. And in one of these are the sketches I made that day in the Temple of which I told your excellency."

Vom Stein set down the portrait, and his eyes looked into La Salle's. "This signifies that you are ready for the undertaking."

La Salle bowed slightly. "I am at your excellency's service, provided always that we find the man capable of playing the part."

"We shall find him. You may depend upon that. And, as you've said, this will help us in our search." The tightening of those thin lips seemed to promise that the man would be found if all Europe had to be ransacked for him.

From what we know of the Freiherr vom und zum Stein we need not doubt that, being resolved upon it, he would have found the man had he been left free to do so. But one evening five days later von Ense, pallid and shaking, came to La Salle's lodging with dreadful news. The great Prussian minister was caught in Fouché's vast network of espionage. A courier of his had been seized and a letter to Spain intercepted, the terms of which betrayed the secret alliance and gave more than an indication of Prussia's growing strength. The surrender of vom Stein to French justice had been demanded of the King, and vom Stein was in flight from Prussia. If he fell into Napoleon's hands his death was certain. Von Ense, himself, was packing up. If he remained and his share in vom Stein's plots were brought to light, he would probably have to face a firing-party.

And so the only profit that La Salle made where such rich rewards seemed to await him was a vellum-bound copy of the mémoire written by Marie-Thérèse Charlotte de France, now Duchess of Angoulême.

Chapter 2

The Heir to the Lilies

With the abortion of vom Stein's conspiracy before it had begun to move, La Salle sinks once more out of sight, and for the best part of the next six years there is again a hiatus in his history. When next he comes to the surface it is in Paris just after the Restoration.

Of that Restoration, or, rather, of the overthrow of Napoleon which made it possible, we find, when all is sifted, that the architect-in-chief was the Freiherr Heinrich Friedrich Karl vom und zum Stein. He fled for his life from the wrath that pursued him, but not from the task which had provoked it. In St Petersburg, where he ultimately found shelter, he became the very soul and brain of the coalition against Napoleon, and it was his hand that guided the riposte by which the Czar laid low the Emperor of the French.

France had drawn a breath of relief when at last the colossus crashed from his pedestal. With an enthusiasm growing to delirium it had displayed the white cockade and summoned its legitimate sovereign from Hartwell in England to come and resume the misgovernment and the errors for which his family was distinguished.

From the outset Louis XVIII had himself in false perspective. The Charter of St Ouen in which he promised France a constitution, he regarded as a noble concession from a king to his subjects, instead of what it actually was – the permission accorded him by the provisional government to enter Paris. So as to vindicate the Divine Right he had to insist that he had granted a constitution and not accepted one. Nor could he admit that he had been recalled by the people, because he had never lost his hereditary rights, and had never ceased to reign from the moment in 1795 when (upon receiving news of the death of his nephew in the Temple) he had proclaimed himself. Accordingly he writes of this year 1814 of his return from exile as the nineteenth of his reign.

Amid full-throated acclamations in the brilliant May sunshine, he rode into Paris in a calèche drawn by eight horses, a vast obese man weighing some three hundredweights, a king of heroic gastronomic powers, credited with ability to swallow a hundred oysters at a sitting and with consuming daily some dozen pints of wine. He appeared to possess no neck. His great head, purple-red of face, under a thatch of white hair, seemed to sit on the épaulettes that adorned his shoulders. He waved his enormous cocked hat in acknowledgment of the roaring plaudits which in reality were less for him than for the niece at his side, whose past tragedy moved the popular imagination to a frenzy of tenderness.

The people spoke of her as the Orphan of the Temple, the very designation which vom Stein in his shrewd estimation of French sentiment would have given to the pretender he had conceived. It served to show with what loving affection France was ready to enfold Marie-Thérèse Charlotte.

This was to be modified when, as soon happened, France became better acquainted with her and realized the harsh aridity of her soul. The indignities, privations, sorrows and insults suffered in the Temple might not have sufficed to curdle her nature without the sequel. Released at the end of 1795, at the age of seventeen, she had been conveyed to Vienna, to her mother's family, there to discover that she had merely exchanged one form of captivity for another. Closely guarded, for four years every effort was made to coerce her into marrying the Archduke Charles, so as to gratify the ambitions of his brother the Emperor, who hoped thus to establish for him a claim to the throne of France. For four years in a loveless disillusion, starved of affection and even of such companionship as she would have chosen, she resisted. And then, when the Emperor finally yielded, and allowed her to go to the poverty-stricken, make-believe Court of her exiled uncle, Louis XVIII, again she found herself a mere political pawn. Falsely urged that it was what her parents would have desired, she was swept into marriage with her cousin of Angoulême, who was only half a man. Thus perished her last hope of that happiness so bitterly earned by years of suffering and wretchedness.

Little wonder, then, that her soul had curdled within her, as her very features showed. The beauty which La Salle had seen in the child of sixteen in the Temple was no longer discernible in the soured woman of thirty-six who came back to Paris in 1814. The face that once had been softly rounded and so gentle of expression had grown harsh and angular. She was tall and thin, haughty of bearing, and showed herself almost insensible to the thunder of acclamation with which she was welcomed by a people generously eager to make amends to her for all that in her youth she had undergone in Paris. Stiffly upright, and scarcely responsive, she sat beside that obese man, her lean figure tightly sheathed in a gown of silver lamé, her sharp features shaded by a little English bonnet, which drew smiles from the Frenchwomen among whom the large hat was in vogue.

To blare of trumpets and roll of drums, with regiment upon regiment of troops that had lately been the Emperor's, the procession crossed the Pont Neuf and passed the statue of the founder of the Bourbon dynasty. Here sycophancy had extolled the inglorious living in terms amounting to insult of the glorious dead: "Lodovico reduce Henricus redivivus."

The old servants of the Bourbon monarchy, to whom a steadfast loyalty had brought suffering and privation, accounted this their hour, and flocked to Paris, so as to garner where they had so unstintingly sown. Amongst the least of these was La Salle, who had lived by shifts, and with whom the world had not gone well. He came back to a Paris that bewildered him, a Paris very different from that which he had left so many years ago. He found now a

superficially gay, bright, care-free, pleasure-seeking city, still reflecting
the glories of the Napoleonic era, which had changed the face of it,
as it had changed the face of Europe.

He found himself here a lonely stranger. His deeds had been
performed in shadow, and his name, he knew would command no
attention. But there was de Batz to speak for him, and who today
should stand higher in the royal favour than that devoted tireless
champion of the royal cause in the years of its adversity? Confidently,
in quest of his old friend and chief, he directed his steps to the
Tuileries, which he found transmogrified like all the rest, its approach
embellished by the Arc de Triomphe of the Carrousel, to the glory of
the Grande Armée.

But the Tuileries knew nothing of the Baron Jean de Batz. From
official to official he wandered, in deepening amazement. In turn
each shook his head. De Batz? They had never heard of him.

Never heard of him! To La Salle it was incredible, a source of
swelling indignation, an offence. What men were these who had
never heard of Jean de Batz, the peerless knight whose deeds were
almost fabulous, who had organized a desperate attempt to rescue
the King on the day of his execution, and another to deliver the
Queen from prison, which would have succeeded but that she would
not leave her family; de Batz who in the rising of Vendemiaire had
exposed himself to the grapeshot of General Bonaparte, and who
had led every reactionary revolt; that man of fantastic courage and
incredible address, that hero of romance, the like of which no
romancer had ever imagined? And they had never heard of him,
these pimps at the Tuileries who took their ease in the royal plenty.
It passed belief.

At long last La Salle's persistence produced some result with
Monsieur de Blacas – one of the new men whose swords were as
virginal as their master's. The letters that he wrote to this royal
favourite, lately created a Duke, with the whole of the sovereign
power concentrated in his hands, won him a brief interview with the
great man's secretary.

He was coldly received in a room of gilded furniture, silken tapestries and pretty pictures, by an insolent, fleshy ecclesiastic, the Abbé Fleuriel. The cavalier tone assumed with him by this upstart he could tolerate. He, after all, was of no account politically or otherwise. But the cavalier tone in which the fellow alluded to de Batz stirred him to an indignation which he could not contain.

At the request of the Duke de Blacas, the Abbé had given himself the trouble – thus he described it – of looking through the dossiers of that multitude which was urging claims on the ground of services rendered to the monarchy, and he had been so fortunate as to discover the dossier of Colonel Jean de Batz, Baron of Armanthieu, if this was the person in whom Monsieur de La Salle was interested.

"I should not have imagined," drawled La Salle with the utmost insolence he could command, "that the claims of Monsieur de Batz were under the necessity of being urged, or that the records of his deeds would have to be sought in a dossier."

For answer he was subjected to a prolonged and haughty stare, intended to awaken in him a sense of his monstrous impertinence. He sustained it, thankful that his exterior, his well-cut coat and black satin stock, his creaseless buckskins and polished Hessian boots, at least lent him an air of prosperity which the facts certainly did not justify.

At last the Abbé recovered sufficiently to be able to pursue his supercilious announcement. "I have had a note made of the address which the dossier contains. It is here."

La Salle received it with eagerness, whilst Fleuriel, turning a page of the document he held, condescended to continue: "As I take it that you are one of the friends of Monsieur de Batz, you will be interested to know that the commission graciously appointed by Monsieur le Duc de Blacas to examine the claims of those servants of the monarchy whose careers were broken by the Revolution, reports very favourably upon the services rendered by Colonel de Batz." With fatuity he added: "It is probable that we shall be able to employ him."

"Probable, is it?" said La Salle, who boiled under his cool exterior. "And it required an investigation by a commission to discover the royalist activities of Monsieur de Batz? Really, Monsieur l'Abbé, I should have thought they would have been known to every scavenger in France."

"Ah! To every scavenger perhaps."

It was La Salle's turn to stare the other down, to render him aware of his unpardonable coarseness. Then he spoke quietly.

"You take advantage of your cloth, you scoundrel. If you were not an ecclesiastic I should give myself the pleasure of boxing your ears."

With cold disdain Fleuriel tinkled a bell on his table. A lackey entered at once.

"This person to the door," he said.

La Salle departed to the address he had received, and there in the garret of a decrepit house in the Rue du Vieux Colombier, in abject poverty, he discovered the preux-chevalier, the knightly gentleman who for years had held his life in daily peril in the service of the Bourbon cause. He found him emaciated, pallid, and unkempt. The figure once so trim and upright, that he had never seen other than dressed with a flaunting elegance that was a defiance of sansculottism, was now in the last stage of shabbiness, and this room, high up under the tiles, was almost bare of furniture. A deal table, a deal chair, an iron camp-bed with soiled and tattered coverlets, a bare floor, supplied the environment in which, under the Bourbon Restoration he had laboured unremittingly to promote, the once fastidious de Batz now had his being.

The two men stood staring at each other, pain in La Salle's eyes, mistrust in the other's. Then the Baron spoke.

"If you've come to collect a debt, monsieur, faith, you can see for yourself what means I have to pay you."

"Jean!" cried La Salle.

"Eh?" The Baron peered at him, frowning. "Who the devil may you be?"

"Is it possible that you don't know me? I am Florence."

"Florence? Florence!" The Baron sucked in his breath, then took his visitor by the shoulders and turned him so that the light fell more fully upon that pallid countenance. "My God! How you've changed!"

"Twenty years is a long time, Jean. It has made some changes in us both."

"But, death of my life, I should have known the voice. It still holds all the expression of your sluggish soul. Florence! Could you bear to embrace me, Florence? Or am I too filthy?"

When that was over, de Batz drew him in at last, and closed the door. Within the room he stood considering him with a crooked smile. "And so you've come back at last? You've come back to the plenty awaiting those of us who risked our necks to serve the Bourbons. I hope the sight of me does not discourage you. I sun myself, as you see, in the gratitude of princes. But sit down, Florence. Sit down since you've come, and tell me of yourself." He waved him to the only chair and, himself, found a seat upon the bed. "Tell me that you have painted great pictures; that you are a Court painter in Austria or Prussia. It was from Prussia, I think, that I last had news of you."

La Salle shook his head. "David was right, I think. He must have been. Art has disowned me. I live by my wits with the varying fortunes that attend the adventurer. A widespread passion for gaming, rooted in human greed, is the weakness I have chiefly exploited. At least I haven't starved."

"Exploiters of human weaknesses seldom do. There is so much weakness to exploit. Those who perish are the fools who live by a code of honour, who are loyal to ideals invented by rogues for their own protection."

"You shall shave and dress, Jean, and we'll go and dine at Foy's or Février's whilst we exchange accounts of ourselves."

"To shave is easy. But as for dressing, it is Verneil's day."

"Verneil's day?"

"You remember Verneil: the Vicomte Gaspard de Verneil, who plotted and worked with Rougeville to rescue the Queen from the

Conciergerie." De Batz sighed. "How near that was to succeeding! And how infernally near was Verneil to leaving his head on the scaffold for it. I dare say the poor devil has come to regret that he didn't. He is another who ruined himself in the service of the monarchy, and now luxuriates like me in the royal gratitude."

"So that was Verneil. I remember. And he too... But what has this to do with dressing yourself?"

De Batz made a wry face. There was bitter humour about the firm lips and in the dark eyes, still lively under the grizzled brows.

"Faith, we're neighbours in this garret, and we share our possessions as in the old days we shared our risks. We have one coat and hat between us. So when one goes out, the other stays at home. And this is Verneil's day out."

"Name of God!" said La Salle, and stared in horror.

"What would you? It's the fate of heroes in retirement."

"But to be reduced to that! I burn with shame for you."

"Burn away, my good Florence. Myself, I haven't even the energy to do so much. I am all but finished. Bit by bit I have sold everything I had, just so that I might sometimes eat. All the rest, my strength, my wits, my courage, my fortune and my very life were spent in the service of the King. And my fortune was considerable. Today the only thing remaining is my sword. There it hangs. The hilt is of silver. It might fetch two or three hundred livres. But I can't bring myself to eat it. I am not yet a sword-swallower. Besides, I may have a better use for it."

La Salle had risen. He moved to the door. "Get yourself shaved whilst I am gone. At least I can supply you with a hat and coat, so that you may come and dine with me."

"Sheer waste, my Florence. They'll go to the Mont de Piété tomorrow for a quarter of their value."

But Florence was already going down the stairs.

That evening in a coat of tolerable fit the Baron dined with La Salle at Février's in the Palais Royal Gardens. The fare was princely, and the wine was a mellow, fragrant vintage of de Batz's own country, than which, he vowed, the world produced none better. It was wine that renewed courage, tempered age and grief, and set aglow the vista of what yet remained of life. So swore de Batz when first the wine was brought. But when he had drunk he showed no sign of any such magic having been wrought in him.

"I suppose," he said, "there's so much gall in me that not all the wine from the Garonne could wash my blood sweet again. For all that I gave, all that I have had is a vague promise that employment may presently be found for me in my colonel's grade. Meanwhile, starvation seems the only way to escape my creditors. For, trusting to royal gratitude, I have permitted myself to run into debt."

"My purse is at your service, Jean."

"That you should say it suffices."

"But I mean it."

"To be sure you do. But to what purpose should I avail myself of your generosity? If you gave me all your purse, what should I face when I had used it? A mere postponement, Florence, is not relief."

"You have not considered that in the meantime relief might come from your debtor. From the King."

De Batz laughed, and then threw up the floodgates of his accumulated bitterness. "From that pretty piece of flesh? That vat of tallow? There is neither sense nor sensibility in the hog. He is all vanity and self-sufficiency, a crowned buffoon who pampers those whose only service has been to flatter him, the idle and safe companions of his exile, who never drew a blade or took a scar to set him on the throne he always coveted.

"Whilst some ten thousand officers of the old nobility who have bled for their principles and have been ruined by the Revolution are struggling with starvation on half-pay, it is the Blacas and the Jaucourts who are the men in power, whilst Bonapartists, Jacobins, and even some of the regicides responsible for his brother's death find favour and affluence under Louis XVIII. Perhaps he feels that he owes these last some reward for having enabled him to gratify his consuming ambition for the pomp of kingship.

"Monsieur de Talleyrand, the revolutionary Bishop of Autun, who has since unfrocked himself, directs his foreign policy. He has actually pensioned Robespierre's sister, and Fouché – you remember Fouché, the Oratorian Professor, the mitrailleur of Lyons – would be his minister of police today but for the opposition to his appointment offered by the Duchess of Angoulême. And, anyway, in his place we have his friend, the Baron André."

"Madame Royale has some influence, then. I wonder that you have not written to her. Impossible that she should not remember your name and what you did: the attempt to rescue her, together with the Queen, Madame Elizabeth and the little King, from the Temple."

"Ah, that! I wrote. I was answered by a secretary, in cold terms that her highness would place my letter before the King. And then – nothing. To the restored King I am as inconvenient as any other creditor to a man who has not the honesty to pay his debts. Take warning, my dear Florence. Never serve an ideal. If serve you must, serve a man. But first make sure that he is a man. If I had given Bonaparte one half the service I have given the Bourbons, I should have come by a dukedom, like Fouché. But then Bonaparte was a man. He may yet come back. Stranger things have been seen in our time. Already he is regretted, particularly by the Army. Either he will return or there will be another revolution. This Bourbon cannot last."

La Salle was dejectedly thoughtful. "If only that boy had survived! If we could have produced him when Bonaparte fell, how different affairs would be!"

To La Salle the Baron's answer was more startling than anything he had yet said. "Would they? I wonder. Not, believe me, if Louis XVIII could help it. Even before the Restoration, when the rumour ran strongly through France that Louis XVII was alive, it was reported to me that this man, this King of France, was reviving by innuendoes the old scandal of his own ignoble fabrication on the subject of the legitimacy of his nephew. It was an expression of his panic lest the rumour of survival should be true, and this child should rise, as it were, from the grave to bar his way to the throne."

"But was he not informed of the facts? Did you never convey to him the news I sent you from Geneva?"

"No. I had sent him word of the escape. But my messenger was never heard of again. No doubt he fell into the hands of the government. Before I could find another messenger, I had your word of the boy's death. To report his escape after that seemed hardly worth while. So His Majesty remains in ignorance of what I could tell him now to set his doubts at rest. If these doubts torment him, as I hope they do, he is well served for his heartless neglect of so many of us."

La Salle's face was dark. "On the whole, then, it is perhaps as well that the boy was drowned, and it would avail me little to base a claim to royal gratitude on my part in rescuing him from the Temple. You make me realize that, save for seeing you again, my return to France has been a waste of time and effort. And I could well have forgone the pain of seeing you thus, Jean. Men are not good. It was you who told me that twenty years ago; and I have seen little since that does not confirm it."

"Twenty years!" de Batz echoed. "Twenty wasted years! You, at least, are not so old but that you may still profit by the lesson they have taught you. As for me..." He raised his glass and surveyed for a moment the wine that glowed like a purple jewel against the candle-light. "In another and a better world I shall hope to be more fortunate." He drained the glass. "After all, there are compensations in touching bottom. There, at least, we no longer fear to fall."

Not until the morrow, when he went again to seek him, did La Salle grasp the full tragic significance of those words. Jean de Batz was dead when La Salle reached the garret in the Rue du Vieux Colombier. He had stabbed himself with the silver-hilted sword, the only one of his possessions that he had not sold, because, as he had said yesterday, he might yet find a better use for it.

Chapter 3

The Counterfeiter

It is probable that nothing in La Salle's forty-one years of life had shocked him so profoundly as the ignoble end of a man whom he had ever regarded as a model of nobility, an incarnation of devotion to an ideal. It filled him for a season with a wrath that advanced the corrosion of his nature. If he had been of a strength to try conclusions with that paltry Prince whom he regarded as no better than the murderer of the noble de Batz, he would have spent the last ounce of that strength in seeking to avenge the Gascon gentleman. But since this was a task beyond him, he made haste to shake again from his feet the dust of a Paris in which he could neither find nor desire a place.

Like de Batz, and perhaps more fervently, from what he had learnt in this brief repatriation, he too could wish that he had served Bonaparte. In the Corsican's service there had always been room for men of brain and nerve, and they had gone far. To wit – amongst so many – that same Fouché whom de Batz had mentioned, the sometime Jacobin, the pitiless Republican pro-consul and ruthless persecutor of aristocrats, now Duke of Otranto, lord of great estates and of a wealth that was counted in millions. The arts, too, had flourished under that master-man, as they had never flourished before in France. But for La Salle's early Bourbon entanglements and the furrow they seemed to have ploughed for him, he might now, at forty-one, be comfortably settled in the world instead of doomed to wander through it as aimlessly as the Shoemaker of Jerusalem. That he viewed things thus, bears witness to the cynical change that grief and resentment had wrought in his nature, and the complete sloughing of such ideals as in the past he might have harboured. That he was ever really an idealist it is impossible to believe.

His wanderings now took him back to Prussia. He may have been induced to this by the relations he had established there. The woman who had given her life for him had been a Prussian. Or he may have thought to reopen association with Karl Theodor von Ense, and through him to reach the Freiherr vom Stein once more. For vom Stein was now a person of European consequence. He might remember that La Salle had found favour with him once for a difficult enterprise and be again disposed to employ him.

Of painting I do not believe that he even thought in those days. He was too hard pressed for money, besides which the spirit in which art is to be pursued had been cast out of him.

He reached Berlin to find that von Ense was no longer there, and without von Ense's support he had little hope of reaching vom Stein. He tried it, nevertheless, but failed.

And so from Berlin he drifted to Brandenburg, and there, in the autumn of that same year, we find his name once more in the police records, and discover him once more at his old trade of keeping a faro bank.

This time the trouble that brings him to the Rathaus is concerned with the utterance of base coin. It was raised one evening by a punter at La Salle's table, who set up an outcry that nine thalers out of ten which the croupier had just paid him were false.

"Where have I landed?" this punter demanded angrily. "In a den of coiners?"

There were in all nine gamesters present, apparently all of them men of the bourgeois class, and they fell at once to examining the money before them. In a moment two of them were protesting that there were false thalers amongst it, which the bank had paid them.

"It's as I said, then," clamoured the first. "This is a coiner's den."

Now, it happened that a deal of base coin was circulating at the time in Brandenburg. The police were excited on the subject, and an accusation of uttering it could not be taken lightly, especially by the keeper of a gaming-house, which of all places was the likeliest for this kind of traffic.

As the hubbub rose about him, La Salle instantly perceived his peril. He raised an imperious hand to calm the storm, and imperious, too, was the tone he took.

"Gentlemen! If you please! Whatever base coin has passed across this cloth has first come to the bank from one or another of you. Those of you whose consciences are clear will be well advised to co-operate with me in discovering the source of this muddy Pactolus. Of my interests, I can, myself, take care. But you have your own to consider, and, above all, the State's. I will beg, gentlemen – nay, I must insist – that not a single coin be removed at present from the table."

It was not only the authority of his manner that calmed the excitement, but the clear good sense of his demand.

Of the nine gamesters, eight at once withdrew their hands from the table and sat back. The ninth, a heavy, rough-looking fellow named Naundorff, kept his elbow on the cloth and his chin in his hands, in an attitude that seemed to shelter and guard the pile of silver heaped before him.

As much from this as from La Salle's recollection of the course of the play – for who keeps a faro bank must have his wits about him – it was to this particular punter that he first gave his attention.

"You, sir," he said. "You have won once only. Five thalers were paid to you on the deal before last."

"No, no," the man was beginning a denial, when his immediate neighbour came to support the banker's assertion, as did one other of those present.

La Salle's glance had flashed a message to the croupier, who at once had stepped to Naundorff's elbow.

"There may, then," said La Salle, "be five base thalers in your pile. If so, the bank will need to go further so as to prove its honesty. Permit my croupier to examine the money."

"Lieber Gott! Do you insult me with your suspicions?" The florid countenance, under a mop of black kinky hair, became inflamed, the little eyes malevolent. By trade a clockmaker, he spoke the harsh dialect of an uneducated man.

"Sir, there is no suspicion. The matter must be sifted, and the course of your fortunes makes you an easy subject for elimination." La Salle nodded to the croupier. "If you please, Fritzli."

Fritzli, an active, humorous lad, laid a hand on one of Naundorff's protecting arms. It merely served to render his resistance the more fierce.

"Devil take you! You shall not meddle with me. I'll not allow it. I'll…"

His harsh voice was drowned by the protests of the other players. One of them went to Fritzli's assistance, to hold Naundorff back, whilst another rang the coins one by one upon the table. There were five good silver thalers. All the remainder were false.

Although La Salle would have avoided police intervention on his premises, he was powerless to resist the insistence of the company. The police were fetched – two officers, who searched Naundorff on the spot; and no fewer than fifty more base thalers were discovered distributed about his person. They took him away, and La Salle heard afterwards that, the fellow's house having been ransacked, moulds and presses had been found to complete his incrimination as a counterfeiter.

At his trial six days later at the Rathaus, La Salle attended as a witness.

There was excitement over the case in the town, and the courthouse was crowded when the Frenchman took his stand to give evidence against the luckless clockmaker.

He was answering the last of the president's questions when his glance alighted upon an eager face in the foreground of the crowd at the barrier, the face of a young man who appeared to be following the proceedings with a strained anxiety. Something in that face so arrested La Salle's attention that he neglected to answer the question asked him until it had been sharply repeated.

Then his eyes sought that face again. Surely at some time he had known this man, or someone very like him. When he left the witness-stand, he took a seat in court whence he could observe the fellow. He judged him to be somewhere about thirty years of age. He was of middle height, slight, and delicate. His countenance was lean, narrow, and careworn, framed in a cloud of dark-brown hair, of unusual length for the times, completely covering his ears. The nose was boldly carved and high-bridged, the nostrils pinched. The eyes, under arched brows, were pale and wistful as a dog's. He wore a shabby, short green coat over a coarse shirt, his legs were gaitered, and his general air was unkempt and neglected.

Having studied him in detail, La Salle decided that he had never known him, that it was merely a case of some elusive likeness creating the impression of a former acquaintance. He would probably have thought of him no more had not circumstances, as he was leaving the court-room, come to reawaken his interest.

Among the last to depart, after Naundorff had been removed under sentence of five years' imprisonment, he observed and overheard that same young man in conversation with one of the guards.

"But I must see him," he was protesting. "I must see him." He spoke – and this imperfectly – a sluggish low-German, very different from the clipped speech of Prussia, and there was a wildness in his air.

"Of course," the guard mocked him. "You have only to wait until he comes out of prison. What's five years, after all? A little patience, my good sir."

"I beg you not to laugh at me. I am in great trouble through this man. It must be possible to see him."

"Not now. Too late. You should have come yesterday, before he was sentenced. Then it might have been possible."

"Oh, my God! My God!" The young man wrung his hands in tragi-comical distress.

The soldier, growing impatient, began to hustle him. "Get along. Get along. Out of here."

Listlessly, dejectedly, the stranger turned away. He was moving with dragging feet towards the door when a lazy voice drawled almost in his ear in French: "Can I be of service?"

His sudden turn was in the nature of a jump. The pale eyes dilated as they looked into La Salle's queer, pallid, masterful countenance, and again the face shocked La Salle by its resemblance to some other face into which once he had looked. Answering that stare of consternation, La Salle explained himself, marvelling the while that a man with such a nose should display so poor a spirit.

"You are French, I think?"

"No, no." The quick repudiation of that nationality in itself suggested alarm. "I am a Neuchâtellois."

"Almost the same thing." La Salle smiled. "It makes for a sort of compatriotism, and, faith, compatriots abroad should assist one another. You seem in some trouble. Could I help you?"

This courtesy was met by distrust. "You are very kind to a stranger." He spoke French with the accent of a peasant of the Jura, thus confirming the nationality he claimed.

"Here we are both strangers," said La Salle. "You were asking, I think, if you could see the prisoner, this counterfeiter Naundorff."

"Could I?" Mistrust gave sudden place to eagerness. "It means so much to me. I have come so far to see him. I arrived in Brandenburg only last night, and only to learn that he had been gaoled. Surely even if he is a prisoner..." Wistfully the pale eyes pleaded.

"It might be contrived. Come. We will inquire. The Praefektur is just here."

He went down the steps; the stranger swung along beside him with reviving hope.

An under-officer scratched his head to La Salle's inquiry. The prisoner had been taken to the cells. It might be possible to see him on an order from the Prefect. But not without it. And the Prefect had just left. He would not be there again today. If the gentleman would come again tomorrow, the under-officer, a kindly fellow, thought it might be contrived.

"Until tomorrow, then," said La Salle, and he clapped the stranger on the shoulder. "March, my lad. You shall come and dine with me."

The arched brows arched themselves a little more. Mistrust returned to those prominent pale eyes. "You are good, sir. Very good. But why should I dine with you?"

"What the devil! Have you no appetite, then?"

"That is not the question." There was a sudden queer access of pride.

"Faith, it's the only question that's relevant."

"Sir, I do not disparage your manifest goodness. But I do not accept a favour which it is beyond my power to return. I am at the end of my resources."

"Then you are the more in need of what the gods may send you. Come to dinner."

He had wanted to laugh at that sudden assumption of dignity by this shabby fellow in his green jacket and long leather gaiters, at the care with which he seemed to pick words that in themselves hardly went with the peasant accent in which they were uttered. For the rest, he could not have told you whether sympathy or curiosity dictated an insistence that was not to be denied.

Yielding almost helplessly to his masterfulness, the young man allowed himself to be shepherded across the square and into the eating-house of the Bär, to a recessed table in the rather crowded common-room.

La Salle made short work of ordering in his languid but compelling way. A dish of eels stewed in white wine, with roast goose to follow; succulent and nourishing food to put heart into a man when washed down by a flask of Rhenish. He plied his guest with questions whilst they ate, and at first was freely answered. He learnt that his name was Charles Perrin Deslys, that he was a clockmaker from Le Locle, in which there are more clockmakers even than in Geneva, and that his business with Naundorff was that the German had some effects belonging to him which it was of the utmost importance that he should recover.

Now, it did not seem to La Salle that the fact that both were clockmakers sufficiently explained the connection, since one was established in Le Locle on the slopes of the Jura and the other in Brandenburg. So when he judged that the wine had mellowed his guest to the extent of rendering him communicative, he pressed to know exactly how they had come to be associated.

"It happened six months ago, in Madeburg. We met in the prison hospital there. I had been arrested as a deserter from the Imperial Army. It was an error. For my uncle had bought me out; that is to say, he had bought a substitute for me. In the end this was verified, and I was released. But the law moves slowly, and in the meantime I was ill. Naundorff was in the bed next to mine in hospital. I was deeply distressed by my arrest, which was ruining all the plans I had made, and I was very desolate and lonely. Naundorff was kind and sympathetic. We became close friends. And then there came a time when I thought I was going to die. I gave him my full confidence, and entrusted to him some papers I had and some other things. Days of unconsciousness followed. When I recovered, Naundorff had gone. I got well again; but it was fully a month before I was, at last, released. I set out to find Naundorff, but I could discover no trace of him."

He paused there, and passed a hand over his brow, thrusting back the damp hair that clung to it. La Salle waited, scenting a mystery in this stranger who shaped his sentences with the lucidity and vocabulary of a cultured mind, yet always with the rough accent of a Jura peasant.

Presently Deslys resumed, a weariness in his voice. "I do not wish to think that Naundorff is a villain, or that he would swindle one who had so fully trusted him. When he left the hospital he would believe, as did others, that I was dying, and he would naturally suppose that I died soon after. So why should he leave any trace by which I might reach him? For four months I have been seeking him, using up the little store of money that I had. A week ago in Berlin I found a clockmaker, at last, who was able to tell me that Naundorff was in Brandenburg. I came at once. I arrived here only last night, to learn that he was under arrest. And now..." He took his head in his hands. "Oh, my God!" he groaned as before. "Unless the prefect will let me see him tomorrow, I shall have to wait five years. Five years! The thought is not to be borne. It will break my brains."

There was a good deal that La Salle could not understand. "But even if you had found him, he might no longer have this property of yours. If he's a villain, and since he's a coiner..."

"He has it. He has it." Deslys was vehement. He met La Salle's frowning, searching gaze, and under it he seemed to grow afraid, his eyes filled again with mistrust.

"But in God's name, what is it that he has, then, that is so valuable?"

The young man looked away. Something froze in him. His tone changed. "Oh, but of value to me alone."

"In that case why fear his villainy? Every man is honest when dishonesty is unprofitable."

The prominent eyes came back to look full and squarely into La Salle's across the table. "Have you never found malice in men for its own sake?"

La Salle laughed. "Faith! I wonder that I came for a moment to forget it. But tell me this: What was it brought you to Prussia in the first instance? What were you seeking here?"

Suspicion was stronger than ever in the lines of that narrow face. "Oh, I wanted to see a little of the world. But, sir, I weary you with so much talk of myself. My story can be of no great interest to you. A poor return, indeed, for your kindness to a benighted stranger."

There was a cold tone to the courteous words which made of them a clear request to leave the subject. Deslys turned his profile to La Salle, and as the Frenchman saw it in silhouette against the leaded panes of the window behind the clockmaker he suddenly caught his breath in amazement. It awoke in him the memory of the cruel sketch in profile David had made of Marie-Antoinette from a window of the Rue St Honoré on that October day of 1793 when she had been carted to the guillotine.

A queer thought assailed him in that moment. By merest chance he had come upon the man who should have been under his hand when the Freiherr vom Stein was seeking an impersonator of the dead Louis XVII.

It was not, perhaps, too close a likeness under analysis. That beak of a nose was nothing like the short stumpy nose of the little King. The face itself was of a different build, long and narrow where the other's had been softly rounded, and the hair was of a chestnut brown instead of yellow. The eyes, too, he thought, should be a deeper blue. But there was likeness enough to serve, and if some features did not match, there were sufficient that did. This fellow was actually hare-toothed, and there was a dimple in his chin.

Their eyes met. La Salle smiled. "Have you ever been told that you are very like the Queen of France?"

The brows were lifted a little higher. "Is there a Queen of France? I thought she died in England."

"Not that one, faith. The real Queen. The one that was guillotined. Marie-Antoinette."

Deslys continued to look at him, and his face was blank. "And you find me like her? No. I have never been told that. But I have been told that she was beautiful. I think you must want to laugh when you say that I am like her."

"Had you been as like King Louis, I should have asked you had your mother ever been to Court."

Chapter 4

The Errant Clockmaker

No doubt that likeness was alone responsible for La Salle's continued interest in Charles Perrin Deslys. Of Deslys we suspect that he tolerated it for purely selfish motives.

On better acquaintance he proved to La Salle a queer, puzzling creature, alternating dignity with awkwardness, boldness with shyness; uneasy mistrust would stare out of his pale, rather plaintive eyes even when he was soliciting assistance. An unstable spirit displayed itself in odd nervousness, in furtiveness and reticences, in revelations of weakness alternating with suggestions of strength; in flashes of irritability, in petulance and a more or less abiding melancholy.

La Salle summed up his accurate first impression of the man when much later he said: "I perceived that somewhere at some time someone must so have hurt his soul as to destroy for ever his trust in man. I think this drew me to him, as to one who was much in my own case, although the effect in each of us was so widely different; for whilst in me disillusion had begotten hardness and an insensibility of which I was all too conscious, in him it had resulted in a sapping of his will."

His actual person was attractive; and yet he was a man whom it would have been difficult to hold in real affection, because of something in him that repulsed it, and this not merely unconsciously but in very spite of himself. I suspect that La Salle, thus fortuitously met, went as near as any man to loving him. But that came later. In what he did on the morrow of their first meeting, he was no more than fulfilling the task he had undertaken. Betimes he hailed the clockmaker from his mean inn and took him off to the Praefektur, and Deslys was thankful because of a need he ever experienced to lean on someone else. For the mistrust that was the keynote of his character extended even to himself.

So by crazy, tortuous streets of mediaeval houses that were all gables, turrets and projecting timbered upper storeys, they came through the bustle and clamour of the Molken Market and the wider space of the Saint Anne Strasse, to the gloomy Gothic building that housed the Prefect.

For an official he proved amazingly accessible. An hour and a half was all the waiting, in the draughty stone hall between doorway and courtyard, to which these clients were subjected. And he proved no more discourteous than most of his kind. A large, bald man in a blue frogged coat, he merely scowled and roared at them as if they were a couple of pickpockets.

Had Deslys gone alone, he would probably have fled at once. But the imperturbable La Salle had long since learnt to look coldly upon noisy bluster. It was the silent man who made him wary.

Quietly he stated the object of their visit. The Prefect roared more violently. He flung some scraps of blasphemy at the pair, assumed them to be associates of the scoundrel Naundorff, and probably engaged in the same nefarious industry.

"That is true only of my friend," said La Salle, at which the Prefect was not the only one to gasp.

"Potzeufel! You admit it?"

"That he is a clockmaker. Why not?"

"A clockmaker! Oh, I see."

La Salle let his laughter ring out with calculated disrespect.

"You see? God be praised! You thought I meant a counterfeiter. Ah, but that is droll, Lord God!"

The Prefect banged his writing-table. "Cease that noise. I'll have no laughter here. You need waste no more of my time. The prisoner Naundorff left Brandenburg this morning. There is nothing to be done."

Deslys' gulp of disappointment may have stimulated La Salle's insistence. "Could we not go after him?"

"To the fortress of Harzburg? Impossible!"

"Ah!" La Salle bowed to him. He turned to his stricken companion, and was inspired. "Come. It means only a slight delay. I will write to the Freiherr vom Stein at once. I warned you it might be beyond the powers of a mere Prefect."

The mere Prefect's beady eyes were suddenly busy with La Salle's exterior, and now that he took the trouble to examine it, his provincial eyes noted its correctness, noted too the quiet authority of that singularly pallid face under the glossy black hair divided by its curious bar of white. It seemed credible that such a man should speak with easy confidence of writing to the all-powerful Minister.

"Stay a moment, gentlemen." There was a muted note in the erstwhile bellowing voice. "You named the Freiherr vom Stein."

La Salle looked down his nose. "I must be at the trouble of writing to him since there is no other way of serving this young protégé of mine in his need."

"You...you have the honour of the Baron vom Stein's acquaintance perhaps?"

"His acquaintance, certainly." La Salle was languid. "Possibly some influence in that quarter, too. It shall be tried."

The Prefect actually came to his feet. "But, Excellency, it may not be necessary to trouble the Lord Baron for so little. After all, I could issue an order to the governor of the prison."

"You might have said so before," La Salle complained. "However..." He found himself a chair.

"It but requires – a mere formality, but they insist upon it in all cases – that the order shall state the business upon which the prisoner is to be seen."

"Of course, of course. There you are, my dear Monsieur Deslys."

The Prefect sat down again, and took a sheet of paper and a pen.

"Your name, sir, if you please."

The young man roused himself from a state of dismay. "Charles Perrin Deslys."

The Prefect wrote. "French, I suppose?"

"No. From the Principality of Neuchâtel."

"Ah! Occupation? Oh yes. Clockmaker, you said. And the business on which you wish to see this man Naundorff?"

"It...it is of a personal nature."

"One understands that. But it must be declared."

Deslys was ill-at-ease. "He possesses some things of mine. Things that I entrusted to him some time ago. I wish to recover them. I want him to tell me where they are to be found."

"Yes. Quite reasonable. Yes. But these things? What sort of things?"

"I am not at liberty to say." He became surprisingly resolute.

The Prefect laid down his pen. "Herr Deslys, I must assure you that it is necessary. The regulations are clear."

Deslys stood stubbornly mute. La Salle came to his assistance.

"Surely, Herr Praefekt, to recover personal possessions should be a sufficient declaration."

The official shook his head. His expression became consequential.

"Consider, Excellency, that this man Naundorff is under sentence for a grave offence. Your young protégé is admittedly of the same trade. The same trades afford the same opportunities. No reflection, you understand. I merely say to you what might be said to me to aggravate the offence I should be committing if I neglected this compliance with the regulations."

La Salle inclined his head. "Understood. My young friend will remove the difficulty now that he perceives the necessity."

Deslys did not take it kindly. "They are papers," he said impatiently. "Mostly papers."

"Ah, mostly. What does 'mostly' cover?"

"Oh, but nothing of any account – a trinket, a personal trifle."

"Look you, sir. This will not do. I have to think of myself. It is no light thing to issue such an order as you request. I must know the nature of those papers."

Deslys' hands worked nervously on the brim of his hat. Then he spoke petulantly. "I can't tell you more. These things are my property, and I have a right to them. The law should uphold me in that and not make difficulties."

Vainly did the Prefect protest that the difficulties were not of the law's making, that the Herr Deslys was not being reasonable. Obstinately the young man refused to help himself on the terms he was offered.

"There is no more to be said, then," the Prefect deplored at last. He addressed La Salle. "It but remains for you to write to his excellency the Minister of State. He may do for you what is beyond my poor powers."

It was their dismissal. The Prefect escorted them to the door, professing himself their very obedient servant. Outside, Deslys clutched his companion's arm.

"You will write to the Minister?"

"Write...?" La Salle looked at him. "Faith, why not?"

"Was it not in your mind to do so? Or don't you really know him?"

"Oh, I know him and he should know me. Or, at least, he should remember me when I recall myself to him."

"And you'll write?"

"Why, yes. But don't build on it. Ministers of State rarely show any alacrity to oblige poor devils like you and me."

The letter, composed with care, was dispatched that day, and for a week they waited in vain for an answer, Deslys in a dejection that increased daily, La Salle, who knew his world, without surprise.

Whilst they waited, Deslys, upon La Salle's insistence, had left his mean inn and had come to share La Salle's quarters. It had followed out of a desperate confession by Deslys that he was without means to pay for his lodgings and that for as long as he remained in Brandenburg he must endeavour to find work at his trade.

"Who will give you employment for a few days?" La Salle asked him. "Bah! Fetch your things from the inn. We'll find room for you here."

"I could not dream of it." His show of pride was ferocious. When La Salle insisted, he expressed at great length the impossibility of accepting so much from a comparative stranger. But in the end necessity drove him to yield, to the disgust of La Salle's croupier and partner, Fritzli.

"My dear Florence, you've landed yourself with an escroc. I know the breed. They all talk like that. Very high and mighty. Couldn't dream of accepting. Nevertheless, they always accept. And you can't afford it now."

This might well have been true, for a letter had come to Monsieur de La Salle from the police to inform him that in view of the service he had rendered the State by bringing a counterfeiter to justice, no notice would be taken of the breach of the law which debarred aliens from setting up gaming-establishments in Prussia, but warning him that the severest penalties awaited him if he persisted. Thus his source of income was dammed up and Fritzli was taking his departure.

But La Salle was not warned by his croupier. He kept Deslys with him, and to pass the time of waiting got out his paints and palette, procured a canvas, and set about painting the young man's portrait. He was to confess later that although he was at this time unaware of it, there must already have been stirring somewhere in the recesses of his soul a notion of at least the possibility of what later followed, and that from this arose the impulse to befriend and retain the clockmaker. The inspiration to paint his portrait he attributes to the elusive likeness which had first drawn him to the man. He scarcely knew in what lines it lay, for features and colouring, as we have seen, were all so different from those of the unfortunate lad who had succumbed in Lake Léman. Yet it was present somewhere in that countenance. To capture it and set it down on canvas was a test of capacity which he imposed upon himself.

He thinks that it was whilst he worked on this portrait that gradually the great temptation evolved out of the recurring conjecture of what might have occurred if this fellow had been under his hand when vom Stein proposed the imposture and if vom Stein had been spared the persecutions of Fouché's police. At first he merely toyed, he thinks, with the notion. Speculations upon it formed an amusing day-dream. But as he continued to indulge it, and came gradually to perceive how closely it could be knit and made to hang together by means of all the intimate information in his possession, it passed gradually from a dream into a solid purpose, and lacked only the consent of the protagonist.

The latest news reaching Prussia from France all served to stimulate the rascally notion. The Bourbons – that is to say, the reign of Louis XVIII – could not endure. Contempt and Parisian ridicule were killing the ruling Sovereign. The white cockade displayed with such delirious enthusiasm in May was by August being used to adorn the tails of dogs that ran about the Paris streets. To the Parisians the obese King was now the gros cochon; the card-players spoke nowadays of the cochon of hearts, the cochon of spades, of clubs or of diamonds. His Majesty was become a subject for gross caricatures and grosser lampoons.

Such reports as these made it clear that the days of Louis XVIII were numbered.

This was the hour, and La Salle possessed the man.

The Orphan of the Temple was actually desired in France by all those – and their numbers were daily increasing – who believed in his survival. Let him appear and he would be warmly welcomed even by those who did not think of him as yet. For every impudent impersonator who had arisen, no matter how unlikely, there had been an immediate following, merely from the human readiness to believe what it hopes. What must happen when La Salle presented one whom he had the necessary knowledge convincingly to equip for the rôle for which he seemed by a freak of nature to have been expressly fashioned?

It was a project to disturb at first even the cold imperturbability of him who conceived it. He glowed and froze alternately as he pondered it. He reflected that he stood to lose nothing; for he had nothing to lose; was nothing. If he should succeed he would win a prize the thought of which turned him dizzy.

It remained to suborn Deslys. If he was the common escroc that Fritzli believed him, the task would be easy. But La Salle did not believe that he was an escroc, and he mistrusted Deslys' courage. The prospect might scare him. Clearly the matter was one to be cautiously approached.

By the time the lack of answer from vom Stein was seriously troubling the clockmaker, the portrait was finished.

"Little remains to do," said La Salle one evening, "and I'll leave that little for tomorrow. The light is failing."

Deslys left the sitter's chair and came round to look at his own face staring boldly at him from the canvas. For a long moment he was silent in sheer wonder.

"It is marvellous," he murmured.

"No," said La Salle. "That is not the word. The draughtsmanship is sound, the colour good; the flesh tints could not be bettered by David himself. Yet it fails. The whole is not definite. It lacks character. I have completely missed the things I sought, or, rather, they have eluded me. I am not subtle with the brush." He sighed. "That's why I live by gaming-tables."

"I don't understand," said Deslys. "It is a likeness that speaks. I seem to look at myself."

"Oh, it's like you. Yes. I could make it more like you still; but then, paradoxically, it would be less like you. That is because I lack the touch, the indefinable, mysterious touch that marks the master. Bah!"

"You do yourself injustice, surely. To paint like that!"

"It is to be very near the summit, and yet so far from it that I might as well be in the valley with the mob of worthless daubers. Such talent as mine is not a gift, but a curse. It chains a man to a dream; prevents him from realizing himself in some other channel. I might have been an honest clockmaker like you, Charles, although frankly I think it's more amusing to be a shiftless adventurer."

The allusion diverted the clockmaker's thoughts. "Do you still hope to hear from the Baron vom Stein?"

Grave eyes considered him. "To be truthful, no. I warned you not to hope too much." He turned away to put aside his palette and mahl-stick and drop his brushes into a jar. After a while he spoke again. "It matters very much to you?"

"Much? Just everything." The tone was tragic. "All these wasted months. All that wasted future. To wait, and wait…" The prominent eyes were dog-like again in their wistfulness.

"For what?" asked La Salle, and saw that by his peremptoriness he had sealed the other's lips.

"Oh, for something that would have helped me."

"Devil take your mysteries. Do you suppose I want to steal your secret processes, or the clockwork invention of which this rogue Naundorff has filched your drawings?"

Deslys stared at him blankly. "What makes you suppose that?"

"What else is to suppose? He stole some papers, didn't he? What else should one clockmaker steal from another in that form? No need to treat it as if it were a secret of State."

"No, I suppose not." Deslys sat down weakly. He passed a limp hand across that perpetually damp brow, thrusting back the chestnut hair from it in that queer, characteristic gesture so eloquent of distress. Then he set his elbows on his knees and took his chin in his hands. "You spoke, monsieur, of being chained to a dream. That seems to have been my case too. Now I am awake and facing reality again, and I find reality ugly."

"There's nothing amiss with your vision, then."

"If only I had left dreaming and stayed in the Jura, reality might have contented me. I suppose all desires are illusions."

"No. Only those that cannot be gratified."

"Mine are of those. Just a torment of which I am weary. I long for peace. Peace. It awaits me in the Jura if I will but resign myself. Yet I have spent almost my last thaler and my last ounce of courage in chasing this jack-o'-lantern. Before I can save enough to take me back, I shall have to work at my trade for at least a year among strangers, here in this foreign land. That is if I can find work in Prussia." A sob shook him. His face vanished into his hands. "It breaks my heart."

From across the room – a large room of sparse but solid bourgeois furnishing – La Salle looked at the bowed figure in silence. His lips were set, his eyes vivid with thought. He came slowly across, and set a fine hand lightly upon those bowed shoulders. His voice was soft, its drawl more marked than usual.

"No need for that. If the return to the Jura is all that it needs to comfort you we can set out at once."

Deslys looked up almost in alarm. "We?"

"There is nothing to keep me in Brandenburg. I'll go home, I think. Le Locle lies on the way. We might journey together."

"If you would do that! Once there my uncle would reimburse you."

"That is no matter. I could take you farther and show you something better than clockmaking if you had the will and the courage to go with me." He paused there before adding: "You don't know it, Charles, but in your face you have a fortune which I think I could shape for you soundly and surely."

"A fortune in my face?" He looked scared. "I don't understand. Nor why my fortunes should interest you."

"Because if I made them I should share them. I am no altruist. I know of an enterprise which if undertaken between us would bring us wealth and power such as you have never considered even in your dreams, whatever the inventions of which Naundorff may have filched the plans."

"What enterprise?"

There was only mistrust in the tone of the question. Nevertheless, La Salle turned away to a press in which he kept a few articles that went with him always on his travels – some sketch-books and a slender vellum-bound manuscript accidentally left in his possession by the sudden flight of vom Stein. He took this manuscript and brought it to Deslys.

"First, read this mémoire. Read it carefully. Then we will talk."

Chapter 5

The King-Maker

La Salle, in a flaming dressing-gown and Turkish slippers, was brewing the breakfast coffee on the following morning when Deslys made his appearance. The vellum-bound manuscript was in the clockmaker's limp hands. His eyes looked red in a face more than usually pale. He set the volume down on the table. He spoke very quietly.

"Why did you give me this book to read?"

La Salle was scrutinizing him. "You have found it a moving tale?"

Deslys made his distressful gesture of sweeping the hair from his brow. "Why did you give it to me?" he repeated.

"To inform you of things which in certain circumstances it would be important that you should know."

"In what circumstances?"

"In the circumstances of the enterprise of which I spoke yesterday. The rest of the knowledge necessary I can impart; and it happens that I am the only man living who can; for, setting aside some precious details in that mémoire, I am better informed on the subject of Louis XVII than Madame Royale, herself, I can even correct her errors."

He set a cup for his companion, and poured the steaming fragrant brew. Beside it he placed the dish of butter and a plate on which crisp rolls were heaped. "Break your fast. Then we will talk."

That talk, when it came, took the shape of a lecture from La Salle on the political conditions in France and the contempt into which Louis XVIII had fallen. He warmed to his subject as he advanced, his passion whipped up by the memory of de Batz. The contempt, he explained, had been richly deserved, not only by the errors of his policy, but by the rottenness of the man's heart.

"Men are not good," he said, quoting that phrase of de Batz's which had remained with him as a sort of philosophy of life, "and I expect no great good of any man. I am not good, myself. Not now. But I have a sort of code. This King has none."

He was pacing the room as he talked, whilst Deslys sat before a broken but untasted roll, his narrow countenance almost ludicrous in its bewilderment as he listened to the coldly bitter phrases in which the soul of the present King of France was being dissected. La Salle spared him nothing. He even stressed the possibility that Louis XVIII had reason to doubt that his nephew had died in the Temple, wherefore he was careful to take no steps to ascertain the truth, and if by a miracle Louis XVII were to return to life and appear in France, it would probably be his uncle's endeavour to send him to the fate of an impostor.

"But it might not be in his power," he added. "For the nation would welcome nothing so much as to discover a usurper in Louis XVIII. Legitimists, Bonapartists and even Jacobins would become one in their common eagerness to show him the door."

After that, becoming more practical, he first startled his listener and then reduced him to a condition that seemed to border on terror by advancing his proposal in plain terms.

Still talking, he went to the press from which he had yesterday taken the mémoire, turned over some sketch-books, selected one of them, and came back with it to the table.

"You may dismiss my proposal, but you need not dismiss it out of fear of its failure. I have thought of everything. Failure is almost impossible. It could come only from lack of boldness. And should we fail after all, at least we shall have played for a stake worth winning, a stake that represents almost unlimited power and fortune for us both."

Deslys' hand trembled on the mémoire. If his expression, in its blend of fear and amazement, continued ludicrous, more ludicrous still was the sudden knitting of those arched brows.

"For us both?"

It was his first utterance since the proposal had been clearly made, and it was a question that came as a shock to La Salle. "What else? Or do you conceive me a benevolent imbecile who goes about the world making the fortune of chance acquaintances?"

"But if such a thing should be, if this absurdity should succeed and you could make a king of France, why should you trust him to keep faith with you?"

La Salle did not conceal his sardonic amusement. This clockmaker merely expressed that profoundly suspicious nature of which he had already given abundant glimpses.

"I should confidently trust him to keep faith with me," La Salle drawled, "because it would be infinitely easier to pull him down than to set him up. At his first breach of faith I should pluck off the mask and expose the imposture. That is why I am prepared to trust you. And that is why I am prepared to risk all, even life itself, to make a king of you; because it will never be in your power, as it would be in the power of a real king, to cast me off when my task is accomplished.

"Oh, I know something of the gratitude of princes." He spoke in a sudden surge of passion. "So much, indeed, that if you were really Louis XVII and it were in my power to establish you, I would not lift a finger to help you, but both hands to hinder you."

To the blank stare of the prominent pale eyes that watched him, he added: "I have had experience of these Bourbons and their gratitude." And he went on briefly to tell the ugly tale of de Batz rewarded by destitution for the greatest services man had ever rendered to a prince. "And he was not merely my friend. That gallant gentleman was my ideal, the noble pattern upon which I sought to shape my nature. I, myself, who strove beside him during the Terror, who schemed and fought with him, go neglected, without hope of regaining the patrimony of which the Revolution stripped me, driven to mean, unworthy shifts so as to keep myself alive. But that is nothing. That I could forgive. But never the heartless, cynical, dishonest neglect that drove that great gentleman to take his life. Never, never. I have spoken of the power and fortune that will follow upon the success of this enterprise. For you those are the whole of the stakes. For me they are only a part. Above them, far above them, I rate the satisfaction of thrusting that royal hog from a throne he is defiling."

He checked there, suddenly conscious that passion had swept him along a course of self-revelation far beyond any that he had intended. Instantly, as if a curtain fell, he resumed his habitual languor. The lips that had writhed in anger were quietly smiling; the eyes that had flashed were almost dulled; the brow that had scowled was smooth again.

"I talk too much. I go beyond my purpose, which was to show you why I need not hesitate to trust you. Just as I take you from nothing, so I can reduce you again to nothing if you play me false. Are you answered?"

"Yes," said Deslys simply, and yet with a queer emphasis, "I am answered." He let his chin sink into his loosely knotted necktie, and stared vacantly before him.

La Salle sipped his coffee in silence, standing. He waited a while before rousing the other from the gloomy abstraction into which he had lapsed.

"In terms less uncivil – and you would perceive that I spoke a little in the heat of ugly memories – what I am proposing is a partnership. I bring to it the full knowledge that will enable you to play your part, and also, I believe, the resource to direct and guide you in playing it. You bring a cast of countenance. Look at these." He set before him the open sketch-book. "Compare those faces with that portrait. What do you find?"

But instead of answering him, Deslys, after a glance at the sketches, asked him, "How do you come by these?"

"I made them one day twenty years ago in the Temple Prison."

"You made them?" The clockmaker stared up at him. "You made them?"

"I made them. I've said so. But look at the portrait. Compare it with these. Do you perceive the likeness?"

For a moment Deslys continued to look at him. Then he gave his attention to the portrait.

"A slight likeness. It is in the brow, I think; and the mouth perhaps."

"If the likeness between the portrait and the sketches is not stronger, the fault is mine. It has eluded me because it does not lie in features alone. Yet it more than suffices. No pretender yet has looked so like a Bourbon."

"No pretender yet has succeeded. And I think you said there have been several. What happened to them?"

"Nothing."

"Nothing?" Deslys was incredulous.

"Nothing," La Salle repeated. "I have told you that Louis XVIII may know that his nephew did not die in the Temple, but escaped. In any trial of a pretender there is a danger that this disturbing fact might be established. Let that give you courage."

"Courage? You think that I lack it?"

"I hope that you possess it; and not only the courage but the will to face this adventure, to leave clockmaking and penury and turn towards the dazzling heights to which I can lift you."

Deslys took his head in his hands, and presently, observing that his shoulders were shaking, La Salle's face grew stern with doubt of the rather invertebrate, vacillating nature he discovered in this Jura peasant. But not even on that account would he draw back, so strong seemed the chances of success for a man with such a face. A gamester nowadays, he knew that who risks nothing, wins nothing. It only remained for Deslys to announce that he succumbed to the temptation.

If he was not yet ready to announce it, neither did he reject it. He confessed himself dazed, bewildered. He must take time for thought.

He took two days. They were days of moody, sullen absorption, in which he gave no indication of his leanings. He asked many questions, chiefly concerned with the difficulties that suggested themselves to his nervous mind, but never one to which La Salle could not at once supply the answer.

The last talk they had concerned Louis XVII's escape from the Temple Tower and subsequently from France, in which La Salle related the important part that he had played. It was a tale that ended at the drowning in the lake.

"There is," said Deslys, "or there was, a rumour current in the neighbourhood – I heard it even in Le Locle – which largely confirms your story. But…" He paused, and frowned as he looked at La Salle. "Do you say that you were the man who escorted the young King?"

"One of the men. There were two of us."

"What was the name of the other?"

"The Prussian Baron Ulrich von Ense. He was drowned with the boy. But you shall be instructed in all that, never fear."

Deslys straightened himself and threw up his head. "I don't. You persuade me that you could guide this tremendous adventure. Do I persuade you that I shall not falter?"

La Salle looked keenly into that narrow face, which by a miracle had suddenly become resolute. "It is time to pack and set out," he said.

Chapter 6

Passavant

By steep pathways, through a woodland that was turning golden, came on a day of late September Florence de La Salle and Charles Perrin Deslys. They rode on mules hired in Le Locle, where the post-chaise had set them down at the end of the last long stage from Bâle. They had travelled swiftly, without sparing horseflesh, for La Salle was of the adventurer's temperament in the matter of expenditure, which is never to stint it until the purse is empty. Fortunately the faro table in Brandenburg had been fruitful before the Naundorff incident.

A sturdy, cross-gartered mountaineer, who owned the beasts, strode ahead, leading a third mule, from the saddle of which the travellers' portmantles were slung. He brought them out of the forest gloom to the open pasture-lands of the Jura foothills, and here they halted to breathe the mules.

A half-mile ahead stood a cluster of wooden buildings set in an orchard and dominated by a wide châlet with deep overhanging eaves. Farther back, towering above these slopes, rose a mighty rampart of mountain masses from a black base of pinewoods to a white crest of snow, on which the sunset flung a patch as of blood. Below and behind them the ground rolled away to the valley already in shadow and the metallic shimmer of the great Lake of Neuchâtel in the far distance to the south-west.

Brown cattle moved and grazed on this open pasture-land, and the clank of cowbells was the only sound upon the evening stillness.

La Salle's eyes greedily absorbed the majestic beauty of the scene, and he breathed deeply of the clear, pure air before digging his heels into the flanks of his mule to urge it after the others along the track that led to Passavant, the homestead of Deslys' uncle. The young clockmaker had insisted upon halting here to pay this visit to his only relatives before continuing the journey into France, there to play the fraudulent part in which by now he was well instructed.

He had given La Salle his reasons for this in the course of the account of himself which he had rendered on the way. These Perrins, who dwelt at Passavant, were as parents to him. His widowed mother had died when he was ten years of age, and Joseph Perrin, her brother – still unmarried in those days – had taken the orphan and had given him a home at the farm, where he had worked until the age of nineteen. Then, urged by a desire to see something of the world, he had gone down to Le Locle to learn the trade of clockmaking, so that he might earn some money of his own wherewith to gratify more fully that desire.

As they now drew near to the low wall that bounded the orchard, a woman showed herself among the trees. A moment she stood at gaze, shading her eyes with her hand, for the low sun was almost directly behind the travellers. Then she moved swift and excitedly, and they heard her voice shrill upon the mountain stillness.

"Justine! Justine! Monsieur Charles is here! Monsieur Charles!"

She ran down to the gate, and by the time that La Salle reached it, Deslys was already afoot. He flung a greeting to the woman. "Ah! My good Suzanne!" he cried, and waiting for no more went racing up the pathway towards a girl who came at like speed to meet him. He caught her in full flight as it seemed, held her, and kissed her.

Observing this with interest, La Salle observed also that she was worth kissing; an adorable child not yet twenty, with eyes blue as the gentians on her mountains, a skin like those sun-flushed snowy summits and braided hair that was of the colour of honey.

La Salle slid down from his mule, bared his glossy black head with that queer bar of white athwart it, and bowed from the waist to Suzanne – a deep-bosomed apple-faced peasant of forty or so – who remained at the open gate.

Not knowing whom she might be, he made himself pleasant.

"This good Charles' condonable but egotistical haste leaves me under the necessity of presenting myself. I am Florence de La Salle, to serve you, madame."

The drawling tone that lent an irony to his artificial speech, the elegance of his tight-waisted, full-skirted riding-coat, so unusual in those uplands, and the countenance of him, so unusual anywhere, almost frightened her. She grinned and curtsied in confusion, and respectfully drew herself away a little as Deslys conducted Justine down the pathway to present his new-found friend. He was flushed and bright of eye.

"This, Florence, is my cousin Justine, of whom I have told you."

"But not the half of what you should have told me. Had Mademoiselle been my cousin, faith, I should have found little else to talk about."

He was ingratiatory, but it amused him to perceive that he did not ingratiate. Justine was as shy and mistrustful under his glance as Suzanne, the waiting-woman, had been. Nor was he more of a success with the uncle and aunt, when presently, the muleteer having been paid and dismissed, he made their acquaintance.

Joseph Perrin and his wife came out to receive the travellers on the wide wooden balcony of the upper storey, which was reached by a broad external staircase, whilst a farm-lad, hurriedly summoned, bore their portmantles within doors.

Joseph Perrin, a man in the late forties, was in build a typical mountaineer, short, thick-set, and bow-legged, but his powerful frame was crippled by rheumatism, and he dragged himself stiffly forward with the help of two sticks. His broad, black-bearded face, weathered almost to the colour of walnut, would have been grim but for the winning kindliness that looked out of his liquid brown eyes, set deep under craggy brows. His wife was a small neat woman, gentle of expression, with the placid eyes of the mountain dweller, a soft-toned voice, and smooth fair hair that had faded to the colour of ashes. It was from her that Justine inherited her fine features.

They were manifestly glad to see their nephew, particularly Joseph, who expressed relief from fears that he vowed had been grievously afflicting him. And, peasants though they might be, the courtesy of the terms in which they welcomed their nephew's companion was not of peasant quality. Nor was their dwelling, which was spread upon this upper storey of the châlet, the ground floor consisting of a byre for the cattle. La Salle found himself ushered into a spacious, commodious, low-ceilinged living-room, furnished solidly, plainly, and yet with touches that suggested a certain culture. There was a clavecin in a corner, and there were pictures on the pinewood wainscot – Alpine landscapes which if crude in the eyes of La Salle, yet by their presence implied an aesthetic striving. The air was pervaded by the odour of burning peat from the enormous glazed stove, and some late roses stood in a piece of painted earthenware on a writing-pulpit.

When they came to supper it was in an adjoining chamber, at a long oak table, and they sat down to meat with three farm-hands and the middle-aged Suzanne, who at the same time saw to their needs. The fare was plain and plentiful: neats' tongues, goats'-milk cheese, rye bread, cider of that autumn's crushing, still very sweet, and a sharp white wine of Neuchâtel, provided in honour of the travellers, over which La Salle heroically avoided grimaces.

Had they been expected, said Madame Perrin, the table would have been more bounteously spread to welcome them. But it was like Charles, she added on a note of mild complaint, to appear as suddenly as he had disappeared. He had gone, leaving them all in a state of distraction on his behalf, not knowing, indeed, in all those months whether he was alive or dead. It was not kind.

That was as near to chiding him as she went, and even this she tempered by her gentle smile. Possibly she might have added more had not her husband mildly checked her.

"He is here, safe and sound. Let us be thankful."

La Salle thought that an excessive leniency was being shown that vagrant nephew, but he was disposed to attribute this to his own presence which, as he was not slow to perceive, and as he perfectly understood, was setting a restraint upon them all. The Perrins watched him furtively, and jerked nervously to answer him when he addressed them, whilst the farm-hands studied him frankly with ox-eyed wonder. To all of them this unexplained man picked up by Charles on his travels belonged to another world and was an object of suspicion. He strove by amiability to combat it. But his lightness of comment seemed to scare them, his courtesies to abash them.

The tension eased a little when the farm-hands, shepherded by Suzanne, had departed in a clatter of wooden soles upon a wooden floor. Old Joseph filled himself a pipe, slewed his chair round at the table's head, and with a stein of cider at his elbow began gently to question his nephew: where had he been, what had he seen, what accomplished?

Charles' answers were vague and timid. In the course of these last two weeks there had been a gradual but increasingly rapid sloughing of the boorish awkwardness of manner that mainly troubled La Salle. Gradually his air, perhaps in quick imitation of his guide's, had been acquiring something of quiet self-possession.

Brought back now to his native environment, this thin veneer peeled off. He was once more the rather awkward child of the soil, echoing in his speech the broad peasant accent of his uncle. He related the vicissitudes that had delayed him abroad, the arrest as a deserter, the prison hospital, the loss he had suffered and the weary hunt of the man who was in a sense responsible for it, and the discovery of him at long last, just too late. Mother and daughter listened to his tale with sympathy which, whilst eager, did not match the concern of Joseph Perrin, whose attachment to his nephew seemed to approach devotion.

When he learnt of the loss suffered at the hands of Naundorff, his distress was so deep as to make it clear that he shared with his nephew the secret so jealously guarded by the latter of the nature of those effects.

Deslys brought his tale to a close by a handsome acknowledgment of his debt to Monsieur de La Salle, but for whose generous assistance when his resources were exhausted he would not now be sitting where he was.

In Joseph Perrin this produced an increase of friendliness towards La Salle. Not so in his wife and daughter. They mistrusted what they could not understand. And they certainly could not understand why this calm, self-possessed stranger with the airs of a nobleman should have befriended Charles as he had. His presence restrained them from seeking the explanation; but it did not restrain Madame Perrin from expressing the hope that there was an end, at last, to Charles' restlessness, and that he would now settle down peacefully at Passavant. Justine's eyes were plaintively eloquent with the same hope.

Charles exhibited embarrassment. He had thought, he ventured timidly, of making a journey into France.

There was consternation.

"Charlot!" It was a cry almost of pain from Justine. Her round, moist eyes were all distress.

Perrin's broad weathered countenance had settled into a deeper grimness, but his kindly eyes expressed only concern as they dwelt on Charles.

"Into France!" he echoed. "Can you think it prudent? After what has happened, too?" He shook his head. "Not for me to force your inclinations. Yet you might be wise to listen to your aunt. Peace and happiness are the greatest treasures. You could find them here if…" He broke off. "But I've said all this to you before."

Charles shuffled his feet. "Have patience with me. It is that… in France… I… I have hopes of doing something better than clockmaking."

Still wistfully considering him, Perrin puffed at his pipe as if answered. His wife, however, would not leave the matter there.

"You may do that here, Charles, and you know it. Who talks of clockmaking? You didn't spend your boyhood here for nothing. You know as much of farming as of clockmaking, and we've no son to follow us. There's happiness for you here. Peace, security and abundance. Where else in the world shall you find them?"

"Tush, tush!" Perrin waved the hand that held the pipe. "Don't plague him. He knows what there is for him here if he chooses. But we must not force it on him."

"It's for his own good, Joseph. He's been out in the world, as they say. He has seen the ugly, sinful place it is, and he's lucky to come home unharmed. He's crazy if he thinks that he can find anywhere else the peace of Passavant."

"It's for him to judge," said Perrin. "We can't insist."

Sadly she reproached her husband. "You've always been like that with him. And what's come of it? If he were of my blood I should know how to persuade him."

"No good could come of it unless it were his own wish."

"Well, well. He's your nephew. You know best."

Justine said nothing with her lips, but no eyes could more piteously have besought Charles to heed her mother.

He was sweeping a nervous hand across his brow in his gesture of helplessness. "We...we will talk of it again," he faltered. "I shall, anyway, be here some days, with your permission."

"You don't need our permission, Charles," said his aunt. "It has been your home longer than it's been mine, and it will always be that."

That night, as he sank into the feather bed in one of the neat small rooms of the châlet, La Salle made a vow that the days Charles announced he would spend at Passavant should be as few as he could make them. Charles, he knew, was at that moment closeted in talk with his uncle. Perrin had begged his nephew to remain awhile when the others were retiring for the night, and La Salle had a shrewd suspicion that the elderly peasant's aim was to pursue the arguments against the intended journey. And if the father failed, he feared there would still be the daughter, with arguments of another and more formidable kind. He wondered, indeed, whether Justine might not have been the reason for Deslys' insistence upon this visit to Passavant. In La Salle's eyes all women were dangers to a man's ambitions, distractions from the main aims of a man's life. He wished now that they had not come.

"If Justine," he reflected, "had been more than ten years of age when Charles took to clockmaking, he would probably have been content to go on farming. For at twenty she is dangerously lovely, and much too ready to be loved by Master Charles, which might be very bad for him. If he should count a throne well lost for possession of her, it would not comfort me at all to reflect that he would certainly regret it later. The devil take you, my dear Justine."

Thus with the smell of peat and kine in his nostrils, and the disquieting thought of Justine in his mind, he fell asleep.

Because the restraint which his presence manifestly imposed upon that household produced eventually a restraint in himself, he went off betimes on the following morning with his sketch-book and paint-box, and he did not come back until sunset. They greeted him with relief. They had been anxious on his behalf, fearing that he might have lost his way in the mountains, or have fallen into a ravine. It amused him to think that had this really happened their relief might have been even greater than it was.

There were signs that a storm had passed over the household. Justine's eyes were suspiciously red. Charles was pale and thoughtful, a frown of trouble between his brows. Joseph Perrin was gruff, and his wife, scanning their faces with troubled eyes, was absent-minded and full of sighs.

To distract them, La Salle displayed his sketches, and actually succeeded in arousing their interest in three of the little landscapes he had brought back. Madame Perrin being particularly enamoured of a little scene of a waterfall over a face of rock, La Salle next day, for lack of canvas, procured himself a thin smooth board of oak, and at evening presented her with a picture which he had spent the day in working up from the sketch. It put to shame the crude landscapes that adorned her living-room, and it thawed some of her coldness towards this amiable stranger. Even Justine, in whom he had sensed a hostility far deeper than that of her parents, had a word of flattering wonder for his talent.

When they retired on that second night, his uneasiness urged him to follow Deslys to his room.

He assumed an airy manner. "It is very pleasant here at Passavant and one might enjoyably linger for a lifetime if nothing else awaited a man. We should be pushing on, Charles. Shall we start tomorrow?"

Deslys, sitting on the narrow bed in the act of pulling off his boots, looked up uneasily. "Why tomorrow?"

"Why ever? Unless the Tuileries or Versailles is to be preferred to a mountain châlet with its cows and goats."

"You think that is all the choice?"

"Choice? I thought the choice was made. A sort of bargain."

Deslys leaned forward, elbows on knees, eyes on the ground. "Yes," he admitted dismally, and added: "It would have been better if we had not come here."

La Salle did not mention that the thought had already occurred to him. He answered lightly. "Man would be a happy creature if all his errors were as easy to repair."

To his keen sight it was clear that there was something on Deslys' mind. At last it came.

"My uncle has made me a proposal. You may have caught a hint of it last night; he was more precise when we were alone. And he has renewed it today."

"I understand. But a throne is hardly to be bartered for a cowshed."

"We are not yet on the throne."

"And we are certainly in the cowshed. Shall we say that a cowshed in esse is not worth a throne in posse?" He set a hand on Deslys' shoulder. "Charles, we had better be making our little packages."

"It's not the cowshed, as you call it, that I am weighing against... the other thing."

"Oho! So there is still a choice, after all?"

"No." Charles stood up suddenly, his manner tense. "Of course there isn't. There is just a cowardly weakness. Florence, there can be no retreating."

"Excellent, sire." La Salle made a leg. "The royal spirit."

"Please don't laugh." Deslys was almost fierce.

"I don't laugh. I rehearse. I anticipate, so as to remind you. We set out tomorrow, then."

"Yes. No. Impossible tomorrow. It would be too abrupt. It would give pain."

"If it gives pain tomorrow, it will give pain any day. Possibly the greater the postponement, the greater the pain. So tomorrow is as good as Sunday."

"Or as bad."

"Pessimism or optimism. Which you will, so that we go forward. Shall we say Sunday, then?"

"I think it will be better." He grew resolute. "Yes. We will keep to that, Florence."

But at breakfast next morning, and once more in the presence of the Perrin family, much of this resoluteness seemed to melt away. After the meal, Justine carried him off and from the end of the orchard, whither he went so as to make a sketch of the châlet, La Salle uneasily watched them climbing the slope beyond it to the west until they were hidden by a belt of pines.

Deslys had seemed to hover perilously between reluctance and desire to go upon that intimate excursion, and La Salle was irritably speculating whether Justine's woman's arts would yet prevail in destroying those high hopes of his own to which Deslys was so necessary.

At the mid-day meal, in time for which he was glad to see them return, he drew a good omen from the frown on Justine's white brow. Afterwards, as he was sauntering alone down the track that led to the forest, he heard a quick step behind him. Over his shoulder he saw that it was Justine who followed him. He halted, and turned as if to meet an adversary.

As she came up with him, a little out of breath, his artist's eye found leisure to admire her. She moved with vigorous grace, her slim shapeliness asserting itself even in the native garments that she wore: a red petticoat, short enough to display ankles clothed in white, and a black velvet corsage, above which the swell of her young breasts was veiled in whitest muslin.

She attacked him almost without crying "On guard!" Her only warning was, "I want to speak to you, monsieur." And at once she proceeded. "It is you, monsieur, who are persuading Charlot to go to France." Eyes and voice were alike challenging and fierce. Her lip quivered as she spoke.

"And you are angry with me," said he gently. "That is unjust, because when I so persuaded him I could not know that it would annoy you."

"Ah! And now? Now that you know?"

"I am desolated, mademoiselle, of course."

"That has no meaning. I am asking what you will do."

"What can I do?"

They confronted each other squarely, she seeking to read that baffling countenance, of a calm that had never looked so sinister to any as it looked to her that morning.

"Undo what you have done," she said.

"Undo what is done? Alas! It is to ask the impossible. All the tragedies of life arise because of that. 'Vestigia nulla retrorsum.' So said an ancient who knew his world." And he translated the quotation for her.

It served only to arouse her impatience. "Arrest it, then."

"Can I arrest the arrow that is sped?"

A pallor crept about her lips. Her eyes kindled. "You amuse yourself with words, I think; and I desire you to be earnest, if you please, monsieur. I... We do not wish Charles to go away again."

"Ah!" No tone could have been more gently reasonable. "Not even if it were for his good? For his great good?"

"His good is here at Passavant."

"I might believe it, having seen you."

"I do not ask for compliments."

"I do not pay them. I said that I might believe it; not that I do. But the question is: does he? It hangs on that."

"You mean, in short, that you will not help me. You desire his company."

"Shall you blame me for being of the same mind as yourself?"

"Not that. I desire only his good."

"And I, then, mademoiselle? Can you conceive that I should wish him ill?"

"How do I know what you wish him? How do I know where you are taking him?"

"Shall I tell you?"

"If you dare."

"To win a crown."

That figure of speech, as he knew she must suppose it, was too much for her patience. "A crown of thorns it will most likely prove."

"What crown is without thorns? Yet men will covet them."

Tears of anger rose to her eyes. "You put me off with words – empty, play-acting words that are nothing to the point. I am in deadly earnest, and you mock. You are not kind. You are hard, selfish, cruel. It is written in your white face."

He smiled, and it brought a sweetening wistfulness into his countenance that took her by surprise. "I am forty-two years of age, and more than half of that has been spent in strife, in what those who are given to self-pity might even call suffering. It is a disillusioning process. That is what you misread in my face."

His forbearance quickened in her an immediate contrition. "Forgive me." She touched his arm. Her gentian eyes, grown soft, looked up imploringly. "I am so troubled for Charlot. So distracted. I have a foreboding that if he goes with you I shall never see him again."

La Salle thought that it was very likely. But his words expressed the opposite. "Oh, that! A groundless alarm."

"Not groundless. No. Twice before he has gone away like this, and it has been an agony to me. The first time I was only fifteen, but already he was everything to me, and for a fortnight I never ceased to weep. I thought my life was ended. He was away for nearly a year.

He came home broken in body and in spirit. Thanks be to God we were able to bring him back to health and strength. Then he returned to Le Locle, and a second time, six months ago, he disappeared again, and again I suffered the same martyrdom. But for you, from what he tells us, he might not have come back for a long time; might never have come back."

"That at least should answer your mistrust of me. Hitherto he has gone alone and with poor resources. This time you will know that he has a friend beside him."

"A friend? Are you that?"

"You have his word for it. Not mine."

"But to what end should he go? How is he necessary to you?"

"He is not. Disabuse your mind of that. I am necessary to him."

"For what purpose? If you would tell me, I could judge. Where are you taking him, and to do what?"

"To make his fortune."

The irritation began to creep back into her intercession.

"What is his fortune to you? His fortune is here. My father has shown him that – for my sake. My father knows what Charles means to me, and I have no brother. This homestead, these lands will one day be ours, Charles' and mine."

"Fortune enough for any man," La Salle agreed. "But there are men who do not recognize Fortune when they meet her face to face."

"Will you tell him that?" She was suddenly eager. "Will you tell him that he should be content with Passavant?"

He winced. He had given her an opening, and she was inside his guard, plague take her. He did the best he could. "Oh, but the responsibility, mademoiselle."

"What is that to you?"

"It should be something to you. Would you take the risk of keeping a man here with the wings of his ambition clipped? A caged bird, pining out his life for the wide spaces over which he had dreamed of taking flight? Should you be happy with such a man?"

"My happiness is of little account. It is his that concerns me."

"Would he be happy?"

"I would strive to make him so."

"He would be enviable. Unfortunately he may not realize it."

"He would come to realize it in time. I would make sure of that. I would surround him with such devotion…" She broke off. Her lip was quivering again. She was all womanly weakness. "Will you help me, Monsieur de La Salle?"

He sighed. He was embarrassed, even distressed. Then he remembered that she had called him hard, and smiled inwardly to reflect how very nearly he was being rendered soft by a girl's display of transient emotion.

"Mademoiselle, I dare not."

"You mean that you will not."

He bowed a little, with a slight gesture of helplessness. She looked at him in silence, and all appeal passed from her glance. Her face was a white flame of fierceness.

"Then I must prevail alone, and in spite of you. More than ever must I prevail. For more than ever do you persuade me that you are evil, and that evil will befall Charles if he goes with you. I warn you that there is nothing that I will not do to save him from you. Nothing."

He was almost plaintive. "Mademoiselle, why speak of it as if it were a duel between us?"

"Because that is what it is. A l'outrance!" She drew herself up. "And I warn you that there is no weapon that I shall not use." She stepped close up to him. "You waste your time, Monsieur de La Salle. Charles is not for you. At whatever cost to myself, I shall save him from you."

And on that she turned and left him.

Chapter 7

Pledges

He followed slowly up the slope. He saw her ahead of him, reach the orchard, and, meeting Charles there, pause to speak to him vehemently, her hands upon his shoulders, before pursuing her way to the house.

A few moments later he sauntered through the gateway. His tone was casual. "Have you bespoken the cart to take us down to Le Locle tomorrow?"

Charles displayed limp distress. "Not yet. No. Don't look at me like that. You have no reason for it. We must go. That is inevitable. But not tomorrow."

La Salle turned himself into an image of aggressive patience. "Tomorrow was the day we settled."

"I am only asking for another day. It will make a difference."

"It may make too great a difference. I perceive your difficulties, Charles. But difficulties, believe me, are the more easily removed the more quickly they are grappled. They are of weedy growth if left. If you are really wise, you will ask for the cart for tomorrow."

"Tomorrow is impossible. I have just promised Justine that I will not go tomorrow."

"All the more reason to ask for the cart," said La Salle dryly.

But this annoyed Charles. "Didn't you understand that I have pledged my word?"

"Some pledges are better broken. I've a notion this is one of them."

Charles' frostiness increased. "You are being detestable. I do not break my promises."

"Unless it suits you. For I seem to remember that you made me a promise. And I'll beg you to observe that this household regards me with distrust and dislike. In its eyes, I am a sort of emissary of the arch-tempter, directing your chaste feet along the path of sin. You conceive my comfort here." His tone hardened. "If there are still any doubts in your mind, tell me frankly, and I'll go my ways."

Charles was sullen. "I have just said that we will leave on Monday."

La Salle resigned himself with an uneasiness that increased to alarm on Sunday morning. Justine, who had not addressed him since yesterday's altercation, once more went off alone with Charles, to climb to La Sourdine. Her reckless, defiant air as they departed brought to La Salle's mind the terms of her threat: "There is no weapon I will not use."

At one moment he thought of getting his paint-box and going after them. But already they had too considerable a start, and he might vainly beat the pinewoods all day for their tracks.

They had not returned by dinner-time, nor was there any sign of them upon the mountain-side. Suzanne gave way to alarm, and infected her mistress with it. Madame Perrin was expressing it when her husband became angry at his daughter's continued absence, and denounced it for an impropriety in the circumstances. Then the mother put aside her own anxieties to defend the absent.

The afternoon wore on. Anxiety increased and wrath gave place to it. Towards sunset Perrin was summoning his hands with intent to beat the mountain-side, when the absent pair were descried, just below the pine-belt, descending.

They reached the homestead in the twilight, to be welcomed by the plaintive reproaches of a distracted mother and the thunders of an irate father who dragged himself painfully forth on his two sticks to meet the truants.

Charles was hang-dog and pallid, the girl in a state of febrile excitement. With flushed cheeks and glittering eyes she met parental complaints in a spirit almost of levity. Where, she wondered, was the need for all this garboil? Charles and she, on that heavenly autumn day, had gone perhaps farther than they should have gone. They had climbed all the way to the Crête du Vallon, and, tired, they had rested there longer than they intended. The time had gone so quickly. Oh, but it had not been wasted. This with a triumphant flash of the gentian eyes at La Salle, who remained acutely observant behind a dreamy expression.

At supper she was gay, with that same queer, febrile, excessive gaiety, the last vestige of yesterday's gloom discarded. She talked of what they would do tomorrow and on successive days, as if there were no longer any question of Charles' departure.

The father, grimly thoughtful, seemed content. The mother, however, watched her child with grave eyes, her lips pursed, her womanly intuitions reaching the same conclusion as that to which La Salle's cynical knowledge of his fellow-creatures brought him. Charles, still hang-dog, spoke only when addressed, and could meet the eyes of none.

At bedtime he avoided La Salle, who again would have gone with him to his room for a last word. He was too tired to talk, he said, and La Salle did not employ an insistence which he reasoned could do no good at the moment. Besides, he required no explanations. He knew already all that Deslys could tell him, assuming that Deslys were disposed to be inconceivably communicative.

In the morning, however, he was fully dressed at Deslys' bedside before the clockmaker had risen, and he took a cold, hard tone with him.

"At what hour do we set out?"

Deslys stared up from his pillow. A sudden dread came into his prominent eyes. He sat up. "Oh, my God!" he said, and took his head in his hands.

La Salle, tall and straight beside the bed, looked down on him with baleful eyes, his lips compressed, and waited.

After a moment Deslys spoke again. "It is useless," he groaned. "It will be cowsheds, as you say, for me, Florence. You must go without me. I stay at Passavant."

"The man who does not break his promises," said La Salle, and laughed unpleasantly. "How readily big sentences come from empty souls!" He turned to the door. "God help you, Charles! By your vacillating spirit you might, indeed, be the son of Louis XVI."

"You have not the right to say that to me. You do not understand."

"Don't I?" He stood at the door, straight and tense, an incarnation of scorn. "You fool!"

He thought that all was lost, and he was uttering the last word. But the unexpected answer he received opened yet a way.

"Yes, I think that describes me," said Deslys in misery. "A fool certainly; and a scoundrel too. For, in spite of everything, I can't remain here. I can't. I can't." Petulantly he beat his brow with his clenched hand as he spoke. "There is my duty…my word to you. And… Oh, my God! Whatever I do I must be forsworn."

"Why?"

"Because whilst I've pledged myself to go, I've also pledged myself to stay."

Slowly La Salle came back to stand over him again. "To stay? That is not the pledge at all. Not the material pledge. The pledge that signifies is the pledge to marry Mademoiselle Justine."

Deslys looked up wildly. "You know that? How could you know that? How…"

"Pish! I have eyes in my head. Perhaps you hadn't noticed it. Mademoiselle Justine has been at no pains to conceal what's happened."

"What do you mean?" the other flared.

"That you are succumbing to a remorse for which there are no real grounds. Conceiving yourself a bold, enterprising seducer, you faint with horror of the wrong into which you conceive that your senses have betrayed you."

Deslys stared at him, white and shaking in angry amazement. La Salle smiled upon him compassionately.

"In such a mood of misplaced penitence men have often done that which has ruined their lives."

Deslys recovered himself in part. "Since you have guessed or discovered so much, we may speak clearly. There is an amend to be made – fool that I am."

"A fool without doubt, if you lack the wit to perceive that it was yourself who were shamelessly seduced."

"You shall not say that. My God, you shall not!"

"I'll say it again. Shamelessly, calculatedly, deliberately seduced. For what other purpose did she take you off yesterday to La Sourdine, or the Crête du Vallon, or wherever else you went? You know what passed. Look back on it carefully. Examine the steps that led to it, and decide if they contradict me."

"It is infamous, I tell you! You shall not dare to say it."

"I should not if I were less sure. Listen patiently, Charles. It may help you in your present quandary. The evening before last, down there on the edge of the forest – you may have seen her follow me – she swore that you should not go away with me; that she would fight me for you; and that – these are her very words – there was no weapon she would not use."

"It's a lie! A heartless, shameful lie!" Deslys was hoarse.

"I swear it's true. Unnecessary oath, after all. What did she say to you in passing in the orchard? Does that confirm me?"

Deslys cast his mind back, then, with a groan, he took his distracted head in his hands again. Calmly La Salle continued, playing upon that weak, irresolute nature. "Yesterday when she conducted you to the solitude of those romantic glades, I had a notion what weapon it was her set intention to employ. I knew in what trammels she would trust to your own conscience afterwards to bind you. And in those trammels, my poor Charles, you are now caught, conceiving that you have to choose between being a heartless scoundrel and remaining here to waste your life."

"That is the choice," Deslys agreed. "What do I say? Choice? There is no choice. There is a pledge, a pledge of more than words; a pledge I cannot break. You must see that, since you see so much." He rose, flung himself out of the bed, and perched upon the edge of it. "If I have ruined myself, I have ruined myself. I must take the consequences."

"By which you really mean that you must take the coward's easier way."

He turned sullen now under that sneer. "Call it that if you will. You had best leave me here, and think no more of what we were to do."

But even as he spoke, dejection brought him to the verge of tears. His soul was in rebellion now, against what he accounted a trick of Fate's. In his next words there was a sudden revelation of how fully his heart had become set upon the French adventure. Ever since consenting to undertake it, La Salle had observed with satisfaction his steadily increasing enthusiasm; but not until now did he realize how deeply the notion had become rooted in the clockmaker's otherwise so irresolute soul.

As he spoke, Charles' clenched fists were beating his knees in puerile rage.

"It is a terrible, terrible price to pay for my folly. Terrible. But I must pay it. I have not the courage to default."

"Nor should I urge it." La Salle was smooth again. "What I still urge is that the material pledge is not to cast away fortune and remain here. The material pledge is to marry Justine. That need not be broken. You merely postpone fulfilment until you can return."

Deslys looked up quickly, hope gleaming in his eyes a moment, to be quenched again in bewilderment. "Return? But if we succeed? Could the King of – "

"Oh, sire, the times have changed since your august father's day. There has been a revolution in France. Notions have changed. Half the duchesses in Napoleon's Tuileries came from the fishmarket. His Créole Empress was of no more account by birth than your Justine."

Deslys stiffened. "I am not Bonaparte," he declared amazingly.

La Salle raised his brows. "Believe me, I was in no danger of supposing it. You are much more like a Bourbon. But what a nation has learnt to approve in a Bonaparte it may well approve in a Bourbon too. Such a marriage might actually help him to the good graces of the republicans who are still numerous in France."

When Deslys had thought it out, he extended trembling hands. His voice shook with the excitement stirring in him.

"Florence! If that were possible…"

"The insoluble would be solved. Why, so it is. Display firmness now and all will be well. If you can't, then you are not the man for the great part that awaits you."

But Deslys was lapsing back into troubled thought. La Salle set a firm hand upon his shoulder. "We depart, then, today. It is understood?"

"I… I suppose so," was the fearful, scarcely convincing answer.

"Good." La Salle momentarily tightened the hand upon the other's shoulder, then left him to dress, and went below, whence a fragrance of coffee rose to meet him.

The family was already in the dining-room. Justine, on a window-seat, was dreamily gazing out over the rolling pasture-land to the east. The morning sun set a glinting aureole about her golden head. She turned quickly as the door opened to admit La Salle. Ignoring the darkening of her glance, he included her in his courtly bow, and then her mother bade her summon the farm-hands to table.

"But Charles?" she inquired.

"Yes. What keeps him?" grumbled Perrin.

La Salle was bland. "I think he overslept. I have just seen him. A disturbed night, I fancy." And he saw Justine lose colour under the steady glance of his ironic eyes.

"Disturbed?" said Perrin. "At his age?"

"The romantic age," said La Salle. "And romance is not tranquillizing."

Whilst father and mother thought him merely affectedly sententious, his languid words struck shame and terror into Justine. There was worse in store for her.

"It is with infinite regret, Monsieur Perrin, that I ask you if we may have a cart this morning, to take us into Le Locle."

"What to do there?"

"Alas! To resume our journey after this delightful pause."

There was a spell of astounded silence, broken at last by Justine's shrill assertion. "You are mistaken. Charles is not going."

La Salle was smoothly urbane. "He must have changed his mind since last he told you so. I have just left him."

"You mean that he is going after all? Definitely going?" She was white to the lips.

"That is how I understood him a few moments ago."

Perrin sat dumb, like a man stricken. Not so his daughter. She was on her feet, leaning across the table towards La Salle, her eyes blazing in her white face.

"This is your evil doing!"

"Justine!" Her mother, rising and taking her by the shoulders, sought to restrain her.

"It is! It is!" she insisted fiercely. "It is the work of this evil man. He has Charles in his evil power. I don't know in what wicked schemes he has entangled him. But it is he who is trying to take Charles away to his ruin."

"Mademoiselle" – La Salle's air was sorrowful – "you use the cruel language of disappointed anger. I must not allow it to offend me."

And then Deslys came in to find the ice broken for him and a fine storm gathering, which in a moment was crackling about his head.

The spirit in which he met it surprised La Salle as much as it enheartened him. Like many another normally timid man, the clockmaker, it seemed, could display a desperate courage once he was committed to battle.

He realized, he said, the disappointment he must be causing them. They might suppose that they had reason to account him ungrateful. This, he protested vehemently, he was not. They must know that he had a duty: that he was bound by a pledge he could not break. All this he delivered with something of that sullen brutality in which the weak find refuge when they are confronted with the need to be strong.

"And I?" cried Justine, made reckless, not only by pain, but by her love and fear for Charles and her overmastering hatred of La Salle. "Have you no duty to me? Do pledges to me count for nothing? Will you forsake me now?"

"God of God!" cried Perrin in sudden understanding, opening wide his eyes in which wrath and horror had extinguished the natural tenderness.

Deslys shuffled his feet and hung his head, abject and awkward. "The pledges made to you, dear Justine," he muttered, "are the most sacred I ever made. Be certain that I shall return to fulfil them."

"That you never shall."

"How?" He looked at her, startled, and she played her last, desperate card to save him.

"If you go now, there will be no returning, Charles. If you leave me now, *now*, I shall never want to see you again, for I could never trust you again, never believe in you again, never..." Her sobs suddenly choked her, and her mother's arms compassionately enfolded her.

Deslys' self-command dropped from him like a cloak. Impulsively he took a step forward, hands outstretched. Then he let them fall again, and stood mute and stricken.

In the background, La Salle, self-contained, impassive, was the merest spectator of this conflict, awaiting an issue on which all his hopes were staked, yet which he conceived that no action of his could now influence. It was Joseph Perrin who unexpectedly precipitated decision. His chair scraped noisily upon the wooden floor. He lumbered to his feet, supporting himself upon the table, his weather-beaten countenance purple.

"Grosjean shall fetch the cart at once," he rasped, and raised his voice to call: "Grosjean!"

Justine stirred fearfully in her mother's arms. "Wait, Father! Charles, you can't – "

"Enough!" Perrin banged the table. "He must go since it is his wish."

"Joseph! Please!" the mother cried, in the anguish of her full understanding.

"He goes," Joseph insisted, and to the elderly Grosjean, who entered, he issued his orders for the cart.

"Oh, but, Father, he must not… I can't. You are sending him to his ruin. I know it…"

"You gave him to choose, and he has chosen. Whether he goes to his ruin or not… Let him follow his destiny." His kindling eyes rested on Deslys. "A fine requital, sir, for all that you have had from me, to bring shame upon my poor house. You leave me cursing the day I gave you shelter here. Take you the thought of that to France with you to help you on your way. Go, sir! Grosjean will be waiting for you. Go!" And shaking as if palsied, he sank down again into his chair.

Breaking from her weeping mother, Justine went to him and flung her arms about his neck. "Please, Father… Dear Father, don't let him go like this."

He put an arm about her, and his eyes were moist. Then he stiffened. Grim-faced he looked at Charles, standing abashed and dejected, and with his free hand Perrin waved him peremptorily away.

A moment still the young man hesitated, seeking words that would not come. Then he slunk lugubriously out, softly followed by La Salle.

As they departed thus La Salle leavened with scorn his satisfaction of the manner in which Deslys had followed his instructions. The fellow's egoism, he reflected, was in the Bourbon tradition. As a Bourbon he might yet be a great success.

PART THREE

Chapter 1

The Duke of Otranto

Of all the details to which La Salle had given careful thought, none had engaged him more deeply than that which concerned a sponsor of worldly consequence and influence for his spurious Louis XVII.

Almost from the outset of his search, his mind had turned longingly in the direction of Joseph Fouché, the sometime Oratorian professor of mathematics, the revolutionist, regicide, national representative, guillotiner and mitrailleur of royalists, now Duke of Otranto, landed proprietor on a vast scale, ten times a millionaire, and acknowledged one of the greatest men of State of any time, just as he was probably the greatest time-server and opportunist that ever lived. A man of vast intellect and incredible courage, he was without illusions, without ideals and without convictions. His own interest was the only compass by which he laid a course, and he had an infallible sense of which way the wind was about to blow, so that he was always able to trim his sails betimes.

In office and in stable national conditions, Fouché would have been the last man whose support La Salle would have desired. But partly from what de Batz had told him, partly from what he had gleaned elsewhere, he knew that Fouché, without whose favour the Bourbons could never have returned, had been cheated of his expectations by Louis XVIII.

Blacas, Jaucourt and the other minions to whom the King entrusted the reins feared their own eclipse if Fouché were in power. Ruled by them the foolish monarch had excluded from office the one man who could have kept him on the throne, for Fouché was of a might and influence to render himself at any time the dominant force in the nation. Always in the rôle of a servant, he had always been the master, even Bonaparte's; and he could be so again when the time came. He had so contrived when in office, and he had so abstained from abusing the incalculable power he had built up, that he had assured himself a vast following in every party. He had conciliated and earned the confidence of the royalists by the liberal concessions to them under Bonaparte, for which he took the credit; he had retained the confidence of the republicans, of whom there still were many in France, because whilst serving Bonaparte he yet seemed to stand for republican principles; the Bonapartists, still so numerous, and daily increasing under the fatuities of the Bourbon misrule, gave him their loyalty because in their eyes he remained Bonaparte's supreme man of confidence, and because in his present exclusion he was regarded as a victim of his devotion to the fallen Emperor.

It was not to be imagined that this man of fifty-five, whose life had been one unremitting activity, to whom activity was life itself, could be sincere in the part of Cincinnatus he was playing in retirement on his estates at Ferrières. It was not to be imagined that he had destroyed the incredible network of espionage which he had so laboriously constructed and with which under the Empire he had covered every stratum of society. An organization which had taken so much time and labour to assemble was not to be tossed aside by its creator whilst there was still a chance that he might one day be again in need of it, and whilst it might serve to warn him when that chance occurred.

So as to bring such a man into the arena, thought La Salle, all that was necessary was to place within his reach a likely substitute for the King who had disregarded him, and this before he discovered one for himself, so as to satisfy the demand which the nation was already beginning to raise.

The more La Salle considered him, the more he persuaded himself that Fouché was the man he needed. If Charles Deslys could be imposed, as the Orphan of the Temple, upon the acute intelligence of the Duke of Otranto, they could go forward in the assurance that the imposture was impenetrable, as well as in the assurance that success would be practically certain.

To seek Fouché on such a business required courage. It amounted to staking their fortunes upon a single fall of the dice. But whatever attributes La Salle may have lacked, audacity was certainly not amongst them. And so it was to Ferrières on the River Cléry, within fifty miles of Paris, that in the early days of October he brought a dejected suspiring Charles Deslys.

Periods of abject, conscience-stricken gloom, haunted by memories of Justine, alternated in that unstable clockmaker with periods of feverish enthusiasm for the task ahead. So excessive seemed this eagerness to La Salle that he suspected it of being spuriously worked up, so as to provide an escape from the recriminations of conscience. Meanwhile, La Salle was diligently supplying him with information concerning the early days of the prince he was to impersonate, and sedulously instructing him in deportment. Under this tutelage there was gradually wrought in him such a change as to make it seem that he was actually conceiving himself at times to be, indeed, the Orphan of the Temple.

Invention had been freely employed to supplement the facts which ended abruptly at the drowning in Lake Léman. In the construction of a subsequent history of Louis XVII, Deslys collaborated actively with La Salle and displayed an imagination not to have been suspected in him.

Satisfied that the tale he had to tell was compact and practically impervious to disproof, La Salle resolved to wait alone upon Fouché in the first instance. Thus he could test the ground, and if he found it favourable prepare the mind of the Duke for what was to follow. Therefore, having reached the little village of Ferrières, he left Deslys at the inn at which they had descended, and went forward early on the following morning to the magnificent château of the man whom he had last seen in a sordid lodging in the Rue St Honoré, when he had boasted that all his needs were met by bread and iron and forty crowns a year. This château, grey and majestic, was set in the heart of a vast domain of parklands, pasturage, and game preserves, which represented not a tithe of the possessions of this fabulously wealthy Duke.

The chaise pulled up at the foot of the double flight of steps, and in a lofty hall, paved in black and white marble, hung with trophies of arms and priceless pictures, some of which had formed part of Bonaparte's plunder of Italy, La Salle delivered to a chamberlain in a plain black livery the note he had prepared.

Monseigneur, he had written, *an old acquaintance who dares not flatter himself to have retained a place in your grace's memory, nevertheless has travelled far for the honour of an interview on a matter of the gravest national importance.* And he had subscribed it, *with the utmost submission and respect, Monseigneur's most humble and obedient servant, Florence de La Salle.*

His hopes that it might suffice to gain him admission were not misplaced. He was not even kept waiting. Fouché, Spartan of habits even amid his ducal splendours, was an early riser and an indefatigable worker. And these were days in which there was a deal of work to claim him: the work of upsetting a throne, an art in which he could already lay claim to some expertness. Thus it happened that La Salle and his impostor arrived more opportunely than they could suppose. Under that mantle of Cincinnatus, which Fouché had assumed when excluded from a government to whose creation he had certainly contributed, he waited only until that government should be ripe for the fate to which its fatuity must ultimately bring it.

It was ripe now. Over-ripe. Its unparalleled ineptitudes, resulting from a lack of orientation, had produced a mixture of despotism and anarchy under which the nation lay terrified and angry. A resolute thrust would send it toppling over, and Fouché, still master of the main strands of the web he had controlled as Napoleon's Minister of Police, delayed only to supply the thrust until he should have decided by what government to replace it. A choice of four was confronting him on that October morning when he was sought by La Salle: he might re-establish the Republic, crown the son of Orléans-Egalité, bring Napoleon back from Elba, or set up a regency in the name of Napoleon's son, entrusted in principle to the Empress Marie-Louise, but in fact to a council, in which he would take for his associates the Prince Eugène, Talleyrand and Davout.

Napoleon's return he would favour only in certain conditions, and Napoleon was not an easy man upon whom to impose conditions. Against Louis-Philippe he was prejudiced by the contempt the man's father had deservedly earned. Napoleon II was the candidate most easily imposed. If he were to enter Paris just then on a donkey led by a peasant, he might ride straight and triumphantly to the Tuileries. But the projected regency might give too great an ascendancy to Austria. The re-establishment of the Republic he regarded without favour, merely as a last resource.

He certainly can have had no suspicion that La Salle's note concerned the introduction of a fifth and hitherto unsuspected candidate. But his amazingly retentive memory awoke to instant and complete recollection of a young man who twenty years ago had given his mind some exercise.

The note was brought to him in his study, a lofty room of a rich severity of walnut furnishings against a background of tapestries in tones of blue and grey. It came to interrupt the instructions he was giving the sober Monsieur de Chassenon, the governor of his children.

For two years now Fouché had been a widower. The loss of the homely Bonne-Jeanne, whom La Salle had seen in that shabby apartment in the Rue St Honoré, had been the cruellest affliction that had ever visited this man, who, utterly without any moral sense, as the world understands the term, was yet of an incorruptible austerity in days in which the domestic virtues were little practised. As proud a father as he had been a loving, faithful husband, this erstwhile pedagogue supervised with care and energy the education of his three sons, whose ages ranged between thirteen and seventeen, and of his only daughter, an attractive child of eleven.

He frowned a moment in thought over the note. Then the thin-lipped smile so habitual to him lightened his expression. In a breath he dismissed Monsieur de Chassenon and ordered the visitor to be brought in.

He received La Salle standing, and for a long moment each of those men measured the other with curious eyes, as if without recognition, so profound a change had the years wrought in the appearance of each.

Fouché in his fifty-fifth year looked fully twenty years older. A stoop robbed his tall gaunt figure of its height, and increased the impression of extreme senility conveyed by a bloodless face that once La Salle had accounted attractive. What remained of the reddish hair had faded to a fulvid hue, and was no more than a transparent veil thinly plastered over a yellow skull. He seemed a mere feeble husk of a man, burnt out within. Only the eyes, when the low lids were raised, could restore life to that corpse-like countenance and betray the energy still abiding in a mind that was perhaps the acutest of its day.

In La Salle, Fouché beheld a change even greater, but of a very different order. His well-knit, supple figure had gained rather than lost in vigour, and there was an increase of calm authority in that countenance, also singularly pallid, under a mane of hair as thick as ever and lustrously black, save for that odd wedge of white.

Fouché, at last, was the first to speak. "You are really Florence de La Salle?"

"The same who twenty years ago climbed three pairs of stairs in the Rue St Honoré for the honour of painting your portrait, monseigneur."

"I remember. At least you cannot reproach me with having made you climb any stairs to reach me today. Tempora mutantur, et nos... Forgive me if for a moment I doubted whether you were the same man. But sit down. Since you speak in your note of a matter of national importance, you will not today be seeking to paint my portrait."

"No, Monsieur le Duc. I have come, instead, to show you one that I have painted."

It was not at all the beginning that he had rehearsed, but the Duke's irony had created an opening by which he was quick to profit. He removed the wrappers from the small picture that he brought, and placed a canvas that was about a foot square on the Duke's writing-table.

"Who should you say that is, monseigneur?"

Fouché bent to inspect through his gold-mounted quizzing-glass the composite portrait La Salle had been inspired to paint. It cunningly blended the face of Louis XVII, upon which La Salle had laboured so sedulously twenty years ago, with that of Charles Deslys as he was today. Whilst it was a speaking likeness of Deslys, yet it artfully stressed his resemblance to the prisoner of the Temple. The brown of the hair had been lightened by a couple of shades; the arching of the brows had been slightly exaggerated, and by painting the sitter full face it had been possible to dissemble the high bridge of the nose. Inspired by the Euclidean proposition that any two which are equal to a third must be equal to each other, it was in La Salle's mind that anyone attributing to this portrait the identity he desired for it, could not afterwards fail to transfer that identity to Deslys when he was, as he must be, recognized as the subject of it. In other words, he sought to create an advance impression which would neutralize the points of dissimilarity between the faces of Deslys and Louis XVII.

At Fouché's elbow now he waited anxiously to learn whether the experiment was likely to succeed.

Still studying the portrait, Fouché spoke. "I should say that it is a portrait of the little Capet grown to manhood if I did not suppose that such a thing is impossible."

"The portrait, then, does not lead your grace to suspect that such a thing may not be impossible?"

"What am I to understand?" Fouché straightened himself as far as his curved spine permitted. "Are you sponsoring yet another pretended Louis XVII? And is it to me that you come with so puerile an imposture?"

In the sudden flame of the eyes, La Salle had his first glimpse of the forces still alive within that cadaveric exterior. But his own bold glance did not falter under this scorching scrutiny.

"Did any of those impostors look like this, Monsieur le Duc?" And he tapped the picture with his forefinger.

"Tut! What argument is there in a fortuitous likeness?"

"None, if that were all. But there is a good deal more. It must be known to some that the widespread rumour that Louis XVII escaped from the Temple is founded upon truth, and that the child who was buried in the Madeleine…"

"Yes, yes," Fouché interrupted. "All that I know. Chaumette knew it. Robespierre knew it. Barras knows it. Louis XVIII knows it, and one or two more, including probably the Duchess of Angoulême. But what became of him afterwards? What is this fellow's tale, for instance?"

"Perhaps, monseigneur, you had better hear mine first. I was the chief agent of his escape from the Temple. Again, it was I who conducted him out of France."

"You?" Once more the eyes momentarily displayed themselves. "You give me news, Monsieur de La Salle. In what year would that be?"

"He left the Temple in my care on Sunday, the 19th of January of 1794. He left Meudon in my care, travelling to Switzerland, late in June of 1797."

Fouché's face betrayed no emotion of any kind. But his stare was long and searching. At last, still with no word spoken, he turned aside to the bell-pull, and rang. Then once more he waved his visitor to a chair.

"Pray sit down, monsieur. It happens that I have with me at present one of my former agents, who knows more about this than any man in France today." To a lackey who entered he gave an order. "Desire Monsieur Desmarets to come to me at once."

To La Salle that name, long since forgotten, conveyed nothing. But he was without uneasiness, for so far he was upon firm ground. He sat down to wait, and Fouché seated himself also, at his writing-table, whence he directly faced his visitor. Watching La Salle from under those sleepy lids, he spoke slowly, in his thin, dry voice.

"The last time that I had the honour of entertaining you, you sought me on the pretext of painting my portrait. For it was, of course, a pretext. I wonder would you tell me now, when it can no longer matter, what was the real object of that visit?"

"Very willingly. And it is odd that you should ask me that question at such a moment." How odd it was Fouché was to realize when he had heard a tale that was in full accord with the claim that La Salle had just made.

Fouché listened attentively. "I see," he said. "And then, having failed with me, you seduced Chaumette. Yes. It might be. Ah! Here is Desmarets."

The stocky frame of the man of fifty who came in was broader than of old; his shaven face was redder and heavier, and his hair was grizzled. Nevertheless, La Salle recognized him at a glance.

"Ah! My old friend, the catchpoll, of Volant and Geneva."

Desmarets stood arrested, taken aback. "You have the advantage of me, sir." He was curt.

Fouché enlightened him. "It is Monsieur de La Salle. Monsieur Florence de La Salle. Do you remember him? He has changed a good deal. But take a close look at him. He claims that it was he who conducted the little Capet out of France."

"That is certainly not true." Desmarets was very positive.

"But take a good look at him," Fouché insisted. "I have said that he has changed."

"No need to look, monseigneur. The man who conducted the young King out of France was the Baron Ulrich von Ense."

"He has an excellent memory, you see," said Fouché to La Salle.

193

La Salle smiled. "Not so excellent if he has forgotten the third man in the party, the man who by leading him astray, travelling alone in the yellow berline along the road to Châlons, made it possible for the Baron von Ense and the child to cross the frontier."

That disturbed the confidence of Desmarets. His beady piercing eyes considered La Salle anew. But in the end he shook his head. "I have too good a memory for you, monsieur. That man's name was certainly not La Salle. It was…"

"Husson," La Salle flashed in. "Gabrile Husson, described on his passport as a chocolate-merchant's clerk, travelling to Switzerland on business. Stir that excellent memory of yours, Monsieur Desmarets."

Desmarets' countenance betrayed that it was stirred already. "If you can tell me," he said slowly, "how the Baron and his charge contrived to give me the slip at Sallières, you might persuade me."

La Salle told him.

"The stage-coach! Ah, pardieu," said Desmarets, crestfallen. "And I never thought of that." Then he laughed. "Faith, you leave me no choice but to believe that you are the man. You played a shrewd, bold game. A pity that you should have had your pains for nothing, and that Fate should have intervened to drown the little Capet."

"Was the body ever found?"

"Von Ense's was."

"I know. I buried it. I was at the lakeside when it was brought ashore. So were you, Monsieur Desmarets. It was the last time that I saw you. But it is of Louis XVII that I am speaking."

Desmarets shrugged. "There was evidence enough without a body."

Fouché's voice came sharp and thin. "I am much obliged to you, Desmarets. No need to detain you now."

When the policeman had bowed himself out, the Duke smiled his sour, thin-lipped smile. "Monsieur de La Salle, I do not like to make mistakes, and I do not think that I have made many. Yet in the case of yourself, whom I am seeing now for the second time, I have been twice mistaken. It is humiliating. I could not forgive myself if it were to happen a third time. You said to Desmarets that the body of the boy said to have been drowned in Lake Léman had never been found. You will have an explanation of that."

La Salle braced himself. Hitherto he had walked confidently upon the solid ground of fact. In shifting now to the treacherous ground of fiction he must appear to walk as confidently. The tale he now told was the tale that had been carefully prepared in collaboration with Deslys.

It ran that when the boat in which von Ense and his charge were escaping across the lake came to founder within hail of Lausanne, one boat had put off, despite the storm and the descending darkness, to attempt a rescue, and the rescuers had come miraculously upon the boy at the point of exhaustion, clinging to an oar, which had been sufficient to bear up his light weight.

In the easterly gale that was blowing, however, they found it impossible to regain the shore at Lausanne. To persist in attempting it would be to invite the fate of the boat that had foundered. So, allowing themselves to drive before the storm, they came at last ashore under the lee of a promontory near Morges, some ten miles to the west. The rescued child's condition made them seek shelter for him at once, and by great good fortune they took him to the house of the parish priest at Morges. The boy, stripped of his wet clothes and wrapped in a blanket before the stove in the presbytery kitchen, quickly revived.

His first thought was that his danger from the Republican agents in pursuit was as real as that which he had escaped, particularly now that his protector was lost. His fears were fully shared by the priest to whom he gave his confidence. That kindly man swore the rescuers to secrecy – there were two of them – and sent them with a tale of failure back to Lausanne, where it was already being feared that they too were lost. The priest kept him at the presbytery that night, and on the morrow quietly and secretly took him back to Lebas' house in Geneva. Lebas, aware that French agents might stop at nothing to repossess themselves of the person of the young King, at once perceived the advantage of allowing the belief in his death to persist.

His own house being suspected and watched, Lebas smuggled the boy out of Geneva and conveyed him to the homestead of his widowed sister, Madame Perrin, at Deslys in the hills, until arrangements could be made for him. Lebas expected to concert these with La Salle when he arrived. But La Salle, under his mistaken impression, left Geneva without again seeking Lebas. The boy stayed on, endearing himself to the widow Perrin Deslys, as she was known from the name of her little farm, and passing for her nephew. Two years later she died, and the boy, by Lebas' contriving, was taken to the Jura, to the farm of her brother-in-law, Joseph Perrin of Passavant. There he found safety and shelter, passing, of course, as Perrin's nephew until such time as it should be safe and proper for him to come to life again.

At that stage of his narrative La Salle made a halt. Before proceeding further with this relation of marvels, he desired some indication of the effect produced thus far. The corpse-like countenance of Fouché remained, however, inscrutable.

"And then, sir? Continue, please. Unless you pretend that for twenty years the King of France was content to be a cowherd in an Alpine pasturage."

"Oh no." La Salle was relieved. From the invitation to continue he assumed that so far no flaw had been detected in his narrative. And the worst was over. From inventions which no records of fact could confirm, he passed now to events that were true at least in the main and verifiable part.

"The young King realized, of course, that there was nothing to be done by him or for him in France as long as the Revolution lasted in the form of the Directoire and the Consulship, or afterwards, when it was finally succeeded by the Empire. For some years he remained, then, on that homestead in the mountains, at Passavant. Then a curious trait of heredity manifested itself." This was an embellishment which La Salle was proud of having conceived. "Like the martyred King, his father, he displayed a taste and a talent for mechanics. He prevailed upon Perrin to send him to Le Locle as apprentice to a clockmaker, and he acquired there, I believe, some skill in that trade.

Meanwhile, he waited patiently, watching for a change in France that might supply him with his opportunity to disclose himself. He wrote to his uncle, Monsieur de Provence, who had proclaimed himself King under the style of Louis XVIII. But that letter, if it ever reached its destination, remained unanswered. He wrote to his sister when she was at the Court of Austria with the same lack of result. Possibly it was believed that he was but another of the impostors that were constantly arising.

"But when the fall of Bonaparte sounded for him the hour of decisive action, he set out at once to resume the journey to the Court of Prussia which the Geneva events had interrupted some seventeen years before."

And now La Salle launched himself boldly upon a story, blending a deal of fiction with a little fact, which he and Deslys had jointly and carefully composed. The facts were supplied by the lad's arrest as a deserter in Germany; the illness which led to his being sent to a military hospital; the meeting there with Naundorff and the friendship that sprang up between them culminating in his entrusting Naundorff with certain papers and other effects with which Naundorff had gone off at a time when it was not supposed that Deslys would survive. The fiction lay in the nature of the papers which had vanished with the Prussian. Concerning these Fouché heard now that the Baron von Ense, with a foresight that was highly commendable, but not at all extraordinary considering the importance of his charge, had taken care to provide as far as possible so that in the event of his own death or of his becoming accidentally separated from the young King, the boy should have no difficulty in establishing his identity. He had supplied him with certain papers, including a full account over his own seal and signature of the manner of the escape from France, and amongst other things with a seal that had been the property of Louis XVI and with a sum of money in gold to help him on his way. To these, at the Baron's request, Lebas had added a confirmatory letter, duly witnessed. Under that signature the boy had been made to append his own, which he could repeat so as to supply a final proof to any doubter.

Such in La Salle's present account became the nature of the effects consigned by the King to Naundorff, and so lost to him. He had carried them until then sewn in the collar of his coat. Since it was unthinkable for him to go on without those credentials he had set out upon a frenzied search for Naundorff. La Salle paused there, to add dramatically: "It was in Prussia – at Brandenburg – that I, who had kidnapped him from the Temple in '95 and carried him out of France in '97, met once more this King whom for seventeen years I had been supposing dead. To see him again was instantly to recognize him."

The almost lipless mouth of the Sphinx at the writing-table delivered itself tonelessly of four words which La Salle expected.

"A singular coincidence that."

"No coincidence at all, monseigneur, when all the circumstances are considered. It was this Naundorff who supplied the link." And now, back on the solid ground of actual fact, La Salle related in detail the manner of that meeting. "In this," he ended, "the Brandenburg police will support my story."

"It is ingenious," said Fouché, "and I could wish that it were true, which is not to deny its truth. For I will confess to you that at every point upon which it happens that I am already informed – and they may be more than you are supposing – your account agrees with my information, just as it did with Desmarets'."

If the admission was matter for relief and even surprise to La Salle, he was not on that account thrown off his careful guard.

"I am more fortunate than I could have hoped."

"But why, I ask myself, should you come to me, who am living quietly in retirement, aloof from the public scene?"

"For that very reason, Monsieur le Duc."

"You misunderstand me, I think. I have no concerns in these days beyond the cultivation of my acres and the education of my children."

"With the assistance, of course, of Monsieur Desmarets."

Fouché smiled at the impertinence. "Beware, my friend, of rash conclusions."

"It has been my practice, Monsieur le Duc."

"Yet you seek me, of course, with a hope of some kind. Might not that be rash?"

"On the contrary. I accounted it prudent." He leaned forward, an elbow on his knee. "I seek you, Monsieur le Duc, because this is the hour and you are the man."

"Oh no, no. From what you tell me, it is you who have the man."

"Put it that way if you please. I was thinking of his sponsor."

"And you pay me the compliment of offering me that rôle? Decidedly you have come to flatter me."

"Shall we be frank, Monsieur le Duc?"

"Great God! Dare you suggest that I am not frank?"

"Perhaps, then, it is I who fail. Let me put all my cards on the table. You, monseigneur, who played a leading part in the great Revolution and in all the lesser revolutions that have followed it, are as aware as I am of the emotionalism of the people. If the Orphan of the Temple were to come forward now, in this moment of national disillusion and of disgust with the present rulers, that emotionalism would sweep him irresistibly to the throne."

The thin voice was dispassionately critical. "It is possible. The Orphan of the Temple. That in itself is an appellation to stir the emotions."

"It needs, however, that he be sponsored by a man of State in whose judgment the nation's faith is established. That, Monsieur le Duc, you must already have perceived, is why I come to you." And greatly daring he added: "To offer you the chance to stand by Louis XVII where you would have stood by Louis XVIII had he possessed the necessary discernment."

"I see. I am to thank you, then, for a favour where I was so fatuous as to suppose that you sought one."

La Salle parried the faint sarcasm with stern dignity. "Monsieur le Duc, there is no question here of seeking or bestowing favours. What I offer amounts to a bargain."

"I perceive it. A man of your discernment will perceive also that there are other candidates to the throne which Louis XVIII should shortly be vacating."

"But none with a better title. And none whom it would be easier or more profitable to set up."

Fouché did not immediately answer. He took up the portrait once more, and silently studied it awhile. Then, setting it down again, he reclined in his chair, his elbows on the arms of it, his fingertips together, his eyelids drooping until the eyes seemed closed. For some considerable moments he remained thus, as if asleep or dead. Then the lips parted to ask a question.

"Where is this King of yours at present?"

"Close at hand. At the Inn of the Lilies at Ferrières."

"Hardly a suitable lodging for majesty. Still, a King who has been a cowherd will hardly be too exigent, and the title of the house is perhaps an omen. Do you believe in omens, Monsieur de La Salle?"

"As much as you do, Monsieur le Duc."

"Yes. I should judge you practical. Therefore you will see that your proposal is fraught with certain hazards. Even without the final judgment, which could only follow upon acquaintance with this risen dead of yours, the matter is not one upon which decision may be taken without some thought. The night, they say, brings counsel." The eyelids rolled back, and the eyes, so singularly alive in that dead face, blazed again momentarily upon La Salle. "You shall have word from me tomorrow, monsieur, at your inn."

Chapter 2

Enter the King

"The fox is all but in the trap."

Thus, back at the Inn of the Lilies, La Salle wound up his account of what had passed at the château.

His hopes, you see, were high. But hardly high enough to prepare him for the terms of the note that reached him at noon on the morrow.

Monsieur, the Auberge des Lys, as I told you yesterday, affords no lodging suitable to the rank of your august companion. Therefore, apartments have been prepared here, which, with the rest of the Château de Ferrières, I take the liberty of placing unreservedly at his disposal. I shall await the honour of welcoming you at Ferrières in the course of the day. My carriage will await your convenience.

I subscribe myself with the most profound esteem,

Otranto.

A carriage upholstered in blue velvet, a ducal coronet on the panels, drawn by four magnificent black horses, with coachman and two footmen in the Otranto livery, stood waiting before the humble door of the mean inn.

La Salle, with a set countenance, handed the note to Deslys. Deslys, less master of his nerves, turned white, began to shake, and lost breath as he read.

"It is unbelievable," he muttered.

"Until one holds the explanation."

"The explanation?"

"The character and history of Monsieur Fouché. He has never cared very much who held the symbols of power, so long as power, itself, was held by him. Statecraft and intrigue are the breath of his life. Under his mantle of Cincinnatus, chagrin is gnawing at his entrails. Already he is busy with plots for a return to power. Desmarets' presence tells me that. He knows that the days of the present Bourbon are numbered. He does not mean to remain in rustication when the gros cochon crashes to his ruin. The successor shall be of Monsieur Fouché's appointing. There are several candidates, he says. You see how much he has considered. This note proves that to each of them his personal ambition perceives some objection. You, Charles, come to him in the hour of his need as a gift from God. I invite you to admire my sagacity in deciding that the Duke of Otranto is the man for us."

"But without having even seen me!" Deslys stood pallid, with beads of nervous perspiration on his brow. His mounting fears, now that the great moment was at hand, stripped away the veneer with which La Salle had been overlaying him in these past weeks. His air, the pitch of his voice, his very accent became once more those of the awkward peasant La Salle had met in Brandenburg. "To take his decision upon no more than a portrait and the account you gave him!"

La Salle's indolent smile displayed itself. His drawling voice was charged with amused scorn. "I see that you do not yet understand. You are so opportune an instrument for Monsieur Fouché's hand that complete conviction of your genuineness may not preoccupy him. He has critically considered your history. It is plausible, even compelling, and without gaps. Presented by a man with your face it becomes irresistible. If it should happen that it does not quite convince Fouché, at least it leaves him no doubt that it will convince others, particularly when he sponsors you."

"You mean that he's a scoundrel?" Deslys was shocked.

"Just like you and me."

"But to be prepared to support a fraud!"

"When did he hesitate to do so? Once in minor orders, then a professed atheist. Mathematician, man of science, Oratorian, Jacobin, regicide, national representative, terrorist, Thermidorean, senator, despot, architect and pillar of imperialism, Grand Cross of the Legion of Honour and Count of the Empire. These are the milestones of the road he has travelled from the Oratory to the Duchy of Otranto, from a squalid garret in the Rue St Honoré to the ducal splendours of Ferrières." He laughed. "Fouché is an emancipated soul. In his immense and tranquil contempt of his fellow-creatures he recognizes neither good nor evil."

Thus La Salle explained him and his present attitude, and yet withheld an explanation far more probable to his all-embracing vision. He remembered vom Stein's scheme to set up a pretender merely for the purpose of overthrowing Bonaparte, this pretender to be unmasked and discarded once the sole purpose for which he had been set up should be accomplished. This might well be Fouché's present plan; and since La Salle's main object, too, was the overthrow of the ingrate who occupied the throne, he was for the moment content.

Deslys, however, with no suspicion of these things, made no concealment of the nausea with which La Salle's revelation filled him. "The horror," he ejaculated, "of leaning upon such a man!"

"Horrible, indeed, to gentlemen of our honesty. Yet consider the security. For it may well be that, like myself, Fouché is ready to serve a pretended Bourbon where he would not serve a real one. He had no more cause than I to love the members of that shabby race. Besides, a pretended Bourbon is more easily shown the door if he does not behave himself and show a proper gratitude."

"That reminder is unnecessary." There was a sudden asperity in the clockmaker's tone. "I am not likely to forget my debts."

"It is not a reminder. It is an explanation. But we keep the Duke's horses standing, and the day is cold. Let us be making our packages, my lad."

They were soon made, these packages, and far though they may have been from royal, yet royal was the welcome awaiting Deslys at Ferrières.

Fouché, himself, gaunt and bowed, bareheaded in the chill of that day of October mists, stood on the wide threshold at the head of the double flights of steps to receive him. His keen piercing eyes played for a moment on that face so queerly reminiscent of Marie-Antoinette's, then the tall, emaciated frame was bent still lower, and the weak voice murmured, too low for any ears but those of Deslys and La Salle, "Sire, my house is signally honoured."

Never was speech more pregnant with significance. Never was so much said in so few words. Never had La Salle been more taken by surprise. The effect upon Deslys was almost magical. La Salle, watching him furtively and not without apprehension in this critical moment, beheld him, like the actor inspired to perfection by the audience's unstinted acceptance of him in the character he portrays, so far settle himself into his rôle that his personality seemed to change.

Since in the presence of the servants he could not extend his hand to be kissed, neither would he offer it to be grasped. He contented himself with bowing, his manner admirably blending courtesy with condescension.

"We are fortunate," he said, and to all but Fouché the pronoun would convey that he spoke for himself and his companion – "we are fortunate, Monsieur le Duc, in a hospitality we shall study to deserve."

His nervousness was masked in dignity. That his voice should shake a little could be attributed to emotion, whilst the excellent choice of the few words uttered almost dissembled the peasant accent.

He was conducted by Fouché to a salon forming part of a noble suite placed at his disposal on the first floor. Here, having dismissed the servants, the Duke, to La Salle's continuing amazement, expressed with less reserve his satisfaction at the trust with which he was honoured. Whilst he attentively studied his guest, yet the quiet, matter-of-fact tone in which he opined that the task ahead of them would offer little difficulty in the conditions that prevailed, implied that he took his claims for granted. After that came some counsels, to show how much thought he had already bestowed upon the matter.

"Until we are ready to proclaim you, sire, which is to say, until we have completely mobilized our forces, it will be prudent that Your Majesty's real identity should continue veiled. For the present, sire, you will remain Charles Perrin Deslys as hitherto. Or perhaps by dropping the plebeian Perrin, retain only the name of Deslys, a name which by an oddly fortunate circumstance comes to strike the imagination in the proper manner. From all those whom I am confident of rallying to your support, you will be pleased to content yourself with a manner of no greater deference than would be due to the simple rank in which you appear. If this, sire, deserves your approval, I will beg, in your own interests, to be excused from again addressing Your Majesty in the terms I am now employing until we shall have succeeded in raising you to your proper place."

"I approve entirely. I commend your prudence, Monsieur le Duc."

Fouché bowed, and passed on to the next point. "Although we shall work quietly, sire, it is not in my mind to work slowly. There is no time to lose because in no case can Louis XVIII last much longer.

"It has always been my way to move as swiftly as is consistent with prudence. Already here, this evening, you will meet a few of those whom I count upon making your supporters. There will be, first of all, my neighbour, Colonel the Chevalier de Chaboulon, an émigré of Condé's army who has shed his blood freely in the Bourbon cause. His lands, confiscated by the Revolution, are today in the hands of an army contractor who was in his time a henchman of Robespierre's. The Chevalier is in poor circumstances; but all his claims for reparation have fallen upon deaf ears. Another, in the same case, whom you will also meet tonight is the Marquis de Sceaux. These two are representatives of a class the whole of which you may confidently expect to find at your side. And there are tens of thousands of them today under this purblind, heartless and ingrate government. Then, amongst others, you will meet the Duchess of Castillon-Fouquières and her daughter, ladies who honour me with their friendship, and who are permitting me to make to them here at Ferrières some poor return for hospitalities enjoyed at their hands some years ago, in the days of my senatorship at Aix. But for your long exile, sire, I should not have to tell you that the Castillon-Fouquières, one of the oldest families of Provence, once sovereign princes in the Rhône Valley, are allied in blood with the House of Bourbon, claim, indeed, an even greater antiquity. Where they lead, be sure, sire, that many will follow, and with them loyalty to the rightful King is a religion above every interest.

"There will be some others. But these I have named – the Marquis de Sceaux, the Chevalier de Chaboulon, and Mesdames de Castillon-Fouquières – you may regard as important representatives of the two classes upon which your success will mainly depend.

"For the moment, sire, that is all with which I need to trouble you. In a day or two I shall hope to submit a definite plan of action. In the meantime I will beg you to regard Ferrières as your property, and all within it as Your Majesty's dutiful servants."

He bowed himself out, and his two guests were left alone in that elegant salon of silken upholsteries, gilded wood, soft carpets and glittering lustres.

La Salle, relaxing with an explosive sigh from his stiffly deferential attitude, sat down unbidden in the presence of thoughtful majesty.

"It's a miracle," murmured Deslys.

"I work miracles," La Salle explained, with a twist of his lips. Then he laughed softly. "On my faith, I think I was mistaken in Fouché. I watched him closely, and although that death-mask betrays nothing of his mind, yet I believe that he is acting entirely in conviction, and not at all in cynicism. On the whole, Charles, I think that so far we may felicitate ourselves. A good beginning is, in itself, half the accomplishment."

The clockmaker's prominent eyes looked down upon him without favour.

"We may not do so for long unless you employ more circumspection." He spoke with the cold hauteur which had been growing upon him since crossing the threshold of Ferrières. It was the tone of the master. La Salle stared displeasure. "Suppose," said Deslys, "that you were overheard. Suppose that anyone were to enter suddenly and discover you sprawling there in my presence."

"Name of a name, my dear Charles! We are not at Passavant. One does not burst in upon a gentleman without knocking."

"I'll ask you to remember that I am not your 'dear Charles' any longer."

La Salle frowned, irritated by the sudden frostiness of the tone. There was a significant hardening of his own as he answered: "Have no anxiety. I shall remember my part for just so long as you remember yours. Henceforth I fill the rôle of secretary to Monsieur Charles Deslys. I shall look to the future for my wages."

"It would be foolish to misunderstand me." Deslys' tone was more conciliatory. He came over to La Salle and set a hand on his shoulder. "Be sensible, my friend, rather than sensitive. You must perceive the necessity."

La Salle's perception of it was displayed that evening in his self-contained demeanour when they came to the brilliantly lighted salon of honour for the presentation by Fouché of those few whom he had announced.

Scant though might be the wardrobe of the two adventurers, La Salle's foresight had included in it a dress of ceremony for each of them, and although they took heavy toll of his rapidly diminishing resources he had practised no misplaced economy in this particular. Deslys' short, slight figure had never looked so elegant as in the blue coat, black satin breeches, silk stockings and ruffled shirt in which he made his appearance that evening at Ferrières. He gathered added distinction from his powdered head, which, if an almost obsolete mode, was still permissible. La Salle had insisted upon it with the object of dissembling the dark colour of Deslys' hair, intent upon avoiding any false note when creating the first impression. La Salle's own moderately tall and vigorously slender frame was all in black, even to the stock which he affected and which heightened the pallor of his face.

The guests assembled in haste for the occasion, apart from the Castillon-Fouquières, who were on a protracted visit to Ferrières, amounted to no more than a half-dozen nobles of the neighbourhood, three of whom were accompanied by their wives. Although they all addressed the clockmaker as Monsieur Deslys, it was at once manifest from their demeanour when presented that to each had been confidentially imparted the amazing secret of his identity. If any of them approached him in doubt notwithstanding the assurances received from Fouché, it was apparent to the narrowly vigilant La Salle that such doubts were instantly dispelled by the meeting. The eyes that rested searchingly on Deslys' countenance announced in their expression how startling they found the likeness to Marie-Antoinette, which the powdered hair had singularly stressed.

Deslys' manner, too, was in the main satisfactory. A certain nervousness was no more than natural. The vestiges of the rustic awkwardness which La Salle had been labouring to efface ever since that first meeting in Brandenburg might be attributed to the gracious modesty of one who was conscious that his rank still awaited universal acknowledgment. His broad accent, explained by the manner of his rearing, was largely overlaid by that natural odd felicity of expression which had been a source of wonder to La Salle from the very outset of their acquaintance.

Observing him as he acknowledged the low bows of the men and the sweeping curtseys of the ladies, La Salle congratulated himself upon the fruits of the laborious tuition to which he had subjected his pupil.

Madame la Duchesse de Castillon-Fouquières was the first to be presented, a majestic woman in the middle forties whose air brought to mind the stately glories of Versailles.

She was followed by the Chevalier de Chaboulon, a lean, hard-bitten, grizzled man who looked the soldier that he was. Grave and reticent, his was a figure to inspire confidence. In sharp contrast was that other returned émigré who was similarly a sufferer from Bourbon ingratitude, the Marquis de Sceaux. An olive-skinned man of forty, of a good height and an incipient corpulency, his thick black hair flecked with grey, his eyes vividly blue under heavy black brows. Although there was no boldness in his features, which were too small for his face, yet he imposed himself by his air of energy and consequence.

He employed towards the guest of honour an outspokenness which none of the others had ventured, whilst at the same time taking advantage of the supposed King's incognito to be the first to speak.

"You make a very timely appearance, sir. Be sure that you will not want for friends in France."

At the patronizing tone, La Salle looked down his nose at the Marquis; Fouché's face became more markedly expressionless; Deslys gravely smiled.

"I am aware, sir, of how deeply my family is in your debt already."

Presuming upon this, the Marquis became almost aggressive. "My scars are my only decorations."

Fouché softly intervened. "Monsieur de Sceaux has a just grievance. He feels strongly."

"He may rest in confidence," said Deslys, "that the future will make amends to him, as it must to all who have suffered for their loyalty."

The Marquis bowed low in acknowledgment of what he took for a pledge.

And then the double doors of the salon were thrown open by a lackey and Pauline de Castillon-Fouquières appeared upon the threshold.

Tall and slimly built, save for a generous fullness of the breast, her height and slimness stressed by the straight lines of her high-waisted gown, she was all a shimmer of white satin, against which three red camellias at her waistband looked at a little distance like a splash of blood. Her hair, dressed flat and clear of her brow, à la Ninon, was of a rich red auburn, and her skin of the warm whiteness that so often accompanies such hair. Very upright, and with a carriage which was almost rigid, she was of a hard and glittering loveliness that must anywhere command attention.

Conscious of the effect which she produced, mistress of the histrionic art of self-display, she paused a moment under the lintel, to regard with regal pride those to whom she offered herself for survey. Then her eyes, of a hazel almost green, coming to rest upon Deslys, she swept forward with a sudden eager swiftness, yet without loss of any of her rigidity.

As the doors closed again upon the retiring lackey, she sank in a rustle of billowing satin at the clockmaker's feet. An assumption of diffidence came to lower her brilliant eyes.

Fouché's soft voice named her to Deslys, who, bending, extended a hand to raise her. Disdaining to respect the incognito as the others had done, she bore the hand to her lips before it could be withdrawn. As she rose, her eyes meeting the young man's rather sombre gaze, she spoke with throbbing fervour.

"Sire, you are heaven-sent to console and uplift a faltering kingdom. God save Your Majesty."

There was utter silence broken at last by Deslys when he had mastered the emotional disturbance it was seen that she had produced in him.

"Mademoiselle, I forgive this momentary lifting of a veil which prudence demands should remain lowered yet awhile, on the condition that the gracious offence is not repeated. My name, if it please you, is Charles Deslys."

It was well done, despite the peasant accent: a rebuke without sting, which went to enhance him in the eyes of all present and brought a gratified surprise and relief to La Salle, who in Deslys' momentary disorder had beheld the signs of panic. This cowherd out-royalled Royalty.

When presently Fouché confidentially commended to him Deslys' deportment, he had a ready answer.

"It's just atavism. No misfortunes or sordidness of circumstances can stifle what is bred in a man's blood and bone."

Chapter 3

Anxieties of Monsieur de Sceaux

Monsieur Charles Deslys rode with Mademoiselle de Castillon-Fouquières through the park of Ferrières in the pale sunshine of a mild November day. He was wrapped against the chilly weather in a bottle-green greatcoat, the high collar of which was of astrakhan. His munificent host had placed at his disposal a wardrobe and a valet, besides horses to ride, a master-at-arms to fence with, fowling-pieces and gamekeepers should he care to amuse himself in the preserves, and whatever else might serve to increase his comfort and beguile his brief leisures.

These provisions had followed upon a short interview with La Salle, of whom the Duke had solicitously inquired the state of the royal treasury. La Salle had answered candidly.

"I am at once the farmer-general of the taxes and the only taxpayer. It is a state of things that could lead to one condition only, and that condition has been reached. The treasury is empty."

Fouché nodded understandingly. "A loan becomes necessary. I will open at once at the Bank of France an account for half a million in the name of Charles Deslys." La Salle held his breath, lest a gasp should betray him. "Meanwhile, your drafts against it for your immediate needs will be honoured by my steward here."

La Salle suppressed the enthusiasm of his acknowledgments, and drew for the royal needs as became an intendant of the royal finances.

Deslys when informed of this sudden accession of wealth annoyed La Salle by remaining languid.

"Saperlipopette!" was his peculiar oath of disgust on this occasion. "Do you know that you become daily more offensively royal, Charles? At this rate you will walk into the Tuileries as unconcerned as if it were the cowshed at Passavant."

The mention of Passavant turned the young man's languor into gloom. He looked into the mirror before him as if he were looking into space, and frowned at his image there.

"Passavant!" he said, and sighed lugubriously. "I wonder what they are doing there now. I wonder what Justine is doing."

"Whatever they may be doing, they are not supposing that there is already half a million to your name at the Bank of France, which is what you should be thinking about instead of glooming."

Nevertheless, in gloom he had continued. But this morning, as he rode with Mademoiselle de Castillon-Fouquières, his melancholy was dispelled, and he was troubled by no thought of Passavant, until Mademoiselle, herself, turned his mind thither. So that he might gratify her curiosity touching his history, she had lured him to talk of himself, as only a woman can lure a man. The tale he told was much the tale that La Salle had told Fouché, saving that he named no individuals and no places.

The lady, an erect figure of regal grace in her close-fitting riding-habit, interjected now a question, now an inarticulate crooning sympathy. They had been so close, these two, in the week since his first appearance at Ferrières, that already the brief acquaintance possessed the intimacy of an old one. She was of those whose imagination invests with glamour the personality of a king, and from the moment when first she had greeted him with her daring disdain of subterfuge, she had remained under a spell of her own weaving. She had attached herself to him with the characteristically arrogant assumption of right of one whose claims to pre-eminence had never seriously been questioned. The only person who ventured to question them now was the Marquis de Sceaux, and this because, being bred in Courts, he was quick to apprehend the danger to a demoiselle's good name in too close an association with a royal personage in posse or in esse. In this he was not being merely altruistic. Monsieur de Sceaux had been caught in the web of Mademoiselle de Castillon-Fouquières' glittering witchery. That it was a frosty glitter but rendered her the more desirable in his eyes. Although forty and greatly impoverished, yet he was a considerable personage, and he had never found that women regarded him as unattractive.

During the month or so that Mesdames de Castillon-Fouquières had spent at Ferrières, he had made such progress with Pauline that they were already on the eve of a betrothal when the advent of Charles Deslys supplied a distraction which the Marquis could not regard as other than untimely. At the very moment when the daughter was riding in the park with Monsieur Deslys, the Marquis was venturing a mild remonstrance with the mother.

The Duchess received it between dismay and amusement. "Can you possibly be misconceiving attentions which express the fervent loyalty we should all share with my daughter?"

"We may share the loyalty, madame, but your daughter takes care that none of us shares the company of...ah... Monsieur Deslys."

Madame de Castillon-Fouquières frowned in her majesty upon the disgruntled Marquis. "It is hardly gallant, monsieur, to attribute to my daughter attentions more properly attributable to Monsieur Deslys. Pauline has always been a model of circumspection."

"It would be the more unfortunate, then, if she were to depart from it at the very moment when it becomes most necessary."

"I am under no apprehension that Pauline will ever depart from it. She is my daughter."

Rebuked, he went off with his troubles to Fouché, but found no sympathy. Fouché, impenetrable, refused to understand that anyone could find matter for scandal in the simple fact that Mademoiselle de Castillon-Fouquières should be riding with Monsieur Deslys.

"It is not the riding that troubles me – name of God! – but what may come of it."

"What do you foresee, my dear Marquis?" wondered the innocent Fouché.

"Mademoiselle de Castillon is a woman."

"A very beautiful woman."

"She will have the weaknesses of her sex."

"Oh, I hope not. Let us hope not."

"Hope won't avail, Monsieur le Duc."

"In that case, my friend, we have still faith and charity. Practise them."

The Marquis understood that he must take matters into his own hands, and this as soon as the lady should return from her ride. It demanded some patience, for the lady was in no haste to return.

In an age in which sensibility was in the mode, Mademoiselle de Castillon-Fouquières was as abundantly supplied with it as she was lacking in real sentiment.

Her large green eyes grew moist at the tale of the hardships suffered by the young King, who looked to her so royally handsome as he rode at a walking pace beside her.

He checked, suddenly aware of the tenderness of her tear-filmed glance.

"You are moved, mademoiselle!" he exclaimed in contrition. "I should not have harassed you with so wretched a tale."

"A tale of wretched things endured," she corrected, "but not a wretched tale. A noble tale. A tale of fortitude such as only real greatness can display."

"No, no. What I have endured is, after all, the lot of the great majority of mankind."

"But not of men born as you were born. Your patience in adversity is a great augury for your reign. Cruelly schooled as you have been, you will make a great king when you come to your own. I do not presume, I hope, in saying that."

"Presume!" he protested, and laughed the notion away.

"At least you had the fortune to fall into generous, charitable hands. What was the place where your youth was spent?"

It was La Salle's teaching that there should be no departures from truth save where necessity compelled them. But possibly he did not even think of that as he answered simply: "A farm called Passavant, on the spurs of the Jura, above Le Locle." And he went on to tell of Joseph Perrin and his wife, who had been as parents to him, and of Justine, who believed herself his cousin. His tone grew wistful as he spoke of them.

"Ah, yes," she said. "How well I understand your gratitude! In other hands what might not your lot have been! I shudder to think of it."

"Some day," he said, very thoughtfully, "I shall hope richly to repay them."

"It would be your first thought. You are like that. I know." Impulsively she leaned across and placed her hand on his. "May that day be soon. That is my prayer for you, who are so worthy." And then, suddenly aware of this fresh and great presumption, she hastily withdrew her hand and in confusion hung her handsome head. "I forget myself," she murmured.

"All that you need to forget at present is that I am anything more than Charles Deslys."

"Ah, no. For then I should have to change when the events compel me to remember that you are something more. And I should detest to change."

He looked at her, so slim and straight and coldly proud of mien. "Yes," he said. "I should judge you steadfast."

"You shall never find me other in my loyalty, sire."

"Sh!" he admonished her. "That title must not be spoken." But he smiled. "Besides, I am not yet accustomed to it. Once I was Monseigneur le Dauphin, then the Citizen Capet, then the Sieur Deslys, as I remain at present."

This he might remain, so far as the form of address was concerned; but no form of address was to obscure the fact that he was King of France. It was very present in the mind of Monsieur de Sceaux, who, having watched ill-humouredly for her return, detained her in the hall when it took place at last.

"Are you prudent, mademoiselle, in giving so much of your society to Monsieur Deslys?"

She stiffened perceptibly, with an upward thrust of her chin. But her tone was coldly demure. "It had not occurred to me that it could be imprudent."

"No, no." He was indulgent. "That I understand. But now that I mention it, you perceive for yourself that it is…ah…hardly circumspect."

"I do not perceive it."

"You do not?" He seemed surprised. He pursed the mouth that was so absurdly small in so large a face. "The dangers of innocence!"

"I am not quite a child, monsieur."

"Not quite. No. And yet in some things, yes. An adorable child, Pauline. Adorable. You'll be guided by my riper judgment."

"I am not aware that I am in need of guidance."

Here were signs of an independence very disturbing to Monsieur de Sceaux. "You know, my dear Pauline, how much you are to me; in what reverence I hold you. I could not suffer you to be held in less by any man."

"Be sure that no man will until I give him the right to do so. And that will be never."

This was better, and pondering her as she stood, so straight in her cold pride, it carried conviction to de Sceaux. "I am sure of it. But there remains the censoriousness of the world. It is as a beast of prey, lying in wait to pounce upon and rend such lovely things as a maid's fair name. I beg only that you will beware of it."

She smiled serenely. "I have the vanity to conceive myself secure. For the rest, Monsieur Deslys commanded me to ride with him."

"Commanded?"

"Is not that how you would describe his invitation?"

"I see. And you were glad to obey?"

"As eager as you would have been in my place. I should be either more or less than human if my interest in him – my curiosity, if you prefer it – were not profound."

"Yes," the Marquis conceded. "That, too, I can understand. And has he gratified it?"

"Very fully. So moving a story." She softened as she spoke, and set a hand familiarly upon his arm. "He spoke of the tribulations he has suffered, how from being Monseigneur the Dauphin he became first the Citizen Capet and then the Sieur Deslys, working on a farm at Passavant in the Jura, and afterwards as a clockmaker in Le Locle."

"As a clockmaker. An odd taste in a prince."

"Heredity, I think. Have you forgotten that Louis XVI amused himself as a locksmith?"

"Ah, yes. And the farm-labouring? From whom did he inherit that?"

The faint sneer surprised and wounded her. She looked at him sharply. "That was imposed upon him by cruel necessity, when he lay concealed at Passavant, passing for a nephew of the Perrins. I do not think his fortitude and patience in adversity can be reverenced too deeply. What an example was set by this King, living by the sweat of his brow, to so many of his nobles who preferred to parade their misfortunes so as to move the charity of foreigners."

Monsieur de Sceaux quivered, stabbed to the soul of him by that sharp reproach. He dissembled his hurt in an increase of pompousness. "So long as you keep your admiration within prudent bounds all will be well," said he.

Stiff and straight, her riding-whip held horizontally in her two hands, her greenish eyes measured him coldly. "I'll ask you to be plainer, Monsieur le Marquis."

"But, my dear Pauline, how is it possible to be plainer? Must I remind you that he is a grandson of Louis XV and great-grandson of Louis XIV? Isn't that enough?"

"I am not aware that Mademoiselle de Castillon-Fouquières descends from either Madame de Montespan or Madame de Pompadour."

"Both might have remained honest women if they had not crossed the King's path."

"That is an interesting theory. You should develop it."

He was reduced to exasperation. "Do you refuse to understand that I am telling you to be warned by the fate of those ladies?"

"I suspected it, yet I hesitate to believe that anyone should flatter me by supposing that I belong to the class of women from which a King's mistress is chosen. I thank you, sir, for so choice a compliment."

Her sarcasm cut him whilst it partially reassured him. "My dear Pauline, you will forgive me if out of my deep solicitude I…"

"Venture upon insult," she concluded for him. "If I had a brother, sir, I might ask him to continue the discussion with you. As I have not, it must be abandoned, greatly to my regret."

With the faintest inclination of her head and the bitterest of little smiles she turned and left him to gnaw his lip again in anger.

Chapter 4

Symptoms

Ten days Monsieur Charles Deslys abode at Ferrières, whilst the ground in Paris was being rapidly prepared for him, and from the calm of the surface none could have suspected the turmoil of activity in the depths.

The police of Louis XVIII was so notoriously incompetent that a current gibe for anyone who displayed ignorance of some notorious fact was, "You must be in the police." Possibly, at a time when it was controlled by the Baron d'André, who was, himself, a creature of Fouché's, some of its blindness may have been deliberate. Certain it is that it appeared to remain unaware of the activities directed from Ferrières, which was within easy reach of Paris. There were daily comings and goings in an almost constant stream between the Duke of Otranto's château and the capital. Desmarets was heavily engaged in marshalling agents whose function it was to reconcile the uneasy Republican party to a change of monarchy not yet defined, with assurances of a constitution, the letter of which they should approve and the spirit of which would be rigorously observed. Colonel de Chaboulon was no less active in the ranks of the great army of émigré nobles and soldiers like himself, towards whom the reigning monarch was scandalously neglecting his deep indebtedness. The enlistment of the Bonapartists was being craftily pursued through the women of the new nobility of Bonaparte's creation, which at the

Bourbon Court was being subjected to mean and stupid insult, upon the example set by the vinegary Duchess of Angoulême. The leadership of this part of the movement was entrusted by Fouché to the Princesse de la Moskowa, the wife of Marshal Ney, who had been reduced to bitter tears by the studied slights of which she had been the victim at the Tuileries. And the Princess had not lacked for vindictive coadjutors in her task.

The Faubourg St Germain, the stronghold of the nobility of the old régime, had not yet been touched. This most difficult part of the recruiting was to be in the influential hands of the Castillon-Fouquières when presently they moved with Fouché to the Hôtel d'Otranto in Paris.

Meanwhile the vast preparations already on foot were being directed from Ferrières by the ever calm and somnolent valetudinarian, of whom his guests saw little until the evening. All day he sat quietly at work in his study, sometimes with Desmarets and sometimes with Chaboulon, both of whom came and went with almost impudent regularity, but nearly always with La Salle, who proved himself so alert, shrewd and indefatigable, and endowed with such a gift of intrigue, that very soon he proved indispensable to the master intriguer with whom he laboured.

It was on the very eve of their removal to Paris that Fouché sought of him information and co-operation in a matter of more than ordinary delicacy.

He broached the subject abruptly in his thin, expressionless voice. "I suppose that our Monsieur Deslys is clear of all feminine entanglements. I mean, that it has never happened to him to take a wife in the course of his wanderings."

"If so, he has never confided in me."

"But one forms impressions. Should you suppose it likely?"

"Quite definitely, no."

"I am relieved. Although, of course, in such a case as his, these things can be arranged, and a previous marriage can always be declared morganatic." He paused a moment before quietly continuing. "You will have observed that a strong attachment appears to be forming between Monsieur Deslys and Mademoiselle de Castillon-Fouquières."

"I have wondered if they are not together more than I should account judicious if I were the lady's mother."

The ghost of a smile flitted across the Duke's cadaverous face. "Madame de Castillon-Fouquières' notion of what is judicious is governed by a high ambition."

"She will not be supposing that her daughter might be Queen of France?"

In reply La Salle was to hear the very argument he had once employed with Deslys.

"I see that you have prejudices. Are they not, perhaps, a heritage from the old monarchical days? The Revolution swept away a good many shams among the rest. We have seen a Créole of only moderate birth by the ancient canons, crowned and accepted Empress of the French. Mademoiselle de Castillon-Fouquières is of a lineage at least as old as that of the Bourbons."

"What you are really telling me, Monsieur le Duc, is that you perceive no obstacle to such a union?"

"Oh, much more. I am telling you that Madame de Castillon-Fouquières sees none."

"Does her view matter, then?"

"Enormously. I depend upon her to enrol the Faubourg St Germain under our banner. The support of the old nobility is of the first importance, and the Duchess possesses great influence. She has spoken to me today. She complains that if the close association of her daughter with Monsieur Deslys should be continued in Paris, her daughter will be gravely compromised unless there should be honourable circumstances to account for it. She does not forget to remind me that her influence with the Faubourg St Germain would naturally be much more actively exerted if her daughter's interests were bound up with the success of them. At the same time she asserts that a union between her daughter and Monsieur Deslys would go a long way towards establishing him. She argues, not unreasonably, that so full a proof of the acceptance of him by the house of Castillon-Fouquières would ensure the unquestioning acceptance of him by lesser folk."

La Salle sniffed. "In short, Madame la Duchesse offers a bargain. Monsieur Deslys shall have her full support if he consents to marry her daughter."

"That is too brutal. No, no. Loyalty is loyalty, and Madame de Castillon is stoutly loyal. Be sure of that. But at the same time, human nature is human nature, and Madame's nature is human. Intensely human."

"Permit me a question, Monsieur le Duc."

"As many as you please, my friend."

"What would be your own view of the expediency of such a marriage?"

Fouché pursed his thin lips and put his head on one side. "In the times in which we live – still, to a great extent, revolutionary times – I see nothing in it to shock public opinion. Therefore, there can be nothing against it. In favour of it there is that unquestionable influence of the Castillon-Fouquières with the old nobility, and some of this influence might be lost if we were to return an answer that would be regarded as a rebuff."

"I am to take it, then, that you would approve?"

"My dear La Salle, I seldom approve or disapprove of anything. I point out what is expedient, and I confess that this marriage might advance our aims. It remains, of course, to obtain the consent of Monsieur Deslys. It should not be difficult once he is assured of the political advantages of such a marriage. That, my dear La Salle, is where I must depend upon you. Since we go to Paris tomorrow, you will oblige me by losing no time."

La Salle considered. "Is my advice permitted?"

"Oh, but invited, my friend. Cordially invited."

"Then I would counsel delay. If the proposal should be repugnant to Monsieur Deslys, he may feel at this stage that he can still draw back. If we allow the association to continue yet awhile, his innate chivalry will compel him to go forward once it is pointed out to him that Mademoiselle has been irretrievably compromised."

"Yes. That is well reasoned. Explain to me only how I am to induce patience in the Duchess."

"By frankness. By telling her just that."

The low lids rolled back from Fouché's pale eyes. For a second, they glowed with admiration. "My dear La Salle, do you know that sometimes you startle me?"

But the delay, the extent of which was now left to La Salle's judgment, was not unduly protracted. He accounted that the time was ripe just one week after they had installed themselves in the Hôtel d'Otranto in Paris. It was the princely mansion of the Rue Cerruti which had belonged to the financier Laborde, but which never in all its opulent history had known such stately and crowded receptions as it housed in the last three days of November of that year 1814.

The Duke of Otranto was not a person who could move unnoticed. His sudden and ostentatious return to Paris, from a retirement associated with disgrace, inevitably gave rise to a score of rumours. The most insistent of them was that he was about to be restored to favour.

At the Tuileries Louis XVIII and his favourite, the Duke de Blacas, in infatuated ignorance of the real reason for that sudden return, found the rumour exceedingly amusing.

Fouché, whilst seeming flagrantly indiscreet, took these first steps in the adventure with the extremest circumspection, closely guided by the information derived from his own personal police, which, admirably organized, penetrated everywhere.

If any government agents had introduced themselves to the Hôtel d'Otranto they would have found only that a certain Monsieur Deslys, befriended by the Duke of Otranto, was paying assiduous court to the famous and high-born Mademoiselle de Castillon-Fouquières, and probably owed to this circumstance and to her undisguised favour the celebrity which seemed suddenly to attach to him and the esteem which he enjoyed in that environment. The assemblies which paid homage to him were made up of persons eminent in all political parties, drawn together under Fouché's roof by that singular man who, whilst mistrusted and even despised by every group, yet knew how to deserve the consideration of the individuals composing each. Here old revolutionists who had made their way in the world, such as Thibeaudeau, Réal and Barère, rubbed shoulders with returned émigrés, Cazalès, Clermont-Tonerre and Chénedollé. Old Lebrun was here, now Duke of Plaisance, who had been Napoleon's Governor-General of Holland, but could find no employment under Louis XVIII, and Davout, the ablest of all Napoleon's marshals, now Duke of Auerstadt and Prince of Eckmühl, a man in the middle forties who would not have accepted service under Louis XVIII if it had been offered him. And there was the gallant, handsome Ney, the Prince de la Moskowa, who was in the service of the reigning Bourbon, but burned with resentment of the slights his wife had suffered at the Bourbon Court. There was Ouvrard, that magician of finance who had furnished the millions required by Bonaparte as First Consul, and who was yielding now to Fouché's persuasions that he should lay the foundations of a still vaster fortune by supplying the millions that were necessary to Louis XVII.

With these mingled such great ladies of the old régime as the Marquise de Vaudémont, the Marquise de Custine, the Princesse de Béarn, Madame d'Auguié, who had been a lady-in-waiting at Versailles, and Madame de Rambaud, sometime lady-in-waiting to Monseigneur the Dauphin.

With a single exception, not one of those who had known the little Dauphin in the days of his infancy at Versailles failed to recognize him now in this Monsieur Deslys; and the fact that he dared not at once proclaim himself to his uncle, Louis XVIII, was responsible for a further subsidence in the decaying foundations of the usurper's throne.

Madame de Rambaud, forewarned by Fouché, yet full of scepticism, had been so completely conquered when face to face with the pretender that she had almost swooned. Considering the position she had held as official cradle-rocker to the Dauphin, it occurred to very few that her recognition in the man of thirty of the child of seven she had last seen might possibly be mistaken.

Some few, however, may have remained in doubt, and one there was, a Monsieur Roger du Chatenay, an erstwhile captain in the royal bodyguard of Louis XVI, who was overheard to say that he was not to be deceived by any such imposture, however much a credulous old woman might be the victim of it.

In the breast of Monsieur de Sceaux – who was of those who overheard him – that phrase was as a seed on fruitful soil. The Marquis, who had also transferred himself to Paris, was on the verge of distraction as a result of the ever increasing intimacy between Pauline de Castillon-Fouquières and Charles Deslys.

At the earliest moment thereafter he buttonholed the sometime guardsman.

"I was impressed, monsieur, to hear you so positively denounce this Charles Deslys for an impostor. You will have good grounds for your opinion."

Du Chatenay, a lean, active man of fifty, looked warily at the portly Marquis. Not discerning a possible challenger in that genial person, he confirmed himself. "It is not to be thought that I would express such an opinion lightly. What evidence are we offered to support the fantastic story you will have heard from Monsieur d'Otranto? The evidence of a likeness?"

"It is sufficiently striking," ventured Monsieur de Sceaux.

"If it were much more striking than it is, I should still want something that could be called proof in a matter of such importance to us all. Nature plays these tricks. And is the likeness so striking, when all is said?"

"You do not find it so?"

"Monsieur le Marquis," du Chatenay was sternly impressive, "at Versailles from '88 to the end of '91 I had the honour of being in daily contact with the royal family. Scarcely a day passed on which I did not see the Dauphin at close quarters, and often I spoke to him. My recollections are very clear. His Highness' hair was a bright golden. This man's is a dark brown."

"Hair will often darken with age."

"Scarcely so much. But I have not finished. The Dauphin's eyes were a dark blue. This man's are pale. And then the nose. The Dauphin's was small, straight, slightly tip-tilted. This man's is boldly aquiline. And then his age. If the Dauphin were alive today he would be just twenty-nine. Take a good look at that man, Monsieur le Marquis. He is standing beside Mademoiselle de Castillon-Fouquières. Could anyone judge him to be a day less than thirty-five? And consider his manners and his speech. So little are they natural to him, so often does the mask slip, that I ask myself how anyone can fail to see that we are dealing with an actor, another Hervagault. This man plays a part, and he plays it so indifferently that it should deceive no person of intelligence. I am sorry if we disagree, Monsieur le Marquis, but in so serious a case a man may not compromise with his conscience."

Now, it is unlikely that if to discover an impostor in Monsieur Deslys had not held out to the Marquis de Sceaux a sudden unexpected hope of destroying a formidable rival, he would have attached importance to Monsieur du Chatenay. He would have perceived in him an obviously vain man who from self-sufficiency must always be in opposition to generally accepted views. Jealousy, however, blind to everything else, is always sharp-sighted for what it seeks. It will insist on finding it even in the very teeth of reason. From the hope that a thing may be true, it is but a step to believing that true it is. This step Monsieur de Sceaux all but took within the hour.

They were dancing that night at the Hôtel d'Otranto, and under the glittering lustres of the splendid white-and-gold ballroom circled a throng made up of the beau monde of Paris. Monsieur Deslys did not dance. There had been yet no time to repair this, among many other gaps in his education. He was well content to sit as a spectator. Dressed with quiet elegance, he achieved distinction by the fact that he was almost the only man present who displayed no orders.

Mademoiselle de Castillon-Fouquières spent most of the evening at his side, declining all but occasional invitations to dance, so that her attendance upon him might not be unduly curtailed. She was at his side when the Marquis de Sceaux, fresh from the opinions of Monsieur du Chatenay, moved with his consequential step in quest of her. He beheld her across the ballroom. A diadem binding her smooth red hair, she was a resplendent figure of disdainfully repressed vitality. Languidly she moved a fan of ostrich plumes on which little diamonds sparkled like drops of water. Behind this, ever and anon, she intimately inclined her head to speak to Monsieur Deslys.

The sight of them thus was so infuriating to the Marquis that he could no longer doubt that all this beau monde assembled here by Fouché as the nucleus of a party was being egregiously deluded.

He had enough good sense not to trust himself in his present state of fury to interrupt that too intimate association. What he had to say would be better said tomorrow, by when he should have recovered his equanimity. It would be better said to her mother in the first instance, and he would exercise the authority which he accounted that he derived from the partial understanding that had already existed between Pauline and himself, so as to demand the immediate formal announcement of their betrothal. This would give him the right to put an end to an association that was already supplying a subject for scandal.

The postponement was unfortunate, for this happened to be the very moment judged by La Salle to supply the opportunity for which he had advised that they should wait. Late that night, or very early on the following morning, after the last guest had departed and the last candle had been extinguished in the Hôtel d'Otranto, La Salle sought the luxurious circular boudoir adjacent to the regal bedroom occupied by Deslys. He found him in the act of being put to bed by the smooth, efficient Italian valet who had ministered to him from the moment that he had appeared in the Duke of Otranto's household. Upon La Salle's intimation that he desired a word with Monsieur Deslys before he retired, the valet was dismissed.

"I hope you will not keep me long," said Deslys. "I am tired."

La Salle's sardonic eye appraised him, amused by, whilst yet approving, a manner that daily became more royal.

Wrapped in a flaming satin dressing-gown, Deslys reclined rather wearily on a sofa that was striped in two shades of old rose. The weariness of which he complained was real enough to produce a certain pallor which added refinement to the narrow face. There was a petulance about the full lips and a wrinkle between the arched brows which accorded with the ungracious tone in which he had spoken.

La Salle sank into a deep arm-chair and crossed his legs.

"I have no wish to keep you long, for I am tired, myself, which is not surprising when you consider how I labour all day and more than half the night in your interests. But, of course, you would not think of that. You display so many truly royal characteristics that I am daily more confident of your ultimate success."

Deslys turned a peevish glance with significance to the Sèvres timepiece on the onyx overmantel. "Won't your sarcasms keep till morning?"

"My sarcasms will. But there's something else that won't. Monsieur d'Otranto perceives a certain urgency, a certain gravity, and also a certain delicacy, in the matter on which I have to talk to you. It concerns Pauline de Castillon-Fouquières."

Deslys roused himself from his languor. His frown deepened. "How?" he asked.

"There is no need for alarm. On the contrary, my mission is one that should be very welcome. I bring you what amounts to a proposal of marriage. His Grace of Otranto requests your authority formally to ask the Duchess of Castillon-Fouquières on your behalf for her daughter's hand."

Deslys stared at him now with round eyes of startled horror, the real source of which La Salle may well have guessed. The young man's conscience, lately lulled by the excitements of which he was the centre, and by the spell which the grace and beauty of Pauline de Castillon-Fouquières had undoubtedly cast over it, was suddenly clamant. Justine Perrin, the memory of whom had been blurred of late by the swiftly successive events that bore him ever higher, seemed suddenly to stand reproachfully before him. When at last he found his voice, it was hoarse.

"What need is there for this at present?"

"The need perceived by the Duchess of Castillon-Fouquières."

"Ah!" There was a flash of suspicion from the prominent eyes. "And Pauline?"

"Mademoiselle de Castillon-Fouquières will hardly have been consulted yet. But since she appears to take as much pleasure in your society as you obviously take in hers, I see no grounds for serious fear that she will raise any obstacle."

"Fear!" Deslys laughed shortly, unpleasantly. "It isn't fear that's troubling me." He spoke coarsely, the peasant emerging from the ermine.

"Then there is nothing to trouble you. You are a very fortunate and enviable young man."

Deslys made a gesture of exasperation. "I don't... It is that..." Again he stumbled. Then finding at last the path, he went racing on. "Mademoiselle de Castillon-Fouquières is not of a station to marry the King of France."

La Salle repressed a desire to laugh. "Is Your Majesty proposing, then, to make her the maîtresse en titre?"

This time he was answered in a blaze of wrath. "How dare you ask me that?"

"Because I must know where we stand. In heaven's name don't let us become theatrical. Things have changed a good deal since your alleged father was guillotined. A France that swallowed the Empress Josephine will not strain at Queen Pauline. So you may dismiss that doubt. In fact, I had better tell you that in the pass to which things have come you are not likely ever to be King of France unless you make this marriage."

"I am not to be constrained. I shall marry when I please and whom I please."

"Shall we be reasonable? What king was ever given license to do that? Kings may love where they please, but they marry as they are directed. You are fortunate, it seems to me, in being offered the opportunity to do both."

"Am I?" It was a cry of angry denial.

"Are you not?"

Deslys abandoned argument along that line. "What directs that I marry Mademoiselle de Castillon?"

"Your own conduct and the lady's honour, which you have deeply compromised by the assiduity of your attentions."

"The assiduity has been hers."

"Oh, my dear Charles!" La Salle showed him a shocked countenance. "This is too royal. It is not gallant. It is not generous. You are not to suppose that a Castillon-Fouquières will play Dubarry to your Louis XVII. But only the announcement of your betrothal will now remove the scandalous suspicion of it. Madame la Duchesse has issued an ultimatum in those terms to Monsieur Fouché."

"And why must I obey Madame la Duchesse?"

"Because behind Madame la Duchesse there is the entire Faubourg St Germain – three-quarters of the old nobility of France which she brings to your support."

"She has already brought it," cried Deslys. "It has accepted me."

La Salle vouchsafed him a long, cold stare. Then he broke suddenly into a laugh that was like a whiplash. "Name of God! There are moments when I ask myself whether you are not really a Bourbon after all, a by-blow of some member of that family. You display such a princely regard for the debt incurred, such a princely readiness to default. I suppose that you regard me as a scoundrel, Charles. And I suppose that I am one. But hardly so royally cold-blooded a scoundrel as you."

Deslys came to his feet in a pet. "You shall not speak to me so. I will not tolerate it."

"You'll tolerate a great deal more, or else you'll go back to your cows and your clocks. Sit down and listen to me, my lad. You might cheat the Castillon-Fouquières as you propose. But behind the Castillon-Fouquières there is Fouché. And you'll not cheat Fouché. No man ever did that."

Deslys would not be calmed. He stood wringing his podgy hands. "It is infamous so to constrain me, and I will not be constrained or threatened." He gathered firmness again. "Understand me. There are limits to what I can endure. Fouché will not find it so easy to destroy what he has built for me. Don't let him drive me to defiance, or he may discover his error."

"My dear Charles, please sit down and calm yourself. No good ever comes of heat. Just listen to me. If you were really the Orphan of the Temple, and you could prove it beyond possibility of doubt, defiance of Fouché would still have no result but to destroy you. Fouché is necessary to you. But you are not necessary to Fouché. You are merely convenient, as an acceptable substitute to Louis XVIII. Do not imagine that you are the only available substitute. He could restore Bonaparte, he could bring in the Duke of Reichstadt as Napoleon II, or he could bring in Louis Philippe d'Orléans. He prefers you because as the Orphan of the Temple you are a romantic figure such as the populace is ever ready to take to its silly heart, and still more because he believes that you will prove docile. Supply him with proof that you can be recalcitrant and it will be the immediate end of you. Fouché's only loyalty is to himself."

Deslys sat down heavily, sapped already of the strength he had summoned up. He took his head in his hands. "I am caught in a trap," he groaned.

"Trap? Rubbish! Many a better man would thank God to be caught in such a trap. You grow too exigent. You've lived soft since you've been under my protection, in ever increasing luxury. Already your existence is princely. Already the wealth and homage you command are fantastic to a man of your origins, and you rail against Fate for heaping yet more favours on you."

Deslys lowered his hands, and in the eyes that stared miserably across at him La Salle caught again that beaten-dog glance which he remembered from Brandenburg. "You are mocking me, I think, Florence. Knowing what you know, you must be mocking me. It is cruel. You are cruel, Florence. Hard and cruel, as my poor Justine said. You are inhuman. I wish to God that I had never seen you."

"That is to wish that you were still making clocks in Le Locle or herding cows at Passavant. And that is stupid. As stupid as to call me cruel, when you really mean that I am intelligent. Because I am intelligent and your friend, I cannot find it in my heart to regret that the indiscretion of your conduct towards Mademoiselle de Castillon-Fouquières should have resulted in a situation entirely to your advantage."

He rose, and went to stand over the troubled man, setting a hand familiarly upon his shoulder. "Sleep on it," he said gently. "And in the morning authorize me to tell the Duke of Otranto that he may ask the Duchess of Castillon-Fouquières on your behalf for her daughter's hand. Pauline de Castillon will bring you both power and happiness."

Charles stared before him, his face set in lines of despair.

"I suppose," he groaned, "that in this world a man must pay for everything."

La Salle preferred not to understand him. He patted the shoulder under his hand. "Few men obtain so much for so little, Charles. Good night." He turned to depart.

Deslys sent a sneer after him. "Always the advocate of your own interests, are you not, Florence? It would wreck all your hopes if in the morning I were to announce a different decision."

La Salle smiled from the threshold. "Nevertheless, I shall sleep soundly. You may be reckless in your attachments, Charles, but your conscience is princely. I trust to that."

Chapter 5

Exit Monsieur de Sceaux

Monsieur de Sceaux, coming to the Hôtel d'Otranto on the morrow for a decisive understanding with the Duchess of Castillon-Fouquières, found the ground which he had imagined so firm and solid suddenly crumbling under his feet. The news with which the Duchess greeted him whilst he was still kissing her hand produced that landslide.

For once this splendid, self-assured gentleman found himself entirely out of countenance.

The Duchess beamed upon him, blind to his discomfiture. "You will, I know, my old friend, rejoice with us in the dazzling future that awaits Pauline. You will want to felicitate her. She is in the little salon, there."

Without any sign of the expected rejoicing, and still speechless, the Marquis, almost waved away by the jewelled hand of the majestic Duchess, bowed himself out of the boudoir into the little salon where Pauline was writing. At his approach she looked up with a calm, self-possessed smile of greeting.

"I fall from the skies," he announced, in a strained voice. "If any but madame your mother had told me what I have just heard, I should not have believed it. I am to felicitate you, I am informed, upon a betrothal."

"You are very kind," said the coldly demure Pauline.

"You misunderstand me. I have no felicitations to offer. I am amazed…indignant at this…incredible breach of faith. It is an affront. Nothing less. And it does not comfort me that you will one day probably regret it."

"I am not sure," said Pauline, her fine brows drawing together, "that you are not being impertinent."

"Most pertinent, believe me, unless you choose to ignore that I love you. Are you so heartless that the pledges that have passed between us count for nothing against ambition?"

She laid down her pen and sat round to face him squarely. She remained a miracle of cool self-possession. "You have no right to say that, and you exaggerate grossly when you speak of pledges. It is to take too much for granted. I liked you very well, Monsieur le Marquis, and I should wish to have you continue my friend. But for more than that we are scarcely suitable in age. I am not to be blamed because my feelings are what they are; and, these feelings apart, I am following the wishes of my mother. Ambition is not concerned in my betrothal, and it is an indelicacy to suggest it."

"I am relieved to hear that. As your friend, I am profoundly relieved." His angry sarcasm was not to be missed. "For if it were not so you might find yourself dismally cheated in the end."

Her head rose a little higher on her perfect neck, and the frown returned to her white brow. "I don't think I understand the innuendo. It is an innuendo, is it not? If you would be plain with me, like a good friend."

"To be plain, then, you may find that you have abandoned a substance for a shadow."

She trilled a delicate little laugh. "You certainly have the advantage in substance, monsieur."

He flushed darkly. "You are witty, mademoiselle. You may discover how much I have the advantage in substance when this fellow proves, indeed, to be a shadow. Have you considered that he might be an impostor?"

"I am not given to considering foolishness."

"You are sure that it is foolishness. Well, well. Yet you might remember that there have been not a few Louis the Seventeenths already, each of whom found a following. What do we know of Monsieur Deslys, after all?"

"Really, Marquis! This is worse than a foolishness. You have only to look at him."

"Yet one or two who had the honour of the Dauphin's acquaintance have looked at him without being convinced."

"And the words of these one or two are to have more weight than those of the scores, including Madame de Rambaud his nurse, who recognized him beyond doubt."

"To recognize a child of seven or eight in a man of thirty must always be an achievement."

For a moment she was stern. "How long have you doubted, Marquis?"

"That is nothing to the point."

"True," she cruelly agreed. "Your doubts really matter no more than your convictions."

His large, full face empurpled. "I see that I talk in vain. Indeed, I wonder that I talk at all. You have chosen. That is enough for me. Your very obedient servant, mademoiselle." He bowed low, and withdrew with great dignity.

On the threshold he came face to face with Monsieur Deslys, who arrived. He bowed again, frigidly, and passed out.

Deslys looked over his shoulder after him.

"Monsieur de Sceaux is in a hurry."

Pauline smiled with a twist of the lips. "Let him go. A malicious, foolish man. He had the effrontery to suggest... What do you suppose? That you are an impostor."

That brought Deslys to a sudden standstill, his face blank. Then he shrugged.

"It is inevitable that there should be some to say that." He drew nearer. "Are you not afraid?"

"Afraid? Afraid of what?"

"That those who say so might prevail."

She rose, and his gloomy eyes admired the grace of the movement, the splendid poise of her as she stood with folded hands, a steady smile on her lips. "What then? I am marrying Charles Deslys. Not Louis XVII."

The avowal increased the distress in his countenance, the awkward nervousness of his manner. "You mean that if I were to remain just Charles Deslys you would still not regret what has happened today?"

She lowered her eyes under his stare, and for the first time he beheld in her an access of shyness. "Must you force me to confess it?" she murmured. "Don't you know yet how wholly I am yours?"

He drew nearer still. He took her hand. "Pauline..." he began, and there seemed to choke with an emotion which she misunderstood so completely that she leaned against him, and the proud head with its glory of red-gold hair came to rest upon his shoulder.

"Even if what Monsieur de Sceaux said in his malice should be really true, I should still be yours, and yours only, Charles."

It is to be doubted if he ever clearly understood what happened to him in that moment, for what he did had held no place in his intentions when he sought her. Her propinquity, the utter surrender to him her words avowed, a perfume as of lilac that assailed him from her, all served to intoxicate his senses. With a little inarticulate cry he bent his head and kissed her.

Later, in the circular boudoir that was his own stronghold, he confessed it in shamed amazement to La Salle. And La Salle was so far from understanding his trouble that he smiled, nodded, rubbed his hands, and said: "Perfect!"

In sheer vindictiveness for this, Deslys then announced that Monsieur de Sceaux had suggested that he was an impostor. This roused La Salle from his normal phlegm.

"Ah, that! Name of a name! But he must be persuaded of his error. And at once."

"Pish! What does it matter?"

"Matter? Sacred name of a dog! Do you know nothing of the world? You may shout yourself hoarse proclaiming a man's virtue, and no one pays attention. Whisper a word of his vices and the world is all ears. I must put a muzzle on Monsieur de Sceaux."

"What do you mean by that?" Deslys showed alarm.

"Ask me when it's done. For I don't know yet. It will depend upon this chattering Marquis. My immediate business is to find out where he is lodged. Fouché will tell me."

He was actually turning to go; but Deslys, thoroughly alarmed by his sinister determination, sprang after him to clutch his arm.

"What are you going to do?"

"I am certainly not going to kiss his hands."

"You mean to pick a quarrel with him."

La Salle smiled upon the other's blank terror, and for once his smile was almost tender. "Be easy, Charles. For years I lived by keeping a faro bank for the instruction of fools to my own profit. It has its risks, and I learnt to take care of myself. When I shall have given myself the pleasure of calling Monsieur de Sceaux a liar, he can have either steel or lead from me, at his own choice. But he'll have one or the other."

"Not on my behalf." Charles was vehement. He hung more heavily upon La Salle's arm as he spoke. "Not on my behalf. I will not have it, Florence."

La Salle looked at him steadily. "Just so on a day of August twenty-two years ago your supposed father ordered his Swiss Guard when they were preparing to sweep the Carrousel clear of an insurgent mob. As a result the Swiss were massacred to a man, and Louis XVI was ultimately guillotined."

"What has that to do with this?"

"History is repeating itself. I am your Swiss Guard."

"You are being mad. There is no need for panic. And, anyway, I'll not have murder done."

"Murder! What a word!"

"The only word for what you have in mind, Florence. I will not have it. Do you hear?"

The door opened, and the gaunt figure of Fouché stood before them. Deslys' voice, strident in its vehemence, had reached him as he approached. Under their low lids his eyes looked dead as a snake's; his thin lips were set in their eternal smile.

"Messieurs, what is happening?"

It was Deslys who answered him, without reservations. Some of that answer he cut short.

"Madame de Castillon has already told me. That is why I am here."

When Deslys went on to disclose the subject of his altercation with La Salle, Fouché's grin grew broader. "Heroic. Certainly heroic. But as certainly unnecessary. What harm do you conceive this fool can do?"

"What harm?" said La Salle. "He can carry a tale to the Tuileries that will make a fine stir and probably put several of us in prison. That is all."

"Really, Monsieur de La Salle, for a man of your wit you are guilty of a curious oversight. Shall we sit down?"

He waited punctiliously until Deslys had found a chair, then sank, in his feeble, weary way, to another. He spoke looking up at La Salle, who chose to remain standing. "Can you really suppose that of the hundreds who have come here and who have been admitted to the secret of Monsieur Deslys' identity, not one will already have betrayed us to the usurper? But what faith in human nature for one who knows his world as you do!

"Louis XVIII is fully aware by now of the presence in my house of his nephew, or, as he would say, of one who pretends to be his nephew. This is not an assumption. I have better means of knowing what passes at the Tuileries than the Tuileries has of knowing what passes at the Hôtel d'Otranto!"

He paused, and, looking from one to the other, seemed to enjoy the amazement he had summoned to both countenances. Then he coughed under cover of his bony, almost translucent, hand, and his thin voice continued.

"Actually, nothing could suit us better than an arrest. There are no lettres de cachet nowadays. The Revolution made an end of that. Arrest must be followed by public trial. And a trial would accomplish in a day what may require weeks and possibly even months by the methods I am pursuing." He sighed. "But I suspect that the usurper fears this as fully as we could desire it. I have good reason to suspect it. Monsieur d'André, so as to prepare evidence for the confusion of any false Louis XVII, lately gave orders to open the grave of the boy from the Temple buried under that name in the Madeleine Cemetery in '95. An order from the Tuileries compelled him to desist." He smiled again. "You see? The Count of Provence fears that such an exhumation might disclose the fact that whoever was buried in that grave was not his nephew. But if an arrest were made, an inquiry must follow, and I should take care that it began in the Madeleine Cemetery. The result would be so to strengthen the case of any pretender that the reigning Bourbons would have to look to themselves. I say the reigning Bourbons because I do not imagine that the Count of Provence is alone in this. His brother d'Artois is at present heir to the throne, and Madame d'Angoulême's husband is next in the succession. They desire no more than he does to witness the resurrection of Louis XVII.

"Nor yet is that all. At the Hospital for Incurables in the Rue de Sèvres there is an old woman who is an early acquaintance of yours, Monsieur Deslys, and of yours too, La Salle: the Widow Simon. She has long since been asserting that Louis XVII did not die in the Temple. Lately she has been relating in detail the manner of his evasion, details which accord perfectly with those you gave me, La Salle. A few days ago she was visited by a high functionary of the Minister of Police and warned under threat of severest penalties not to repeat this story.

"So you see, my dear La Salle, how unnecessary is the action you propose."

"Have you considered that I might precipitate matters by drawing a challenge from Monsieur de Sceaux, with full publication of my motives: that I have given him the lie for declaring Monsieur Deslys an impostor?"

"It has occurred to me. But all things considered, I should prefer to explode the bomb in my own time, unless, of course, our hand is forced."

Chapter 6

The Impostor

It was the unexpected that eventually forced the hand of the Duke of Otranto and compelled him to depart from the leisurely methods by which he was preparing the ground.

Early in January he was waited upon by three Bonapartists: the loud blustering Savary, whom he despised, accompanied by La Valette and Exelmans, of whom he had no very high opinion. The business on which they sought him supplied the explanation of reports he had lately received of activities in Elba. They came as the representatives and practical leaders of a group plotting the return of the Emperor, and their aim was to engage the assistance and support of this man of crises, this metteur-en-scène of Thermidor and Brumaire. Boldly they invited him to join them in overthrowing a government which appalled and exasperated the nation.

Suspecting that in seeking him they acted upon instructions from the Emperor, to whom they would report his attitude, and having learnt from life's uncertainties that there is no profit in opposing possibilities however remote, Fouché was entirely sympathetic. At the same time, he described the movement as premature. The nation was ripening fast for a change of government, but it could not yet be considered ripe, and he warned them of the dangers of precipitancy. In the proper season he would be happy to talk to them again. On that, having dismissed them under the favourable impression that they could count upon him when the time came, he immediately set to work to anticipate the change for which they plotted by the change at which he aimed. Loyalty to Fouché was, as La Salle had told Deslys, the only loyalty that existed for him. He had no faith at this stage in any plot to restore the Emperor, particularly if he were not, himself, at hand to guide it, and he had every reason to suppose that his own power would be more assured with a plastic Louis XVII than with a masterful Bonaparte. But in possession of definite information of the existence and extent of the plot, he perceived in it possibilities of distracting the nation's attention from the Orphan of the Temple at the very time when he desired it to be concentrated upon that personage.

In view of this emergency, he so far departed from the methods by which he had proposed to prevail, that he considered recourse to military measures, and to this end enlisted the co-operation of Drouet d'Erlon, who commanded the Sixteenth Division in the north.

Drouet, thoroughly disaffected, was not difficult to persuade. At a given signal from Fouché he would march upon Paris and seize the Tuileries, trusting to Fouché's influence with the National Guards either to bring them to revolt or at least to ensure that they should remain neutral.

So Drouet d'Erlon went off to Lille to his work of treason, and meanwhile the Duke of Otranto provided in a manner entirely characteristic against the Bonapartist danger to his schemes.

Although excluded from office and disdained by Louis XVIII, yet from time to time he had adopted the apparently odd course of sending his criticisms of government measures, sometimes to the King, sometimes to the Count of Artois, sometimes to the favourite Monsieur de Blacas, pointing out not only the error committed, but the inevitable and disastrous consequences to be expected if it were not speedily corrected.

You conceive that this was inspired by no kindness to a government that had slammed the door in his face, but by the desire to bring that government to understanding and regret of such a blunder. In this aim he certainly succeeded; for whilst his letters were contemptuously ignored, the certainty with which his prognostications were fulfilled had ended by arousing in those dullards an awed wonder of the uncanny acuteness of his political vision.

He sent now a note to the King's brother, in which he employed the phrase: "Your Ministry of Police knows nothing of its business, since it knows nothing of the plots by which His Majesty is threatened." And he followed this up by paying a visit to the Ministry of Justice, where he was respectfully received by the Chancellor Dambray, who besought him to disclose to what plot or plots he alluded in that note.

"That is the object of my visit," he replied. "I invite you to compare your police system with that which I established. For ten years nothing could happen in France without my instant knowledge of it. Now your police are the last to know what is taking place, even when it doesn't need a policeman to perceive it."

Dambray, alarmed by the sinister suggestion behind the words, chilled by that personality, of an almost reptilian coldness, ventured no resentment of the rebuke.

"But what, then, is happening, Monsieur le Duc?"

Fouché delivered his message. "The island of Elba is under no proper surveillance. Go and tell Monsieur de Blacas at once from me that if the present want of vigilance on the coast of France is allowed to continue, you may count upon having Bonaparte back with the swallows and the violets. That is all, Monsieur Dambray."

He departed with his tight-lipped smile, leaving alarm behind him, and a sudden haste on the part of the government to take measures which should thwart any interference with Monsieur Fouché's own plan to overthrow that same government. The obvious benevolence towards it to which his warning bore witness did for a moment lead it, further, to discredit all rumours of sinister intentions centred round a certain Monsieur Charles Deslys, to whom the Duke of Otranto was known to be dispensing a lavish hospitality. This, however, was not to endure long, for returning from his interview with Dambray, Fouché sent for La Salle.

"Immersed as you are in politics," he said, "you are neglecting your art. That is waste, and I detest waste. It is high time that a painter of your talent exhibited in the Salon."

"That has long been my opinion," said La Salle.

"Then here is a commission for you. It is for two pictures which no man living is better qualified to paint. The first, a large canvas of the late Royal Family in the Temple, giving particular prominence to the Dauphin. The second, a portrait of Monsieur Charles Deslys. What do you say to it?"

La Salle's astonishment was followed by a glimmer of understanding. "It may precipitate a crisis."

"Your quick grasp of things is a perpetual delight to me. I will have a studio prepared for you at once. All that you may need shall be placed at your disposal. Depend upon me to see not only that the pictures are exhibited, but that they are hung side by side. If that does not release the deluge that is to wash away the reigning Bourbons, then, my friend, the years devoted to the public service have taught me nothing.

"You will lose no time, La Salle. I should like to have this little palace revolution over before Monsieur de Talleyrand returns from Vienna." He said nothing of Napoleon returning from Elba. "One other recommendation, La Salle: you will paint Monsieur Deslys' portrait with all the clever little impostures you employed in the picture with which you first enlisted my own interest." His smile broadened. "You will paint him in ceremonial dress and with powdered hair. This – also one of your clever little ruses – will dissemble a colour that might be accounted too dark, and it will emphasize his likeness to Queen Marie-Antoinette."

When La Salle communicated this to Deslys, it set the clock-maker staring. "But does he believe in me, or does he not?"

La Salle made a dubious lip. "At first I thought he did; then I thought he didn't; then I thought he did. Oh, my friend, if I could tell you what Monsieur Fouché believes, my name would not be La Salle. It would be God."

And there you have the secret history of the manner in which per saltum and quite fortuitously Florence de La Salle achieved that fame as a painter of which he had long since abandoned all hope, and of which – it must be confessed – he was certainly not deserving.

When as a result of the irresistible wire-pulling of the Duke of Otranto those two pictures came to be exhibited in the Salon, the questions, within a week, on the lips of everyone not previously acquainted with the two men thus advertised were, "Who is Monsieur Charles Deslys?" and "Who is Florence de La Salle?" To the first of these questions the answer was instantly and spontaneously supplied.

They were creditable paintings. As a result of the assiduous and varied labour devoted to the subject, from the days of David's atélier, twenty years earlier, La Salle never painted anything better than the picture entitled *Portrait of Monsieur Charles Deslys*. Indeed, he never painted anything as good. *The Royal Family in the Temple* is also representative of his best work. He was at pains to make it so. For the purpose he visited the Temple again and made numerous sketches; he collected portraits of Louis XVI, and of Marie-Antoinette, and helped himself freely to what he needed from them. For the portrait of the Queen there can be no doubt – although this was not noticed at the time – that he borrowed shamelessly from Vigée Lebrun, which is why, next to the Dauphin's, hers is the best portrait in the group. Much inferior to these are his portraits of Madame Royale, for which he seems to have depended mainly upon the sketches he had made in the Temple, and of Madame Elizabeth, the discovery of models for which cost him a great deal of time and labour.

February had been reached before the pictures were exhibited. Meanwhile, the preparation of the ground had gone steadily forward.

Drouet d'Erlon at Lille awaited marching orders, and at hand such eminent soldiers as Ney and Davout were ready to support Charles

Deslys' claim. But Fouché still hoped to avoid recourse to military measures. He counted upon so shaping public opinion into acknowledgment of Deslys as the Orphan of the Temple that Louis XVIII would be constrained by it to surrender the throne to him. And the crowning assault upon public opinion was delivered by the exhibition of La Salle's two paintings.

From the ever-increasing crowds that flocked to see them in the Salon, the news flamed out through every class and section of Paris, and began thence to spread into the country, that Louis XVII had escaped from the Temple prison and was alive.

With the fantastic stories invented by the public so as to explain this portent we are not concerned, but with the events that followed upon the exhibition. They came quickly, which was what Monsieur d'Otranto expected; but the course they ran was not at all in accordance with his calculations. For once his prescience was at fault. The government of Louis XVIII, stricken as it seemed with a paralysis of panic, displayed no sign of life in the presence of the rapidly spreading conviction that Louis XVII had come back to claim his own. The only feeble counterblast that might be attributed to it was an attempted revival of the old ignoble scandal of the Dauphin's illegitimacy. It was as if Louis XVIII meant to take his stand upon the ground that even if the son of Marie-Antoinette had survived, there was no claim he could advance, since Louis XVI was not his father.

But a slander which had been eagerly adopted by revolutionaries glad of anything that might bring the monarchy into disrepute, made no headway against the emotional tide in favour of the Orphan of the Temple, regarded as heaven-sent to deliver France from a government that it disliked and despised.

Never since coming to Paris had Charles Deslys in any sense practised concealment; but never – and this at the urging of Fouché – had he displayed himself so freely as when the exhibition of his portrait in juxtaposition to the picture of the Royal Family had drawn all eyes to him and rendered him the dominant topic of conversation in Paris.

When he rode now in the Bois or along the old Cours la Reine, as he did on fine days, commonly accompanied by Mademoiselle de Castillon-Fouquières and followed at a distance by a couple of mounted grooms in the Otranto livery, the passers-by stood still, not merely to stare, but many of them to salute him. At the Opéra and the Théâtre Français he was now a regular attendant, and one night, a fortnight after the Salon sensation, his appearance beside the Duchess of Castillon-Fouquières and Pauline, with La Salle in attendance, supplied the occasion for a demonstration. Upon his entrance two-thirds of the audience rose, faced his box, and remained standing until he had taken his seat. One suspects that Fouché was not entirely innocent of having engineered this display, and that a numerous claque in his pay was dispersed through the audience to supply a lead for those who chose to follow it.

Deslys behaved with a calm that La Salle found admirable, contrasting in this with Pauline de Castillon-Fouquières, who, still preserving her rigidly upright carriage, yet quivered and sparkled with excitement at this foretaste of the royal honours she was destined to share.

It was very odd, La Salle reflected, that Deslys, impulsive, hasty and emotional, could yet preserve in the face of this homage a self-possession to be expected only in one born, whilst Pauline, so cold and hard and normally imperious, should betray the extent to which she was moved by these attentions. The truth is that, ambitious and expectant though she had ever been, she found herself on a threshold of achievement far transcending her loftiest aspirations. Not all the arrogant pride of her nature could render commonplace to her the fact that she was likely to become Queen of France, she who three months ago had complacently been accepting the prospect of becoming a marchioness.

She was in an intoxication that melted a little the frozen splendour of her bearing, and it is to be doubted if she bestowed a thought on the impassioned and unfortunate de Sceaux, so summarily dismissed. She might at least have been grateful to him for having made no trouble and for having quietly departed. For de Sceaux had completely vanished. It was not merely that he had dropped out of the society she frequented; he had left Paris on the day after his last interview with her, according to the information of Fouché, whose vigilance was unremitting.

If to the world in general Pauline de Castillon-Fouquières could graciously unbend from her austerity in those delirious days, to Deslys she gave proof of a tenderness and womanliness which played havoc with his reluctant senses. Despite himself he had come gradually under the spell of her beauty and her matchless poise, and now her fond displays on his behalf of a palpitating muliebrity were to him as the incredible condescensions of a goddess turned worshipper. He was at once exalted and tormented by this evidence that what he regarded as purely a marriage of convenience was considered by her an affair of the heart.

A climax was reached on the night of that demonstration at the Opéra. Back at the Hôtel d'Otranto, in her mother's boudoir, during one of those rare moments when she and Charles were alone together, she cast from her in her intoxication the last vestige of her normal hauteur. Flushed of countenance, a feverish glitter in her magnificent eyes, she took him impulsively by the shoulders.

"Charles, why do we wait? Is it your wish that we should?"

Disconcerted by this sudden onslaught, troubled too because unable to escape the allurements of a woman so desirable, he avoided her glance and faltered in his fencing answer. "There are wishes other than mine to be considered."

"Are there? I do not know them. Sire," she addressed him, as if to remind him of what he was, "you are the master. It is for you to command."

"Not yet. I am not yet crowned. Are you forgetting it?"

She removed her hands from his shoulders and stepped back. The splendid eyes were misty. "Why are you so unkind?"

"Unkind!" His distress deepened at that accusation. "My dear, I am all kindness. We do not know what we may yet have to encounter, what unsuspected obstacles may yet defeat me, and so cheat you."

"Cheat me? How could I be cheated if you love me? So long as I am not cheated of that, what else matters?"

She came to him again, all womanliness, and again set her hands upon his shoulders. Of a height, they stood eye to eye. "Do you know me so little even now that you can suppose I ask anything but love of the man I marry?"

He winced, startled at once by the avowal and the utter frankness of its terms. If on the one hand he might take pride in the conquest of so rare a woman, on the other there was the abiding distress of having awakened passion where he had conceived that no more than a political marriage was expected of him. Out of this conjunction of emotions was born a wistful regret that it should be so, and a reluctance – blending chivalry with weakness – to handle other than gently the love that was offered him. He must pay the price of the thing he had done by leaving her under the fond illusion which she so artlessly revealed.

"Of me," he evaded, "you have the right to ask something more."

She shook her head. Her smile was a miracle of tenderness. "There is nothing more, nothing greater."

And then a further troubling of his senses made it easy for him to play the very perfect, gentle knight. "My dear!" He took her by her slender waist, drew her close and bestowed upon her the kiss that she invited. "Never," he said, and in this at least there can be no doubt of his sincerity, "was woman more clearly designed by Heaven for a throne."

"Are your thoughts still for making a queen of me, when all that I ask is that you make a wife of me? And this, Charles, you may now make me when you will."

Sounds of Madame de Castillon-Fouquières' approach set them apart and rescued him, as he supposed, from a position of difficulty. Pauline spoke tonight from a heart surcharged with emotion. Tomorrow, her normal poise recovered, she would hardly be likely to renew an invitation to an immediate wedding, which he found as embarrassing as it was flattering. And very possibly had she waited until the morrow it would have been precisely as he surmised. But from that same surcharge of emotion, and assuming that if his assent had not been expressed, it was only because the advent of her mother had robbed him of the opportunity, she flung him into fresh confusion by informing the Duchess that they had taken the decision to be married at the earliest moment, betide what might.

The Duchess, who was also under the spell of that demonstration in the theatre, saw no reason to oppose them. At the same time, she reminded them that their station in life scarcely permitted them to approach the altar like any ordinary pair of lovers. Considerations of State were involved, and whilst she did not imagine that they would really offer obstacles, yet she must take the night for thought before giving her consent.

For Deslys, too, the night was one for thought, so troublesome that in the middle of it he rose, sought La Salle's room and aroused him from his peaceful slumber.

"I want you to make me a promise, Florence. When I am King I shall require you to travel to Passavant to Justine, to tell her what has happened to me. When she knows that I am King she will understand. She may cease then in her heart to reproach me for pursuing the course of my destiny."

La Salle blinked and frowned at him in the dim candle-light. "Do you break into my sleep for this?"

"I am troubled, Florence. Deeply troubled."

"You have a conscience, then, after all? And it possesses the common habit of awakening in the silent watches of the night, does it?"

"I have come to you for help, Florence. Don't jeer." He was gently reproachful. "Things have happened to disturb my mind. I shall never have peace until Justine knows all the truth, until I am assured that she understands. And you could make her understand. It will be something to have your promise that you will do this for me when the time comes."

So as to be rid of him La Salle gave him that promise. But the marriage, the prospect of which had so disturbed Deslys' mind, was none so imminent as he supposed. When the Duchess, taking Deslys with her, went to place the project before Fouché on the following morning, he uncompromisingly opposed it. If, on the one hand, Deslys was relieved, on the other, he was profoundly irritated by the display of that mastery which Fouché knew how to exert when most he professed to serve.

"The notion, sir, is most untimely. It must wait until the more serious business is settled."

Out of his irritation, Deslys actually found himself insisting upon the very step he desired to postpone. "To me there is no business more serious than just this."

"You hear him, my friend," the Duchess remonstrated.

"Oh, I hear. But, with respect, I counsel a correction of these fevers. Marriage may be contracted any day. A throne can be reached only when the moment serves. It is a journey upon which encumbrances are not desirable."

"You consider Mademoiselle de Castillon an encumbrance?" Deslys was bristling.

"It is not polite," said the Duchess.

But Fouché was not affected. "Anything is an encumbrance that may dim the popularity of a man to whom popularity is of the first importance."

"How can Pauline dim that?" demanded the indignant mother.

Fouché exhibited his tight-lipped grin. He continued to address himself to Deslys. "Once you are King, you may marry as you please in reason. In these times, as I have already had the honour to point out to you, and with the precedents that exist for condescension, no opposition to Pauline de Castillon-Fouquières is to be apprehended. But if when you come forward openly as a claimant you are dragging a wife at your heels, a good deal of prestige with the populace will be lost to you. And the populace counts for a great deal in these times. Add to this that marriage is in itself a distraction; and distractions at such a time are to be avoided." His tone hardened. "I beg of you, sir, in prudence to dismiss the thought until we are at the Tuileries."

Charles looked into that cadaverous face and was taken with a sudden hatred of the eternal smile which made of his countenance a transparent mask of obsequiousness upon an indomitable will. Baffled, defeated, humiliated by the sense of his own weakness in the presence of that formidable mastery, he sullenly abandoned an insistence which had merely been evoked by opposition.

Nor was this by any means the only clash of wills between them in those days of confident waiting for the rising tide of national emotion to sweep Deslys upward to the throne.

Fouché was busy upon a partial remodelling of the constitution, the charter which had been imposed upon Louis XVIII; and, profiting by experience, he was so strengthening and clarifying its terms that no king should ever again find it easy to disregard them, as Louis XVIII had done. Upon this he laboured unremittingly, so that when the hour struck he should be ready with a new charter that should confirm the hopes with which France would be hailing the advent of a new monarch.

Deslys lent himself very willingly to the project, conceiving that it would be for him to work it out in conjunction with Fouché. His avowed notion was that this charter should be the expression of his will, and that Fouché's experience should be employed merely to guide him in the terms of it. He was soon disillusioned. It was Fouché's mind and Fouché's will that the charter was to express, framed by him in collaboration with the four men he selected to form the nucleus of the new government that should presently arise. True, he made none of these provisional appointments without consulting Deslys. When, however, Deslys found that there was not one amongst these four of whom he could approve, whilst there were two of whom he violently disapproved, and when nevertheless they were brought in to form the embryonic cabinet, he realized in resentment that the consultation had been the merest mockery.

The first to whom he objected was Michel Ney, submitted by Fouché to be his Minister for War. He was at a loss for arguments with which to assail Ney's competence, and knew himself incapable of forming a judgment upon it. But he also knew that he did not like Ney, and he said so bluntly, conceiving that this should be enough.

Fouché raised his brows. "That, sir, is regrettable. The loss to your councils of the Prince de la Moskowa would be so serious that I venture to ask you to be more explicit."

They sat in Fouché's nobly appointed study, a lofty pillared chamber, lined in cedar where it was not lined with books. The Duke was at his writing-table, a choice specimen of cabinet-making of the days of Louis XV encrusted with chiselled ormolu; Deslys, in an arm-chair, faced him, whilst La Salle, who had also been brought into the discussion, leaned in the embrasure of one of the tall windows, little more than an interested observer.

Deslys shifted uncomfortably. He had no desire to be explicit. His dislike of Ney was personal and instinctive. Ney's manner towards him had wounded a vanity of which in these days he was giving ever-increasing signs. The red-headed, handsome son of the soil who had risen to be one of Napoleon's greatest marshals lacked courtly graces. He had served a genius who was authority incarnate, and no lesser claimant to a throne could ever awaken his respect. Perceiving in Deslys neither the strength nor the ability which he demanded in any man by whom he would choose to be commanded, he had been at no pains to pretend himself impressed by this prospective monarch.

"It is just that I should not be happy to work with him."

"If that is all, a little patience, sir, will overcome it." Fouché was smooth as silk. "The Prince de la Moskowa is a great figure in France; a romantic figure; he strikes the imagination vividly. 'The bravest of the brave' is the proud title his achievements have won him. You cannot dispense with him, sir."

"But must I, then, have persons about me whom I do not like?" His tone grew petulant.

Fouché continued to smile. La Salle, observing, considered that a little of this was all very well; but Deslys must not overdo it. So he held himself in readiness to apply the brakes should the career become too headlong.

"Believe me, sir," purred the Duke, "it is more important to have about you men you can trust than men whom you like."

"I could never trust anyone I did not like."

"To that the only answer I can make is to remind you that your uncle's downfall will certainly be due to his indulgence of his personal likes in his ministers. Let me urge that as a warning. A single favourite can do a king more harm than a dozen mistresses."

"I am not asking for favourites. I am asking for men towards whom I can feel friendly. That is all. Why not Davout, for instance? He is well born and a man of great ability, of much wider knowledge and experience than the Prince de la Moskowa."

"The Duke of Auerstadt?" Fouché pursed his lips. "An excellent suggestion. He is certainly all that you say, sir. And he is of a shrewdness and sagacity that fully justify the preference." He paused, and Deslys knew that Fouché merely humoured him, cloyed his palate before administering the bitter draught. "Unfortunately, Davout is a difficult man; a little too masterful; not easily managed. It has always been his fault and it has greatly detracted from his merit. His birth?" Again the thin lips were pursed, as if in dubious thought. "I wonder if even that is an advantage. There has been a revolution. Something remains of the sentiments it begot. Ney's appointment would be a proof of the liberality of your views, sir. Decidedly, I think, you must choose Ney. It is not in my power to advise you better. We will say Ney, then, for the Ministry of War." And he set down the name on the sheet before him, without waiting for a reply. "Let us pass on to the finances. There the choice is easy. Indeed, it is no matter of choice at all. Ouvrard is our man, of course."

"Ah, that, no!" The resentment stifled in the case of Ney exploded violently now. "That, no!"

Fouché who had been about to write the name, paused and looked up.

"But whom else, sir?"

"I don't know. But someone else it will have to be."

Fouché rubbed his nose reflectively. He sighed. "That would be enough for me if only I could think of anyone else. But I know of no one as skilled in finance as Ouvrard. He can work miracles."

"He is a thief," said Deslys uncompromisingly. "A gutter-bred swindler who has amassed millions by impudent robbery of the State."

Fouché permitted himself to look amazed. "To whom have you been listening, sir?"

"To the voice of common report. All the world knows what I have just said. You cannot pretend ignorance of it, Monsieur le Duc."

There was more truth in this than Deslys, himself, could suspect; for a deal of Fouché's vast fortune had resulted from his association with Ouvrard. Nevertheless, Fouché remained impassive. He laid down his pen and rested his elbows on the table.

"In a long and active life, sir, I have learnt to mistrust nothing so much as the voice of common report. So deep is this mistrust that whenever a common report reaches me, I begin to assume that the opposite is probably the truth."

"But this man has been gaoled for his dishonesty."

"Bonaparte was not always scrupulous. That should not prejudice you, sir. Against the voice of common report let me set some facts within my knowledge. In Brumaire of the Year VIII, when Bonaparte seized power and established the Consulate, there was not a crown in the national treasury, not enough to pay for the hire of couriers to carry into the provinces the news of the change of government. The bankers of Paris were summoned to the Consul's aid. But they had no courage. Three millions was all that they could be coerced into offering. Then Ouvrard came forward and saved Bonaparte's situation by pouring ten millions into the exhausted treasury."

"Where did he find them?"

"We can return to that if you consider it important. For years it was Ouvrard who by the sagacity with which he handled the finances averted the bankruptcy that constantly threatened Bonaparte. Is it not enough for us that that Colossus thought fit to lean upon this banker? And not only Bonaparte. The splendours of the Bourbon restoration were due to the financial assistance Ouvrard supplied."

"For which, no doubt, he would see that he was richly compensated."

"But of course." Fouché looked straight at Deslys, and he was not smiling now. There was a sudden rasp to the thin voice. "Is it not your notion, sir, that the men who help you to your throne should be worthy of some recompense?"

Deslys flushed. His glance fell away in confusion from Fouché's steady eye. "Oh, but naturally. Naturally," he faltered, uncomfortably conscious always of that stern regard.

"Very well, then." And the masterful rasp was still present in the Duke's voice. "In the matter of Ouvrard we cannot forget that help has already been forthcoming." He turned over some papers, and consulted one of them. "At this moment you are in his debt to the extent of four millions."

Deslys jumped. "Four millions! Four millions? I am in his debt for that? But how, sir? How?"

Fouché's smile was now patient, tolerant. "How do you conceive, sir, that the underground campaign by which we have all but established your identity has been conducted? How do you imagine that I have kept myself so minutely informed in your interests of everything that happens in every rank of society? This entails the employment of an army; and armies must be paid, especially civilian ones."

"Why was I not told of this?"

Fouché shrugged. "It is not usual for a prince to trouble himself about minor details of organization, or to go into the accounts. But if you wish to do so, the accounts are there and scrupulously kept. Besides, there are at this moment funds to your credit in the Bank of France amounting to over a million."

"And this is the first I hear of it?"

"Really, sir! Is that quite reasonable? Have you lacked for anything proper to your station? Clothes, servants, horses, jewels for presentation? Only last week there was a diadem for Mademoiselle de Castillon-Fouquières procured at a cost of two hundred thousand francs. How did you imagine that these things were obtained for you?"

Chapfallen, Deslys stared into the grinning death's head. "I thought that you…"

"That I supplied such sums?"

"Oh, but only as loans, of course."

"I should not have hesitated if I had not seen that I could serve you better by attaching to your fortunes a man who is a magician with the touch of Midas. So I brought in Ouvrard." He took up the pen again, and dipped it. "And you will end, sir, by being thankful that an appointment foregone by the circumstances is now irrevocable. So that is settled." He wrote whilst he continued to speak. "For the affairs of the Interior I have thought of Monsieur d'André, a man who has worked under me and in whom I have utter confidence." He waited.

"A policeman, is he not?" said Deslys sullenly.

"No better training-ground than the Police for the Ministry of the Interior. I take it that you agree." He wrote again. "And now we come to an appointment for which the right person is less obvious. The portfolio for foreign affairs. Have you any idea, sir?"

Deslys, sitting huddled together, gloom on his brow and a sense of hopeless impotence in his soul, had no ideas and had come to understand that it would nothing matter if he had. "No," he answered simply.

"And you, La Salle?"

"I know of only one."

"You mean yourself perhaps."

La Salle laughed. "Indeed, no. I mean Monsieur de Talleyrand."

"Of course. The ideal. A diplomatic genius. Unfortunately his absence in Vienna leaves us without any idea of his possible attitude towards Monsieur Deslys. You laughed just now when I asked if you had yourself in mind. Yet I was not jesting."

He was sincere enough. The talent for intrigue which he had so clearly discerned and admired in the painter, made La Salle a man after Fouché's own heart. He turned to Deslys. "What should you say to La Salle, sir?"

The browbeaten Deslys looked from one to the other of them blankly.

"I don't think I am qualified to hold an opinion. Florence's experience of affairs does not seem very extensive."

"If you will take my word for it, sir, natural astuteness ranks above experience."

"Florence is certainly astute," said Deslys listlessly.

"I should prefer to be called intelligent," drawled La Salle. "It is less suggestive of the fox."

"Ah, but foxiness is the desired attribute of a minister for foreign affairs. That is why Monsieur de Talleyrand succeeds so well." Fouché looked at Deslys again. "I am waiting, sir," he reminded him.

Deslys made a petulant gesture. He was at the end of his patience. "Oh, by all means if you two are agreed."

"But not unless you also agree, sir."

"You were not so gracious in the cases of Ney and Ouvrard."

"Necessity was more relentless. Besides, you will remember that in each case I was at pains to secure your agreement." And he went on quickly: "We say Monsieur de La Salle, then."

"I suppose he must have something."

"Naturally," said the imperturbable Fouché.

"But I'd like it graciously bestowed," was La Salle's acid comment. "God knows I've earned it."

"I beg your pardon, Florence. I did not mean to be ungracious." Deslys got up and made his troubled gesture of brushing the hair back from his brow. "I am tired, I think. I will leave you. You do not really need me."

"A moment, sir." Fouché detained him. "I should like your approval of myself for my old office. The Ministry of Police. It is the capacity in which I am persuaded that I can best serve you."

Thus Fouché helped himself to what he wanted. Deslys wondered idly what would happen if he were to venture to refuse him the appointment. "Very well, Monsieur le Duc," was all that he said.

"Then all that we need at the moment is settled. I will notify these gentlemen of the choice with which you honour them, and summon an early meeting for the discussion of initial measures." He rose, and bowed respectfully. La Salle held the door and followed Deslys from the room.

In the privacy of the gold-and-pink boudoir, the storm repressed in Deslys' bosom found vent as he paced furiously to and fro.

"He will notify these gentlemen of my choice! My choice! Ouvrard, the thief. Ney, the upstart sabring peasant. André, the muckrake. My choice!"

"You are forgetting me, Charles," said La Salle. "I await my designation."

"You!" Deslys glared contempt at him. "You know what you are." Then he raged on. "Was it for this that you brought me here? To be browbeaten, overborne, tyrannized by that soulless regicide?"

"Now, here's gratitude. Oh, most princely. What the devil do you think I brought you for? Haven't you enough? A million in the Bank of France today; a throne tomorrow, and the loveliest lady in the land for a wife. God's death! Are you really a prince by any chance, or are you a cowherd turned clockmaker? Buffoon!"

"That's it. That's what I am. Buffoon. That's what you're making of me, you and Fouché between you. A puppet moved by the strings of a couple of scoundrels. A wretched actor."

"But in a noble part. And don't overact it, my lad, or you may find the stage collapsing under your feet, or the audience pelting you with garbage."

"Oh yes. I am to do as I am told. I am to be docile, without will, or mind, or soul; otherwise…"

"You can go back to your mountains and your cows. Just so. We brought you here to play the prince, not to be a prince. Remember it, to save yourself from being ridiculous."

Deslys stood before him white and breathless. "If I were to go back to my mountains and my cows, what would happen to you? Where would you be?"

"Where fortune and my talents have at last placed me," was the unexpected answer. "The most famous painter of the day, besieged by beauty, talent and nobility, all craving to be painted by me. Do you suppose I could bewail the loss of a portfolio with that in my grasp? Do you imagine that I am agog to pursue the ignoble trade of politics when I may live nobly in the service of the arts?"

Deslys continued to stare at him. "I see. Faith! You and Fouché are a well-matched pair. You should run well in double harness. Each of you cares for no interest but his own."

"Whilst you consented to come and play the Orphan of the Temple merely so that you might make my fortune." La Salle laughed, lazily and without heat. "Just as it was for her own good that you turned your back on that girl in the mountains that you betrayed."

"My God! You villain! If you say that to me again, I'll strike you." He was livid, and he shook with passion.

La Salle coolly shrugged. "My dear Charles, you make it necessary to be brutal so as to bring you to a sense of realities. You accuse me of being an egotistical self-seeker. Perhaps I am. But can you discern nothing more in me? Are there no risks in what I am doing for you? If I were just an egotistical self-seeker, having found fortune in my art, rather than jeopardize it I should wash my hands of this imposture. There are a dozen ways in which I could prick this bubble and leave you to pay the penalty. A self-seeker I may be, also a scoundrel, as you've said. Oh, I don't dispute it. But it is not for you to reproach me on either ground. For what else are you?"

"I?" Deslys sprang to his feet, his limbs shaking, his face livid, his eyes blazing. For a moment he stood so, glowering upon the cool, mocking La Salle, a man struggling with something within him that was stronger than his powers to repress it. Then like an explosion of his very soul he answered: "I am the King of France."

La Salle continued to survey him with critical amusement. "Of course, Your Majesty. I have been at pains to make you that. I have reversed the processes of our old friend Chaumette. He took a king to make of him a man. I have taken a man to make of him a king. But he who makes the idol does not usually worship it."

"You don't understand," Deslys raged at him. "It is true what I say. True. I am the King. The only imposture I have practised is the imposture practised upon you. Upon you, who by an irony proposed it. I am Louis-Charles, the son of Louis XVI, I am the man you kidnapped from the Temple, the mart you conducted out of France."

La Salle's eyes were no longer mocking. They were angry. "Come, come, my lad. Leave these buffooneries. You don't imagine you can dupe me with my own inventions? You don't…"

"Your inventions? You fool! You don't even suspect how little you supplied of those inventions. You never perceived that where you thought you were instructing me, it was really I who was instructing you. In all that chain of events between my arrival in Geneva in '97 and our meeting at Brandenburg last summer, is there a single link that was not supplied by me?"

"You contributed a deal, but…"

"I contributed all. *All.*"

"If you did, what then? It only proves that of the two you were the more fertile liar. But you are not fertile enough to…"

"Listen to me. Listen!" Deslys was violent. "Do you think I would make such an assertion if I could not prove it?"

"Prove it? You can prove it! Excitement has turned your brain, I think."

"I'll prove it in a dozen ways. I'll begin with this: something which you certainly never told me, something which you may have forgotten, but of which I will remind you; if your memory fails, I can find something else." The words had poured from him in a torrent that left a froth upon his lips. Now he grew quieter, his speech slow and impressive. "That day in the Temple when you were making sketches. At one moment, whilst we were waiting for Marie-Thérèse,

Hébert – I can see the mincing dandy now – passed behind you, looked over your shoulder, and took your sketch-book from you. He brought it to the table and drew the attention of Chaumette and Pache to the sketch you had just made. Chaumette adjusted his spectacles to study it, and he commended it. But Pache, when it was shown to him, brushed it rudely aside. And what he said, like a coarse-minded fellow for whom art had no purpose or significance, was: 'Don't pester me with such trifles.' I wonder, do you remember Hébert's answer? You can hardly have forgotten it. 'This is not a trifle, Pache. Futurity may account it a historical document. A pity that you have no culture, Pache.' Those, I think, were his very words. Have you forgotten?"

La Salle, in stupefaction, was pondering that white, excited face, almost as if he were seeing it for the first time. "I had forgotten," he admitted, and his voice was oddly hushed. "But I remember now. And you…" He broke off. "Oh, but… You have come by this knowledge in some odd way that I cannot yet…"

"Do you want more? I can supply it. There were little incidents upon that journey to Geneva which you have not mentioned, but which are clear in my memory. And there is more than that. Heaven set upon me brands that are unmistakable when it planned my unhappy destiny; as if providing me with ineffaceable means to prove myself when the time came. Do you know nothing of those personal signs I bear? They were noted in the Temple register. They were known to every conventionnel. Have you never heard of them?"

La Salle was darkly frowning, stirred less by Deslys' assertions than by the wild fury that was returning to his manner. Staring at him as he mouthed and ranted in his violence, he recalled what were those signs to which Deslys alluded, and the eccentric, peasant length of the clockmaker's hair, which he had failed to induce him to modify, suddenly assumed an odd significance. Abruptly he stepped forward, and with the rough impatience of one who tears the mask from an impostor, he seized the wings of that hair and lifted them clear of the ears they covered.

Deslys stood stock still to let him have his way.

La Salle sucked in his breath at what he saw. The left ear was deformed, its lobe abnormally large, just as he knew it had been with Louis-Charles.

He let the hair fall and stepped back again, in silence, visibly shaken out of his normal calm. Deslys followed him up, thrusting a leering face into his own.

"And here on my thigh," he said, "the veins have traced the pattern of a dove, head downwards, like the emblem of the Order of the Holy Ghost, of which I am by right of birth Grand-Master. You may see it when you will if you still doubt, you presumptuous fool."

"This is fantastic," said La Salle weakly.

"No. It is true."

"Impossible! Impossible!" La Salle was in revolt against his own momentary doubt. He was frenzied in his turn. "If there were a grain of truth in this, why should you not have told me before? Why should you not have declared this to me at once? Could a man pretend to be himself? Is that the absurdity of which you hope to convince me? If you were real could you have concealed it?"

"You made me," Deslys answered him.

"I made you? I made you consent to be an impostor when you had only to tell me that you were actually the man I asked you to personate! Ah, name of God! That is too grotesque, my friend."

"Have you forgotten what you said to me at Brandenburg? Have you forgotten your declared hatred of the Bourbons? Have you forgotten your fierce declaration that if I were really Louis XVII, and it were in your power to help me to my throne, you would not lift a finger so to help me, but both hands to hinder me? You disclosed, then, a twofold purpose, of which the lesser was – or so you seemed to represent it – the achievement of fortune by a fraud. The greater purpose was to use me as a tool for your vengeance upon Louis XVIII. Have you forgotten all that? I regarded you then as an agent directed by Heaven unwittingly to bring me to my own. You presented yourself in the moment of my deepest despair. Could I then destroy the chance you offered by acknowledging myself a member of the family you had vowed to ruin?" Deslys laughed without mirth. "I kept silent. I accepted the rôle of impostor in your eyes, and so became one, using you for my ends who thought only of using me for yours. That is all. Believe it or not. Where you have placed me now, your belief matters nothing. It is beyond your power, as you suppose, to pull me down again if I am not docile. For truth once perceived is indestructible." And with another fleering laugh, trembling, shaken, exhausted, he flung himself upon a couch.

La Salle turned away, his face set, and paced the room in silence for some moments. It required no more to convince him of the monstrous comedy in which he had played so blind a part. A deus ex machina who knew not his own functions until the work was done. Things hitherto odd and obscure, which he had explained only in part to his own satisfaction by depending upon eccentricities of mind in this puppet of his, were gradually emerging clearly from the mist which had enveloped them. He began to understand Deslys' conduct at Passavant, and his stifling of conscience where Justine Perrin was concerned. He saw where else he had misjudged this man, and how little he need have been surprised either by his apparent stupidity at times or by his sharp vision and what he supposed his ready invention at others.

At last he came to a halt squarely before this new-found king. Outwardly, at least, La Salle was now calm once more.

"How much of the tale we told Fouché is true?" he asked. "I mean, the tale of your rescue from the lake and your later adventures, the papers with that fellow Naundorff, and the rest."

"It is practically all true. You only imagined that you invented some of the tale. Actually I supplied it all, piece by piece, either by correcting your inventions or by furnishing what you supposed to be original ones. It all happened just as you have it. It was a priest of Morges who took me back to Lebas in Geneva, and for the very reasons we have given, Lebas induced his sister, who was a widow and childless, to give me shelter. In a sense she adopted me, and when she died two years later I was sent to her brother-in-law at Passavant."

"And the papers and things with Naundorff?"

"Are just as I said. In addition, there was amongst them a letter written by Lebas, witnessed and confirmed by the priest who took me back to him, setting forth the story of the misadventure on the lake, and announcing how it was proposed for the time being to conceal me. Lebas is dead. But possibly that priest might still be found. He was a young man, I remember, and his name was Blancard."

"Then if Naundorff could be made to give up these papers, there would be additional proof of your identity?"

"Undoubtedly. But who will need it now?"

La Salle continued to ponder him, and never had Deslys seen so blank a look on the painter's countenance.

"You are convinced, I think," he said gently.

And then La Salle laughed his old sardonic laugh. "Convinced of the incredible," he said. "And all this while..." He broke off impatiently. "What does that matter now? I'll ask your patience whilst I readjust my ideas, sire."

At the title, used for the first time without mockery, Deslys rose and came to set a hand upon his arm. "You'll stay with me, nevertheless, Florence?" he pleaded weakly. "I am so little fitted to walk these ways alone. It is a duty I cannot shirk. Yet I must have fled from it had you not guided my faltering steps."

"In the path of truth, supposing it the path of falsehood. Oh, I shall be at your side for as long as you require me. The going will be easier now."

Chapter 7

Brother and Sister

In a room on an upper storey of the Hôtel d'Otranto, Florence de La Salle was at work upon a portrait of Mademoiselle de Castillon-Fouquières. You know the picture, arresting by its crafty composition, of a slim, tall woman in a high-waisted gown of shimmering black, of an austere loveliness of face, with unfathomable eyes, a braid of her red hair set like an encircling crown upon her low white brow, seated, very erect from the waist, in a tall arm-chair of the time of Louis XIII, upholstered in crimson velvet.

The room was lofty, well lighted by its tall windows and very sparsely furnished. It contained no more than a tall Italian cabinet of ebony with ivory inlays and a couple more of such massive chairs as the one that the sitter occupied. The wood mosaics of the floor were bare save for the rich Eastern rug on which Mademoiselle de Castillon-Fouquières' chair had been placed.

Charles Deslys, otherwise Louis-Charles, was with them, lounging in a chair, vaguely observing the last touches La Salle was putting to a portrait that might be considered finished. He had been dragged thither by Mademoiselle de Castillon-Fouquières. He had gone reluctantly, and reluctantly he remained, lost in dreamy abstraction until the Duke of Otranto came to interrupt the sitting and to carry him away to the ducal library.

He announced to him that the Council, composed of the ministers chosen, had held its first meeting, and it had decided – that is to say, the Duke of Otranto had decided – that the time for overt action had arrived. His grace had decided also what form this action should take, and he made it his present duty to convey the decision to the King in whose name it had been reached.

"It becomes necessary, sir, more definitely to force the issue. Your following is now strong enough to warrant it, and there can be no profit in waiting. It becomes plain that from the Tuileries no action is to be expected until we compel it."

"Very well," said Louis-Charles. His manner was decided. "It is what I would wish. This waiting becomes nerve-racking." He flung himself into a chair. "Let us consider what is to do."

"It is considered," he was dryly informed. "Your Council has decided that you should write a letter to Her Highness your sister."

Louis-Charles frowned. "I should have thought that the matter was one for my decision."

"For your ultimate decision, sir; naturally. But this is what your Council considers desirable."

"Then why to my sister? Why should I not write to my uncle?"

"The Council takes the view that a letter to Her Highness is more likely to produce an answer. It counts upon feminine emotion and impulsiveness, and it has more faith in the honesty of Madame Royale than in that of the Count of Provence."

Louis-Charles considered. "Very well," he said at last, "I will write to her. I will write tomorrow. I will take the night to think of the terms."

Fouché, lean and bent by his writing-table, cleared his throat. "We did not wish, sir, that you should be at so much trouble." He took up a sheet of paper.

"The letter has been drafted for you. I trust that you will approve of it." And he brought the sheet across to Louis-Charles.

But Louis-Charles was slow to take it. "It has been drafted? A letter that I am to write to my sister?" The frown between the arched brows was deep. Indignation was darkening the colour in his face.

"Oh, but a political document wrapped in a brotherly letter. If you will glance at it, sir, you will see, I think, that it is precisely what you would wish to write."

"And if I do not? What then?"

Fouché's smile did not falter. "Need we anticipate? If you will be so good as to read, sir."

There was an insistence which Louis-Charles could not withstand. Sullenly he took the sheet, and read:

Madame my Sister, If the news of my survival and presence here in Paris has not yet reached you, I can only suppose that it is deliberately being kept from you by those whose first duty should be to acquaint you with it. If it has reached you I conclude from the absence of any sign from you that it has failed to carry that conviction which I can confidently promise to afford you at a personal interview.

I hope that this letter will induce you to accord me that interview with the least possible delay. I would not have the world suppose that there is on your part any reluctance to test the claim of one who signs himself

Your brother,

Louis-Charles.

Having read it twice, he sat a moment in thoughtful silence. Fouché standing over him, waited patiently.

"It is not," said the young man at length, "the letter that I should wish to write. There are explanations to offer which she cannot disregard."

"Those will follow at the interview."

"But what if that interview is not accorded?"

"It will be."

"You are a prophet as well as a statesman, Monsieur le Duc."

"No, sir. But a very good policeman. Let me tell you something. You already know that at the Hospital for Incurables in the Rue de Sèvres there is an old acquaintance of yours from the Temple – the

Widow Simon. Until your uncle's police set a gag of fear upon her, she missed no opportunity of publishing the fact that you had been smuggled alive out of the Temple. Two days ago Madame d'Angoulême, accompanied by another lady, went in disguise to visit her. To what end, sir, do you suppose?"

Louis-Charles' manner betrayed excitement. "If that is true…"

"I can depend upon my information."

"She will have gone to question her about me, you think?"

"That was my conclusion."

"Two days, you say, since she saw the Widow Simon. Two days. And having heard La Simon's tale, she yet makes no move to see me."

"That is what renders this letter necessary."

Louis-Charles gave him back the sheet. His countenance was flushed. "Never," he declared. "Never will I write to such a sister."

Fouché was coldly sympathetic. "I can understand the feeling, sir. Nevertheless, the letter must be written."

"Must?"

"I mean that your interests must be served."

"They shall be served in some other way. My dignity will not suffer me to do this."

"What other way would you suggest, sir?"

"There are the courts of justice, open to the meanest subject who accounts himself wronged."

Fouché smiled, sighed, and shook his head. "That will be our last, not our first, recourse. It is upon popular sympathy that you must build, and popular sympathy is too commonly bestowed upon the defendant. That is why I prefer that the Count of Provence should proceed by arresting you. Once we begin to establish your identity before the Courts, we shall make it clear that your survival was known to him throughout and suppressed by him, and he will be smothered in odium for prosecuting you."

"But it is not what I wish. I should detest to pursue such vindictive methods."

"Have you nothing to avenge, sir?"

Louis-Charles looked at him without affection. "Are you not perhaps pursuing a vengeance of your own upon a king who disdained to employ your talents?"

Fouché did not so much as flinch. "If that were so, the profit would still be yours."

"Oh, and yours as well. Yours and your friends'."

"Do you grudge their wages to your servants? But we were talking of this letter."

"That matter is finished. I will not write it."

Fouché raised his shoulders slightly. Beyond that he betrayed no impatience. "Sir, I should not presume to press it if there were an alternative. Your Council is persuaded that there is not."

"My Council! You mock me, I think, with my Council. You mean your Council. What had I to do with the appointments? It is a council of your creation, to do what you consider proper."

"In your service, sir."

Louis-Charles rose abruptly, driven to exasperation by that bloodless countenance, that frozen, relentless calm. "You profess yourselves my servants, but you take the tone of masters. You coerce and constrain me. You deny me all initiative. You treat my wishes with contempt, and impose your own upon me."

"Is this quite just, sir? Can you point to a single act of mine that has not resulted to your advantage, that has not brought you a step nearer to the attainment of your object? In what case were you when you first sought me? In what case are you now? I do not think that I have served you so badly as to merit your reproaches. But if I have lost your confidence, it can only remain for me to resign the office with which you have honoured me."

Translated into blunt terms this meant that Monsieur Deslys could pack his effects and depart the Hôtel d'Otranto. It might mean in addition that all the energies and influence hitherto devoted to establishing him might henceforth be devoted to thrusting him back into obscurity.

Alarm tempered his annoyance. "There is no question of any loss of confidence in you," he grumbled. "What I complain of is the utter lack of confidence in me. In my judgment."

Fouché became human. "Sir," he said gently, kindly, "I am very old in affairs. I have made governments and unmade them. I know my way through the labyrinth of statecraft, and I know something, too, of human impulses. You could do worse than trust to this knowledge."

"But I have just assured you that I do."

"I should value proof of it more highly than assurance, sir. Afford it me by writing this letter, which I should never have brought to you if I had not been in full agreement with the terms of it as your Council has drafted them."

It was the end of the argument. In stifled reluctance the letter was written.

The response to it was swift. On the following afternoon a carriage drew up at the portals of the Hôtel d'Otranto, and after a footman had informed himself that Monsieur le Duc was at home, two ladies alighted from it.

A majordomo came in haste to conduct them up the noble staircase and along a thickly carpeted gallery to Monsieur le Duc's library. He threw open the mahogany doors with the announcement: "Her Royal Highness, Madame la Duchesse d'Angoulême."

As the ladies entered, Fouché, forewarned of their arrival, laid down his pen and rose calm and unhurried from his writing. Tall, gaunt and almost inhumanly impassive, he advanced a step or two to meet them, his eyes veiled. He bowed low to the foremost of his visitors, a tall, angular woman whose narrow face with its aquiline nose and pale red-rimmed eyes was utterly unprepossessing.

Over her high-waisted gown she wore a short spencer of black velvet, trimmed at waist and cuffs with sable, and her face was partly in the shadow of a poke-bonnet à la Pamela. But she wore her finery in a manner that robbed it of all the elegance her dressmaker had conceived. Her hands were tucked into a large sable muff.

She acknowledged the bow by no more than a curt nod.

"I have received a letter from one who appears to be a visitor here, monsieur." Her voice was harsh, its tone disdainful. "I desire a word of explanation from this person."

"Certainly." Fouché bowed again, correct without affability. "If Your Royal Highness will follow me, I shall have the honour to conduct you to him."

"I prefer that you bring him to me here."

She was peremptory. But Fouché in his time had handled and subdued a greater peremptoriness. He opened the door, and held it, the eternal smile on his bloodless lips, the suggestion of inflexibility in his whole attitude. "If Your Highness will condescend, it will be better."

She hesitated a moment; then with an ill-humoured "Come!" to her lady-in-waiting, the elegant little Madame de Brézé, she passed out.

Fouché desired witnesses for whatever was to follow. In the small salon that was known from the decoration of its walls and ceiling as the gold chamber, Mademoiselle de Castillon-Fouquières, who had some small talent in that direction, was making music for Louis-Charles. Her mother and Monsieur de La Salle were of the company. Fouché brought them to their feet by dramatically announcing the Duchess of Angoulême.

Her Highness advanced with the quick, mannish stride that was habitual to her, then checked suddenly, her head thrown up in haughty displeasure at seeing so many. She was about to express her annoyance when her glance fell on Louis-Charles, and the sight of him struck her dumb.

He stood deathly pale and visibly trembling in an intensity of emotion, his eyes devouring this harsh, lean, imperious woman of thirty-six, who gave him back stare for stare.

Madame de Castillon-Fouquières and her daughter sank to the ground in the lowest of unheeded curtseys. Beyond Louis-Charles, La Salle, an elegant figure in a tight-waisted black frock, watched keenly even whilst bowing.

But the tired red eyes of Marie-Thérèse beheld only Louis-Charles.

It was over twenty years since she had last seen her brother, and this on the dreadful occasion of the confrontation at which La Salle had been present in the Temple Tower. In the young man before her she could discover little trace of the chubby-faced, merry, fair-haired boy of 1793. But the countenance that she did behold was even better known to her, for it was very near akin to a countenance that her mirror showed her daily. To the others present, the likeness between those two was no less arresting. Saving the red-rimmed eyes and the fairer hair of the Duchess, both countenances displayed the same essential features. The narrowness, the aquiline nose, the high, arched eyebrows and the hare-teeth combined to make up that extraordinary resemblance. And to La Salle the oddest circumstance here was that whilst they so closely resembled each other, yet neither of them resembled the child from which each had grown.

Because of the agitation she displayed, it was the more startling that when at last she spoke, her words gave no sign that his appearance had so much as set in doubt the preconceptions in which she came. The harsh voice was hostile.

"Is it you who call yourself the Duke of Normandy?"

A smile of odd, disdainful wistfulness crossed his white face. He spoke very quietly. "No, madame. I have not called myself by that name since my father died in '92."

No rehearsed effect could have been more impressive. La Salle, who still must be looking upon Louis-Charles in part at least as his creation, watched him with an artist's pride in a fine piece of work. Her Highness was momentarily out of countenance. When she recovered, a bitter sneer writhed on her thin lips.

"Who do you pretend was your father?"

"I assert that he was also yours, madame. I am your brother and the King of France."

With livid fury in her face, she swung to Fouché.

"A chair," she croaked.

Fouché made haste to advance one, but as she moved to it, Louis-Charles spoke again, and his voice, too, had grown harsh. "You will sit in my presence, madame, when I give you leave."

La Salle wanted to laugh. If the fellow failed to reach the throne, there was a career awaiting him at the Théâtre Français.

She checked a moment, and flashed him a glance of unutterable contempt.

"Can audacity and imposture venture quite so far?" She reached the chair and sat down, whilst Madame de Brézé, looking scared and nervous, went to stand behind her.

"Before this interview ends, madame," said Louis-Charles, "I shall hope to receive your apologies for a want of respect that might have waited until the imposture is proven."

"It needs no more proof than I already possess."

"That can only be because you desire conviction."

Her chin went up. A flame of colour swept across her face. He went calmly on. "If you are convinced, as you pretend, why do you trouble to remain?"

"So that I may question you."

He drew himself up. His pallor was passing, and as he grew steadier he assumed a majesty of demeanour such as Louis XVI had never known. "I am not to be questioned in that spirit. Or in any spirit. You have leave to withdraw, madame, taking your convictions with you."

She turned to Fouché. "I trust to you, Monsieur le Duc, to protect me from more of this insolence."

Fouché came forward, washing his knuckly hands in the air. Behind his smiling mask he was perturbed. Things were not taking at all the course he had hoped. This interview was no better than a duel. His tone was conciliatory, although his actual words would not appear so to Her Highness.

"Are you not perhaps a little intransigent, madame? To denounce beforehand as an imposture the thing you are here presumably to investigate is to render your visit worse than futile."

She eyed him sourly. "To listen to you, sir, one might imagine that there is still a revolution in France."

"To listen to you, madame, if you will suffer me to say so, one might imagine that there had never been one."

"You say that to me, Monsieur Fouché?" Her tone was now of a scalding bitterness. It seemed to fling in his face all that through his kind she and hers had suffered, all the torment and humiliation of those dreadful years which had hardened this unhappy woman into what she was.

"It has always been my endeavour not only to follow the path of reason but to point it out to others." He paused a moment, during which she stared at him stonily. Then he spoke again on an easier tone. "Why not begin by being frank with us, madame? Two days ago Your Highness paid a visit to the Widow Simon at the Incurables."

"How do you know that?" she shrilled.

"I have my little methods." He smiled. "If you guessed the extent of half my knowledge, you would not suppose – if you do suppose it – that I should house an impostor."

"Not to serve your own ends?"

"Oh, madame! This is to palter. I am not so foolish as to perceive profit in such a fraud."

Louis-Charles turned aside to Pauline and her mother. "Mesdames, I keep you standing. If you please." He waved them courteously to chairs.

Pauline, splendidly regal, flashed him a smile of pride and encouragement. Not until they were seated did he turn again to Her Highness. His voice was quiet.

"I do not know whether what the Widow Simon told you, madame, would be news to you. But I do know that the substance of it must have been that I did not die in the Temple Prison."

There were dark shadows about the eyes that sternly measured him out of her white face. The slight movement of the muff in her lap told of the agitation of the hands within it, and betrayed her struggle for self-mastery. At last her voice came, hoarse, strained, forbidding.

"You will answer me when I speak to you. Until then…do not dare to address me."

A curious change came over his sensitive face. Mechanically, slowly, he repeated her phrase. " 'Do not dare to address me.' Curious that you should say that." He paused there. Then, dropping his words slowly, one by one, he added: "Curious that at this first meeting, after a lapse of twenty years, you should use again the very last words I heard from you twenty years ago in the Temple Tower. 'Do not dare to address me.' Do you remember, madame?"

In a face that was now the colour of lead, her eyes dilated in panic. Then with an exhalation deep and audible she closed her eyes and sank limply back in her chair. Madame de Brézé was instantly at her side in alarm, and Fouché, as instantly, stepped towards her from the opposite direction. She was known to be given to swooning, especially when poignant memories were aroused, and it was feared that she was swooning now. But she summoned her will to combat the weakness. She opened her eyes again slowly, and for a moment only were they vacant. Then she was sitting forward once more, looking squarely at Louis-Charles, and the harsh voice was heavy with scorn.

"You have been well schooled."

"Schooled?"

"Schooled, you impostor. But not well enough. For if you were really he whom you pretend to be, the memory of that hideous day in the Temple Tower is the very last you would evoke to move me." Passion rang ever harsher in her voice as she proceeded. "I had lived through evil cruel days before, and I have lived through many evil, cruel days since. Vile, incredible days. But none so vile and so incredible as that. And you would know it if you were Duke of Normandy. Never would my brother dare to speak of it, lest it should scorch him with shame as it does me even now."

She had awed her listeners by the fierce bitterness of her manner, saving only La Salle. Only he, perhaps because, having been present at that scene twenty years ago, he possessed full knowledge of her meaning, was vouchsafed a glimpse of the tortured workings of the

Duchess of Angoulême's mind, understood what the others did not even begin to suspect.

Charles, with a drawn face of misery, spoke at last in his own defence. "Must I bear full responsibility for something which I did not understand, for reciting a lesson which had no meaning for me at the time? I was a child of seven, cruelly corrupted, half drugged with brandy. You know these things, madame. But who else knows them today? By whom could I be schooled, as you say?"

"By whom? There was no lack of witnesses to that scene. Chaumette, for one." And she turned to the Duke of Otranto. "He was your friend, Monsieur Fouché, was he not?"

Fouché, sharply stung, met scorn with scorn. He broadened his smile. "It is not so easy to persuade us that you persuade yourself, madame."

"That is an insolent speech. It is worthy of a Jacobin."

He let that pass. "But can you persuade yourself that you are not face to face with your brother? Does your mirror give you no assurances?"

"Is a chance likeness to become a proof?"

"Not alone. No. But since you know that your brother did not die in the Temple – "

"I do not know it," she interrupted vehemently.

He spread his hands. "Shall we say, then, that you do not know that he died there? You were not informed of it at the time of the pretended death. You were in the room above, yet you were not called to identify the body, nor was any other single person who had known your brother in life. And there were many available. Tison, for instance, who had known him well, was himself a prisoner in the Temple. Instead, great care was taken that amongst those called to identify the body of a dead boy as that of Louis Capet there was not one who had ever known him alive. I know because I was of those responsible for that precaution. Is there no clear inference to be drawn from it?"

"You know as well as I do that all this is negative."

Fouché leaned forward. He spoke slyly. "But what the Widow Simon told Your Highness would be positive enough."

"An old woman in her dotage, haunted by illusions."

"Will the Courts take that view? Besides, the Widow Simon is not the only survivor who can testify to the escape. There is actually a man present in this room – one whom you will hardly remember, but who may be able to recall himself to your memory. Monsieur de La Salle!"

La Salle stood forward, and so well hitherto had he effaced himself that her attention was drawn now for the first time to that erect, well-knit figure in its close-fitting black, and the singularly pallid face between the high black military stock and the lustrous black hair with its queer wedge of white. He answered her inquiring frown in his slow, drawling voice.

"Your Highness may perhaps recall that on that day which has been mentioned, the painter Louis David – who would be known to you – was of the attendance in the Temple Tower. A young man, a pupil of David's, was with him, making sketches of those present. I was that young man, madame. I can still show you the sketch-book. For it has a historical value and I have carefully preserved it. Shall I fetch it?"

"I will not trouble you, sir," she coldly denied him. "I will take your word for its existence, and for the rest. It is valuable evidence." Her smile became more sharply cruel. "Evidence of the preceptor who out of his own memories has supplied this impostor with the materials he required."

This was a stroke inside the guard of those who championed the cause of Louis-Charles. La Salle, disconcerted, questioned Fouché with his glance. Fouché took a step towards Her Highness.

"Let us pass on," his thin voice croaked. "We shall yet find something to which there is but one explanation. If there is no definite knowledge of the survival of Louis XVII, ask yourself, madame, why did your uncle arrest the exhumation which a too zealous police minister had ordered of the body buried as Louis XVIII's in the Cemetery of the Madeleine."

"It is not within my knowledge that His Majesty did so. But if he did, what then? Suppose that it is true that my brother escaped, and that another was buried in his place, does that prove that he is alive now?"

"I am concerned at the moment only with the good faith of Your Highness' uncle."

"Do you mean the King, sir?" she flashed.

He remained cold as ice. "Believing as I do that the King stands here before you, it follows that I mean the Count of Provence."

"Monsieur! You dare to go so far!"

"I merely express what must naturally be inferred. But do not let us fall into quibbles. There are things upon which I am reluctant to touch. Yet I must, if the truth is to prevail. The Courts may have to touch upon them in the end, and then the scandal will be public. Years ago, at Versailles, a calumny was set on foot that struck at the Dauphin's right of inheritance. I do not say who invented it. That shameful scandal has lately been revived. I must ask myself what could be responsible for this but a fear that King Louis XVII, who is known not to have died in the Temple, may be at hand to claim his own."

She rocked in fury; her eyes were blazing in a distorted face.

"Must I listen to these infamies? Do you dare to say, Monsieur le Duc, that the King...that the King... Oh, I cannot go on. There are things that are not to be spoken."

"I know, madame." Fouché was suddenly gentle. "I beg you to observe that I have categorically accused none. I have merely stated the known fact of the current rumour, and pointed out the purpose it might have."

"His Majesty shall be informed," she threatened.

He bowed in silence, and then La Salle made bold to speak, addressing himself to Fouché, and startling them by the suddenness of his intervention.

"Her Highness very properly desires to begin at the beginning, by being first persuaded that His Majesty Louis XVII escaped from the Temple. Any inquiry must naturally start there. The evidence of the Widow Simon Her Highness dismisses as that of an old woman in her dotage. But in recounting the escape it is hardly possible that the Widow Simon will not have mentioned my part in it."

Her Highness looked at him haughtily. "Your part in it? Do you pretend to have been in that too? You are – are you not? – the painter of those two pictures in the Salon. I begin to perceive the link that joins you to this plot."

"Then the Widow Simon did not mention me by name? She will, at least, have described the means employed: that His Majesty was concealed in the handcart piled with household effects and linen belonging to the Simons, who were removing on that January night from the Temple."

"That was the tale. Yes. What then?"

"I was the man who trundled the cart into the street and away from the Temple. After that the Widow Simon knows no more of the King, for he remained with me. It is because of this that I can tell Your Highness, as I can tell the world, the rest."

That shrewd reminder that what he told her he could tell the world compelled her to listen to his tale, which briefly covered the events of Louis-Charles' life down to the escape from France with the Freiherr von Ense in '97.

The mention of that name brought from her the first interruption.

"Whom, did you say?"

He repeated the name. Scorn smiled on her thin lips. "Why, the Freiherr von Ense is not yet forty. At the time of which you speak he was a child in his teens."

"Your Highness is thinking of the present Baron. I speak of his uncle, who was drowned in Lake Léman, who sacrificed his life to your brother."

Her lips parted, and she leaned quickly forward to reply. Then checked, and sank back again in her chair. "Continue, sir," she commanded.

But Louis-Charles intervened, curt and peremptory. "It is not necessary to continue. There are limits to my patience." His voice rose a little. The haughty stare of Her Highness had no power to subdue him. "If I still command any, it is not in my own personal interest, but in that of the Bourbon name. Monsieur d'Otranto has spoken of the Courts, and of what must be brought to light if we have recourse to them. So as to spare Monsieur de Provence the odium that must then fall upon him, I hope that he will prefer to acknowledge me for Louis XVII when Your Highness tells him I have persuaded you – as I am confident that I shall – that I am your brother."

"You are confident to persuade me of that? You are confident indeed."

"I am, madame." And he went on. He subdued his voice, but under its quiet tone vibrated the emotion stirring him. It cracked the veneer which in the last few months he had been so rapidly acquiring, and whilst his words remained well chosen, his accent was once more at least suggestive of the Jura peasant.

"The instance I cited of an intimate passage between us, madame, twenty years ago, you dismiss on the ground that others were present by whom I have since been schooled. Let me, then, speak of something more intimate still, something to which there were no witnesses to school an impostor. Let me recall that day of January when the guns announced to the four of us huddled together in that room on the second floor of the Temple Tower the passing of the King, my father."

He made a pause there, as if to choose his words, or, perhaps, to await her permission to proceed. But she merely stared at him in an agitation too deep to be concealed. Her bosom was in tumult, she seemed to have a difficulty in breathing, and in her blenched face there was again an expression of panic. The others waited in utter silence, awed by the sense of impending drama.

On the overmantel of the onyx fireplace with its gold inlay, the Sèvres clock ticked out a dozen seconds before Louis-Charles spoke again.

"Let me remind you of the group we made. It was a cold, foggy morning; you will remember that. My mother occupied the arm-chair near the stove, beside which a pile of wood had been stacked. I knelt on one side of her – on her left – you on the other. Aunt Babet stood before us, so near that by putting out her hand she could have touched me, as presently she did. At the sound of the first gun, my mother uttered a low, shuddering moan and sank forward, her face in her hands. But when the reverberations had ended, she suddenly sat up very stiff and straight. She might have said, 'The King is dead. Long live the King!' Instead, the exact words she chose were: 'The King is with God.' And then, placing her hand on my head, she added: 'God be with the King!' At that, Aunt Babet – "

He broke off. Her Highness had fainted.

Chapter 8

The Key

Louis-Charles sat with La Salle in the circular boudoir, waiting. They had left the unconscious Duchess of Angoulême to the care of the ladies, and Fouché had remained at hand, in the ante-chamber, ready to wait upon Her Highness so soon as she should have recovered.

Louis-Charles, without elation, had expressed the opinion that he must now have set all doubts at rest. La Salle, haunted by a phrase that Her Highness had employed early in the interview, still entertained misgivings, but kept them for the present to himself.

For close upon a half-hour they sat in a silence of so gloomy a thoughtfulness in Louis-Charles that La Salle did not venture to break it. At last Louis-Charles got up and moved restlessly about the room. He spoke suddenly, giving some indication of how his thoughts had been trending.

"If my unhappy father could have chosen his destiny, I think he would have been content to be a locksmith. Why, then, should I who inherited his mechanical aptitudes, and was vouchsafed by destiny the occasion to employ them, seek to battle my way to a throne? And how ignoble is this battle! Thwarted by one egoist, assisted for his own purposes by another, and scornfully opposed at the end by the people of my own blood."

"I thank you for the place you assign to me in that charming gallery," drawled La Salle.

Louis-Charles swung upon him, showing a tortured face. "I was thinking of Fouché, not of you. But even you, Florence – " He broke off. "Oh, my God! How gladly would I exchange this kingdom for the knowledge that I possess one true friend, one devoted heart glad to help and serve me from affection and not for his own profit."

"I'll not invite your contempt by protestations, sire. But setting me aside, you seem to me less than grateful to Fate if you forget Mademoiselle de Castillon."

"Pauline!" He hung his head. La Salle had touched a chord that awoke more sorrow than joy. "Ah, yes! Pauline. Yes, Pauline at least cares something for the man I am, and little for the King that I may be. I have the proof of that. God knows, it might be better if it were not so."

There was a tap, and the door opened. Fouché stood on the threshold. Louis-Charles sprang towards him.

"Has she recovered?"

"She has recovered, sire, and she has gone."

"Gone?" The young man's face darkened. "Gone? Without seeing me again? After... Oh!"

For once Fouché was not smiling. "She left a message for you. 'Tell him,' she said, 'that I must have a little time in which to readjust my ideas. When I have done so, I may see him again.'"

"May see me again? She may see me? But what does it mean, then?"

Fouché had quietly closed the door. He came forward, raising his shoulders. "Do not ask me that, sire, for I do not know the answer. I merely repeat her message."

"But after the proof I have given her!" Louis-Charles seemed stupefied.

"Not so welcome, perhaps, that proof," came the dry voice of La Salle, and both swung to him for an explanation.

He was thinking of the phrase that had revealed so much to him, but which apparently had remained meaningless to the others. He repeated it slowly, word for word.

" 'If you were really he whom you pretend to be, the memory of that hideous day in the Temple Tower is the very last you would evoke to move me.' That is what she said. And she added: 'Never would my brother dare to evoke it, lest it should scorch him with shame as it does me even now.' " He paused. "Does that convey no message to you? Do you perceive there no indication of the workings of a soul that is arid, rancorous, and unforgiving?"

"Ah!" said Fouché softly. "And I allowed that to pass me by."

"Non semper arcus…" La Salle began, and broke off the quotation.

Louis-Charles, bewildered, looked from one to the other of them.

"But what is it? What does it mean?"

"It is, I think, the key to the situation," said La Salle. And seeing the continuing blankness of Louis-Charles' expression: "I must explain, I suppose," he added. "You remember what was done on that day in the Temple Tower, sire; on that day which Her Highness describes as hideous; the thing which must, in her view, still so scorch her brother with shame that he would rather forgo a throne than evoke it. There was an infamous lesson recited parrot-like by a child of seven who did not know what he said, and who was befuddled at the time. All that Madame d'Angoulême can bring herself to consider is that that recitation, those depositions concerning which she was confronted with you on that day and soiled with questions from which she has never yet succeeded in cleansing her memory, had for result to send Queen Marie-Antoinette to the scaffold, and to send her there besmirched with the last infamy."

"Oh, my God!" cried Louis-Charles, and sank loosely to a chair, his head in his hands.

La Salle came to set a soothing hand upon his shoulder. "It is all false, sire. False as Hell. Monsieur le Duc here knows that. He knows that the Queen's death had already been determined, and that no depositions of yours contributed anything to the real indictment, save... Hébert's embellishments. But there is no power on earth will ever persuade Madame Royale of this, and no power that will ever bring her to forgive. That is what I gathered from her declaration. It leaves me convinced that she would actually prefer to see an impostor on the throne, rather than a brother whom, in her rancorous obsession, she regards as a matricide."

Fouché, chin in hand, slowly nodded. "Your sight is long, La Salle. You point out something that I had not suspected. And you are right. Where we looked for an ally we have found an enemy."

"But do you mean," cried Louis-Charles, "that because of this obsession she will bear false witness? I can't believe it."

"You need not believe it," said La Salle. "She will never bear false witness consciously. But the inextinguishable rancour in that otherwise empty heart will father so strong a hope that her brother is dead that she will prefer any evidence of it, however shallow, to evidence of his survival, however strong."

"I think that expresses it," Fouché agreed. "When Her Highness shall have readjusted her ideas, it is odds that she will still be on the side of her uncle, Monsieur de Provence."

A sudden fury flamed in Louis-Charles' eyes; the blood returned in spate to his countenance. "Then I am to be despised and opposed for having unconsciously done what this man is ready to do consciously so as to exclude me from the throne."

"That overstates it," said La Salle.

But the more cynical Fouché refused to take so generous a view.

"Do not let it trouble you, sire. We are strong enough to prevail against all the Bourbon brood, their stupidities and wickednesses. Madame d'Angoulême would be Queen of France one day if you were set aside. She will not be charitably judged when it is remembered that her husband, after d'Artois, is next in the succession. Your day is coming, sire."

"Do I want such a day at such a price?" he cried, and, surrendering to the anguish that filled him, fell to sobbing like a child.

Chapter 9

Pauline

It was left for the stately, queenly Pauline de Castillon-Fouquières to combat the bitterness and dejection into which Louis-Charles had fallen. She chose to do so by explaining Madame Royale to him out of a knowledge of events, affairs, and human nature which took him by surprise.

It was the last day of February, a mild day of bright sunshine and soft southern breezes that would have graced the month of April.

Shaken by the events of the morning, he could not be induced to ride in the Bois, as had been planned. So she took the air with him in the garden of the Hôtel d'Otranto, where the buds were already breaking on the azaleas. A fur pélérine about her shoulders, her perfect face in the shadow of a fur-trimmed bonnet that completely hid the ruddy glory of her hair, she paced slowly at his side, and the rather hard note of her voice was muted as she reasoned.

"You must judge more mercifully, Charles." He would always, it seemed, be Charles, as he had been in childhood to the guards at the Temple. "You must remember what Madame Royale has suffered."

"It is the excuse of every rogue," said he, "that we are what life has made us. Are my sister's sufferings greater than mine?"

"Perhaps she has plumbed greater depths of disillusion."

"She has never been denied. She has come into her own without opposition."

"But at what a price! Consider those dreadful years in the Temple, when one by one the members of her family were taken from her, three of them to go to the scaffold."

"Was that not my fate too?"

"Consider the terrible indignities she suffered in those years."

"Did I suffer less?"

"Her age and sex made a difference. There were hands to minister to you. She, a princess of the blood, was her own servant, constrained to sweep her own floor, make her own bed, and the rest. Confined alone in that tower, her only exercise was to walk quickly round and round the room for an hour each morning. And she was seventeen at the time. I never see her walking now, always with that oddly quick, hurried step, but I think of that. Her captivity endured much longer than yours, and it did not end even when she left the Temple. In Vienna, her uncle kept her virtually a prisoner when she was delivered to him. No Frenchman was allowed to approach her. She saw only the companions the Emperor desired for her. The restoration of order in France was leading to the restoration of property. Your death assumed, Madame Royale's was an enormous heritage. It might become yet greater. Amongst the many ancient institutions swept away for ever would be, it was supposed, the Salic law. In an ultimate Bourbon restoration, Madame Royale might become Queen of France. She understood this and her uncle's interest in her when she found herself being coerced into marriage with his brother the Archduke Charles.

"It was out of similar motives that Monsieur de Provence, who had proclaimed himself Louis XVIII, strengthened her resistance to the Austrian marriage by the false assurance that the wishes of her dead parents, which she must regard as sacred, were that she should marry her cousin Angoulême, whom she had never seen.

"Conceive the feelings of that unfortunate girl when she understood that she was a mere counter of no personal account in the ambitions of those from whom she had all the more right to expect tenderness in view of what she had undergone. She may – poor soul! – have woven a romantic dream about Angoulême, and this may have lent strength to her determination to resist the wooing of the ill-favoured Archduke. At last, after years of this persecution, the Emperor, abandoning hope of constraining her, packed her off to Louis XVIII at Mitau. There fresh, and perhaps even more bitter, disillusion awaited her. Within two or three days of her arrival at that starveling Court, maintained by the grudging charity of the Czar, they married her – ever under that falsehood of her parents' wishes – to the rachitic, degenerate Angoulême. That was to set a tombstone upon all her feminine hopes.

"Can we wonder, when we reflect how ruthlessly she has been sacrificed to calculating, soulless ambition, that she should be so cold and hard and rancorous? You may have suffered much, but at least your heart has been allowed to remain your own. You have been free to love where you would, and to choose the partner of your fate."

She waited for him to say something, to offer up one of those protestations which in such circumstances should come so readily to a lover's lips. But he paced on in silence, his head bowed, his eyes upon the ground, a cloud upon his brow which seemed to have deepened at her last words. She spurred him with a question.

"Is that not something that should teach you mercy?"

"You certainly help me to understand," he admitted. "Perhaps I understand the better because I too have known the bitterness of feeling myself a puppet handled by others for the service of their own greed."

She frowned a little in a disappointment she was, however, too wise to express.

"Once you are King, you can make an end of all that," she assured him. She took a hand from her muff to set it on his arm. "I shall know how to help you, dear Charles. Always can you count on me."

He looked at her at last, and in his prominent eyes there was that dog-like, pathetic expression that La Salle had observed so frequently in the early days of their association. "That I could never doubt," he answered her in all sincerity. And then, conscious that this was scarcely enough, he added with no less sincerity, "In all the world, Pauline, I could have found no woman worthier to be my Queen."

She lowered her eyes under his gaze, in which, if there was no passion, there was at least admiration and affection. She seemed to draw a veil of humility over her natural haughtiness. "I shall pray to be worthy, Charles, not only of the King, but of my lover."

"Ah!" It came from him almost in a cry of pain, the source of which was entirely misunderstood. She hung more heavily upon his arm. She swayed towards him with a little fluttering sigh. They had passed within the shelter of a little space, enclosed by tall yew hedges, over which a marble faun presided. Yielding to her invitation, he kissed her eyes and then her lips. His voice came choked.

"You teach me to pity that poor starved sister," he said.

"Now I am happy, Charles," she murmured. "Hold me close, dear love."

He obeyed, and, in his arms, her eyelids lowered, a heavenly smile on her lips, she renewed her vows of unalterable fidelity. "We are indissolubly one, Charles, you and I, betide what may. Malice can no more rob you of your inheritance than of my love. You will prevail. For your own sake; not for mine, who am nothing, of such account only as I may become through your love." She lay against his breast, looking up at him with an adorable shyness such as none had ever seen in those blue-green eyes, habitually so cold and proud.

"I loved you from the moment when I first saw you, Charles," she murmured, as if to enrich for him this surrender of herself. "And those were unhappy days for me."

"Unhappy?"

She gave him a wistful little smile. "My fears made them so. If only I had not known that you were King of France, it would not have been so. Kings marry as reasons of State dictate, and that frightened me. I could almost have prayed then that you might never come into your own, since it seemed to me that I must lose you if you did. It's a confession of disloyalty. Do you forgive it, sire?"

He smiled. So deeply was he moved, so much had he endured that day, that he was almost in tears before this demonstration of a love so freely bestowed and, as it seemed to him, so little merited. "The man is greater than the king," he answered her, sadly conscious that he made artificial phrases. "Disloyalty to the king can be no crime when it is rooted in loyalty to the man."

"The man, dear love, can always count upon my loyalty," she vowed, and offered her lips to his kiss again.

As he led her back to the house after these passages which violated all the accepted canons of royal wooing – but then, of course, there had been a Revolution – his emotions baffled definition even by himself. He discovered in them a mingling of happiness and unhappiness, of exaltation and dejection, of tenderness held in leash by conscience. But he was comforted, at least, by a better understanding of his sister, now that the causes had been laid bare of the bitter effects which La Salle had so mercilessly exposed.

But it is to the key supplied by La Salle that we must have recourse in reading the subsequent part of Madame Royale in these transactions.

We conclude, then, that Her Highness departed from the Hôtel d'Otranto in an anguish of mind surpassing anything that her deeply troubled life had known. She felt herself confronted with evidence of what to her was the worst horror imaginable, that her brother, whose infamous depositions had sent her mother to the scaffold, had survived and might yet come to reign in France. Yet in spite of what she must account a proof of it, her warped sense of right and wrong obstinately refused to believe in what she could regard only as a triumph of evil.

The Freiherr von Ense had been mentioned at that terrible interview, and the name had impressed her as that of a new arrival at the Prussian Embassy in Paris, one who had lately presented himself at the Tuileries. If, as La Salle had declared, this was the nephew of that Freiherr Ulrich von Ense who had lost his life whilst escorting her brother out of France, he must have some knowledge of that mysterious affair. Therefore, before distressing her uncle, Louis

XVIII, with an account of the events at the Hôtel d'Otranto, Madame Royale decided to command the presence of this von Ense.

He happened to be absent from Paris when the summons reached the embassy, and it was three days before he received and obeyed it. In those three days several things had happened.

Fouché, having taken a night for thought after the visit of Madame Royale, had reached the conclusion that it was become more imperative than ever to pursue a forcing policy.

The course he proposed was clear and straightforward. He would formally announce to Louis XVIII the presence in Paris of the legitimate King, who had already given irrefutable proof of his identity to Madame Royale, and invite the reigning Prince to a further examination, in public or in private, of the further proofs which the Council of Louis XVII was prepared to submit, to be followed by an abdication in his favour.

So as to be armed against all emergencies, this presentation of what amounted to an ultimatum should synchronize with the arrival in Paris of the Sixteenth Division under Drouet d'Erlon. Meanwhile, he would take the necessary steps to ensure the co-operation of the National Guard, or, at least, its complete neutrality, so as to avoid bloodshed and reduce disturbance to a minimum.

Requiring a little time for this, he summoned the Council to meet two days later, which would be the first Thursday in March, so as to consider and give effect to his project.

Chapter 10

Inventions of Monsieur de Sceaux

If Fouché had heard in those days of the sudden return to Paris of the Marquis de Sceaux, it is not likely that amidst his preoccupations he would have paid much heed to that insignificant person.

Like Madame Royale, the Marquis de Sceaux, in the fervour of destructive investigation, had perceived in what he had been told of Louis-Charles a thread which it might be profitable to pursue. Much in the same spirit in which the Duchess was seeking von Ense had Monsieur de Sceaux sought the Perrins at Passavant. From the results he obtained it is to be assumed that he went very craftily to work to win the confidence of those simple, honest souls, and he never suspected that he had not won it completely where Joseph Perrin was concerned.

In Revolutionary days the identity of Louis-Charles had been dangerous not only to himself but to any who harboured him. Afterwards, under Napoleon, it had been even more dangerous, if the execution of the Duke d'Enghien after seizure on foreign soil could be taken as an indication of the likely fate of any Bourbon prince within Bonaparte's reach. Therefore that identity had been a secret so fearfully guarded by Perrin that he had not shared it even with the wife whom he had married a year after the boy had come to him. If she had sensed a mystery about this lad and the peculiar consideration which he was shown by Joseph, who yielded to his whims and accorded him liberties that were unaccountable, yet she accepted him as the son of Joseph's dead sister-in-law, whom she had never known.

Now, it was not likely that Joseph, who had kept that secret so well for so many years, would betray it to the first Frenchman who came to Passavant manifesting interest in Louis-Charles. Something de Sceaux had been able to pick up in Le Locle, where he began his investigations on the way up. A queer unsettled fellow, they there pronounced this Charles Perrin Deslys, who had been apprenticed clockmaker to Rudolph Lehmann. Lehmann, upon being visited, was contemptuous on the score of his sometime apprentice. He suspected him of not being quite right in the head; gave himself airs, and at times assumed an irritating manner of superiority with his betters. Also he suffered, seemingly, from a wander-fever, and he had a trick of disappearing for long spells. Lehmann believed that he was absent at present, had been for some months; and he let it be understood that he would not be greatly perturbed if Le Locle never saw him again. The fellow didn't appear to know whether he wanted to be a clockmaker or a farmer; for when at home, he was sometimes one, sometimes the other. The pure truth was that he was just a good-for-nothing vagabond.

Enriched and encouraged by this information, the Marquis, dropping his title and calling himself simply Georges de Sceaux, pursued his journey into the Jura. He came to snow-clad Passavant as a new-found friend of Charles Perrin Deslys on a matter very closely concerned with him, and he observed attentively the effect of this announcement.

Under cover of the dense black beard Joseph Perrin's lips closed like a trap, to be guessed from the grimness of that naturally grim face; the softness went out of the deep-set brown eyes which from under their craggy brows stared hostility at the portly, pompous visitor.

"No matter concerned with him can concern us," he growled.

The anxiety which de Sceaux's words had summoned to the pallid, wistful face of Justine changed to acute distress at those harsh words. In Madame Perrin's gentle countenance, too, the trouble deepened. She put out a hand to find her daughter's. But Justine at that moment left her side to speed, pleading, to her father's.

"If he were ill! If he were in need of us!" she cried, and thus supplied the watchful Marquis with a cue to help his indifferent wits and to amend the tale he had prepared.

The Revolution which had changed many things may have brought to those unfortunate men of birth who had been put to odd shifts to save their skins and keep their body and soul together, habits of duplicity and deceit; or else the Marquis de Sceaux was one who, whilst born a gentleman, was yet born without those lofty attributes on which the pride of his class was rightly founded. For so as to serve the aims which brought him to Passavant, he appears to have had recourse to just as much falsehood as he found necessary.

The short altercation which followed between father and daughter, and in itself supplied him with some precious information, gave him leisure and material to adjust his inventions to the circumstances he found.

Forcefully Perrin had declared that whatever trouble might have beset his nephew was now his nephew's own affair and a just punishment of heaven upon him for his sins.

"It is my affair too, Father," she had answered him with a decisiveness that matched his own.

"Yours? Are you shameless, then? Have you no sense of your wrongs?"

The mother came to set a protecting arm about her. "Don't, Joseph. She has been hurt enough."

Joseph snorted angrily. "She doesn't seem to realize it. To be still concerned with that worthless ingrate…"

"Sh! Joseph! Joseph!" She reached for his shoulder with her other hand, to repress him, especially in the presence of a stranger, to whom they were disclosing too much of their own affairs. "Be charitable with her."

"I am asked to be charitable with him," Perrin complained. "We are only poor peasant folk, I know, but…" And there he checked on the brink of the indiscretion into which his emotions were betraying him. "…But we have our feelings and our pride for all that."

He looked up at the stranger, who leaned against the table, quietly observant. "And, anyway, we do not even know what is this trouble."

"It is – alas! – as mademoiselle your daughter has surmised. This unhappy Monsieur Deslys is ill." Quickly here he had readapted the fiction with which he came prepared. "And that is scarcely the worst of it. The worst is the nature of the illness and the consequences it has brought down upon him."

Justine faced him wildly. "He is not… You do not mean…that his life is…in danger?"

"Not from his illness. No. Merely from the errors into which it has led him. Oh, do not unnecessarily distress yourself. It is not too late. All can yet be arranged if we act promptly. It is fortunate that I should have interested myself in his case; fortunate that I have some little influence, too. I have asked Monsieur de Blacas – Monsieur le Duc de Blacas is His Majesty's chief minister – and I have obtained not only a respite for your nephew, but a promise that he will be surrendered into the care of his own family. That is what brings me here."

His vagueness drove Justine to exasperation. "But what is it, sir? What is it? You do not tell us. I beg you, in charity, to be precise."

It was not, however, in the nature of Monsieur de Sceaux to be precise or yet orderly in his statements even when he was truthful. In the maze of falsehood into which he had now adventured he was of a bewildering confusion. Only gradually did the strands of his statement emerge, and when arranged in their proper order made the following pattern:

Charles Deslys had drawn upon himself the attention of the police of Paris by an insane claim based upon no more than a cast of countenance remotely resembling that of some members of the House of Bourbon. There existed people foolish enough to believe that the late Dauphin, or Louis XVII, as he became before his death, had actually escaped from the Temple and was alive. Like several other foolish impostors before him, Charles Deslys was setting up the preposterous pretence that he was the Dauphin. Engrossed in his subject, Monsieur de Sceaux did not observe the pallor that overspread the weathered face of the master of Passavant. Steadily he pursued his narrative.

If he had supposed that Deslys was no more than an impostor, he would have left him to the fate he deserved. But at an early stage of their acquaintance he had formed the clear opinion – and he had some experience in these matters – that the young man was afflicted by a mental aberration. Possibly it had been fostered and deepened by a painter scoundrel named La Salle and other ill-intentioned persons who for their own ends were trading upon the poor lad's weakness. Anyway, in this persuasion Monsieur de Sceaux had exerted himself to avert the terrible consequences with which, as they might well suppose, Deslys was threatened. He had been arrested, of course, but Monsieur de Sceaux had succeeded in convincing Monsieur de Blacas of the poor fellow's affliction, and, as a result, he was happy to say, instead of having been sent to La Force or some other prison, he had been placed in a *maison de santé*, where, whilst detained as a prisoner, he was yet treated as an invalid. With unconscious humour Monsieur de Sceaux mentioned that this house was in the Rue Cerruti. There he would be kept for one month, of which nearly the half had already elapsed. If within that time some member of his family would come forward to take charge of him and would give an undertaking to conduct him home and place him under proper restraint, no further proceedings would be taken, and he would be allowed to depart in the care of that relative.

They must understand that to this remarkable concession, due entirely to Monsieur de Sceaux's influence with and representations to Monsieur le Duc de Blacas, two factors had materially contributed: the government would prefer not to give the matter the publicity of proceedings which might inspire other impostors, and the offender, not being a French subject, would be removed out of France.

Failing, however, compliance with the conditions within the specified time, ordinary criminal proceedings would follow, with results upon which Monsieur de Sceaux need not insist. Nevertheless, he did; for he added that Charles Deslys would be fortunate if he were sentenced to nothing more than imprisonment for life.

Such was the specious tale, gradually extracted by question and answer, by which Monsieur de Sceaux hoped to lure some member of Charles Deslys' discovered family to Paris, there to convert him willy nilly into a witness for the prosecution, and so ensure for Deslys the terrible fate from which it was his pretended desire to rescue him.

It produced a consternation in his audience which in the case of Justine was blended with gratitude towards this rare friend in need, but in the case of her father deepened by his knowledge that in the claim of Louis-Charles there was no mental infirmity beyond the folly of having gone to Paris to prefer it without a single shred of evidence to support him.

It did not surprise Joseph Perrin to learn of the part played by La Salle, for Louis-Charles had given Perrin his confidence on that first night of his return to Passavant. Perrin had then done his best to dissuade him from an adventure to be undertaken under auspices so questionable, representing to him that only ill could come of it. With sound sense and a philosophy of outlook scarcely to be expected in that rustic mind, he had pointed out the peace and happiness to be found in a simple existence aloof from the world's unceasing strife. He had begged Louis-Charles to renounce an origin which hitherto had been no more than a source of torment, and to give himself peace. All the signs were that Fate was against him in the quest for the rights of his birth.

At first his arguments had seemed to be prevailing. But in the end Louis-Charles, in an exaltation, had declared that whilst he could relinquish without a pang the rights derived from his birth, he could not relinquish the duty it imposed upon him.

Perrin's rejoinder that the duty of ruling over so unruly a race as the French could as well be discharged by his uncle as by himself, had been met by an assertion that what was known of his uncle's misrule rendered his duty all the more insistent. It was almost as if in that exaltation he saw himself as the saviour for whom France was waiting. Therefore go he must at whatever sacrifice, availing himself of whatever means should offer, which was why he seemed to lend himself as an impostor to the schemes of La Salle.

After that as a last resource, in his concern for the lad, Perrin had enlisted the aid of Justine to persuade him to remain at Passavant, had sought to exploit to that end the obvious affection binding those two. So that whilst he had afterwards cursed Louis-Charles for his ill-requital of all that he owed to Passavant, yet in the depths of his just soul he had taken upon himself some of the blame for what had happened.

If some rancour abode in him, yet it was not of a degree to bring him – as it might have brought another – to account Louis-Charles well served by the terrible situation in which Monsieur de Sceaux informed them that he now found himself. Besides, the habit of guarding and protecting Louis-Charles – always in his eyes a romantic figure deserving of infinite compassion for all that he had suffered at the hands of Fate – had become ingrained in Joseph Perrin's nature. Because of this, whatever the wrong done by Louis-Charles to him and his, he could not bear now the thought of leaving him to perish.

In one particular, however, this self-sufficient gentleman from Paris inspired his shrewd senses with an indefinable mistrust. He gave it utterance.

"I am asking myself, sir, how the association of a gentleman of your world with my nephew could have come about."

But for this Monsieur de Sceaux had prepared himself. "You must see that it was precisely into my world that he would be brought by the adventurer La Salle. I made his acquaintance through some misguided friends of mine whom La Salle had persuaded of the honesty of his preposterous claim. It is astounding that there should be such people. But what would you?" He shrugged. "Men, even intelligent men, can be unbelievably credulous."

The explanation was not one to strain belief. Frowning darkly in thought, Perrin stroked his beard.

"Monsieur, it is a great thing that you have done, to undertake this journey for the sake of a man who is nothing to you."

Monsieur de Sceaux did not know whether this implied a doubt. But he answered boldly.

"I am a Christian, I hope. And I am susceptible to compassion. I could not stand idly by and see this unfortunate man destroyed."

"Nevertheless, an act of rare nobility. A truly Christian act, indeed. It is beyond mere thanks. But what to do? It is all terrible. God knows we may have little cause for goodwill towards him. But imprisonment for life…perhaps the scaffold…"

Justine's cry of terror interrupted him. "Oh, my God!"

"What to do? What to do?" groaned Perrin.

For one wild moment he thought of declaring to this stranger that in the claim he made Louis-Charles was neither mad nor fraudulent. But of this he realized in time the futility. Its only possible result would be to bring scorn upon himself for a foolish attempt to buttress an impostor.

"There is one thing that you can do, monsieur," said the Marquis, "and that I have shown you. The way is open. You have but to follow it, and if you do so, you may dismiss your alarms. My assistance naturally continues at your disposal."

Justine was on her knees beside her father. "You hear," she cried. "You hear."

He frowned down upon her upturned pleading face. Marking the lines of care which these last months had brought to it and remembering the source of them, his heart grew hard again.

"I hear. Yes. What then? Do you conceive that we have a duty to him still?"

Her voice was very soft and plaintive. "I know that I need him, Father."

"Ay, ay. You need him. I know. But will he need you?" Exasperation rose in him. "Oh, God! This is to drive a man mad. I don't know why I was ever cursed with the burden of him. And, anyway, what is to do? What can we do? Am I to go to Paris in this state? You see that if I had the will, I haven't the legs. I am in no case to travel, crippled as I am."

"Then let me go," said Justine.

"Justine!" cried her mother in protesting horror.

And in horror of the notion her father frowned on her.

"You? To Paris? Alone?"

Still on her knees, she swung from one to the other of them as she asked, "Is he to die, then?" Her fierceness left them dumb. "You see that there is no answer to that. That with his life at stake you dare not deny me."

"But the dangers, Justine," her mother wailed. "You don't know the dangers, child."

"What dangers? And what of dangers? What of his danger? Can we sit here in peace whilst...? Oh, my God!" She bounded to her feet, and swung white-faced upon Monsieur de Sceaux. "How soon can we set out, monsieur?"

"Wait! Wait!" Her father's voice was harshly imperative. "What's this? Is all settled, then? You cannot go. At least, not alone. Not thus. I might still do much – though God knows why – for a man who no longer deserves anything at my hands. But not that much. What do we know, after all?"

"Monsieur!" It was a bellow of pompous indignation from Monsieur de Sceaux.

Perrin's tone made little of that outraged dignity. "Sir, sir, your good faith may be beyond suspicion, your intentions excellent. But it remains that you are a stranger to me. It remains that I have no more than your word for all this. Not that I presume to doubt your word. But it is a question of my daughter, my only child. I do not know if you are a father, sir. But whether you are or not, would you suffer your daughter to go forth thus alone with a stranger, upon such a journey? Would you?"

Monsieur de Sceaux was still hesitating over his answer when Justine spoke.

"There is no need for me to go alone. I can take Grosjean. Let him come with me for protection. Then you will know that no harm can come to me." She was on her knees again beside her father. "You see that I must go. There is no one else, and whatever you feel about Charlot, you would not wish this dreadful thing to happen to him. Oh, you must not blame Charlot. It is that wicked evil man La Salle who is blameworthy. He possessed some power over him. It is La Salle's evil schemes that have brought this affliction to his mind. It was La Salle who took him away. But for him Charlot would never have gone. I am sure of it. Sure, sure, Father."

She melted him with her prayer. He was persuaded, too, of the truth of her judgment of La Salle and the part he had played in luring Louis-Charles to France.

"I will bring him home, Father," she confidently promised. "And this time all will be well."

He wondered. It might be that Louis-Charles had learnt at last his lesson, and that if she went all would yet end well for her and for Louis-Charles.

He stroked her golden head with a hand that shook. "If you took Grosjean..." He fell to musing.

She put her arms round him and buried her face in his breast.

To his great relief Monsieur de Sceaux saw in Perrin's grim face that he was conquered.

Chapter 11

Re-enter Monsieur de Sceaux

The Marquis de Sceaux arrived back in Paris with his companions on Tuesday, the first of March, the very day on which Fouché was summoning for the following Thursday the Council of Louis XVII to consider and frame the ultimatum to the usurper.

Monsieur de Sceaux put up at the Hôtel d'Eylau in the Rue de Richelieu, and on a pretence of going to ascertain the precise present condition of Charles Deslys, he took himself off to the Rue Cerruti and the Hôtel d'Otranto.

He left behind him a Justine filled with an indefinable uneasiness that was not entirely or solely concerned with Charles. The general vagueness displayed by Monsieur de Sceaux when she sought greater details from him, replies which merely deflected her questions, explaining nothing, inspired her with a growing mistrust of this smooth, pompous gentleman, which was fully shared by Grosjean. Nor was her confidence increased by his disclosure of a rank which it would have been inexpedient to have continued to conceal.

Whilst in vague uneasiness she waited now at the Hôtel d'Eylau, Monsieur de Sceaux was at the Hôtel d'Otranto, asking to be received by Mademoiselle de Castillon-Fouquières. To ensure that an audience be accorded him, he had scribbled three lines of a note, which he now proffered to the gorgeous Swiss who kept the vestibule. The

Swiss, having passed on the note to a lackey, ushered Monsieur de Sceaux into the blue-and-gold antechamber on the ground floor.

Mademoiselle de Castillon read the note aloud to her mother.

"Mademoiselle, Urged by a devotion to be extinguished only with life itself, I have been pursuing investigations abroad, the fruits of which I now beg to be permitted to lay before you, assuring you that they closely concern your happiness and perhaps your very honour.

"My honour," she said, with resentful disdain. "How does my honour concern this man? He was insolent to me once. It is an insolence to imagine that I could consent to receive him again after that." And she pulled the bell-rope, to recall the lackey.

"You will refuse him, then?" drawled the Duchess from the sofa, where she lounged with a copy of *Manon Lescaut.*

"What else? I have my dignity, I hope."

"Dignity is good. But wisdom is still better. There is no wisdom in refusing to hear what spite may have to say. Spite can be so very informing."

"I desire no information from Monsieur de Sceaux."

"It can also forewarn. If he intends mischief, as I should suppose, it would do no harm to have a glimpse of it."

The servant entered. It was Madame who spoke. "Beg Monsieur le Marquis de Sceaux to give himself the trouble of coming up."

Mademoiselle shrugged her white shoulders, visible above the high-waisted sheath of royal blue that gowned her. She moved in her slim stately rigidity to a chair beside her mother, and was seated when the Marquis was introduced. She interrupted his compliments.

"You have a communication to make, monsieur."

It took him a moment to recover from the douche of that cold haughtiness.

"Alas! I would that I had not. But my duty to you... I could not bear that you should be the victim of the fraud that I suspected. I am gifted – or so it is conceded, mesdames – with perhaps more than ordinary sagacity. For my sins, I often perceive what is hidden from others."

"And still more often, no doubt, what is not there at all," said the Duchess sweetly. "It so often happens to you clairvoyant people."

"I would that it happened now. For your daughter's sake I would that it happened now. I should have rejoiced to have found myself in error."

"Would it not be better," said frigid Mademoiselle, "to tell the tale you have come to tell?"

But he stood upon such solid ground that he was not to be disconcerted. "I warn you, dear mademoiselle, that it will shock you."

"Having warned me, please proceed."

He smiled. Let her indulge her pertness if she must. She would be on her knees when he had done. He cleared his throat.

"I have not spared myself in my deep concern for you. I have been to Switzerland, to Le Locle, and on to Passavant in the Jura. You will remember telling me that it was from Passavant that this fellow came who calls himself Charles Deslys. No one else appears to have had the wit to investigate at the source. It was left for me. And this is what I found."

He described the homestead and advanced his evidence that the man, whose full name was Charles Perrin Deslys, was the peasant nephew of Joseph Perrin of Passavant, an impostor like so many others who had traded upon the freak of a likeness so as to set themselves up as the Orphan of the Temple. This one had enjoyed the advantage of being instructed and abetted by an adventurer named La Salle, who chanced to be exceptionally informed upon matters concerned with the late Dauphin.

The tale that should have shattered smugness into consternation was told, and the only consternation was the narrator's. For the audience sat unmoved, Mademoiselle stiff and straight, with the faintest of disdainful smiles on her cold lips, Madame considering him through a gold-rimmed spy-glass with a broader and more languid expression of amusement. He looked from the calm of one to that of the other in amazement.

"You don't believe me?"

"Monsieur le Marquis," said the Duchess, "you are behind the fair. A week ago your tale might have impressed us. Now..." She shrugged her broad shoulders. "We can only deplore your wasted pains. Madame Royale has acknowledged her brother."

In that large face the small mouth fell open. "Acknowledged him? Acknowledged that peasant lout for the Dauphin?"

"For the King," Mademoiselle corrected. "King Louis XVII."

"But I know him to be an impostor. I know it. I know who he is, as I've told you."

"You will not easily persuade Madame d'Angoulême of that. His Majesty supplied proof. Conclusive proof."

"So can I give proof. I bring evidence." He spoke in excitement.

Mademoiselle lifted her fine brows. "Evidence?"

"Witnesses. His own cousin, Joseph Perrin's daughter, and one of the farm-hands from Passavant."

"Take them to the Tuileries, and see what Madame Royale will say to you," Mademoiselle advised him, "If that is all you have to tell us, Monsieur le Marquis, it only remains to thank you for the interest displayed and the vain labours undertaken."

"But it is not all." They were driving him to frenzy. If he could not awaken reason, he might still at least arouse the demon of jealousy. "This girl I have brought all the way from the Jura is soon to be a mother. She comes to claim the father of her child."

That stirred them. "Are you telling us that he is married?" shrilled the Duchess.

"Oh no. This scoundrel was not so conscientious."

The Duchess shuddered, and her dark brows met in a scowl. Her tone was outraged. "Monsieur le Marquis, you forget yourself. To mention such a thing in the presence of my daughter!"

But the daughter's cool cheeks were mantled by no blushing evidence of violated modesty. She even permitted herself a little trill of scornful laughter. "Monsieur le Marquis offers as proof that Monsieur Deslys is an impostor the fact that a peasant girl has been negligent of her honour. Oh, a convincing argument."

Monsieur de Sceaux was dumbfounded. His shocked eyes considered her in unbelief. "Is it possible, mademoiselle, that the dream of becoming Queen of France has robbed you not only of judgment but of delicacy?"

Madame rose in her majesty, large and imposing. "Monsieur le Marquis, I think you left your manners at this place, Passavant, if that is the name of it." She crossed the room as she spoke. "There can be no purpose in detaining you." She pulled the bell-rope.

He shrugged in anger. He spread his large hands. "Oh, as you please; as you please. Persist, then, in your infatuation. The awakening, I promise you, will be the ruder. I thought to save you. It only remains to commiserate you."

A servant appeared.

"Monsieur le Marquis de Sceaux is leaving," said the Duchess.

Monsieur de Sceaux, livid to the lips, bowed himself out. The bows remained unacknowledged. Madame de Castillon-Fouquières looked down her hooked nose at him. Mademoiselle, sitting erect and disdainful, merely thrust out her chin a little farther.

For Monsieur de Sceaux, without hope now of advantage, there still remained the satisfaction of ruining the man who had destroyed his marriage prospects. And he went about it without delay, proceeding exactly as had been mockingly suggested to him. He took himself off to the Tuileries, so that he might dispel the illusions under which they told him that Madame Royale was lying.

He sought immediate audience of Her Highness, and again so as to make sure that it would be vouchsafed, he made use of a note, in which he respectfully begged to be heard upon a matter of the first importance concerned with "the man who calls himself Charles Deslys".

It procured him almost instant admission to the presence of that perturbed and harassed lady. Now that she had recovered from the shock of the disclosure made by Louis-Charles, she was encouraging every doubt that would combat the hideous and inconvenient conviction.

Here, in Madame Royale and Madame de Brézé, he found an audience very different from that which he had just left. He was heard with so much sympathy and eagerness that he begged to be allowed to repeat his tale to the King. This, however, was for the moment denied him.

"There is no need yet to distress His Majesty," Her Highness told him. "Nor do you bring us quite all that we need so as to disprove a claim that is as impudent as it is well supported. But it will help, I think; particularly if I can find elsewhere what more I need so as to explain this man's astounding knowledge. I am waiting for it now, Monsieur le Marquis."

She must have found it that same night; for early on the following morning Fouché received a note in which Madame Royale desired to be informed of the earliest hour at which Monsieur le Duc d'Otranto could make it convenient to receive her.

To the Duke of Otranto, holding now in his deft hands all the threads by which the various puppets of the show he was preparing were to dance when he took up the curtain, this request was very opportune. He conceived the doubts and fears which impelled Madame Royale to seek this fresh interview. It would be convenient for him to receive Her Highness on Thursday, when the Council would be sitting. He would have her brought before it without warning, so that she might supply to responsible persons, who would afterwards publish it, the crowning proof of her brother's survival and identity. And she should depart again to convey the Council's ultimatum to her uncle, the usurper.

Chapter 12

The Dupe

Madame Royale did not come alone on Thursday to the Hôtel d'Otranto at the appointed time. She was accompanied, in addition to her lady-in-waiting, by two gentlemen and an awed and bewildered girl, of whose existence she appeared to remain unconscious after having bestowed upon her no more than a passing glance of a freezing haughtiness.

Into the library, however, where the Council was in session, she chose to be ushered alone, leaving her companions to wait in the antechamber.

The sight of the company, numbering a round dozen, assembled at the long table of gleaming mahogany, took her completely by surprise, and brought her to a frowning halt on the threshold with something of the feeling of having walked into a trap.

From the table's foot, the lean and bent Fouché strode stiffly to meet her, bowing low. The others rose in their places on her appearance and remained standing, all save Louis-Charles, who kept his seat as by royal right.

To reinforce the ordinary members of the Council – Davout, Ney, Ouvrard and La Salle – there were present also Lebrun, Duke of Plaisance, the distinguished lawyer and man of letters who for two years had been Napoleon's Governor of Holland, the Marquis de Sisteron and Roland d'Auguié, men whose notorious disaffection from Louis XVIII disposed them strongly to support the Orphan of the Temple, and whose position and abilities made them welcome on this Council; and there were three others, the Vicomte de Foudras, the Chevalier de Marville, and the Abbé Fleuriot, men of influence and authority whom Fouché had brought in at the last moment.

From the threshold Madame Royale challenged her host. "What is this, monsieur? My request was for a private interview."

Fouché inclined himself again. "Apprehending the subject of the interview, madame, it seemed to me that Your Highness might be glad of this opportunity of meeting His Majesty's Council."

"His Majesty's..." Her red-rimmed eyes raked the ranks of those present. "You go rather fast, Monsieur le Duc."

"It becomes necessary to move, madame."

"I see. The movement may prove unpleasant for you in the end, and for some of these very foolish dupes of yours." She came forward. "However, since you have decided upon a full audience, let us make it fuller still. You will oblige me by requesting the presence of Mesdames de Castillon-Fouquières, so that I may correct in them any impression my last visit may have left. A chair if you please, Monsieur le Duc."

Fouché advanced an arm-chair to a place near his own at the foot of the table. Madame de Brézé placed a cushion, and Her Highness sat down, drawing her fur pelisse about her, as if cold. Monsieur de Chassenon, who had ushered her into the room, went off at a nod from Fouché on the errand she requested. Then the company sat down again, to wait in an uneasy silence.

Louis-Charles at the head of the table, with La Salle immediately on his left, braced himself for the battle of which he had read the declaration in the single malevolent glance his sister had bestowed upon him. He was not in the best of moods for it. The Council had already been in session for an hour, and the various matters debated had led to altercations. The first of these had been between Fouché and Ney. The Prince de la Moskowa disapproved of the military measures taken by Drouet d'Erlon and resented that they should have been decided without reference to him in whose department the matter lay. After that there had been an altercation between Fouché and Ouvrard on financial matters, in which the swarthy, fleshly banker had taken the coarse, overbearing tone that was to be expected from him. There had also been a difference of opinion between Fouché and Davout on the immediate methods to be pursued. And throughout all this, Louis-Charles, as if of no account, had sat ignored by these men who professed themselves his servants and in whom he now beheld his masters. Not once had his opinion been invited, nor had anyone troubled to explain to him any of the matters which he could not yet be expected to understand. He might occupy the presidential seat, but it was Fouché who supplied the presiding spirit, who held the reins of kingly power, who answered everything and disposed of everything.

Once only had Louis-Charles ventured to raise his voice. It was during Ouvrard's wrangle with Fouché. He had asked for light in connection with the reimbursement of a loan that Ouvrard had made. He was answered shortly by Ouvrard in terms intelligible only to a financier, and he was made to feel by that answer that his interruption was stupid and frivolous.

Hence it resulted that his mood was disgruntled enough before the coming of Her Highness. Her advent, her manner, her veiled threat in summoning him to battle imposed upon him at the same time a sense of deadly lassitude.

At long last the uncomfortable silence was ended by the reopening of the double doors and the announcement of Madame de Castillon-Fouquières and her daughter.

Fouché went to meet them. To dispel their surprise at finding themselves in the presence of this assembly, he informed them that Her Highness commanded their presence so that they might hear a communication she had graciously come to make.

They curtsied, first to Madame Royale, Mademoiselle de Castillon achieving it without loss of her stiff, almost hostile dignity, and then to Louis-Charles with a deliberate ostentation that drew a thin, bitter smile to the lips of Her Highness. As they took the chairs which Fouché advanced for them Her Highness spoke.

She possessed the power of rapping out a censure or a retort with a sting to it; but when it came to making a sustained exposition she was as awkward and clumsy as in most other things that she attempted.

"I came here," she said, repeating herself, "so as to correct an impression which I may have left behind me here some days ago. I came to speak to Monsieur le Duc d'Otranto. To disabuse his mind. But I am not sorry to find you all here, since now you may all learn the imposture you are fostering. That is, if you are not already aware of it; if, in fact, you are not all of you partners in this fraud."

She paused there, to find herself silently regarded by fourteen pairs of eyes out of countenances that were set.

"That it is a fraud I am today in a position to prove. It can leave no doubt with any of you. I shall prove it by witnesses – unimpeachable witnesses. And I shall tell you who this man really is; also by witnesses."

As she spoke she jerked a hand forward, to indicate Louis-Charles where he sat silently glooming at her from the other end of the long table. From the remainder of her audience there was still neither sound nor movement.

Fouché had slewed his chair round and a little away from the table, so that he might face her. Never had his low-lidded eyes looked more sleepy, never had the smile more broadly stretched the lipless mouth. He had the air of an evil cat that watches the gambols of an audacious prey, withholding the stroke of the paw that will presently stretch it lifeless.

"Perhaps I had better begin by acquainting you with your impostor's real identity. Monsieur le Duc, be good enough to summon from the antechamber Monsieur le Marquis de Sceaux and the young woman who accompanies him."

Fouché raised his brows without relaxing his smile. For a moment he seemed about to speak, then, containing himself, moved quietly to the door.

Madame de Castillon-Fouquières and her daughter exchanged glances, and in the magnificent eyes of the Duchess there was a gleam of scornful amusement. Madame Royale, they opined, was leaning upon a singularly rotten staff if she depended upon the sort of evidence they knew to be de Sceaux's.

Louis-Charles, raising his eyes as de Sceaux appeared, came suddenly out of his gloomy calm. His hands clutched the arms of his chair and his eyes dilated as they rested upon the girl the Marquis was ushering into the room.

At the same moment the timidly advancing, utterly bewildered Justine beheld him in that seat of honour, and checked, scared eyes returning his own scared stare.

She was simply yet daintily dressed in a bourgeois fashion of ten years or more ago. Her petticoat was striped in two shades of green, a muslin fichu crossed her breast, worn under a short spencer, and a dark-green velvet bonnet, of mob-cap pattern, shaded the winsome face.

She remained at gaze as if petrified before this culmination of all her doubts and misgivings of the last twenty-four hours. Whatever the purpose for which Monsieur de Sceaux had lured her hither, clearly it was not what he had represented.

As she stood there in woeful bewilderment, the Marquis took her by the arm and drew her gently forward. In her nervousness she moved awkwardly. If her scared eyes swept round the ranks of that imposing company, they returned almost at once to the amazed contemplation of Louis-Charles. His arched brows were contracted now, his face was dark. It was impossible for him to suppose anything other than that she had been brought there for the purpose of destroying him.

He heard Madame d'Angoulême's acid voice. "You know this man, mademoiselle. Do you not?"

To Justine it seemed that it was her heart beating in her throat and almost suffocating her that rendered her answer barely audible.

"Yes, madame. Oh yes, madame."

"Who is he, then?"

"He is my cousin."

"But what is his name?"

"Charles Perrin Deslys."

"And where does he come from?"

"From Passavant, in the Jura, beyond Neuchâtel."

"And what did he do there?"

"At one time he helped on the farm. Then he went apprentice to a clockmaker in Le Locle, and became, himself, a clockmaker."

"When was he last with you?"

"Five months ago. In September last."

"Had he been away before that?"

"Yes, madame. In Prussia."

"Did he return alone?"

"No, madame. He brought a gentleman with him to Passavant."

"Do you see this gentleman here? Look round, mademoiselle."

Obediently her timid eyes went round the company. "He is there, madame. Monsieur de La Salle."

"Was it Monsieur de La Salle who persuaded him to leave Passavant again and come to France?"

"Yes, madame. Monsieur de La Salle possessed a dreadful influence over him. It terrified me."

"Had you ever seen Monsieur de La Salle before?"

"Never until he came with Charles from Germany."

"And you had not…"

The resentment that had been steadily swelling in Louis-Charles exploded suddenly. He smote the table with his hand resoundingly, to interrupt her.

"Enough of this." His voice was vibrant. Anger lent him strength. "I am not on my trial, and you shall not put me on it. Not here. In the Courts, when you please. This lady has told you nothing that I have ever concealed, can tell you nothing that is not already known to every one of you, unless Monsieur d'Otranto has been negligent. All this is idle. If I am to be discredited, it will have to be done by other means."

There was a fairly general murmur of approval.

Madame de Castillon-Fouquières looked at Monsieur de Sceaux with a broad sneer. Her daughter, straight and composed, did not look at him at all. Her eyes were approvingly on Louis-Charles.

Fouché made a humming sound at the end of which, "Your Highness wastes her time, I think," he purred.

"I'll waste a little more of it, Monsieur le Duc, in the interests of all of you, so as to save you from further treason and its unpleasant consequences. Monsieur de Sceaux, please be good enough to tell these gentlemen what you have discovered."

But Fouché still interposed. "Madame, you have heard His Majesty protest that he is not upon his trial. It is a protest in which we must all uphold him. If a trial be desired, process may be taken in the ordinary way, publicly before the Courts."

"It will follow if you force it upon us. But I hardly think that any of you will care to face the risk when you have heard all. And do not misunderstand me. It is not out of mercy to you or your impostor that I take this course, but out of concern for my uncle the King and the peace of the realm. I do not wish to add this miserable affair to the troubles that already distract both my family and the nation."

"What happens here, madame, cannot avert that," said Fouché. "That is why I say that this is merely to waste time."

"A moment, Monsieur le Duc." It was Lebrun who spoke. "There can be no disadvantage in hearing what Her Highness believes to be evidence."

"Faith, that's in my mind, too," Ouvrard agreed.

Mademoiselle de Castillon-Fouquières permitted a sound of scornful impatience to escape her.

Fouché looked at them tight-lipped. Then the smile reappeared.

"Lawyers and bankers are by nature cautious."

"So are soldiers sometimes," said Davout. "Her Highness promises to add to our knowledge."

Fouché shrugged, and went to find a chair at a little distance from the foot of the table. He sat down, crossed his slender legs and lowered his eyelids until he seemed to be asleep, whilst at

Her Highness' invitation Monsieur de Sceaux consequentially told his tale.

He had been actuated, he said, by uneasiness and a sense of responsibility towards those friends of his who were putting their whole faith in Monsieur Deslys; and here his bulging eyes sought Mademoiselle de Castillon-Fouquières, and met a withering glance. It was in his nature, he hoped, always to do the best for his friends, even at the risk of being misunderstood. He had gone to Neuchâtel, to Le Locle and on to Passavant; and he related in detail the evidence collected there that the man who claimed to be Louis XVII was a rather poor-witted, eccentric nephew of Joseph Perrin, who had come under the evil influence of a designing scoundrel named La Salle.

"I won't interrupt you now," said La Salle, and his drawl rang sinister. "We'll discuss your description of me afterwards, between ourselves."

Madame de Castillon-Fouquières did not quite suppress an unkind laugh.

The Marquis quivered as if struck. Having recovered he went on calmly to render a full account of what he had found and learnt at Passavant. He had sought, he said, to bring Joseph Perrin to Paris, to claim his nephew. But the old man, too infirm to undertake the journey, had sent his daughter instead, in the care of an old servant from the farm, who could add his testimony if they accounted it necessary. "To what Mademoiselle Justine Perrin had already told them, she could add..." he was ending, when Justine interrupted him.

At last she perceived clearly the real reason for which she had been brought – a dupe – to Paris. Her shyness lost in burning indignation, she sprang from the chair to which the Marquis had conducted her before beginning his account.

"This is infamous!" she broke in upon his speech, and then swung to address the assembly. "This is a trick – a mean, shabby trick. I supposed this Monsieur de Sceaux a gentleman."

"Others have made the same mistake," jeered La Salle, to be instantly hushed by Louis-Charles.

"He came to us pretending that my cousin was in danger."

"My faith, that was hardly a pretence," said Madame Royale.

"I think so. Oh, I think so," murmured Fouché, whose eyes were open again.

"We were told that he was ill – mentally ill – and in great danger. That is the lie he told us. That is how he brought me. That is why I answered your questions, madame – your mean, tricky questions."

Her Highness stiffened; but Justine, her voice growing shriller, went recklessly on. "I was brought here, I now see, so that I might ruin him, so that I might give evidence that would…that would…"

She choked there, and turned abruptly to Louis-Charles, sobs breaking her utterance. "Charlot! Charlot! You don't think…you can't believe that I would have come if I had known…"

And there Louis-Charles, his own eyes moist and laden with sorrow, rising, checked her. "Hush, Justine. Hush, child. Do not be troubled. You have done me no harm. I have nothing to fear from anything that you or anyone can disclose."

De Sceaux laughed aloud. "Not even when she declares that you are her father's sister's child, and that your name is Perrin Deslys – Charlot Perrin Deslys?"

Mademoiselle de Castillon-Fouquières was now watching him with anxious intentness; so for that matter were they all. He sank down into his chair again. His voice was quiet.

"I must have called myself by some name during those years of my concealment. I could not call myself by my own name and continue to appear related to those who sheltered me. This girl was born two years after I was taken to Passavant, and she grew up believing me to be her father's nephew. Even her mother believed me to be the son of Joseph Perrin's sister. Joseph Perrin was not married when I went to him, and he considered the secret of my birth too dangerous to be breathed even to his wife. Is there anything in all this that does not accord with, that does not follow from, what you were previously told?" He sensed an atmosphere of growing mistrust about him, and ended abruptly: "I think Monsieur d'Otranto, at least, is well aware of it all."

"Of as much of it as matters," said Fouché.

"Does it not all matter?" It was Mademoiselle de Castillon-Fouquières who suddenly startled them by that question.

"Not as much as may seem," said Fouché.

"In that case," said Her Highness with sour humour, "we must endeavour to supply something further. Monsieur de Sceaux, be good enough to conduct this young person to the antechamber, and require Monsieur le Baron von Ense to come to me."

Justine stood hesitant, overawed. Monsieur de Sceaux touched her arm, and after a glance of despairing appeal to Louis-Charles, which he answered by a wistful smile, she allowed herself to be led away.

Chapter 13

On Trial

The Freiherr Karl Theodor von Ense, tall, blond, correct and grave, came in quickly, and, with his heels together, bowed from the waist, first to Madame Royale and then to the assembled company. Declining the offer of a chair, which Fouché hastened to make him, he remained standing beside Her Highness.

Across the room, from his place near the head of the table, La Salle was contemplating in amazement this man whom six years ago it would not have been a presumption in him to have called his friend. If the Baron's presence surprised him, it did not bring him the uneasiness it would have brought a little while earlier. Aware now of the genuineness of Charles Deslys' claim, he had no fear of the success of any assaults upon it.

Her Highness presented him. "Monsieur le Baron Karl Theodor von Ense, now attached to the Prussian Embassy in Paris, will already be known to some of you. He is the nephew of a gentleman who was welcome in the old days at Paris and Versailles, and he is in a position to tell you, with the authority of full knowledge, how, where, and when, my brother died."

That phrase had the curious effect of stirring Louis-Charles to exasperation as nothing hitherto had done. There was the bitterness of heartbreak in his voice. "How you must desire to believe that, madame!"

She did not heed him. She looked round and up at von Ense. "Will you tell them, Baron?"

Von Ense stood in view of all, a calm, self-assured gentleman of unimpeachable integrity, with an air that in itself commanded confidence and trust. He told a frank and clear tale, in smooth if guttural French.

Undoubtedly the Dauphin, or, rather Louis XVII, had been smuggled out of the Temple Prison. That occurred in January of '95. For two years after that he had been kept in concealment in France. Then it had been considered best by his friends to convey him to the Court of Prussia. The Baron announced himself in a position definitely to assert this, because it was his own uncle, Ulrich von Ense, who was entrusted with the person of the young King and the mission of escorting him out of France. His uncle succeeded in reaching Geneva with the boy. Here, finding government officers close on their heels, they set out to cross the lake, so as to gain the shelter of the Prussian principality of Neuchâtel. They did this in defiance of a storm that was raging at the time. The boat was lost, and all in it perished, as he had ascertained on the spot. "My uncle, Ulrich von Ense," he ended, "is buried at Geneva."

Then Fouché nodded and spoke. "Yes. And Louis XVII? Where do you say he is buried?"

"In the Lake Léman. His body was never recovered."

"Ah! And how does one prove a death in Prussia without a body? Here in France it is sometimes difficult to prove a death even when a body is supplied!"

Someone laughed a fat, throaty laugh at the sly allusion. It was Ouvrard. "As in the Cemetery of the Madeleine," he said, the great bulk of him shaking with relish of the sarcasm.

But von Ense remained grave. "You will understand that when I received news of the death of my uncle I naturally went at once to Geneva and made the most searching investigation." With slow emphasis he added: "I verified beyond possibility of doubt that all who were in that boat – my uncle, the boy who accompanied him and the two boatmen – were all drowned. The boat foundered within sight of a crowd on the quay at Lausanne. A rescue was attempted but had to be abandoned. Even now, after the lapse of years, I could still bring witnesses from the shore of Lake Léman to swear to this. But there is not the need to go so far in quest of a witness. There is a gentleman seated at your table who can, himself, testify. It is the gentleman who accompanied my uncle and King Louis XVII in that flight, and without whose courage and address Geneva would never have been reached.

"Monsieur de La Salle, I beg you to take your friends more fully into your confidence than you appear yet to have done. Tell them what you told me in Berlin in 1808 about the loss of that boat and all its occupants, the tale which I went to Geneva to verify."

That invitation, delivered with a tinge of irony, made some stir about the Council table, and La Salle, already branded by Justine as a man who had exercised a malign influence over Louis-Charles, found himself under the company's uneasy frowning regard, with the single exception of Fouché, who remained sleepily smiling. But he showed no sign of perturbation as he quietly drawled his answer.

"Since His Majesty, Louis XVII, lives and is here present, it follows that I was mistaken in Berlin, deceived by the information I had received when I reached Geneva. For I did not arrive there with the King and the Baron von Ense. I remained behind, to form, as it were, a rearguard for them."

Lebrun, the grave, elderly lawyer, the latest recruit to the ranks of Louis-Charles' supporters, turned sharply to question him.

"But if you had your information from those who witnessed the foundering of the boat, do you pretend that they too were all deceived?"

"Since the King is here, it follows that they must have been."

"This is to beg the question, sir," said Lebrun warmly. "It does not supply the information we obviously require."

Louis-Charles sat forward, stifling resentment of the mistrust by which he found himself beset. "Let me supply it," he said. And quietly he told his tale. We know that it was not one of those tales that bear within themselves the elements of conviction;

Louis-Charles possessed no natural gift of narrative; the suspicion of those present, increasing as he proceeded, closed about him like a fog, with the result that the tale, such as it was, could not have been worse told.

He ended lamely, and as he sat back, brushing the heavy brown hair from his brow in that familiar gesture of distress, the silence was ominous.

Madame de Castillon-Fouquières, in a condition of manifest agitation, had been clutching the arm of her daughter, who sat in her usual tensely erect attitude, but with a disfiguring frown on her white brow, her eyes fixed upon her betrothed. And their glance was of stern inquiry rather than affection.

Then said Lebrun: "This account might have carried more weight if we had received it before we heard Monsieur le Baron von Ense."

That cold, dry comment brought a dull flush to the pale cheeks of Louis-Charles and a smile of sour gratification to the lips of Madame Royale. But it was Ouvrard who spoke. Suddenly agitated, his big face inflamed, he turned to Fouché.

"In the name of God, Monsieur le Duc, what are we to believe?"

Fouché awoke, and sneered: "That your millions are safe. You need have no fear for them where I stake my reputation."

"Your knowledge and your insight are admitted, Duke," the Prince of Eckmühl interposed. "But you are not immune from error."

Fouché was bland. "Not immune perhaps. No. But neither am I addicted to it. And no one, I think, has ever found me rash. Accept my word for it that there is no error here. If I had entertained a doubt of His Majesty's identity, his tale, which some of you may mistrust, would have dispelled it. For it accords exactly with the knowledge that has been long in my possession."

Madame Royale's red-rimmed eyes flamed malevolently. "What do you say? My God, Fouché, your head may answer for your audacity."

"It will be a change. Hitherto my audacity has always answered for my head."

Ney asked a question. His handsome face was overcast.

"Are we not all forgetting something? One man, at least, must have known what actually happened. Lebas. Is it to be believed that he would not have conveyed the news of His Majesty's survival to those who were most concerned?"

"That thought was in my mind," said Lebrun. "It is not to be believed."

"Of course not," Fouché agreed. "Lebas sent a letter at once, giving an account of the King's survival, to the Baron de Batz, who had organized the escape from France."

"What became of that letter?" cried someone.

"Wait. That is not all. The Baron von Ense will tell you that his uncle was a man of order and system. So as to provide for every eventuality, the Baron Ulrich von Ense wrote a letter in duplicate before embarking for Lausanne, and he sealed both copies. One of these he left with Lebas to be forwarded to de Batz, the other he delivered to the King, together with some other papers and a seal that had belonged to His Late Majesty Louis XVI, to serve him as credentials at the Court of Prussia. This the letter, itself, stated. One of those copies, together with Lebas' letter giving the account of the King's survival, fell into the hands of the police of the Directoire. They were in the State archives when these came into my possession as Minister of Police, and in the archives they have remained, so that they must have been seen there by the ministers of the present occupant of the throne and by that occupant himself."

That statement, which drew a fresh gasp of indignation from Her Highness, made upon the others an impression which was instantly dispelled by Ouvrard, governed now by anxiety for the millions he had advanced.

"And if these documents should not now be found in the archives, you will say of course that they have been destroyed."

There was a sudden full revelation of Fouché's eyes. Their heavy lids rolled back like the membrane from the eye of a reptile, and the malevolent flash of their glance withered the banker. "If they are no longer there, it will be because they have been destroyed," he said. "And that would not be surprising."

With a grunt, Ouvrard sank back and was sullenly silent.

If any other at that table shared the doubt expressed in the banker's innuendo, that other was not La Salle. He was moved almost to laughter at his own fatuity at Ferrières when he had imagined that he imposed a false pretender upon Fouché. At last he held the explanation of why Fouché had so readily believed him.

"In any case," Lebrun was saying, "there fortunately remains the letter that the Baron von Ense gave his royal charge, together with the other documents you mentioned and the seal of His Late Majesty."

Fouché looked along the table at Louis-Charles, who met the glance and read the invitation in it. His high arched brows came together. He was in visible distress. But he braced himself and in forced calm related the circumstances in which they had been stolen from him when he was on his way to appeal to Frederick William of Prussia.

Madame Royale uttered a short, stabbing laugh. "Well schooled, is he not? Well rehearsed! An answer to everything."

Davout was scowling at Fouché. "It comes to this, then: that actually there is no evidence whatever in existence of the identity you have attributed to Monsieur Charles Deslys. Have you been quite fair to us, who have so readily trusted you, Monsieur le Duc?"

And Ney, rearing his red head, rapped out an oath that seemed to support the question.

Fouché, sitting back from the table as he was, threw one leg over the other and grasped the knee in his knuckly hands. "If any here mistrusts my honesty or my judgment, he is at liberty to depart. I have deprecated this placing of His Majesty on trial. That trial shall certainly not be extended to include myself. As for the lack of evidence..." He gave a little shrug of contempt. "Is there no evidence before you in the person of His Majesty? In his countenance and in his close knowledge of all that concerns Louis XVII from infancy? Last week in this house Madame Royale was given overwhelmingly convincing proof that – "

"Wait! Wait!" she interrupted him gustily. "It seemed a proof only because I possessed no inkling of how the knowledge he displayed might have been obtained."

"How could it have been obtained?" In her turn she was impatiently interrupted by her brother. "How could it have been obtained?" He was quivering with anger. "I told you something so intimate, madame, that it could have been known to none but your brother." He turned to the assembly. "I told Her Highness in detail what happened between us in the Temple Tower in the hour of the execution of the King, our father. Let her say whether what I told her was true. And if that is not enough, let her question me, here before you all, upon any other secret matter that could be known only to her brother and herself. That is a ready and easy way to prove me. But first let her say whether what I told her here last week was true. She must admit, as you must all, that it could be known only to her brother."

His pleading yet vehemently confident tone recovered for him some of the ground that he had lost. All eyes turned now upon Madame Royale, who remained coldly scornful.

"Or to someone," she said slowly, "to whom my brother might have related it." She spoke to the company rather than to him, less concerned to answer him than to destroy the impression he had made. "Must I remind you that this Monsieur de La Salle here claims to have conducted my brother out of France? If that is not true, then all the tale's a lie. But if it is true, then Monsieur de La Salle was day after day in the young King's company on that journey. My brother was naturally talkative. Who shall say how much or how little he related to Monsieur de La Salle of what had happened to him in the Temple? And Monsieur de La Salle has been very prominent, the chief figure, indeed, in this imposture. He has been this unfortunate young man's preceptor, fitted for it by the information he possessed. By means of that they were able last week to dupe me for a moment. But now that I understand, what would it avail to apply the tests so brazenly suggested?"

She paused there a moment, and her hard eyes swept over the mute assembly. Louis-Charles found the ground cut from under his feet, and it was ground upon which he had been very confident of being able to take his last stand and there prevail against all comers. La Salle gloomed beside him, sharing his sense of the formidable force by which they were opposed. Only Fouché continued unperturbed and smiling.

"Ingenious!" he mocked.

Madame Royale turned sharply. "Your effrontery is insufferable, Monsieur Fouché. But I have not yet done with you. Knave or fool, you shall take a humbler tone when you have heard what the Baron von Ense has yet to tell you." She looked up at the tall blond Prussian. "If you please, Baron," she commanded.

And La Salle, perceiving quite clearly what was coming, felt himself turn cold and the heart shrink within him.

Chapter 14

Sacred Duty

"In the year 1808," began von Ense, "that great statesman the Baron Heinrich vom Stein was being driven by despair, as will be known to most of you, to make use of any means for the overthrow of the Emperor Napoleon, so as to deliver Prussia from his grasp. It happened that a year earlier a copy of an intimate mémoire by Madame Royale of her captivity in the Temple Tower had come into his possession. It had been sold to him by a Russian spy who had obtained access to the original during Her Highness' sojourn at Mitau. It contained such close details of the captivity that it supplied a valuable vade mecum for any impostor who might attempt to impersonate Louis XVII.

"It also happened that Monsieur de La Salle was in Berlin at the time, and under my hand. He had been, to my certain knowledge, closely associated with Louis XVII; he was extremely well informed on Parisian matters at the time of the young King's captivity; he knew the Temple Prison intimately, and he had been the chief agent of Louis XVII's escape, first from the Temple, and, later, from France.

"With such means at hand, the Baron vom Stein was inspired with the notion of setting up a spurious Louis XVII so as to embarrass Napoleon and perhaps lead to his overthrow. Monsieur de La Salle was charged by vom Stein to discover a suitable person, of a plausible cast of countenance, and by means of Madame Royale's mémoire, supplemented by Monsieur de La Salle's own knowledge, to school him in the part he would be required to play."

The stillness about the table was deathly. The gravity of every countenance told of the profound and shattering impression made by von Ense's revelation, which appeared to supply so complete and damning a confirmation of Madame Royale's indictment.

Fouché, his eyes completely veiled, had never looked more cadaverous. He seemed to have ceased to breathe. Louis-Charles, benumbed by what he learnt now for the first time and by his intuitive perception that the company's earlier incipient mistrust had suddenly been converted into hostile conviction, looked in despair at La Salle, and La Salle's luminous eyes, grown dull with pain for Louis-Charles, returned the despair of that glance.

Suddenly on the silence rang the angry quavering voice of Madame de Castillon-Fouquières. "Well, sir? Why don't you give him the lie?"

Louis-Charles looked up and across, and his glance met Pauline's. What he beheld there, the utter lack of sympathy with him in a moment of such dreadful need, chilled him to the soul. Its inscrutability baffled him. She sat very still, with folded hands, her head high and perfectly poised. Only her pallor and the quickened heave of her breast betrayed her inward disquiet.

"That is for Monsieur de La Salle," said Louis-Charles in answer. "For myself I can only say that I know nothing whatever of this."

It gave La Salle a cue. "And that, sirs," he cried with vehemence, "is the truth. His Majesty has no part or concern in anything that may have been concerted between the Baron vom Stein and me."

"You admit, then, that this was concerted?" asked Lebrun, disgust and condemnation in his tone, whilst disgust and condemnation were in every eye now turned upon La Salle.

He shrugged ill-humouredly. "You have heard."

Ney addressed von Ense. "Can you carry your tale no further, Monsieur le Baron?"

"Not much further. All that I can add is that whilst Monsieur de La Salle was seeking his man, the Baron vom Stein was constrained to flee for his life from the wrath of Bonaparte. Therefore we must suppose that the project was abandoned at the time."

"At the time," Ney made echo, whilst Davout was saying: "Unless, of course, Monsieur de La Salle chose to pursue it for his own account."

"That is an assumption."

"But an irresistible one," thundered back Davout.

Ouvrard was banging the table with his great fist. "Name of God, Fouché, have you nothing to say?"

Again Fouché seemed to awaken. "Only to deplore your lack of manners. You forget the presence in which you find yourself." His gesture included Louis-Charles with Madame Royale.

"Presence! You want to laugh! And this dirty work of La Salle's, then?"

"It is unfortunate. It creates an atmosphere of suspicion. But fact is not destroyed by suspicion. Fact is obstinate. It thrives in any atmosphere."

"When established," said Lebrun gravely. "In the meantime, what have we? An identity sponsored by a man convicted of imposture."

"Monsieur le Prince!" cried La Salle, in rebuke.

"Is it less than true?"

Fouché intervened. "You'll include me in the indictment. For the identity is sponsored by me too."

"Ha! By you, Fouché!" The Prince of Eckmühl's tone was almost an insult.

But it never touched Fouché, as indifferent to censure as to approval in his settled contempt of human opinions. "If you need more, I shall see that you find it, in the Courts."

Madame Royale, who with the faintest and sourest of smiles on her lips surveyed the havoc she had made, turned her hard glance upon him. "If you have the folly to invite them, the consequences be upon your own head. You know something now of the evidence you will have to answer."

"Does Your Highness imagine that I shall be at a loss to answer it?"

"You will answer it with your head, as will this unfortunate young man by whose imposture you hoped to climb back to power." She rose, and held herself stiffly, her head high. She looked down the table at Louis-Charles. "Monsieur Deslys, do not misunderstand me. Not out of mercy for you, but only so as not to distress the peace of the realm, I accord you two days – forty-eight hours – in which to leave France. On the expiry of that time I shall request His Majesty to order your arrest. The end of the adventure you can guess."

All had risen save only Louis-Charles. Retaining his seat, he looked up at her with eyes of sorrowful contempt.

"Although it is impossible," he said, "that you can have forgotten that morning when you said after our mother, 'God be with the King!' "

Momentarily it again shattered her assurance and turned her white, whilst Fouché was adding: "Be persuaded, madame, that I do not sponsor impostures. And be persuaded that we stand firm. Firm and confident. For against facts malice is powerless."

"Malice!" She choked on the word. "To whom do you impute malice?"

"To whom, indeed?" Lebrun demanded, supporting Her Highness. "It is foolish, my friend, to see malice in unbelief after what we have all heard."

Hearing that, Madame Royale accounted her task accomplished.

"The door, Monsieur le Baron," she said.

Von Ense sprang to open it. She passed out, moving with her quick, mannish stride, and the Baron followed her.

She left behind her a gloomy, angry silence that was broken at last by La Salle, speaking through his teeth, venting the rage that boiled in the depths of him.

"I shall have two words to say to the Marquis de Sceaux before tomorrow morning."

Then the storm broke, precipitated by that futility from the one man who in the general view should be prepared to receive rather than to utter threats. It was Ouvrard who supplied the first peal of thunder.

"Much good that will do towards saving your dirty neck, you scoundrel."

"You are safe from me, Ouvrard," sneered La Salle, meeting insult with insult. "I don't fight with usurers."

"Do you call me that?"

"I practise restraint. Bonaparte called you a thief."

Ouvrard swore foully at him for answer. "At present," he ended, "I seem to have fallen among thieves. What I want to know, Fouché, is who is to refund me my three millions, the three millions advanced on your word so as to forward the fortunes of the Orphan of the Temple. By God, Fouché, if you default with me – "

"Silence!" Fouché hissed at him, and the contemptuous gleam of his eye fell like a blight upon the corpulent financier. "Is there no grain of gratitude in all that well-nourished carcase? Have you forgotten, you miserable wretch, that if I had not stood between you and Bonaparte's wrath you would be in the gutter now? – which, after all, is your proper place. Out of my house!"

"And my money, then?"

"I'll make myself responsible. And I'll make you rue the day you asked for it. Go!"

"He does not go alone, Fouché," said Lebrun.

"I have said that I care nothing who goes with him. It is a test."

Lebrun bowed stiffly and went out at once. Ouvrard rolled after him.

Davout and Ney, who had drawn apart, now also took their leave. The peasant-born Prince de la Moskowa had no word to offer. But Davout sought to temper his withdrawal.

"I think too well of you, Fouché, to suppose that you have not been duped."

"Ha! To be sure, credulity has always been my weakness. All the world knows that."

But even the reminder in that gibe did not check the secession.

D'Auguié, and the Abbé had each a polite word of valedictory regret. The others followed, one by one, each with a farewell for Fouché, none with a word or a look for him who an hour ago had been their accepted King, until at the long table were left only Louis-Charles, with La Salle on his left, his elbows on the mahogany, his fingers in his thick smooth hair, and Fouché, standing afar, at the foot of it, and miraculously still smiling.

For spectators they still had Madame de Castillon-Fouquières and her daughter. But now Mademoiselle de Castillon rose languidly. Although white to the lips, her composure was perfect.

"I think, madame, we have waited longer than was necessary. Shall we go?"

The Duchess came up violently, shaking from head to foot. She was as red as her daughter was white. She spluttered in wrath to see the magnificent world her imagination had built laid in ruins about her.

"God forgive you, Fouché. I don't know whether you are a fool or a villain."

He made her no more than the Caesarian answer: "Ah! You too!"

But Louis-Charles, coming out of a stupor, was suddenly on his feet.

"Pauline!"

Mademoiselle de Castillon-Fouquières was already moving down the room towards the door. She did not appear to hear him, for, calm and stately, she continued on her way.

"Pauline!" he cried again, anger blending with the pain in his voice.

It was the Duchess who answered him. "Impudent impostor! Have you the effrontery still to address my daughter? Isn't it enough that you have made her a butt for ridicule?"

"Mother!" Mademoiselle de Castillon-Fouquières had paused in the doorway. She used a tone of remonstrance. "Can it serve any good purpose to talk?"

"No. My God, I suppose not! Nothing serves any purpose." She rolled after her daughter. But before Fouché she paused again. He confronted her with his bland smile, his eyes half veiled. "God will punish you for this, Fouché, you grinning devil. I shall leave your house at once. And I hope they'll hang you, you wicked regicide."

She went out, slamming the door so violently that the windows rattled.

"Regicide!" Fouché was plaintive. "And I seek to make a king."

Louis-Charles had sunk down again into his chair, his white face drawn and haggard. He looked at La Salle, who still sat with his head in his hands.

"Well, Florence? Why do you stay?"

La Salle lowered his hands, looked up and then round. "What? Are we three all that remain of the pleasant company that was here? I heard a fish-wife railing a moment since. Has even the lovely, the fond, the ardent Pauline, who was to have been Queen of France, forsaken us? Is the comedy really played out, then, Monsieur le Duc?"

"On the contrary," said Fouché. He paced slowly up to the head of the table, drew up a chair, and sat down on Louis-Charles' other side. "The curtain is about to rise. The real comedy is about to begin. It will be played for Your Majesty's entertainment by the buffoons who have just left us. I promise you that they will afford the groundlings abundant amusement. The seat in which you will attend the performance will be the throne of France."

Louis-Charles shook his head, looking straight before him. "That dream is over," he said.

"Never suppose it for a moment, sire. I still hold the trumps. I always make sure of them before I begin to play. If I did not disclose them today, it is because they can be disclosed to better advantage presently."

"There is no presently. That is all finished."

"Sire, I do not talk at random. Have faith in me. Don't forget the letters of the late Baron Ulrich von Ense and Lebas to de Batz, to which we may possibly be able to add the papers and the seal in the possession of Naundorff. I can find ways to penetrate a Prussian prison."

"You know that the letters to de Batz are in the hands of the government. They can be destroyed if they have not been destroyed already."

Fouché's smile grew broader. "Do you imagine that, having discovered those letters, I really left them in the archives? That was never my way with documents so precious. What the government possesses are copies. The originals are among my papers, and the original of Ulrich von Ense's letter is sealed with his arms and his signature attested by two witnesses. A careful man, the late Baron. Then, too, we can bring Joseph Perrin to Paris. Lastly, though perhaps first in importance, nature and chance, as if foreseeing your need, have placed certain signs on your body. Unmistakable signs, to which several existing documents attest. Your vaccination marks are peculiar: in the form of a triangle, as I had occasion to verify once at Ferrières. Oh yes. I took my precautions before I sponsored you. On your right thigh there should be a network of veins tracing the design of a dove, as if you came into the world with the insignia of the order of the Saint Esprit upon you. And then Your Majesty's ears. By your leave, sire."

He leaned forward abruptly, and before Louis-Charles could guess his intention, as La Salle had once done, he had raised the heavy wing of chestnut hair that always concealed the young man's left ear. He nodded as he let it fall again.

"I wonder that Your Majesty never thought to mention these matters to your sister. They should be enough for any court of law, even if we had not all the rest." He looked across at La Salle. "Have we trumps enough?"

Now that he was shown how complete was the knowledge in Fouché's possession which had guided him in recognizing Louis XVII, La Salle was reassured. It mattered nothing that he should be a discredited witness. His evidence would not be necessary.

But Louis-Charles, an incarnation of dejection, merely seemed to sneer.

"The only fortunate thing in all this wretched business, Monsieur le Duc, is that you have not yet played those trumps."

"Faith, yes," La Salle agreed. "It will render the sweeter the revenge on the fools who have forsaken you."

"What should that profit me? Justine Perrin came here to save me from danger, as she supposed. She has saved me. From the danger of being a king. That is at an end."

"At an end?" quoth Fouché.

"Definitely at an end. I have no wish to go on."

"Are you mad?" cried La Salle. "With the crown as good as on your head?"

Fouché pronounced himself deliberately in his thin voice. "It is not a matter of what you wish, sire. This is a duty imposed upon you by your birth."

"So I deluded myself for years. To that idea I almost sacrificed my life, my chances of happiness, my peace of mind; for that I strove and suffered more than you could ever guess. Only here, at close quarters, on the very threshold of the throne, do I perceive the damnation to which I would dedicate myself." He spoke with a passion that gathered intensity as he proceeded. "To be a king. What is it to be a king? Haven't I discovered it? It is to be a slave of men's greed and ambition, a puppet tricked out in all the panoply of power, to be used for the ends of others, to dance as the strings are jerked, but denied all self-expression, unable to count upon a disinterested friend or a loyal mistress. My God, what have you shown me? What have I found? Of all the supporters who crawled, fawning, about me there was not one who was not moved by self-interest."

The passionate torrent of recrimination rolled on.

"You, Monsieur d'Otranto, using me as a forlorn hope for the recovery of the power that is as the breath of your existence, to afford you the voluptuousness of avenging upon the reigning Bourbons their neglect of you. That hard, stony-hearted woman who is my sister and hopes one day to be Queen of France, resisting conviction of my identity because of what she might lose by it, so jubilant to have found grounds to justify her in regarding me as an impostor that she will not give a glance at anything that might unsettle that conviction. An uncle, who with every reason to know that his nephew escaped from the Temple and from France, refuses all investigation that might establish his own usurpation; a man who would labour to suppress me without examining my claims, who might even proclaim me a bastard if he could exclude me from the throne by no other means. A woman betrothed to me, who as lately as yesterday lay palpitating against my breast, swearing a devotion to the man upon whom you have seen her brutally turn her back when she no longer sees the King in him."

"A man who to all appearances was an unmasked impostor," Fouché gently reminded him.

"Would she have believed that quite so readily if the love she protested had been the love of anything but power? Though the whole world turned against me, a woman who loved me – me, Charles Deslys, or Louis Capet – would have rallied to me in my hour of humiliation, instead of showing me that the love reserved for kings is prostitution.

"Everywhere, everywhere, it is the same. La Salle here – "

There La Salle interrupted him. "Of your charity, leave me out of your accounts. If I played the rogue, at least I thought myself the partner of a rogue."

"Ah! That is interesting," said Fouché, with a suddenly odd attentiveness.

But La Salle went on. "I should have handled things differently if I had known from the outset that you were really the King. Yet I should have known. There were signs enough, as I now realize."

"But your eyes were so fixed upon the fraud that you could not perceive the reality. You should have begun where you ended: by looking at my ears. But it was a providence that you did not; a providence that you sealed my lips. It has ended by saving me from Hell."

"I see," Said Fouché, and looked curiously from one to the other of them. "I see. Your bitterness, sire, is readily understood. But it will pass. What will not pass is your duty to the place into which you were born. That is not to be dismissed on any grounds. It imposes upon you, as you have, yourself, felt, a sacred charge to which you dare not be false. Or dare you?"

Louis-Charles pondered him very solemnly. "This from you, Fouché," he said at last, "one of those who sent my father to the guillotine!"

But Fouché's reply was ready. "Because I conceived it necessary to the service of France, just as I conceive it necessary to the service of France to place you on the throne. France needs you." He was vehement. "With that dull, infatuated usurper at the helm the ship of State will founder. Not merely the monarchy, not merely the Bourbon cause, but the State itself. Louis XVIII is doomed. When he falls — and that will be very soon – the nation, without a rallying-point, will be torn by factions. Will you so far play the traitor to your birth and your blood as to suffer that to happen? Will you indifferently stand aside whilst anarchy is let loose and the Paris kennels run once more with blood, when by supplying the needed rallying-point, as your sacred duty is, you may avert this evil? Dare you consider only these paltry scratches which your pride has suffered? Dare you?"

It was one of those rare moments in which Fouché revealed the force which had placed him where he stood. His words, his tone, the solemn earnestness of his countenance, caused even La Salle to ask himself whether he had not done him a cruel injustice in attributing to him no motives but those of self-interest.

As for Louis-Charles, his rebellion was subdued by the magic of that fierce sermon on his kingly duty. The ideal amounting to obsession borne from childhood in his breast was restored once more from its momentary repudiation. He could perceive only that the course so clearly pointed out to him as that of stern duty was not to be avoided. Conscience would not permit it, whatever his inclinations in this hour of bitterness, whatever bitterness there might yet be in store for him.

He hung his head in an access of shame. He had no words in which to answer the indictment of his defection.

Fouché, watching him narrowly, struck home to break down the last misgiving. "Depend upon me, sire. There shall be no more humiliations for you. I will approach things by another road; I will employ the evidence in my hands not merely as defensive bucklers, but as weapons of offence. I will carry the war into the enemy camp, and in all their lives the fools who forsook you today shall find nothing to regret more bitterly. I ask only a night for reflection. By tomorrow morning I shall have a clear plan of the campaign upon which I propose immediately to embark."

Louis-Charles made a sound that was either a sob or a groan. "I have no choice, it seems. I must abandon my hopes."

"Your hopes?" said La Salle.

"Of returning to Passavant."

"To herd cows?"

"Or to make clocks at Le Locle, applying the only thing of value inherited from my father – his mechanical ability."

"From your father, sire," said Fouché, "you inherited a throne."

"That was the tragedy of him. Had he not been, as I am, the victim of his birth, he might have lived a happy locksmith, instead of perishing a tragic king. I was beginning to dream for myself the emancipation fate denied to him. But now…of what use are words?"

"Of none, sire," said Fouché. "We must pass to deeds."

Chapter 15

Ave Atque Vale

The battle fought within the conscience of Louis-Charles which ended in his surrender to the will of Fouché had been more fierce and bitter than either Fouché or La Salle was in a position to perceive.

Justine Perrin had held the very centre of that brief dream of his of returning to Passavant. The sight of her that day, even before she had stirred him by displaying a loyalty that showed how far was her gentle soul from harbouring rancour, had revived the poignant grief and self-contempt, amounting in their aggregate almost to despair, in which he had last left Passavant in obedience to the relentless beckoning not, indeed, of La Salle, as was supposed, but of the ideal of sacred duty. There had arisen from his soul, to sweep away every other consideration, a neap-tide of tenderness for this girl who had so readily hastened to Paris on the false tale of his need for her, ready for any sacrifice to serve a man who had very deeply wronged her. He contrasted the conduct towards him of this peasant-girl whom he had abandoned with that of the high-born lady he would have made a queen, who after passionate vows of affection for the man rather than the king, could not even stay to hear him in his own defence. With shame of himself there had been mingled relief that, disowned, he might now step out of the royal shackles he had inherited and find peace in devoting the remainder of his life to making amends to

Justine if she would take him back. When she knew all, he thought that she would understand, and to understand is always to forgive. This had been the one sweet alloy in all the bitterness the day had brought him.

But it had been an idle dream from which Fouché's lofty, forceful admonition had awakened him. Like a galley-slave, he must take up again the oar to which destiny had chained him.

Even so, however, it was intolerable that Justine, at present within easy reach of him, should be allowed to depart again without a full understanding of the forces that had so relentlessly shaped his conduct in the past. Without the balm of her forgiveness, his sensitive conscience now would never give him peace again.

He informed himself of the address she had given to the driver of the hackney in which she had departed alone from the Hôtel d'Otranto, and in the splendours of one of the ducal carriages he had himself borne that afternoon to the modest Hôtel d'Eylau.

He discovered her in the act of packing, the massive middle-aged Grosjean in attendance, lending her what assistance he could.

Over the ravages of weeping on her countenance an expression of terror was spread at sight of him, and as if suddenly drained of strength, she sank into the nearest chair. Grosjean discreetly effaced himself.

Louis-Charles went to her like a hurt child to its mother. He fell on his knees beside her, and without a word uttered, buried his face in her lap. Thus he remained for a spell in which terror continued her only emotion. At last, timidly, gradually, she bent forward over him, her lips quivered into a pathetic little smile, and with the lightest of touches her hand caressed his chestnut head.

"You are not angry with me, then?" she murmured to this man who had come to implore her not to be angry with him.

"The King of France is on his knees to you, Justine," he said, without suspicion that he was being theatrical. "Let that explain me. It is the truth, Justine, the simple truth, although I know that it must seem incredible to you."

De Sceaux's tale had been that Charles Deslys was out of his senses, the victim of an hallucination that might easily destroy him. Setting aside the falsehoods touching the circumstances in which as a consequence he found himself, what she had seen that day had confirmed the cardinal fact, short of the alternative explanation that he was a rogue intent upon a vast imposture. And now this histrionic assertion to her that he was King of France confirmed it further, and increased her trouble. But the next words with which he broke upon a shocked silence, the source of which he may have guessed, were even more startling.

"Your father, Justine, knows that it is true. He has always known it, from the hour I was entrusted to him, before you were born, before he was married. It has always been a secret too dangerous to be shared with any, even with your mother. But now...now those dangers are overpast, and he may tell the world the part he has played in my preservation."

The incredible assertion brought a succession of questions from her. His replies exhibited no taint of delusion. They were so clear and ready that gradually the incredible grew credible. Little by little she recalled instance after instance of a queer deference which her father had shown him, of an inexplicable patience with him in his failings – failings which in the light of what he now told her were scarcely so to be regarded. She remembered, too, incomprehensible allusions from her father, to which the present disclosure certainly supplied a key. And so, at long last, whilst he still knelt there, she came into an amazed belief in his extraordinary tale. Perhaps his explanation of his conduct towards her went some way towards settling that belief.

"When I so cruelly left you at Passavant, I was more cruel to myself even than to you, Justine. For I love you, Justine. Honestly, sincerely, deeply, as I shall never love again. And I never loved you more than on that day of my departure with La Salle. But to be born a king is to be born into a strait-jacket. By that birth and the duties it imposes, kings are set apart. They may not love and mate as ordinary men; for being in reality masters of nothing, who seem masters of everything, they are not masters even of their destinies. I should have remembered it. Love should have helped me to remember. For love should never wish to hurt, and I – God knows – have brought you naught but needless pain."

"But not by loving me, Charlot. Oh, not by loving me. Never reproach yourself with that, for it is what sanctifies us. What I have suffered does not matter now, for I too loved honestly. I… I sought to save you from Monsieur de La Salle, not understanding. My failure in that is what hurt me most. For myself…"

"My dear!" he murmured.

"You must not kneel, Charles. You must not."

"Let me be. I want you to understand before I rise."

"I understand," she assured him. "All is clear now."

"No. Not quite all. Not yet." He did not look at her, but kept his eyes upon the buckle of her belt. "I have been the sport of self-seekers, as is the case, I suppose, with all men of my kind. For their own profit there have been many who were ready to take up my cause. And there was a lady to whom they betrothed me, who shamed and tormented me by vows of affection which in my simplicity I believed were honest, but which have been proved as false as all other vows with which the favour of a king is sought. From that marriage, at least, I am now saved, for this lady has been quick to abandon me now that I have been touched by the breath of suspicion. For that I may thank God. Yet it is very little. For it does not set me free. I am to fight for this throne. That sacred duty has been made so clear that I must despise myself if I am false to it. It will not be a difficult battle. But it is a battle for bondage. To have broken the shackles of that betrothal brings me no nearer to you, my Justine; for I must marry, as I must do all else, as the State requires of me, not as I would."

"I understand," she said, and stroked his head again. "How could I not understand? You are the more dear to me for that. You are good, Charles. I always knew that you were good."

"Good! Mother of Mercy! I am neither good nor bad. I am nothing: a lay figure to wear a royal mantle. If I were really anything, I should be imploring you to take me back to your heart, Justine; to let me come back with you to Passavant, there to live out my life with you, free and unfettered."

"Take you back to my heart, Charlot! You have never left it. You never will. But Passavant can never be for you."

He groaned. "There was a moment today when I believed that it could be. I fought for liberty, Justine; for liberty and you. But I was overborne, browbeaten. I was made to see reasons why I must take up the place that is mine; they frightened me with the horrors that would lie on my conscience if I did not. It broke my heart, I think, to yield. What can I say to you, my dear?"

"No more, Charles. It needs no more." She took his face between her hands, forced him now to look up into her eyes. "I love you and you love me. Enough in that to keep me strong, yes, and happy. God be with you always, Charlot. Always, my dear!" She stooped and kissed him. Her arms went round him, and she drew him against her breast as a mother might have drawn her child. "Sh! Comfort you, my dear," she crooned to him. "What must be, must be. To rebel is to suffer to no purpose. Resignation will come. At Passavant we shall always think of you with love. We shall pray for you. Let that knowledge give you strength."

Thus she whom he had come to console turned to minister consolation, and by her very attempts, displaying as they did her sterling worth, merely increased his sense of loss, the aching loneliness in which at last he tore himself away and went back to the Hôtel d'Otranto and his duty.

Chapter 16

The Man of the Circumstances

These events took place on Thursday the 4th of March of that memorable year 1815. The night which Fouché had said that he would require for thought may well have proved one of the busiest of his busy life. Until the flames of the guttering candles were turning pale in the grey dawn of Friday, he was bowed over his writing-table at work. La Salle spent the night at the Duke's elbow, acting as a consultant, and Monsieur de Chassenon, at a side-table, shouldered the very heavy secretarial burden imposed upon him by these preparations. Thus the late March daybreak found them. And if then, at last, they suspended their labours, it was for no more than a couple of brief hours. By ten o'clock on that Friday morning Fouché and La Salle were again closeted in the library of the Hôtel d'Otranto, for a last survey of the night's work before giving it effect, and so as to receive the reports from the little army of scouts entrusted last night by Fouché with the task of reconnoitring in those salons of the Paris beau monde, where the events of yesterday would supply the inevitable topic and where views would be expressed on the scene with Madame Royale and the subsequent desertion of Louis-Charles by his Council.

These reports proved eminently reassuring. In one particular they presented a singular, encouraging unanimity, very flattering to Fouché. The general impression among the great mass of supporters of Louis-Charles was that the members of the Council had acted rashly in not waiting until the other side of the story had been fully heard and examined. The majority accounted it inconceivable that so astute a man as the Duke of Otranto would either be so rash as to father a fraud of such a magnitude as this, or continue in the highly perilous position of supporting the pretender after Madame Royale's revelations unless he had very solid grounds for believing that the pretender's claims could be established beyond possibility of question. In any other case, he would be supplying his rancorous enemies at the Tuileries with irresistible weapons for his annihilation. And Fouché would take no chances of that. It was remembered that, always the man of the circumstances, he was always on the winning side. Such was the general faith in this that the story of La Salle's having once been employed by Prussia to manufacture a spurious Louis XVII was being generally discredited.

Reassured that the ground lost yesterday was more apparent than real, since the great body of Louis-Charles' supporters remained unshaken in their belief in him, Fouché passed at once to the measures which he accounted necessary so as to force the issue.

Persuaded as he was that the Tuileries would make no move, whatever tale Madame Royale might have told her uncle, it became necessary openly to attack. It was the cruder method; but there was no longer a choice. Therefore he sent for General Lallemand, and dispatched him to Lille, where Drouet d'Erlon, with the Sixteenth Division, held himself at Fouché's disposal. The orders to d'Erlon were to march his regiments at once on Paris and occupy the Tuileries.

La Salle's apprehensions that this would inevitably lead to bloodshed, the extent of which remained incalculable, Fouché had met by a confident assurance that he could depend upon the support of the National Guard, and thus avoid conflict. To provide for this was the next of the measures to be instantly taken.

Meanwhile he gave a final editing to the manifesto on which they had laboured far into the night. It was to go to his own printers that day, so that the placards might be ready for publication immediately upon the arrival of d'Erlon and his troops.

The Duke's writing-table was a litter of documents which had made contribution to the manifesto. These had come from a secret cabinet contrived behind the books, in one of the bookcases, and the chief amongst them were those which went to prove the survival of Louis XVII and his history after the flight from France. They included the letters from Ulrich von Ense and Lebas to de Batz, which had been intercepted by the police of the Directoire, whose endorsement upon them, stating the time and circumstances in which they had been seized, placed their authenticity beyond question; there was the independent confirmation of the flight from France supplied by the twenty-year-old report of Desmarets, signed by him and one of his associates, and similarly attested by its endorsement. And there was a mass of lesser documents assembled from various quarters relating to Louis XVII's escape from the Temple. There were notes of documents to be sought in Prussia, notes of the means and provisions for bringing at once to Paris such witnesses as Joseph Perrin and his servant Grosjean, as well as the parish priest at Morges and the clockmaker with whom Louis-Charles had worked at Le Locle. Desmarets' lieutenants were to set out that very day on the quest of those persons.

In deepening amazement La Salle had reviewed the array of evidence marshalled before him by Fouché bearing witness to the thoroughness of the methods of the great policeman upon whom he had so fatuously supposed that he could impose a fraud. Well might Fouché with confidence order d'Erlon to march on Paris, trust to the support of the National Guard, and edit with the lucid pedantry of the sometime Oratorian professor the manifesto that was to inform the French nation of the advent of its legitimate King, since he possessed the means to render his claim irrefragable. La Salle's flattering comment drew a thin smile from Fouché. The statesman leaned back in his chair, bringing his fingertips together.

"I do not often prophesy. Never unless I am rather more than sure. And in all my life I have never been so sure of anything as that before the end of the month Louis XVII will be at the Tuileries."

By the eternal irony of the gods it was at this very moment that there came a tap on the door. The appearance of a lackey drew a clucking sound of annoyance from Fouché.

"I told Monsieur de Chassenon to give orders that I am not to be disturbed."

"Yes, monseigneur. So Monsieur de Chassenon told Monsieur Desmarets. But Monsieur Desmarets insists upon seeing your grace at once."

"Desmarets!" Fouché frowned; he paused before adding with a touch of impatience: "Bring him here."

Desmarets advanced at once from the antechamber, thrusting before him a man whose riding-clothes were dusty and splashed, whose boots were caked with mud; he was unshaven, unkempt and blear-eyed. Desmarets, white with excitement, named him to Fouché, superfluously, for he was well known to the Duke.

"It is Volant, monseigneur, my agent, from Antibes."

"Volant!" Fouché's voice was querulous. "Why are you here? Why have you left your post?"

Volant staggered forward on legs that were stiff from the saddle.

"You should guess, Monsieur le Duc." To La Salle it seemed that scorn of the question rendered his tone familiar. "There could be one thing only to make me do that. The Emperor."

"The Emperor!" The Duke's thin voice went shrill. "Bonaparte?"

"He landed in the Gulf Juan five days ago; on the first of the month. I have killed two horses and melted the shoes of a half-dozen others to be first in Paris with the news."

Fouché's eyes were wide open for once; so was his mouth; his jaw had dropped in the intensity of his surprise.

"Bonaparte in France!" he said at last. "My God! To arrive at this moment!" He got up in his sudden perturbation, paced away from the writing-table, and back to it again. He stood there, his frame more bent than ever, a man momentarily at a loss. He took up the manifesto upon which he had been at work, and held it a moment as if reading it, though it is to be doubted if he saw it at all. Then he let it fall again, drew himself stiffly up, and he was once more his imperturbable self.

"Masséna is at Marseilles," he said reflectively. "That he will march to join Bonaparte is almost certain."

"Certain, monseigneur," echoed Volant.

"Ah! You gathered that. What else did you gather in the south?"

"That it will not hesitate to rise for him. Provence is in a state of joyous excitement."

Slowly Fouché nodded. "And after the south, the west, the east and the north, or all that matters in those four quarters." He cackled a mirthless laugh. "They will know the value of my warnings at the Tuileries. Faith, Bonaparte could scarcely have chosen the moment better for himself."

"Or worse for us, I suppose," La Salle deplored.

Fouché waved one of his thin, bony hands in dismissal. "You may go, Volant. Get some rest. You, Desmarets, wait in the antechamber, I shall have orders for you."

"Here's a fine bolt from the blue," said La Salle, tight-lipped, when the door had closed upon the agent.

Fouché did not seem to hear him. He let himself drop into his chair at the writing-table and with his chin in the folds of his cravat sat like a man stricken, lost to all consciousness of his surroundings. For a spell La Salle respected that preoccupation. But at length he broke into it.

"I could conceive no more damnable complication."

Fouché stirred, as if the voice had awakened him. "Eh? Oh, ah, complication." Abruptly he gathered up the papers concerned with Louis-Charles and thrust them back into the portfolio from which they had been taken.

"Complication?" He shrugged. He was himself again. "It merely means that another and stronger Perseus has arisen to slay the fat dragon at the Tuileries."

"How does that help us?"

"Isn't it all that really matters?"

"To you, Monsieur le Duc?"

"Oh, and to you. Was not that all your aim? To pull down this silly tyrant who has no memory for his friends, who does not pay his debts?" He swept the last of the papers into the portfolio, made fast the tapes that closed it, and carried it to the bookcase that concealed the secret recess. La Salle became aware of something symbolical in this.

"That," he replied, "may once have been my aim. But since it was, we have formed new loyalties."

"Loyalties? My dear Florence, in politics a man can have but one loyalty."

"To himself?" sneered La Salle.

"To his country," said Fouché, with a smile that made a mock of the lofty falsehood. He flung the portfolio into the recess, slammed the door, which merged invisibly into the panelling, and swung the section of the bookcase back into position.

Then he stepped back to his table, sat down, took up a pen and wrote rapidly.

La Salle watched him in frowning silence for some moments. "If you have made up your mind to a course of action, Monsieur le Duc, I should be glad to know what it is."

"So you shall." He set down the pen and tinkled a little silver bell.

A footman answered the summons almost immediately.

"Monsieur Desmarets," said Fouché, in the act of folding the note he had written. And when Desmarets was fetched, he proffered it to him.

"You must carry this yourself, Desmarets," he said. "General Lallemand set out two hours ago for Lille. Ride after him. This letter is his authority to act upon the instructions he will receive from you. These are – pay attention – to order in my name General Drouet d'Erlon to march his regiments south at once, so as to join forces with the army Bonaparte will have assembled by the time d'Erlon comes up with him. Lest he hesitate, let him be told that his pretext and sufficient excuse hereafter if things should not go as we expect, is that he took this action so as to oppose Bonaparte's advance. Is that clear?"

"Perfectly clear, monseigneur."

"Then away with you. Return to me here at the earliest. I shall have need of you."

Desmarets bowed perfunctorily and went out.

La Salle roused himself from the stupor into which he was flung by this swift, cynical verification of the suspicion that he had been resisting.

"It is thus that you are loyal to France," he said with reckless sarcasm.

"As I understand it," said Fouché without resentment. He hunched his narrow shoulders. "It is not what I should have preferred. But I must accept what Fate sends. Unless Bonaparte has lost his wits I shall be back at the Quai Voltaire in charge of affairs before the end of the month."

La Salle stepped to the table and leaned upon the edge of it, looking down upon Fouché with eyes of wrath. "And Louis XVII, then? He matters nothing to you?"

"That question is irrelevant. What signifies is whether he matters to France. Now that Bonaparte is here, nothing could be more certain than that Louis XVII will matter nothing. There is no hope for him."

"Therefore you abandon him without a pang?"

"What do you know of my pangs? You are less acute than usual, my dear Florence. It is not I who abandon Louis XVII. It is Fortune."

"Ah, yes. And you follow Fortune, to be sure. That has ever been your part."

"Has it not been yours? And why should it not still be yours? In the service of Bonaparte intelligence and enterprise are given their due. You would find it very different from the service of the Bourbons."

La Salle, white-faced and looking wicked, was breathing heavily.

"You have every right, I suppose, to regard me as a scoundrel. But I do not readily turn my coat or my skin."

"I do not know why you should be wanting in respect for me," complained that man of State of whom resentments were almost unknown. "But you are, and you are wrong to be; for I have as much regard for your ability as I have contempt for your character, and at need you will always find me your friend. And the friendship of Joseph Fouché is not to be despised even if you should elect to live by your brush rather than by politics. A Court-painter now, at the Imperial Court – "

The opening of the door and the entrance of Louis-Charles interrupted him.

Fouché pushed back his chair and rose. "I was about to seek Your Majesty," he said.

Pale and dejected, Louis-Charles bore upon him all the signs of a sleepless night; there were dark circles about his eyes and upright lines of pain between his arched brows.

Fouché made haste to advance a chair. Louis-Charles sank into it listlessly, and wearily swept a hand across an aching brow. Fouché stood over him.

"You must prepare yourself for a shock, sire. I have received information of extraordinary gravity."

Louis-Charles looked up, suddenly startled, to receive the news conveyed to him in a dozen pregnant words. After a moment's fixed stare of astonishment, during which the shattering announcement was absorbed, his expression became one of relief, as if from the exordium he had feared something worse.

"I see." Without particular interest, he asked: "What do we do now?"

"What is there to do, sire?"

"That is what I am asking you."

"Nothing remains. Bonaparte is in France. That he will reach the throne again is certain. Whether he will last depends upon whether he has learnt discretion. I can't imagine it, because natures do not change. But whether he last or not, he is certainly here; and being here, there is no room today for a competitor, however sound his claim. In short, sire, it becomes necessary to postpone your affair."

"Postpone it?"

"It would be sheer madness to put it to the test at such a time. Your Majesty will see that."

"Yes, I see." He was very quiet. "It means, then, that I am to go?"

"Your Majesty will perceive the danger of continuing in France." Fouché was coldly formal, displaying no emotion in tone or manner.

"But yesterday when, myself, I would have gone, abdicating everything, you insisted upon the responsibilities attaching to my birth. You made me understand how dishonourable it would be to go; that it was my sacred duty to remain at whatever sacrifice."

"And I might still so insist; for, indeed, duty demands great sacrifices from each of us, as long as there is a chance of fulfilling it. Here there is no such chance. Duty cannot demand that a man should choose deliberately to face a firing-party, which is what would happen to you at the hands of Bonaparte."

"But with the evidence of my identity..."

Softly Fouché interrupted him. "The identity of your cousin, the Duke of Enghien, required no evidence. Bonaparte perceived in him a menace to his own security on the throne: a much more remote menace than you would be. Bonaparte has not come back to France so as to establish the claims of Louis XVII. You may take my word for that, sire."

Louis-Charles' bewildered eyes went beyond Fouché in quest of La Salle, where he leaned silent against the window-frame, a thunder-cloud on his brow. "You say nothing, Florence."

"Nothing, sire." La Salle was grim. And grim was the humour with which he drawled "The situation is one for Monsieur le Duc."

"And you, Monsieur le Duc, are ready to capitulate."

Fouché bowed a little, spreading his hands. "Sire, I am no longer of an age to serve abstract ideals and to lead forlorn hopes. I do not advance where I see inevitable defeat."

"Did you ever?" La Salle asked him contemptuously.

But Fouché merely grinned. "The assumption that I never did flatters my intelligence. You, sire, if I may presume still to advise, would be better out of France without delay. You face a menace of a very different order from that of Madame d'Angoulême's forty-eight hours."

For a moment Louis-Charles contemplated the ground. Then he stood up, and startled them by his sudden laugh.

Their alarmed glances seemed to ask whether the shock had turned his wits. It did not seem conceivable that a man in his position should laugh if he were sane. That was because they could not guess the vision that had come to him during that long moment of silent thought.

He had seen himself delivered of the fetters of a duty which had grown increasingly odious in a measure as he had advanced in it, until recent events had shown him that he had neither the fortitude nor the will to discharge it. He had consented to go on as the galley-slave consents. Emancipated now by circumstances, he saw himself free at last to live his life as he listed, and by so living it to make his peace with his conscience. Imagination, racing ahead of the present moment, sent him hot-foot after Justine, who would already have set out on her journey back to Passavant. Such good speed would he make that he saw himself overtaking her perhaps before Troyes was reached, and in a room of some inn thereabouts, falling on his knees and putting his head in her lap again, as yesterday, and yet so differently. For now there would be no farewell tears, no heart-break. Now, instead of separation, as yesterday, there would be reunion. Delivered from the yoke to which nothing should ever make him lend his neck again, he came to her free, as he had never yet been free in all his life, with the tranquil freedom resulting from definite frustration of a sincere attempt to perform his duty. Done with dreams and will-o'-the-wisp pursuits, he came to offer himself as a mate whose whole ambition in future would be to labour for her happiness and the prosperity of Passavant.

And in fancy, so sure was he of her love, he felt himself already gathered again, as yesterday, to her young breast, and he ached on a sudden with the yearning to realize that sweet imagining. It was out of this yearning that he answered Fouché.

"I will not lose a moment in following your advice. The time to make a package, and I will take my leave."

That package was soon made. Of the prodigal contents of chests and wardrobes to supply the needs of a king, he took no more than could be contained in a single portmantle for his immediate wants. He exhibited at parting some distress concerned with money. But Fouché, anxious to deal generously with a man so reasonable as to make no trouble, cut short his diffidence.

"Ouvrard has stolen millions from the State. And you have the word of your great-grandfather, Louis XIV, that you are the State. It will be good for Ouvrard's soul to make some little restitution. Supply your needs freely, sire."

But this he would not do. "Lend me a thousand livres to enable me to reach Switzerland. I will repay you when I can."

La Salle he embraced at parting. "You have been so much in my life, Florence, from its earliest days and in all its fateful ones, that I can have only kindness for you and gratitude. Perhaps if I were really good, myself, I should regard you as a scoundrel."

"And mingle contempt with affection. I understand. And if I were really wise, I'd go and herd cows with you instead of staying here to paint bad portraits."

"Seek me some day at Passavant," Louis-Charles begged him. He waved to them from the window of the post-chaise in which he went racing away from a throne in the pursuit of Justine and happiness.

Then in silence, side by side, La Salle and Fouché crossed the marble vestibule and ascended again the staircase of honour.

"See," said Fouché, "how ill-founded was your indignation with me. I glow with the sense of a worthy action done in removing from his shoulders the mantle of a king and sending him forth in freedom to become a happy man."

La Salle's laughter startled him. It had none of its habitual sluggishness. It was sharp and staccato.

"Thus, undoing all that I had done to convert a man into a king, you have achieved the early aim of your friend the Citizen Chaumette, which was to convert a king into a man. The wheel has come full turn. And so we end where we began twenty years ago, and all that has happened in between becomes of no account."

"Life," said Fouché quietly, "is often like that."

Rafael Sabatini

Bellarion

Bellarion, a young man set on joining the priesthood, is diverted from his calling to serve the Princess Valeria. He remains with her for five years, serving her faithfully despite her cold response. Yet when the time comes for him to leave, they both find that the passion and romance of Italy has left its mark...

Captain Blood

Captain Blood is the much-loved story of a physician and gentleman turned pirate.

Peter Blood, wrongfully accused and sentenced to death, narrowly escapes his fate and finds himself in the company of buccaneers. Embarking on his new life with remarkable skill and bravery, Blood becomes the 'Robin Hood' of the Spanish seas. This is swashbuckling adventure at its best.

Rafael Sabatini

The Gates of Doom

'Depend above all on Pauncefort', announced King James; 'his loyalty is dependable as steel. He is with us body and soul and to the last penny of his fortune.' So when Pauncefort does indeed face bankruptcy after the collapse of the South Sea Company, the king's supreme confidence now seems rather foolish. And as Pauncefort's thoughts turn to gambling, moneylenders and even marriage to recover his debts, will he be able to remain true to the end? And what part will his friend and confidante, Captain Gaynor, play in his destiny?

'A clever story, well and amusingly told' – *The Times*

Scaramouche

When a young cleric is wrongfully killed, his friend, André-Louis, vows to avenge his death. André's mission takes him to the very heart of the French Revolution where he finds the only way to survive is to assume a new identity. And so is born Scaramouche – a brave and remarkable hero of the finest order and a classic and much-loved tale in the greatest swashbuckling tradition.

'Mr Sabatini's novel of the French Revolution has all the colour and lively incident which we expect in his work' – *Observer*

Rafael Sabatini

The Sea Hawk

Sir Oliver, a typical English gentleman, is accused of murder, kidnapped off the Cornish coast, and dragged into life as a Barbary corsair. However Sir Oliver rises to the challenge and proves a worthy hero for this much-admired novel. Religious conflict, melodrama, romance and intrigue combine to create a masterly and highly successful story, perhaps best-known for its many film adaptations.

The Shame of Motley

The Court of Pesaro has a certain fool – one Lazzaro Biancomonte of Biancomonte. *The Shame of Motley* is Lazzaro's story, presented with all the vivid colour and dramatic characterisation that has become Sabatini's hallmark.

'Mr Sabatini could not be conventional or commonplace if he tried'
– *Standard*

Made in the USA
Lexington, KY
16 May 2011